Liza Marklund is an author, publisher, journalist, columnist, and goodwill ambassador for UNICEF. Her crime novels featuring the relentless reporter Annika Bengtzon instantly became an international hit, and Marklund's books have sold 12 million copies in 30 languages to date. She has achieved the unique feat of being a number one bestseller in all five Nordic countries, as well as the USA, and she has been awarded numerous prizes, including a nomination for the Glass Key for best Scandinavian crime novel.

The Annika Bengtzon series is currently being adapted into film.

Neil Smith studied Scandinavian Studies at University College London, and lived in Stockholm for several years. He now lives in Norfolk.

D0413058

Also by Liza Marklund

THE BOMBER
EXPOSED
RED WOLF

and published by Corgi Books

By Liza Marklund and James Patterson

POSTCARD KILLERS

VANISHED

Liza Marklund

Translated by Neil Smith

CORGI BOOKS

TRANSWORLD PUBLISHERS
61–63 Uxbridge Road, London W5 5SA
A Random House Group Company
www.transworldbooks.co.uk

VANISHED
A CORGI BOOK: 9780552160957

First published in Great Britain in 2004 by Pocket Books
Corgi edition published 2012

Copyright © Liza Marklund 2000
English translation copyright © Neil Smith 2012
Map © Tom Coulson at Encompass Graphics

Liza Marklund has asserted her right under the Copyright, Designs and
Patents Act 1988 to be identified as the author of this work.

Addresses for Random House Group Ltd companies outside the UK
can be found at: www.randomhouse.co.uk
The Random House Group Ltd Reg. No. 954009

The Random House Group Limited supports The Forest Stewardship
Council (FSC®), the leading international forest certification organization.
Our books carrying the FSC label are printed on FSC® certified
paper. FSC is the only forest certification scheme endorsed by
the leading environmental organizations, including
Greenpeace. Our paper procurement policy can be
found at www.randomhouse.co.uk/environment.

Typeset in 11/13pt Sabon by
Kestrel Data, Exeter, Devon.
Printed and bound by
CPI Group (UK) Ltd, Croydon, CR0 4YY.

2 4 6 8 10 9 7 5 3

A Note to the Reader

Chronologically, the events in this book follow on from those of my previous novel, *Exposed*. However, although the Annika Bengtzon novels form part of a series, they can just as easily be enjoyed on their own.

Enjoy!

Liza Marklund
January 2012

A Note on the Currency

Calculated at a rate of 10.3 Swedish Krona to the pound, the monetary figures in this book would convert approximately as follows:

10kr = 97p	500kr = £48.50
50kr = £4.85	1000kr = £97
100kr = £9.70	2000kr = £194
200kr = £19.40	3000kr = £291

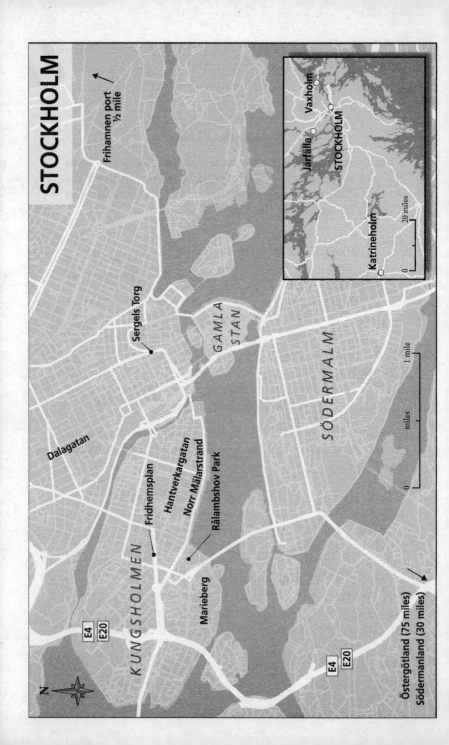

Prologue

Time has stopped, she thought. *This is what it's like to die.*

Her head hit the tarmac, and she blacked out momentarily. Fear vanished, along with all sound. Only silence remained.

Her thoughts were calm and clear. Her stomach and pelvis were pressed against the ground, ice and gravel against her cheek and in her hair.

How strange, the way things turn out. How little you can actually predict. Who could have guessed that it would end up like this? A foreign shore, far away in the north.

Then she saw the boy in front of her again – his outstretched arms – and her fear returned. She heard the shots, the sobbing that went with them, and felt helpless.

'Sorry,' she whispered to the memory of her brother. 'I'm sorry I was so weak, so pathetically useless.'

Suddenly she felt the wind again. It tugged at her bag, hurting her. Sound returned. One foot was aching. She became aware of the damp and cold coming through her jeans. She had simply fallen, she hadn't been hit. Her mind went blank again, but one thought remained: *Get away from here.*

She struggled onto all fours but the wind forced her back down. She tried again. The buildings were making the squalls unpredictable, sweeping in mercilessly from the sea, and along the road.

I have to get away from here. Now.

She knew the man was somewhere behind her. He was blocking the route back to town. She was stuck.

I can't just stay here in the glare of the headlights. I've got to get away. Anywhere but here!

A fresh gust of wind took her breath away. She gasped and turned her back to it. More headlights, bright yellow, turning the grey, grimy surroundings into gold. Where could she go?

She picked up her bag and ran with the wind behind her towards a building by the water. A long loading bay ran the whole length of it. There was a mass of wreckage that had blown to the ground, what on earth was it? A staircase? A chimney! Furniture. A gynaecologist's chair. A Model T Ford. An instrument panel from a fighter plane.

She struggled onto the loading bay, dragging her bag behind her. She wove between bathtubs and school-desks, finally crouching down behind an old desk.

He's going to find me, she thought. *It's only a matter of time. He's never going to give up.*

She curled herself into the foetal position, rocking and breathing heavily, covered in sweat and filth from the tarmac. She realized she had walked right into the trap. She wasn't going to get out of this. All he had to do was walk up to her, put the revolver to the back of her head and pull the trigger.

She peered cautiously under one of the sets of desk-drawers. All she could see was ice and warehouses, bathed in the yellow of the headlights.

I have to wait, she thought. *I have to work out where he is. Then I must try to escape.*

After a few minutes her knees began to ache. Her thighs and calves grew numb, her ankles were sore, particularly the left one. She must have sprained it when she fell. Blood was dripping onto the quay from the cut in her forehead.

Then she saw him. He was standing by the edge of the loading bay, three metres away, his harsh profile dark against the yellow. The wind carried his whisper with it.

'Aida.'

She shrank back and screwed her eyes shut, now a small animal, invisible.

'Aida, I know you're here.'

She was breathing through her mouth, silently, waiting. The wind was on his side, silencing the sound of his footsteps. The next time she looked up he was walking along the other side of the road, beside the fence, his weapon discreetly concealed under his jacket. Her breathing accelerated, coming in irregular bursts, making her feel giddy.

When he vanished round the corner and went inside the warehouse she got up, jumped down onto the tarmac and ran. Her feet were thudding, louder than the wind, her bag bouncing on her back, her hair blowing in her eyes.

She never heard the shot, just sensed the bullet as it whistled past her head. She started running in a zigzag pattern, making abrupt, illogical twists and turns. Another whistling sound, another turn.

Suddenly the ground stopped and the raging Baltic Sea took over. The waves were enormous. She hesitated for just a second.

*　　*　　*

The man went over to the place where the woman had jumped and looked out at the sea. He peered intently, his gun poised, trying to see her head among the waves. Hopeless.

She'd never make it. Too cold. The wind was blowing too hard. Too late.

Too late for Aida from Bijeljina. She had overplayed her hand. She was too alone.

He stood there for a few moments, the wind coming right at him, firing crystals of ice into his face.

The sound of the Scania truck starting up behind him was carried away, never reaching him. The vehicle disappeared silently into the yellow light.

PART ONE

I am not an evil person.

I am simply the result of my circumstances. We are all born into the same life, the only difference between us is our situation: genetic, cultural, social.

I have killed, that much is true, but that is not terribly interesting. The interesting question is: does a person who is no longer really alive actually deserve to carry on living? I know my own views on this, but they don't have to correspond to anyone else's.

I could be regarded as violent, but that does not necessarily have anything to do with evil. Violence is power, in just the same way as money or influence are power. Anyone who chooses to use violence as a tool can do so without being evil. But a close relationship with violence does not come for free, you have to leave your soul as a deposit. And on this point the terms of the deal vary, of course. In my case there wasn't much to hand over.

The gap that is left is then filled up with the conditions for violence. Evil is one of them, despair another. Revenge, and rage, and, in a few sick cases, pleasure.

And I am not an evil person.

I am the result of my situation and circumstances.

Sunday 28 October

1

The Securitas guard was alert. The chaos left by the previous evening's hurricane was everywhere – toppled trees, sheets of metal and plastic from the roofs and walls of the warehouses, their contents scattered by the wind.

He braked sharply as he entered the Frihamnen port area. In the broad, open space facing the water lay the innards of a fighter-plane cockpit, some medical equipment and sections of a bathroom. It took him a few seconds before he realized what he was looking at: wreckage from one of Swedish Television's props stores.

He didn't see the dead bodies until he had switched off the engine and undone his seatbelt. Oddly, he didn't feel fear or horror, just genuine surprise. The black-clad corpses were lined up in front of the wreckage of a staircase from some cancelled TV series. Before he had even got out of the car he knew they had been murdered. It didn't take great powers of deduction. Parts of the men's skulls were missing, and a sticky substance had run out of their bodies onto the icy tarmac.

Without a thought for his own safety, the guard got out of his car and walked over to the men. They were no more than a couple of metres away. His reaction was one of astonishment. The corpses looked extremely odd – their eyes had partly popped out of their sockets, and their tongues were hanging out a bit. *Like Marty Feldman's younger brothers*, he thought. Each had a small mark towards the top of his head; each was missing an ear, and, as he'd already noticed, parts of their skulls were missing.

The living, breathing man stared at the two dead ones for a while; he was later unable to estimate for how long. His stare was broken when a lingering gust of the storm swept between the grain silos and knocked him to the ground. He put his hands out to break his fall and one of them landed in the spilled brain tissue from one of the bodies. The feeling of the cold, sticky goo between his fingers made him immediately, violently sick. He threw up on the bonnet of his car, then tried frantically to wipe off the mess from his fingers on the material of the front seat.

The regional police communication centre on Kungsholmen in Stockholm received the call from Frihamnen at 05.31. The news reached the *Evening Post* newspaper three minutes later. It was Leif who called.

'Car 1120 is on its way to Frihamnen, along with two ambulances.'

At that time of the morning, forty-nine minutes after the deadline for material and twenty-six minutes before the presses started rolling, the newsroom was, as usual, in a state of concentrated creative chaos. All the editors, red-eyed by now, were hammering away at the last headlines, polishing the text on the front page, finalizing picture captions and correcting typos. Jansson, the night-editor, was busy checking the final layout and firing the pages off to the printers.

This morning, the staff member taking tip-offs from

16

the public was the nightshift's copy-editor, Annika Bengtzon.

'Which means?' she said, scribbling furiously on a Post-it note.

'At least two dead,' Leif said, then hung up so he could be first to give the news to the next paper. Anyone who was second with a tip-off got no payment.

Annika stood up and put the phone down in the same movement.

'Two dead out in Frihamnen; could be murder, unconfirmed,' she said to the back of Jansson's head. 'Do you want it in this edition?'

'Nope,' the back of his head said.

'Do you want me to give it to Carl and Bertil?' she asked.

'Yep,' the back of his head replied.

She headed off towards the reporters' corner, the yellow note sticking out from her finger like a flag.

'Jansson wants you to check this out,' she said, offering her finger to one of the reporters.

Carl Wennergren took the note with a look of derision.

'Bertil Strand is here if you have to go out,' Annika said. 'He's down in the photo lab.'

She turned on her heel and left before Carl had time to reply. Their relationship wasn't exactly cosy. She settled back on her chair, an empty feeling in her head. It had been a rough night, and she'd had to make a lot of goal-line saves. A hurricane had swept in over Skåne in the far south the previous evening, and was working its way up the country. The *Evening Post* had put a lot of effort into covering the storm, and it had paid off. They had managed to get reporters and photographers on the last plane from Stockholm to Sturup in order to strengthen the news team in Malmö. Their journalists in Växjö and Gothenburg had been working through the night, and they'd also received a lot of material from freelancers, both pictures and text. Everything had landed on the night-desk, and it had fallen to Annika to pull together the articles. Which meant that she had rewritten every single one so that they matched and fitted the context of the pieces. Yet her name still wouldn't appear anywhere in the paper, apart from at the bottom of the factual box-out she had put together about hurricanes earlier on. She was just a copy-editor, one of the many journalists who are never seen.

'Fucking hell!' Jansson suddenly roared. 'There's no yellow on the cover picture. Fuck . . .'

He stormed off towards the picture desk, yelling for the picture editor, Pelle Oscarsson. Annika smiled weakly. Oh, brave new world. Digital technology should have made everything faster, safer, simpler. In actual fact there was a little gremlin who appeared each time they sent their files to the printers, eating up one of the colour files at irregular intervals, usually the yellow one. If the error wasn't discovered in time, it resulted in some very odd pictures in the paper. Jansson claimed that the colour-eating monster was the same little bastard who lived in his washing-machine and kept eating single socks.

'Bloody technology,' the night-editor mumbled as he headed back to his desk once catastrophe had been averted and the picture file resent.

Annika was tidying her desk.

'Well, we got there in the end again, didn't we?' she said.

Jansson slumped onto his chair.

'You did a damn good job tonight,' he said, nodding appreciatively. 'I saw the original texts. You did really well, pulling them together like that.'

'Well, I guess it worked,' Annika said, embarrassed.

'Who were those dead bodies out in the harbour?'

Annika shrugged. 'Don't know. Do you want me to check?'

Jansson stood up and headed towards the smoking room.

'Please,' he said.

She began by calling the emergency call centre.

'We've sent two ambulances,' the duty-officer confirmed.

'No police vans?' Annika wondered.

'We considered it, but the call came from a security guard. We sent ambulances.'

Annika was making notes. Police vans were only sent to pick up bodies if it was absolutely certain that the victims were dead. Police regulations stated that they could only request a van if the victim's head was separated from the body.

She had trouble getting through to the police emergency response centre. It was several minutes before anyone answered. Then it took another five minutes before the duty-officer was free to talk to her. When he finally got to the phone he was clear and concise.

'We've got two dead,' he said. 'Both male. Shot. We can't yet say if it was murder or suicide. You'll have to get back to us later.'

'They were found at Frihamnen,' Annika said quickly. 'Does that tell you anything?'

The duty-officer hesitated.

'I don't want to speculate at this point,' he said. 'But you can work it out.'

When she hung up she knew the paper would be dominated by the double murder for days to come. For some reason two murders weren't simply twice the size of a single murder, but much, much bigger.

She sighed and thought about getting a cup of coffee.

She was tired and thirsty, and it would help. But caffeine at this time of day would leave her wide awake for hours, staring at the ceiling while her body ached with exhaustion.

Oh, what the hell, she thought, and headed for the drinks machine.

The coffee was hot, and it did help. She sat back down and put her feet up on her desk.

A nice little double murder out at Frihamnen. Oh well, such was life.

She blew on the coffee.

The fact that the victims had been shot meant that this wasn't just some drunken bust-up. Drunks killed each other with knives, fists, kicking, or by chucking each other off balconies. If they ever had access to guns they would sell them to buy more drink.

She emptied the plastic cup, then went to the water fountain to refill it.

Two men, which meant it was unlikely to be a murder followed by a suicide, not out in Frihamnen in the middle of a hurricane. And the motive probably wasn't jealousy. So that left the coast clear for the sort of speculation that journalists find much more interesting. Something criminal – anything from biker gangs to the mafia and dirty money. Or some political motive. International connections.

Annika went back to her desk. She was sure of one thing. She wouldn't get anywhere near this case. Other people would end up covering it for the *Evening Post*. She gathered up her outdoor clothes.

At weekends there was no dedicated morning team in the newsroom, which meant that Jansson would have to stay until the later editions had gone to press. Annika's shift ended at six o'clock.

'I've had enough of this now,' she said as the night-editor walked past. He looked exhausted, and would have been happy to see her stay.

'Aren't you going to wait for the paper to arrive?' he said.

The first bundles arrived from the printers by courier fifteen minutes after the presses started to roll. Annika shook her head, called a taxi, stood up and put on her coat, scarf and gloves.

'Can you come in early tonight?' Jansson called after her. 'To help clean up after this damn hurricane?'

Annika pulled her bag up on her shoulder.

'Like I've actually got another life.'

2

Thomas Samuelsson gently touched his wife's stomach. The old hardness was gone. Since Eleonor had become branch manager at the bank she hadn't had time to go to the gym as often as she used to.

He let his hand gradually circle downward, past her navel, until it reached her crotch. His finger slowly followed the groove down to her thighs, feeling the hair and dampness.

'Stop it,' she muttered, turning away from him.

He sighed, swallowed, rolled onto his back, his lust thumping like a hammer. He put his hands behind his head, staring at the ceiling, and heard her breathing settle into a slow rhythm again. She never wanted to any more.

Annoyed, he threw back the covers and walked into the kitchen naked, his cock deflating. He drank some water from a dirty glass, put coffee into a fresh filter, poured in some water and turned on the machine, then went to the bathroom. In the mirror his hair was sticking up in all directions, giving him a look of irresponsibility more suited to his actual age. He sighed, rubbing his hair with his hands.

It's too early to have a midlife crisis, he thought. *Way too fucking early.*

He went back to the kitchen and stood staring out to sea. It was dark and wild. The night's storm was still evident in the foam and waves, and the neighbours' sundial had toppled over by the French windows.

What on earth's the point? he wondered. *Why are we doing this?*

A great wave of melancholy swept over him, but he was aware that it verged on self-pity. Feeling the draught from the window and thinking of the shoddy workmanship, he shivered, sighed, then went and got his dressing-gown. It was a present from his wife last Christmas, green, blue and burgundy – expensive – from the NK department store. There were matching slippers, but he had never used them.

The coffee machine gurgled. He got out a mug with the bank's logo on it and turned on the radio, just in time for the news. The words filtered through his dark mood and the coffee, hitting their target randomly. The hurricane sweeping over the south of Sweden and the damage it was causing. Electricity supplies disrupted. Insurance companies promise prompt payouts. Two men dead. The security zone in southern Lebanon. Kosovo.

He switched it off and went into the hall, pulled on his boots and went out to fetch the newspaper from the mailbox. The wind tugged at the pages and forced its way through the towelling dressing-gown, chilling his thighs. He stopped, shut his eyes and took several deep breaths. There was ice in the air, the sea would freeze over before too long.

He looked up at the house – the beautiful, architect-designed villa that her parents had had built for them. There was a light on in the upstairs kitchen, the lamp above the table, designed by someone whose name he couldn't remember. The light was greenish and cold, like an evil eye watching over the sea. The façade of the house looked grey in the morning light. His mother always said it was the most beautiful house in Vaxholm. She had offered to make curtains for every room when they moved in. Eleonor had declined, politely but firmly.

He went back in. He flicked idly through the different sections of the paper, and ended up, as usual, at the property pages. A five-room flat in Vasastan, with an old tiled stove in every room. A two-room apartment in Gamla stan, a penthouse with exposed beams and stunning views in three directions. A wooden farmhouse outside Malmköping, with electricity and running water, at a bargain price!

He could hear his wife's voice in his head: *Day-dreams! You'd be a millionaire if you spent half as much time on the share market as you do looking at property adverts.*

She was already a millionaire.

He felt a sudden sense of shame. She meant well. Her love was rock-solid. He was the problem, he was the one who was lacking. Maybe she was right, maybe he really was having trouble dealing with her success. Maybe they ought to go to that therapist after all.

He folded the paper neatly again. Eleonor didn't like it to be messed up. He put it on the little table they used for post and magazines. Then he went back to the bedroom, slid out of the dressing-gown and back under the sheets. She shifted in her sleep when she felt his cold body. He pulled her to him, blowing on the soft skin of her neck.

'I love you,' he said.

'Me too,' she mumbled.

Carl Wennergren and Bertil Strand arrived at Frihamnen a little too late. As the photographer parked his company

Saab they saw the ambulances pulling up inside the cordoned-off area. The reporter couldn't help swearing. Bertil Strand always drove so carefully, sticking to the speed limit, even though there wasn't a soul in sight. Bertil registered the unspoken criticism and felt irritated.

'You sound like an old woman,' he snapped.

They plodded over to the police cordon, the distance between them clearly marking their annoyance with each other. When they caught sight of the lights of the police cars and the figures moving about, their differences faded and work took over.

The cops were quick today, the storm must have got their adrenalin pumping. The cordon covered a large area, from the fence to their left, all the way to the office building far to their right. Bertil Strand gazed across the area, impressed. So close to the centre of town and yet completely alien. Good light, clear but still soft. Wonderful shadows.

Carl Wennergren buttoned his oilskin coat. Damn, it was cold.

They couldn't really see the victims – their view was blocked by debris, police officers and the ambulances. Wennergren stamped his feet, hunched his shoulders, his hands deep in his pockets. He hated the morning shift. The photographer hauled out his camera and telephoto lens from his rucksack and slid off along the cordon. At the far left of the tape he got a couple of decent shots, uniforms in profile, the dark corpses, plain-clothed forensics officers.

'Finished,' he yelled before long.

Carl Wennergren's nose was red, a little drop of transparent snot hanging from the end. 'What a fucking awful place to die.'

'If we're going to get anything into the late edition we'd better get going,' Bertil Strand said.

'But I'm not done yet. I haven't even started.'

'You'll have to call from the car. Or the office. Just soak up a bit of local colour that you can spice it up with.'

Bertil Strand walked off towards the car, his rucksack swinging. The reporter followed him. They sat in silence all the way back to Marieberg.

Anders Schyman clicked to close the news agency's website. It was like a drug. You could set the site to arrange updates by subject: domestic, foreign, sport, features, but he preferred to have it all. He wanted to find out about everything at once.

He walked round his cramped, aquarium-like office to loosen his shoulders. He sat down on the leather sofa, picked up that day's paper, the hurricane special, and nodded in satisfaction. His plan had succeeded. The different departments had worked together just as he had suggested. Jansson had told him that Annika Bengtzon had done most of the practical coordination, and it had worked bloody well.

Annika Bengtzon, he thought with a sigh.

The young copy-editor had somehow come to be associated with his position on the paper in an entirely coincidental but regrettable way. He and Annika Bengtzon had arrived at the paper only a fortnight apart. His first battle with upper management had been specifically about her. It had concerned a lengthy fixed-term appointment to the news team, and he had assumed that Annika Bengtzon was the obvious choice. Admittedly, she was too young, too immature, too excitable and too impetuous, but in his opinion she had far more potential than most people. She was naïve, but had a strong sense of ethics, driven by a undeniable belief in justice. She was fast, and she wrote well. And she showed definite signs of being a bulldozer, which was a great advantage for a tabloid reporter. If she couldn't get round a problem she just rode over it.

The board of the *Evening Post* consisted of nothing but white, heterosexual, middle-aged men with nice cars and a good income, the sort of men that the paper was built of and produced for. Anders Schyman suspected that Carl Wennergren reminded these men of themselves when they were younger, or rather he personified the illusion of their own youth.

Eventually he had found a post as copy-editor to cover maternity leave on Jansson's nightshift, which Annika had accepted. He had had to argue with the board before they would accept even this decision. Annika Bengtzon became the defining moment for him to exert his control over the paper. And it had come to a catastrophic end: a few days after her appointment the girl had killed her boyfriend.

She'd hit him with an iron pipe, toppling him into a disused blast furnace in the old steelworks in Hälleforsnäs. Right from the start there was talk of self-defence, but Anders Schyman could still remember how he felt when he first heard, wanting the ground to swallow him up. Then the thought: *Talk about backing the wrong horse.* That evening she had called him at home, quiet, and in shock, to tell him that the rumours were true. She had been questioned and was under suspicion of manslaughter, but hadn't been formally charged. She would be staying at a cottage in the forest for a few weeks until the police investigation was finished. She was wondering whether she still had a job at the *Evening Post*.

He had told her how it was: the job was hers even if other people on the paper might regret the decision, and she wasn't exactly a favourite with the union.

Manslaughter suggested some form of accident. If she was found guilty of causing an accident in which someone lost their life, well, that would be regrettable, but still not grounds for dismissal. If she received a lengthy prison sentence then obviously there would be difficulties extending her appointment beyond maternity cover, she had to recognize that.

When he got to this point she had started to cry. He had struggled against the impulse to yell at her about how monumentally careless she'd been, and for dragging him into the shit.

'I won't go to prison,' she had whispered down the line. 'It was him or me. He would have killed me if I hadn't hit him. The prosecutor knows that.'

She had started work with the nightshift as planned, paler and thinner than ever. She spoke to him occasionally, and to Jansson, Berit, Picture Pelle and a few others, but otherwise she kept to herself. According to Jansson she was doing a brilliant job at night, rewriting, adding text, checking facts, coming up with captions and writing front-page text, without ever making a fuss. The rumours died away, quicker than he had expected. The paper dealt with scandal and murder every day, and there were limits to the amount anyone could manage to gossip about a tragic and accidental death.

The case of the deceased and abusive hockey player Sven Matsson from Hälleforsnäs wasn't a great priority for the district court in Eskilstuna. The prosecution were calling for either manslaughter or causing another person's death. The judgment came shortly before midsummer last year: Annika Bengtzon was found not guilty of manslaughter, but was found guilty of the lesser charge, and sentenced to a supervision order. For a while she was obliged to attend some sort of therapy as part of the sentence, but as far as he was aware the whole thing had been legally concluded for a while now.

The head-editor went back to his desk and opened the news agency website again, checking whether anything had appeared since he last looked. Sunday's sports results were starting to come in, there was the aftermath of the hurricane, and several items repeated from Saturday. He sighed again. Everything just rumbled on, never ending, never reaching a conclusion. And now there was to be yet another reorganization.

The editor-in-chief, Torstensson, wanted to introduce a new layer of management, and to centralize decision-making. This model was already being used by their rival, the other evening paper, as well as several other national media organizations. Torstensson had decided it was time for the *Evening Post* to do something similar and become a 'modern' business. Anders Schyman was at a complete loss. There was every indication that they were heading for disaster. Sales were falling. The accounts didn't look good. The board was increasingly unhappy. The newsroom lurched badly in stormy waters, with poor leadership and an all too fallible radar. The truth was that the *Evening Post* didn't know where it was heading, or why. He had failed to convince everyone of where the boundaries lay, despite large seminars and conferences about the current conditions and responsibilities of the media. Admittedly, there hadn't been any more atrocious and all too public disasters since he arrived at the paper, but the work of repairing earlier damage was going far too slowly.

Something that worried him more than he cared to admit was that Torstensson had dropped a few hints about a new job, something prestigious in Brussels. Maybe that was why he was in a hurry to reorganize the paper. Torstensson wanted to leave his mark, and, God knows he hadn't managed to achieve much with any of his publicity campaigns.

Schyman groaned and impatiently closed the website again.

Something had to happen soon.

3

Gloom was already spreading from the corners when she woke up. The short day had given up while she had been tossing and turning in bed; she really shouldn't have had that last cup of coffee. She took several deep breaths, forcing herself to lie still, and checked how she felt. She didn't have any aches or pains. Her head felt a bit heavy, but that was because of the way day and night had switched places. She looked up at the ceiling, flaking and grey. The previous tenant had used gloss paint over the old distemper, and the whole ceiling was a mess of different colours. She followed the ragged, irregular cracks with her eyes, seeing the shape of a butterfly in the pattern, then a car, then a skull. A single, persistent note started to sound in her left ear – the sound of loneliness, gradually rising and falling.

She sighed, annoyed that she needed the toilet, and got out of bed, the floorboards rough under her feet; they sometimes gave her splinters. She pulled on her dressing-gown, the fabric was silken and cold against her skin, making her shiver. She opened the front door and listened for noises in the stairwell. Nothing but the ringing in her ears. She padded quickly down the half flight to the shared toilet, her feet immediately cold and gritty, but she couldn't be bothered to care.

She felt the draught as soon as she got back into her flat. The thin curtains were fluttering even though she hadn't left any windows open. She shut the door behind her and the through-draught subsided as she wiped her feet on the doormat and went into the living room.

One of the top windowpanes had broken during the night, either blown in or hit by swirling debris. The outside glass seemed to have fallen out in one piece, but the inside pane still had jagged edges and there were shards and putty on the floor under the window. She stared at the mess, then shut her eyes and rubbed her forehead.

Typical, she thought, unable even to start thinking about getting it fixed.

There was a cold breeze round her legs, so she left the room and went into the kitchen. She settled onto the kitchen chair and looked out of the window, into the flat on the third floor of the building facing out onto the street. It was used as a hospitality apartment by some construction company. The bathroom window had frosted glass. The people who stayed there for a night or two never considered the fact that they might be visible when they went to the toilet; as soon as the light went on their wavy outline was reflected through the glass. For more than two years she had seen the company's customers make love, shit and change tampons. To begin with it had embarrassed her, but after a while she started to find it funny. Then she got annoyed; she didn't want to see people pissing while she ate dinner. Now she didn't care any more. There were fewer visitors to the flat and the building looked rundown, hardly very hospitable. Today the window was grey and mute, empty.

A lot of plaster had fallen away from the façade overnight, into the slushy snow in the courtyard. There seemed to be two broken windows on the first floor. She got up and went over to the window, looking at the dark holes below, just like her living room. The kitchen heater warmed her legs, and she stood there until it started to burn. She didn't feel hungry, although she knew she ought to eat something. She drank some water direct from the tap.

This is fine, she thought. *I've got everything I want.*

She went into the living room again, restless, sat on the sofa and pulled her legs up, wrapping her arms round her knees, breathing deeply. It really was quite cold. There was no central heating in the building, and the free-standing heaters she had bought could hardly keep the flat warm even when the windows were intact. The draught had free rein over the largely empty floor. The few things she had bought came from the Salvation Army or Ikea, and she felt no personal attachment to them.

She looked round the room, watching the shadows chasing each other. The clear light she had loved so much to begin with was no longer white. The shimmering white of the walls, which used to absorb and reflect the light at one and the same time, had dried and become mute. Daylight no longer reached very far into the rooms. Everything just stayed grey, no matter how the seasons changed. The air was heavy and thick as clay.

The coarse fabric of the sofa was itchy, leaving marks in her skin, and she idly scratched herself as she went back into the bedroom and crept under the sweat-soaked bedclothes. She pulled the duvet over her head, it was damp under there. She soon warmed up, but there was a slightly stale smell. The rock musician on the ground floor turned his stereo on, and the bass travelled through the walls, making her bed tremble. The ringing started up in her ear again, irritatingly shrill this time, but she forced herself not to get up. It was still several hours before her shift started.

She turned to face the wall, staring at the wallpaper. It had been painted over with thin white undercoat and the old pattern showed through. The neighbours who shared that floor with her came home; she heard them clattering about and laughing. She put the pillow over her head and the laughter became muffled, and the sound in her ear louder.

I want to sleep, she thought. *Just let me sleep a bit longer, then maybe I'll be able to carry on.*

The man lit a cigarette, inhaled deeply and forced the chaos in his brain to calm down. He couldn't tell which feeling was strongest: fury at the betrayal, fear for the consequences, embarrassment at being tricked, or hatred of those who had done it.

He would get his revenge. Bloody hell, they would pay for this.

He finished the cigarette in under two minutes, leaving just a fiery column hanging from the filter like a small turd of burned tobacco. He stubbed it out on the floor of the bar, then waved to order another shot. Just one, just this one; he had to keep his head straight, had to be able to move quickly. He downed the drink, the holster rubbing reassuringly in his armhole. Fuck, now he was really dangerous.

An explanation, he thought. *I need to come up with a fucking good explanation for why it all went so wrong.*

He was about to order another measure but stopped himself in the middle of the gesture.

'Coffee. Black.'

He couldn't make sense of it. He couldn't see what the hell had happened, and he had no idea how he was going to explain it to his superiors. They'd demand that he put it right. It wasn't the bodies that were the problem, even if that sort of thing was never great. Murder victims attracted the attention of the police and meant you had to be more careful for a while. The problem was the lorry. It wasn't enough to track down the goods and return them. No, he would be personally forced to tidy up the mess. Someone had talked. He had to find the shipment, and he had to find the person who had made it disappear.

No matter how he looked at it, he realized that it had to have something to do with that woman. She had to be involved somehow, otherwise she wouldn't have been there.

He drank the coffee the same way as the shot, down in one. It burned his throat.

You're dead, bitch.

4

The lighting in the lift was as cold as ever, making her look like a dead fish. Annika closed her eyes to escape her reflection. She hadn't managed to get back to sleep, so she'd gone out to Rålambshov Park instead, trying to get some fresh air and light, but failing. The ground had been soft, all claggy and brown, churned up by rain and thousands of feet. She had walked in to work.

The newsroom was empty and desolate, as usual on a Sunday. She went over to her desk. The head of news, Ingvar Johansson, was sitting nearby talking on the phone, so she changed her mind and headed towards the crime-desk instead. Her head felt empty as she slumped onto Berit Hamrin's chair and phoned her grandmother.

The old woman had gone in to her flat in Hälleforsnäs to do some washing and get supplies.

'How are you?' her grandmother wondered. 'Have you had much wind?'

Annika laughed. 'Well, you could say that. One of my windows was blown out!'

'You're not hurt?' the old woman said anxiously.

Annika laughed again. 'Oh, don't worry so much! How are things with you? Is the forest still standing?'

Her grandmother sighed. 'More or less; but a lot of

trees came down. The power was off here this morning, but it's back now. When are you coming down?'

Annika's grandmother had been granted the use of a cottage on the Harpsund Estate after many years as the housekeeper of the prime minister's country residence. It was a small cottage without electricity or running water, and Annika had spent all her summer holidays there as a child.

'I'm working tonight and tomorrow night, then I'll come down to you sometime on Tuesday afternoon,' Annika said. 'Is there anything you'd like me to bring?'

'Oh, no,' her grandmother said. 'Just bring yourself, that's all I want.'

'I miss you,' Annika said.

She picked up a copy of that day's paper and leafed through it dutifully. It was pretty good. She was all too familiar with the hurricane articles, and skipped them. Carl Wennergren's piece about the double murder in Frihamnen wasn't up to much, though. The dead men had been shot in the head, it said, and the police were considering suicide. Really? Then came a description of Frihamnen that was almost poetic – Carl had evidently been out and got the feel of the place. It was 'attractively rundown' and had 'an international atmosphere'.

'Hello, gorgeous; *qué pasa*?'

Annika gulped.

'Hello, Sjölander,' she said.

The head of the crime team settled comfortably onto the desk in front of her.

'How are things?'

Annika tried to smile. 'Fine, thanks, just a bit tired.'

The man tapped her amiably on the shoulder and winked.

'Tough night, eh?'

She got up, grabbed the paper and gathered her bag and coat.

'Really tough,' she said. 'Me and seven blokes.'

Sjölander chortled. 'You've got some stamina, haven't you?'

She held the paper up under his nose.

'I was working,' she said. 'So what's going on in Frihamnen?'

He looked at her for a few seconds, brushing the hair from his forehead.

'No ID on the victims,' he said, 'no keys, money, weapons, chewing gum or condoms.'

'So their pockets were emptied,' Annika muttered.

Sjölander nodded. 'The police have nothing to go on; they don't even know who the victims were. Their prints aren't on any Swedish database.'

'So they've got no ideas? What about their clothes?'

The head of crime went over to his desk and switched on his computer.

'Outer clothes, jeans and shoes from Italy, France and the US, but their underwear had Cyrillic writing on it.'

Annika looked up.

'Foreign designer clothes,' she said, 'but cheap, locally produced underwear. The former Soviet Union or Yugoslavia, or Bulgaria.'

'You're keen on crime stories, aren't you?' he said with a grin.

He knew. They all knew. She shrugged.

'You know how it is. You never lose the habit.'

She turned and walked over to the night-desk. She could hear him chuckling behind her. *Why do I play along?* she wondered.

She switched on the computer to the right of the night-editor, curling up her legs on the office chair and settling down with her chin on one knee. Maybe she ought to check if anything had happened. She waited patiently for the programs to load, then opened the news agency's website, reading, checking, clicking.

'Hey, Bengtzon, what's your extension number?'

She looked over her shoulder and saw Sjölander waving a phone at her. After she'd called out her number, he shouted back, 'Some bird wants to talk about social services, something about women in trouble. I can't take it right now. And it's your sort of thing, isn't it? Can you take it?'

She closed her eyes and took a deep breath .

'My shift hasn't really started yet,' she said. 'I was planning to—'

'Are you going to take it or shall I get rid of her?'

She sighed.

'Okay, transfer her.'

A voice, calm and cool: 'Hello? I want to talk to someone in confidence.'

'You're always protected when you talk to a newspaper,' Annika said, her eyes still checking the news agency website. 'What's this about?'

Click, click, a draw in the local derby.

'I'm not sure if I'm talking to the right person. It's about a new organization, a new way of protecting people who have had death-threats.'

Annika stopped reading.

'Really?' she said. 'How?'

The woman hesitated. 'I've got information about a unique way of helping people under threat to get a new life. Most people don't know about this way of doing it, but I've been given permission to release this information to the media. I'd like to do this in a calm, controlled way, which is why I was wondering if there's anyone I could talk to at your paper.'

She didn't want to listen, and didn't really care. She stared at the screen: ongoing power-cuts . . . a new rocket attack on Grozny. She leaned her head on her hand.

'Could you send the information by post or fax?' she asked.

The woman was silent for a long time.

'Hello?' Annika said, ready to hang up with a sense of relief.

'I'd prefer to meet the person I talk to face to face, in a secure setting,' the woman said.

Annika slumped over her keyboard.

'That isn't possible,' she said. 'There's no one here right now.'

'What about you, then?'

She pushed her hair back, trying to think of an excuse.

'We'd have to know what this is about before we send anyone out,' she said.

The woman at the other end fell silent again. Annika sighed and tried to end the call.

'Well, if there wasn't anything else, then—'

'Did you know there are people living hidden lives, right now, here in Sweden?' the woman asked quietly. 'Woman and children who have been abused and threatened?'

No, Annika thought. *Not this*.

'Thanks for calling,' she said, 'but I'm afraid this isn't a subject we can look into this evening.'

The woman on the other end raised her voice.

'So you're just going to hang up? You're just going to ignore my work? Do you have any idea how many people I've helped? Do you really not give a damn about women in trouble? You journalists, you just sit there in your offices without a clue what society really looks like.'

Annika felt dizzy, suffocated.

'You don't know anything about me,' she said.

'The media are all the same. I thought the *Evening Post* would be better than the big morning papers, but you don't give a damn about abused and vulnerable women and children.'

The blood suddenly rushed to her head.

'Don't you dare presume you know what I think,' Annika said, far too loudly. 'Don't make statements about things you know nothing about.'

'So why won't you listen?' The woman sounded grouchy.

Annika put her hands to her face, waiting.

'This is about people who are isolated,' the woman at the other end of the line went on. 'Their lives have been threatened, they're terrified. Wherever they try to hide, there's always someone or something that means they can be tracked down, a social worker, a court hearing, a bank account, a nursery . . .'

Annika said nothing, just listened in silence.

'Most of them are women, of course. And children, as you can imagine. They're the group most at risk in society. But there are also witnesses who've been threatened, people who've left religious sects or are being hunted by the mafia, journalists who've written big exposés. But mostly it's women and children whose lives have been threatened.'

Annika slowly picked up a pen and started to make notes.

'There's a group of us behind this new organization,' the woman said. 'I'm in charge. Are you still there?'

Annika cleared her throat.

'What makes you different from existing women's support groups?'

The woman at the other end sighed tiredly. 'Everything.

Those support groups receive public funding, but no-where near enough of it. They don't have the resources to do what we do. We're an entirely private initiative, which means we can do an awful lot more.'

The pen stopped working and Annika tossed it into the bin and dug out a new one.

'In what way?'

'I really don't want to say over the phone. Can you meet me?'

Annika slumped in her chair. She didn't want to. She didn't have the energy.

'Bengtzon!'

Ingvar Johansson was looming over her.

'Hang on,' she said into the phone, then held it to her chest. 'What?'

'If you're not doing anything, you can type this up.'

The news-editor was holding a sheaf of sports results from the lower divisions.

The remark struck Annika like a physical blow. What the hell? So they thought they'd get her to do the things she used to do as a fourteen-year-old on the *Katrineholm Courier*, typing results into a table.

She turned away from Ingvar Johansson, lifted the receiver and said, 'I'd be happy to meet you, right now if possible.'

'This evening? Great!'

Annika clenched her teeth, aware of the news-editor's presence behind her.

'Where would suit you?' she asked.

The woman named a hotel in a suburb that Annika had never been to.

'In an hour?'

Ingvar Johansson had gone when she hung up. She quickly pulled on her jacket, slung her bag on her shoulder and checked the car rota. Naturally, there were none available, so she called a taxi. She could do what she liked in her own time, after all.

Type up your own fucking sports results, you chauvinist pig.

5

'Are you ready yet, darling?'

Eleonor was standing with her coat on in the doorway of the recreation room, pulling on her leather gloves.

He could hear the surprise in his own voice.

'What for?'

She tugged at the thin leather, annoyed.

'The business association meeting. You promised you'd come.'

Thomas closed the evening paper and lowered his feet to the heated clinker floor.

'Of course,' he said. 'Sorry, I forgot.'

'I'll be waiting outside,' she said, then turned on her heels and disappeared.

He sighed quietly. It was lucky he'd showered and shaved, at least.

He went up to their bedroom and took off his jeans and T-shirt. Pulled on a white shirt and suit and hung a tie round his neck. He could hear the BMW start up outside, revving impatiently.

'All right, all right,' he said.

All the lights in the house were on, but he had no intention of running round turning them off. He went out with his coat over his arm and his shoes unlaced, slid and almost fell on a patch of ice.

'There is such a thing as grit, you know,' Eleonor said.

He didn't respond, just shut the passenger door and put his hand on the dashboard as she pulled out onto Östra Ekuddsgatan. He knotted the tie on the way. His shoelaces would have to wait until they arrived.

It was already dark. Where had the day gone? It was dying away before it had properly got going. Had it even got light today?

He sighed.

'How are you doing, then?' she asked, friendly again.

He stared out of the window towards the sea.

'I feel a bit rough,' he said.

'Maybe it's that bug Nisse had,' she said.

He nodded, uninterested.

The business association. He knew exactly what the conversation would be about. Tourists. How many, how to get more, how to keep hold of them once they'd come. They'd discuss the problem of businesses that only opened during the short summer months, out-competing the locals who stayed open all year. The good food at The Waxholm Hotel. The preparations for the Christmas market, late-night opening and weekends. Everyone would be there. Everyone would be happy and engaged. It was always the same, no matter what sort of do they were going to. There'd been a lot of art recently. And a lot of parish stuff. A lot about preserving old buildings and gardens. And a lot about other people paying for it all.

He sighed again.

'Come on, cheer up!' his wife said.

'Annika Bengtzon? I'm Rebecka Björkstig.'

The woman was young, much younger than Annika had expected. Petite and thin, she looked like porcelain. They shook hands.

45

'I'm sorry for suggesting such an odd place to meet,' Rebecka said. 'We can't be too careful.'

They walked along a deserted corridor and reached a combined lobby and bar area. The lighting was low, the atmosphere was reminiscent of a state-run hotel in the old Soviet Union. Round brown tables with compact little chairs. A group of men were talking quietly in one corner, but there was no one else there.

Annika had a surreal feeling of being in an old spy drama, and had a sudden urge to flee. What was she doing here?

'I'm glad we could meet so quickly,' Rebecka said, sitting down at one of the tables and glancing cautiously over her shoulder at the men on the far side of the room.

Annika muttered something inaudible.

'Will this be in tomorrow's paper?' the woman asked with a hopeful smile.

Annika shook her head, feeling slightly giddy from the stale air.

'No, definitely not. It isn't certain it'll get into the paper at all. It depends on what the editor-in-chief decides.'

She sat down, conscious of lying, and avoided the woman's eyes.

Rebecka adjusted her thin skirt and pushed back her hair.

'What sort of thing do you normally write about?' she wondered, trying to catch Annika's eye, her voice sounding light but tired.

Annika cleared her throat. 'Right now I copy-edit and check articles,' she said truthfully.

'What sort of articles?'

She rubbed her forehead.

'All sorts. Last night it was all about the hurricane,

46

and earlier this week I went through a piece about a handicapped boy who was being let down by the local council . . .'

'Ah!' Rebecka said, crossing her legs. 'Then what we do fits in exactly with your area. We get most of our work through local councils. Can I have a cup of coffee?'

A waiter in a grubby apron had appeared beside them. Annika nodded when he asked if she'd like coffee as well, feeling unwell, wanting to go home, wanting to get away. Rebecka leaned against the curved back of the chair. Her eyes were bright, round, gentle, expressionless.

'We're a non-profit charitable foundation, but of course we have to be paid for our work. A lot of the time local social services departments pay our costs. We don't make a penny from any of this.'

Her voice was still gentle, but the words were forceful.

She's a gold-digger, Annika thought, looking up at the woman. *She's doing this to make money from vulnerable women and children.*

Rebecka smiled. 'I know what you're thinking. And I can assure you that you're wrong.'

Annika looked down, fiddling with a toothpick.

'What made you decide to call us, and why tonight?'

Rebecka sighed quietly, wiping her fingers on a paper napkin she took from her bag.

'To be honest, I was really only calling to see what the situation was. I was reading the articles about the hurricane, and I saw the phone number for the newsroom. We've been talking about trying to publicize what we do for a while, so I decided quite spontaneously to call.'

Annika swallowed.

'I've never heard of you,' she said.

The woman smiled again, a smile as fleeting as a draught blowing through a room.

'Until now we've never had the resources to deal with the influx of cases we know would follow any publicity, but now we've got them. Right now we've got the means and the opportunity to expand, so this feels like the right time to go public. There are so many people who need our help.'

Annika pulled her notepad and pen from her bag.

'So tell me how it works.'

The woman glanced round again, and wiped the corner of her mouth.

'We come in where official organizations can't quite cope,' she said slightly breathlessly. 'The only reason we exist is to help seriously vulnerable people to make a new life. For three years we've been working tirelessly to make the system successful. And we're now confident that it is.'

Annika waited in silence. Then, 'How?'

The waiter brought their coffee. It was dark and bitter. Rebecka put one of her napkins between cup and saucer, then stirred the drink.

'Our society is so computerized these days that no one can get away from it,' she said when the waiter had sailed off again. 'Wherever these people turn, there's someone who knows their new address, new phone number, new bank account, new tenancy agreement. Even if all this information is kept secret, they still have medical notes, social security records, a legal history, tax records, financial details. All sorts of things.'

'But can't that be sorted out somehow?' Annika asked cautiously. 'Isn't there some way of removing addresses from the system, getting new ID numbers and so on?'

The woman sighed again. 'Yes, there are various options. The problem is that they don't work. Our group has come up with a way of erasing people's histories completely. Did you know that there are over sixty official databases that practically every Swede appears in?'

Annika made a surprised noise. The coffee really was disgusting.

'I spent the first six months just identifying all these databases and registers. I worked out ways of getting round them. There were a lot of questions, and the answers weren't always easy to find. The methods that we've worked out are completely unique to us.'

These last words were left hanging in the air. Annika took another sip of the liquid, spilling a bit as she put the cup down again.

'Why did you get involved in all this?' she asked.

The silence was deafening.

'I was threatened myself,' the woman said finally.

'How?'

Rebecka cleared her throat, paused, dabbed at her wrists with a paper napkin.

'I'm sorry, but I'd really prefer not to go into it. It brings it all back. I've worked hard to get my new life, and I want to use my experiences to help others.'

Annika looked at Rebecka Björkstig, so cool and so soft at the same time.

'Tell me about what you do.'

Rebecka took a cautious sip of coffee.

'The organization is set up as a non-profit-making foundation under the name Paradise. What we do isn't really that remarkable, we just give people who have been threatened their everyday lives back. But for someone who has been stalked – someone who really knows what terror is – normal everyday life is paradise.'

Annika looked down at her notebook, embarrassed by the cliché.

'So how do you do that?'

The woman gave a quick smile, sounding confident now.

'The Garden of Eden was a safe place,' she said. 'It was surrounded by invisible walls that kept evil at bay. That's how we work. The client comes to us, and they pass through our hands behind an impenetrable barrier. They get erased, so to speak. So when anyone tries to track our client, no matter how they go about it, they hit the same brick wall: us.'

Annika looked up.

'But aren't you frightened?'

'We're aware of the risks, but the Paradise Foundation is in turn impossible to find. We have several different offices that we move between. Our telephones are routed through exchanges in different districts. There are five of us working full time at Paradise, and we've all been erased. The only way into Paradise is via an unlisted phone number.'

Annika looked at the little porcelain woman as she sat there unconsciously fiddling with a napkin. The woman was completely wrong in this setting, so pure and white against the shabby bar and dowdy decor.

'So how do you erase someone?'

Someone turned on a ceiling lamp somewhere behind Rebecka's head, casting a shadow over her face and making her expressionless eyes look like black holes.

'I think we should leave it there,' she said. 'I'm sorry, but I'd like to wait a while before releasing any more information.'

Annika felt a mixture of disappointment and relief, and let out a deep breath. Rebecka Björkstig pulled a card from her bag.

'Talk to your editor and see if you can write about what we do. If you get the go-ahead, call me, this is our secret number. I'm sure I don't have to tell you to be extremely careful with it.'

Annika swallowed and muttered something that sounded like agreement.

'If you can get authorization to publish, we can meet again,' Rebecka said, getting up, petite and bright, yet still in shadow.

Annika gave a meaningless smile and stood up. They shook hands.

'Well, we'll probably speak on the phone, then,' she said.

'If you don't mind, I'm in a bit of a rush,' Rebecka said. 'I look forward to your call.'

And then she was gone.

The waiter glided over to their table. 'That's fifty-five kronor for the coffee.'

Annika's thoughts were racing as she took a taxi back to the office. The suburbs flew past outside the dirty windows, industrial estates, unrelenting blocks of flats, main roads and traffic lights.

What did Rebecka Björkstig actually look like? Annika realized that she had already forgotten, and that her memories were vague and elusive.

Vulnerable people, abused women. If there was one subject she ought to avoid writing about, this was it. She was permanently disqualified.

What was that thing Rebecka had said about the Garden of Eden? Annika searched her memory, but she couldn't remember. She took out her notes, leafing through and trying to read in the flickering yellow light of the motorway.

That it was surrounded by invisible walls that kept evil at bay.

She put the notepad down and watched the blocks of flats in Blåkulla flash past.

What about the snake, then? Annika thought. *Where did that fit into her theory?*

6

Berit Hamrin was sitting at her desk in the newsroom when Annika got back. She went over and gave her a hug.

'The double murder?' she wondered.

Berit smiled. 'There's nothing like a little mafia turf-war.'

Annika took off her jacket, letting it fall in a heap on the floor.

'Have you eaten?'

They went down to the staff canteen, nicknamed 'The Seven Rats', and both chose the dish of the day.

'Have you got anything on the go?' Berit asked, buttering a piece of crispbread.

Annika sighed. 'I suppose there'll be more hurricane again tonight,' she said. 'And I went out to meet a woman who told me a really weird story.'

Berit raised her eyebrows in interest as she tasted the potato gratin.

'Weird stories can sometimes be great,' she said. 'Can you pass the salt?'

Annika reached back and picked up the salt and pepper from the next table.

'This woman reckoned that there's something called

the Paradise Foundation that helps threatened women and children to get a new life.'

Berit nodded encouragingly. 'Sounds exciting. Is it true?'

Annika hesitated. 'I don't know; she wouldn't tell me all the details. She seemed deadly serious. They've evidently come up with some way of erasing the pasts of vulnerable people.'

She took the salt from Berit and sprinkled some over her own plate.

'Do you think there'd be any problems if I check out a story of this sort?' she asked cautiously.

Berit carried on chewing for a few moments.

'No, not at all,' she said. 'You're thinking of Sven?'

Annika nodded, suddenly unable to speak.

Her older colleague sighed. 'I can see why you might be worried about what others will think, but at the same time it doesn't disqualify you from carrying out your job like any other journalist. It was an accident, and you've got the documents to prove it.'

There was nothing more to say, and Annika stared down at her plate, cutting a lettuce leaf to ribbons.

'Just make sure the bosses know,' Berit said. 'It's easier to get stuff into the paper if the old sods at the top think it was their idea.'

Annika smiled, and chewed her salad. They carried on eating in warm, companionable silence.

'Have you been out to Frihamnen?' Annika asked as she pushed her plate aside and reached for a toothpick.

Berit stood up.

'Coffee?'

'Black.'

She went and fetched two cups.

'It's a messy story,' she said as she handed Annika

her coffee. 'The men may have been Serbs, the police are guessing that it was something to do with the Yugoslavian mafia. They're worried there's going to be an all-out turf-war.'

'Any leads?'

Berit sighed. 'It's a difficult one,' she said. 'The forensics people were out there until it got dark, examining every last bit of grit in an attempt to find evidence and bullets.'

Annika blew on her coffee.

'So do we get to use all those lovely clichés? Execution? Gangland bust-up? Police fear gang warfare?'

They laughed.

'Probably all of them,' Berit said.

She wrote up her notes about the Paradise Foundation, then Jansson put her to work tidying up various pieces about the aftermath of the hurricane. She was starting to feel the effects of working the nightshift, and she kept rubbing her eyes to bring the words back into focus. As luck would have it, the large item about the handicapped boy was edited and ready to go in the paper, four pages about how social services had failed to fulfil their legal obligations and weren't giving the boy the care he was entitled to. It would be a quiet night, maybe even too quiet.

Just before midnight the rest of the nightshift went down to eat. Annika stayed at her desk, to answer the phone and keep an eye on news agency alerts. She was relieved not to have to go. Once the others had gone she hesitated for a moment, wondering whether to slip into a coma or run a few checks. She settled into Jansson's chair, his computer was faster for some reason, and did a quick search for the Paradise Foundation. The computer took its time, and failed to find anything. She tried Paradise on its own, and got a number of results: a travel agency, a Free Church minister in Vetlanda, a film starring Leonardo DiCaprio, but nothing about an organization that helped threatened women and children.

She went back to her desk and checked the news agency site. No breaking news. She dialled the internal number for the archive on the third floor; they had a folder containing the details of various foundations that were registered with the Tax Office. She asked for it to be brought over, but by the time the porter turned up with it she didn't feel like looking through it. Instead, she went for a walk round the office, rubbing her eyes, feeling tired, sluggish, unmotivated. She sat down at her desk again, wishing her shift was over, wishing she could go home. But she knew that she would soon be counting the hours until she could come back to work and get out of her flat. Her chest felt tight, oppressed by a feeling of how pointless it all was.

'Sjölander,' she called, 'do you want me to do anything? A fact-box about the history of the Yugoslavian mafia?'

He was on the phone, but gave her the thumbs-up.

Annika shut her eyes, swallowed, went over to Jansson's desk again and looked up the Yugoslavian mafia in the cuttings database.

To judge by earlier articles, criminal gangs from Yugoslavia had been established in various places in Sweden for several decades, big cities and small towns alike. Their main occupation had been smuggling and drug-trafficking, often using restaurants as a front, but in recent years the business had changed. When the government jacked up the tax on cigarettes a few years ago a lot of them had switched from smuggling drugs to tobacco. A carton of two hundred cigarettes cost between thirty and fifty kronor in eastern Europe, where Scandinavian brands like Prince and Blend were produced under licence. They were shipped either directly to Sweden or via Estonia.

Annika sat for a while reading some of the articles, then went over to Sjölander. He was off the phone and typing with just his index fingers.

'Are we going to say this was an internal dispute among the Yugoslavians?' she asked.

Sjölander sighed deeply. 'Well, that depends on what angle we go for. But it's definitely gang-related, some sort of mafia dispute.'

'Maybe we shouldn't blame any particular national group yet,' Annika suggested. 'There are loads of criminal gangs that have been active here for years. Do you want me to come up with an overview of the different groups and their favourite crimes?'

Sjölander was getting his index fingers ready to strike again.

'Why not?'

Back at her desk, Annika called her source. He answered after one ring.

'You're working late,' Annika said.

'Oh, so they've let you come in from the cold again, have they?' the detective said.

'Nope,' Annika said. 'I'm still frozen out. Have you got time for a few quick questions.'

The man groaned. 'I've got two bodies here,' he said, 'shot through the head.'

'Ah,' Annika said. 'Sounds painful. So are you sure they were from Yugoslavia?'

'Get lost,' Q said.

'Okay. A few general questions about different ethnic gangs. What do the South Americans do?'

'I haven't got time for this.'

'Just some little questions?' she pleaded in a small voice.

The detective burst out laughing.

'Cocaine,' he said. 'From Columbia. We doubled our seizures last year.'

'How about the Baltic States?' Annika wondered, frantically taking notes.

'Partly cigarettes. A lot of stolen cars. We think Sweden's becoming a transit country for the trade in stolen vehicles. Cars stolen in Italy and Spain are driven right up through Europe and put on ferries to the Baltic States and Russia.'

'Okay, what about other groups? You know them better than me.'

'The Turks used to deal in heroin, but in recent years that's gone over to the Kosovan Albanians. The Russians are into money laundering: so far they've invested half a billion kronor in property over here. The Yugoslavians are big in tobacco and alcohol smuggling. They run a few gambling dens and protection rackets. Sometimes with restaurants as their cover. Will that do?'

'Keep going,' Annika said.

'The biker gangs do debt collection and provide muscle for hire. They're all Swedes and other Scandinavians. The porn mafia is run by Swedes as well, but you already know all about that . . .'

'Ha ha,' Annika said drily.

'Financial crimes are almost always carried out by Swedish men. They often collaborate on things like asset-stripping, VAT fraud, that sort of thing. A few of them use heavies. We've also had a few Gambian gangs dealing in heroin.'

'Okay,' Annika said. 'That's enough for a fact-box.'

'Always nice to be able to help,' he said sourly and hung up.

Annika smiled. He was a sweetie.

'What are you doing?' Jansson asked as he came over holding a plastic cup.

'Something creative,' Annika said.

She typed up the material for the fact-box, added her name and sent the file to the shared filestore.

'I'm going to stretch my legs,' she said.

Jansson didn't respond.

The feeling of pointlessness tightened across her chest again.

7

The woman coughed, quietly but persistently. Her head was aching like mad, a throbbing pain from the wound in her forehead. She assumed she must have a slight temperature, to judge by how feverish she felt, and guessed that she might have some sort of infection in her chest or lungs. She had taken the first tablet of a course of broad-spectrum antibiotics at lunchtime. The glowing numbers on the clock-radio beside her bed indicated that it was time to take the second one.

She staggered out of bed, shivering, and looked through her medicines. She found the antibiotics under the plasters, and took a couple of paracetamol for the pain. The pills were old, she'd had them since Sarajevo, and the best-before date was several years ago. It couldn't be helped, she didn't have any choice.

She decided to try to sleep it off and crept back into bed, but she couldn't get back to sleep. A sense of failure gnawed at her. Various scenes flashed before her mind's eye, people died, strange fantasies began to materialize; her fever seemed to be getting worse. And in the end the little boy appeared, arms outstretched, always in slow motion, running, screaming, death in his eyes.

She got up, annoyed, coughed, drank half a litre of

water. She had to get rid of this before they found her. She didn't have time to be ill.

She pulled herself together. What was a little cold compared to what could have happened? The sea had closed over her head, ice-cold and black, all darkness and pain. She had fought against panic, forced her body into action, swimming underwater as far from the quayside as she could, coming up for air, diving again. The waves had thrown her the last few metres towards the quay on the other side of the harbour, her shoulder crashing against the concrete, and she had turned to see him standing there, staring out across the water, a black silhouette against the illuminated warehouse.

She had scrambled up into the oil terminal, laid down between two yellow bollards, and lost consciousness for a while. Fear and adrenalin had shaken her out of her torpor. She had got out of the wind and checked the contents of her bag. After a few tries she had managed to get her mobile working, and ordered a taxi to Loudden oil terminal. The wretched taxi-driver hadn't wanted to let her in his car because she was so wet, but she had insisted and had finally got him to drive her to this shabby motel.

She shut her eyes and rubbed her forehead.

The taxi-driver was a problem. He was bound to remember her, and would probably talk if he was paid enough. She ought to get away from here – pack her things and leave the room at once.

She felt a sudden sense of urgency. She got up, slightly steadier now that the pills had started to work, and pulled on her crumpled clothes. Her coat still felt damp.

She had just put her medicine kit in her bag when there was a knock at the door. Her heart leapt into her throat, fluttering anxiously.

'Aida?'

The voice was soft and low, muted by the door. The cat playing with the mouse.

'I know you're in there, Aida.'

She grabbed her bag and rushed into the bathroom, locked the door, climbed up on the edge of the bathtub and opened the little window. A cold wind burst in. She threw out her bag, yanked off her coat and forced it through the window. At that moment there was a sound of breaking glass out in the room.

'Aida!'

She heaved herself up and shoved her way out of the window, breaking her fall with her arms and doing a somersault. The sound of the bathroom door being broken in came through the window, a shriek of splintering wood. She pulled on her coat, grabbed her bag and ran off towards the motorway.

Monday 29 October

8

She got off the number 41 bus at the last stop, exhaling as she watched the bus glide away and vanish behind a low office block. Everything was quiet, there was no one in sight. Daylight was fading, withdrawing before it had properly arrived. She wouldn't miss it.

She hoisted her bag onto her shoulders and walked a few metres, looking round. There was an odd atmosphere out here among the warehouses and offices. This was where Sweden stopped. A sign over to the left indicated Tallinn, Klaipeda, Riga and St Petersburg, the new economies, the young democracies.

Capitalism, Annika thought. *Taking responsibility for yourself. Privatization. Is that really the answer?*

She turned into the wind and screwed up her eyes. Everything was grey. The sea, the quayside, the buildings, the cranes. The cold, squally drizzle. She closed her eyes, letting the wind batter her.

I have everything I ever wanted, she thought. *This is how I want to live my life. This was my choice. There's no one else to blame.*

She faced the wind again, and it made her eyes water. In front of her was the main office for Stockholm Port Authority, a fine old brick building with various wings and terraces and an irregular roofline. Behind the building loomed the giant silos, phallic, pointing at the sky. The terminal for Estonia was off to the left, and beyond that the water. To the right was a dock lined with cranes and warehouses.

She turned up the collar of her jacket, tightened her scarf and headed slowly towards the office. One of the Tallinn ferries was in port, towering above the port authority building. The Baltic States' window on the west.

As she rounded the corner of the office building she saw the cordons. The blue and white plastic fluttered in the wind off towards the silos, looking forlorn and frozen. There was no sign of any police. She stopped and studied the tongue of land stretching out in front of her. This must be the heart of the harbour. It was a couple of hundred metres long, with huge warehouses on all sides. In the distance, beyond the cordon, she could just make out a parking area for container lorries. The only people in sight were a few men with luminous yellow jackets over by the containers.

She walked slowly over to the police cordon, looking up at the huge silos. Even though she was standing firmly on the ground, their height made her feel dizzy. The top of the silos blended into the sky, grey against grey. She stared up at them until she bumped into the cordon.

Between the silos was a narrow gap untouched by daylight. This was where the two men had died. She blinked into the darkness to acclimatize her eyes, and could make out the dark patches left by their blood. The bodies were found at the opening of the passage, not hidden in the shadows.

She turned away from the site of death and looked round. There were rows of tall floodlights along the quaysides. The whole area must be brightly lit at night, apart from the gap between the silos.

If you were going to shoot anyone, why leave them lying in the glare of the floodlights? Why not drag them into the shadows?

She presumed that it all depended on how much of a hurry you were in.

She lowered her eyes, stamping her feet and blowing on her hands. The slush splashed. What a crap winter. Behind the cordon she could see Swedish Television's props store. She didn't know that was out here.

She walked round the cordon. It was freezing cold, the rain was light but sharpened by the icy wind off the sea. She wound the end of her scarf round her neck more tightly and headed towards the water, following a chain-link fence that marked the boundary with the Baltic. An articulated lorry that had seen better days was coughing up exhaust fumes on the other side and she pulled her scarf over her nose. The fence ended in a heavy gate beside the lines of containers. Three customs officials were checking the last but one lorry of the day. The final one would be the polluting monster behind her.

'So, what are we doing here, then?'

The man was red-faced with cold, a customs office uniform under his luminous yellow tunic. His eyes looked bright and cheerful. Annika smiled.

'I'm just curious. I work for a newspaper and read about the murders out here,' she said, gesturing over her shoulder.

'If you're researching a story, I'll have to refer you to our press spokesman,' the customs officer said, not unfriendly.

'Oh no, I don't write for the paper, I just make sure that what other people write is correct. Which is why it's good to get out every now and then and take a look about – to make sure the reporters aren't messing up.'

The man laughed. 'Well, you've got your work cut out,' he said.

'Like you, I guess,' Annika said.

They shook hands and introduced themselves.

'Have you almost finished for the day?' Annika asked, pointing towards the last lorry as it rolled towards the gate.

The man sighed lightly. 'Yes, I'm almost done. It's been a messy couple of days, with the police cordon over there and all the rest. And all the cigarettes.'

Annika raised her eyebrows.

'Did something special happen today?'

'We picked up a fake refrigerated lorry this morning, tobacco everywhere, in the chassis, in the roof, in the walls. They'd taken out all the insulation and packed the space with cigarettes.'

'Wow,' Annika said. 'How did you find it?'

The customs officer shrugged. 'Unscrewed a panel on the back. There was a bit of insulation, but not enough. There was another panel behind that, and that's where the cigarettes were.'

'How many?'

'You can fit half a million in the floor of a container, and the same in the ceiling and walls. Something like two million in total, at a rough value of one krona per fag.'

'Bloody hell,' Annika said.

'That's nothing compared to the amount that's coming in. There's no end of tobacco being smuggled these days. The gangs have given up on drugs and are peddling cigarettes instead. Since the government put up the tax on tobacco you can make as much profit from cigarettes as heroin, but at much less risk. If you're caught with heroin worth millions of kronor, you'll be in prison for years, but the same value in tobacco gets you hardly any punishment at all. They use padded tarpaulins, loose floors, hollow frames . . .'

'They're pretty inventive, then,' Annika said.

'Yes, you can't take that away from them,' the customs officer said.

Annika grasped the nettle.

'Do you know who the dead men were?'

The man shook his head. 'Nope. I'd never seen them before.'

Annika opened her eyes wide. 'So you actually saw them?'

'Yes. They were lying there when I arrived. Shot right through the head.'

'God, how awful,' Annika said.

The customs officer pulled a face and stamped to get some life in his feet.

'Well, it's about time to shut up shop. Anything else you're wondering?'

Annika looked round.

'Only what's in those warehouses.'

The customs officer pointed to them in turn.

'Warehouse number eight,' he said. 'Empty right now. Number two, at the back there, is the Tallinn terminal and maritime customs. All freight from Tallinn has to go through there and have its papers checked before it gets to us.'

'What sort of papers?'

'Shipping documents – the contents of every container have to be listed. Then they get one of these to show us.'

The man pulled out a bright green sheet of paper with various stamps, signatures, and the letters IN.

'And you check everything?' Annika wondered.

'Most of it, but we don't have time to check it all.'

Annika gave him a sympathetic smile.

'What makes you wave something through?'

The customs officer sighed. 'If you open the back of a lorry and see crates and cartons piled right up to the roof, your heart sinks. If we're going to check something like that, we have to take it into warehouse number seven over there in the container area, and unload the whole thing with forklifts. We've got customs officers who are trained to do that. Not enough, though.'

'No, I can imagine,' Annika said.

'Then there are sealed containers – lorries that are just driving through Sweden without unloading. No one's allowed to remove or add anything to a container like that until it reaches its country of destination.'

'And those are the ones that say TIR on them?'

The man nodded. 'There are other types of seal, but TIR is the most well-known. It stands for "Transport International Routier", and allows for sealed cargoes to pass through countries without customs inspections.'

Annika pointed. 'What are all those containers doing over there?'

He turned and looked at the parking area.

'That's where we keep freight that's waiting to be loaded onto a ship to the Baltic States, or anything that needs to have duty paid on it before it can be brought into Sweden.'

'Can you hire space there?'

'No, you just turn up and use whatever space there is. No one keeps a proper check on what's there. Or why. Or how long it's there. It could be anything.'

'Maybe even the odd carton of cigarettes?'

'That's all too likely.'

They smiled at each other.

'Well, thanks for letting me take so much of your time,' Annika said.

They walked off towards the entrance to the Frihamnen area together. Just as they were alongside the police cordon the floodlights came on, bathing everything in their harsh glare.

'What a waste,' the customs officer said. 'Young lads, probably not much more than twenty.'

'What did they look like?' Annika wondered.

'They didn't have much idea about winter,' the customs officer said. 'They must have been freezing, wearing just their smart leather jackets and jeans. Nothing on their heads or hands either. Trainers.'

'How were they lying?'

'Practically on top of each other, both of them with holes through their heads.'

The customs officer tapped his head.

Annika stopped.

'Didn't anyone hear anything? Don't you have security guards here at night?'

'There are dogs in all the warehouses, apart from number eight, which is empty. They bark like mad if anyone tries to get in. There's been a marked decline in theft and burglaries since they introduced the dogs, but they don't make very good witnesses. I don't know if anyone heard the shots. It was blowing a right storm, after all.'

They swapped business cards and said goodbye. Annika hurried away towards the bus shelter next to the sign to Tallinn, Klaipeda, Riga and St Petersburg. She was so cold her teeth were chattering. Loneliness enveloped her, heavy and wet. She stood there, a grey figure dissolving into the grey scenery. It was too early to go in to the office, too late to go home. Too much emptiness to think about.

9

When the number 76 suddenly appeared from behind the SVEX administration building, Annika acted on impulse. Instead of getting the number 41 back to Kungsholmen she went in to Gamla stan. She got off by the Royal Palace and weaved through the narrow alleys towards Tyska brinken, at the other end of the island. The rain had stopped and the wind had died down. Time stood still between the old buildings, the sound of the traffic on Skeppsbron died away, and her footsteps echoed dully on the frozen cobbles. Darkness was falling fast, colours transformed in the yellow light from the old streetlamps, reduced to small highlights in the circles of light. Black iron. Red ochre. Sparkling hand-blown glass in leaded windows. Gamla stan was another world, another time, an echo of the past. Naturally, her friend Anne Snapphane had managed to get an attic flat next to the old German Church. A sublet, but it was still pretty impressive.

She was home, busy cooking some pasta.

'Get another dish, there's enough for you too,' she said when she had let Annika in and locked the door behind her. 'To what do I owe this pleasure?'

'I've been out and about, I've just come from Frihamnen.'

Annika sank onto a chair under the sloping ceiling of the little kitchen, breathing in the heat and steam from the pan of pasta. The sense of pointlessness retreated, its place taken by Anne Snapphane's rolling stream of chatter. Annika gave mostly monosyllabic responses.

They sat opposite one another, adding butter, cheese and soy sauce to the tagliatelle. The cheese melted, forming sticky tentacles in the pasta. Annika twisted her fork through the food and stared out of the window. Roofs, chimneys and terraces formed dark shapes against the deep blue winter sky. Suddenly she became aware of how hungry she was, and ate until she was breathless, then drank a large glass of coke.

'Wasn't there a murder out in Frihamnen this morning?' Anne said, eating the last of her pasta and filling the kettle.

'Two, yesterday morning,' Annika said, putting her plate in the dishwasher.

'Great,' Anne said. 'So when did you get to be a reporter again?'

She poured boiling water in the cafetière.

'Don't jump to any conclusions. I'm further out in the cold than anyone thinks,' Annika said, walking into the open-beamed living room.

Anne Snapphane followed her with a tray holding two mugs, the cafetière and a bag of sweets.

'But you've started writing again? Properly, I mean?'

They settled into the sofa. Annika swallowed.

'No, I haven't. I just didn't want to be at home. And a double murder is always a double murder.'

Anne pulled a face, blew on the hot drink and took a sip.

'I don't know how you do it,' she said. 'Thank God for relationships and fashion and eating disorders.'

Annika smiled. 'So how's it going?'

'The head of programming thinks *Sofa Talk* is a great success. I'm not quite as enthusiastic. The whole team are working themselves into the ground, everyone hates the presenter, and the director is plotting with the floor manager.'

'What are the viewing figures like? A million?'

Anne Snapphane looked at her mournfully.

'My dear, we're talking about the world of satellite broadcasting here. Viewing shares. Target groups. Only dreary old public service broadcasters still talk about viewing figures.'

'So why are we always writing about them, then?' Annika said, opening the bag of sweets.

'I've no idea,' Anne said. 'You probably don't know any better. And *Sofa Talk* will never be any good unless we get some decent journalists in the team.'

'Is it really that bad? Weren't you supposed to be getting someone new?' Annika said, stuffing a handful of sweets in her mouth.

Anne Snapphane groaned loudly. 'Michelle Carlsson. Can't do anything, doesn't know anything, but looks disgustingly good in front of the camera.'

Annika laughed. 'Isn't that the TV industry in a nutshell?'

'Ha, that's easy for you to say,' Anne said. 'Tabloid journalists in glass houses shouldn't throw stones.'

Anne switched on the television, just at the start of the main news show.

'*Et voilà*, the epitome of pretension,' she said.

'Shh,' Annika said. 'I want to hear if they've got anything on the Frihamnen murders.'

The news began with the after-effects of the hurricane in southern Sweden. The local news team in Malmö had been out filming wrecked bus shelters, barns with their roofs blown off, broken windows. An old man scratched the back of his neck as he looked at the shattered remains of his greenhouse, and said something in such a strong Skåne accent that it should have been subtitled. The scene moved to inside an energy company, where a hollow-eyed spokesman declared that they were doing everything they could to restore power supplies to all their customers that evening. And gave the number of households still without power in Skåne, Blekinge and Småland.

Annika sighed quietly. It was incredibly dull.

Then came a report on the estimated cost of the damage, reckoned to run to many million kronor. A woman had been killed in Denmark when a tree fell on her car.

'Do they actually have trees in Denmark?' Anne Snapphane asked.

Annika looked at her northern Swedish friend.

'I don't suppose you've ever been that far from home, have you?' she said.

Then came subtitled reports from Chechnya and Kosovo. Russian troops, blah, blah, Kosovo Liberation Army, blah, blah. The camera swept over bombed buildings and dirty refugees on the backs of lorries.

'They evidently don't care about your murder,' Anne said.

'It isn't mine,' Annika said. 'It's Sjölander's.'

But, after a short item about something the Prime Minister had said, there was a live report from Frihamnen. The presenter read the details over footage of the space between the silos. They had pretty much the same information that the *Evening Post* had printed twelve hours earlier.

'God, they never manage to come up with anything new,' Annika said. 'They've had all day and they haven't found a thing.'

'They don't prioritize stuff like this,' Anne said.

75

'They're stuck in the fifties,' Annika said. 'They're happy as long as they've got a few moving pictures with a bit of sound. They don't give a damn about the quality of the journalism. Unless they're just incompetent. Their reporters are utterly useless.'

'Amen to that,' Anne said. 'God's gift to journalism has spoken. Hang on, have you eaten all the sweets? You could have saved me a couple!'

'Sorry,' Annika said, suddenly embarrassed. 'I have to go.'

She left Anne in her attic flat and headed along Stora Nygatan towards Norrmalm. The air didn't feel so sharp any more, just fresh and clean. Something inside her shifted, and she felt like bursting into song. She was standing at the pedestrian crossing by Riddarhuset, humming to herself, when a rather short man wheeling a bicycle appeared alongside her.

'I've just cycled all the way from Huddinge,' he said, making Annika jump.

The old man looked exhausted. His whole body was trembling and his nose was streaming.

'But that's miles away,' Annika said. 'Your legs must be made of rubber!'

'Not at all,' the old man said, tears trickling down his face. 'I could ride just as far again.'

The pedestrian crossing turned green. As Annika started to cross the old man followed her, hanging over his bike. Annika waited for him at the other side.

'Where are you heading?' she asked.

'The train,' he whispered. 'The train home.'

She helped him across Tegelbacken and over to the Central Station. The old man didn't have a penny on him, so Annika paid for his ticket.

'Is there anyone to look after you when you get home?' she asked.

The man shook his head, snot dribbling from his nose. 'I've just been discharged,' he said.

She left him by a bench outside the station, his head hanging, the bike leaning against his legs.

The picture was big, spreading over two pages of the paper. It was mostly yellow, the detail sharp and clear. Police in their heavy leather jackets, dark in profile; the luminous white of the ambulancemen; serious-looking men in greyish blue holding hand-tools; debris; the staircase; the gynaecologist's chair.

Then there were the two bundles, lifeless, crumpled, black. So large when they were alive, taking up so much space. They looked so small now, on the ground. What a waste.

She coughed, still shivering. Her fever had risen during the day. The antibiotics didn't seem to be helping. The wound in her forehead ached.

I have to rest, she thought. *I have to sleep.*

She let the newspaper drop and leaned back on the pillows. She got the falling sensation that always preceded sleep straight away, falling backwards, shallow breathing, fumbling for something to hold onto. And the boy, his fear, his screams, and her own infinite inadequacy.

She opened her eyes wide. From the other side of the wall came the sound of conference guests laughing. She had arrived at the hotel at the same time as a coach load of them, and had managed to sneak in as one of the participants. That had saved her for the time being, but not for much longer. If her old medication didn't start to work soon, she'd have to get some proper help. The thought scared her: that would make her so easy to find. She drank some water, her arm stiff and heavy, then tried to concentrate on the article again.

A gangland dispute. Yugoslavian mafia. No suspects, but several lines of inquiry. She turned the page. A picture of a taxi-driver.

She stopped, focused, struggled to sit upright against the pillows.

The taxi-driver, the one who hadn't wanted her to mess up his nice car. She recognized him. He had spoken to a reporter. The article told how he had driven a woman away from the oil terminal that night, wet as a drowned rat. The police were keen to contact the woman for questioning.

For questioning.

She sank back on the pillows and closed her eyes, breathing fast.

What if they'd started an official search for her? That would mean she definitely couldn't seek medical help.

She groaned loudly, panting for breath. The police were looking for her.

Don't panic, she thought. *Don't get hysterical. Maybe they aren't looking for me.*

She forced herself to calm down, and gradually managed to slow her pulse and her breathing.

How could she find out if they were looking for her? She could hardly call and ask, because they'd pick her up straight away. Maybe she could try to find out by pretending she had information, and see if the police gave anything away.

She groaned out loud again, and picked up the paper to read the rest of the article. There wasn't much more to it, and it didn't say if the police were actively looking for her. Then she saw the name at the bottom of the article. The reporter. Reporters sometimes made things up, made out they knew more than they did. But sometimes they knew more than they let on.

She coughed hard. She couldn't go on like this. She needed help. She picked up the paper and read the name again: Sjölander.

She reached for the phone.

10

Annika was just taking off her jacket when Sjölander called her name, waving the phone.

'It's some bloody woman saying she wants help. Can you take it?'

Annika shut her eyes. He was implying this was her subject. *Play along, keep it together.*

The woman on the other end sounded tired and unwell, and she spoke in a thick accent.

'I need help,' she panted.

Annika sat down, suddenly empty inside again, desperate for coffee.

'He's after me,' the woman said. 'He's hunting me.'

She closed her eyes to shut out the newsroom and leaned forward, slumping over her desk.

'I'm a refugee from Bosnia,' the woman said. 'He's trying to kill me.'

Bloody hell. Was she suddenly responsible for all the ills of the world?

The woman muttered something, it sounded like she was on the verge of losing consciousness.

'Hello?' Annika said, opening her eyes. 'What sort of state are you in?'

The woman started to cry. 'I'm ill,' she said. 'I daren't

go to hospital. I'm scared he'll find me. Can't you help me?'

Annika sighed silently, looking round the newsroom to see if there was anyone she could pass the call on to. No one.

'Have you called the police?' she said.

'He'll kill me if he finds me,' the woman whispered. 'He's tried to shoot me more than once already. I can't run any more.'

The woman's strained breathing echoed down the line. Annika felt a growing sense of impotence.

'I can't help you,' she said. 'I'm a journalist, I write articles. Have you tried social services? Or a women's refuge?'

'Frihamnen,' the woman whispered. 'The dead men at Frihamnen. I can tell you about them.'

Annika's reaction was purely physical. She gave a start and sat upright with a jolt.

'What? How?'

'If you tell me what you know, I'll tell you what I know,' the woman said.

Annika moistened her lips and tried to catch sight of Sjölander, but couldn't see him anywhere.

'Come out here,' the woman panted. 'Don't tell anyone where you're going. Don't take a taxi. Don't tell anyone who I am.'

Jansson was standing in front of her when she hung up.

'The Frihamnen murders,' she said by way of explanation.

'Why didn't Sjölander take it?' Jansson asked.

'It was a woman who called,' Annika said.

'Ah,' Jansson said, answering his own phone.

'I'm going out. I may be gone a while.'

Jansson waved her away.

Taking a copy of the Yellow Pages with her, Annika got the keys to one of the paper's cars from Tore Brand's son in reception. She took the lift down to the garage and eventually found the right car. She rested the phone book on the steering wheel and worked out where the hotel was. It was long way out, in a suburb she had never been to before.

There wasn't much traffic, but the roads were slippery. She drove carefully, pretty sure she didn't fancy dying in a crash.

It will all work out, she thought. *It'll be fine.*

She glanced up at the sky through the windscreen.

Someone's watching over me, she thought. *I can feel it.*

Thomas changed the channel to get away from the news, only to find an ill-tempered discussion programme instead. He carried on past an American soap and reached MTV. He realized he was staring at the singers' breasts, their tanned stomachs and flowing hair.

'Darling?'

He heard Eleonor close the front door behind her and stamp the snow from her feet.

'In the recreation room,' he called back, quickly changing back to the news again.

'God, what a day,' his wife said as she came down the stairs, pulling her silk blouse from her skirt and undoing the mother of pearl buttons on her cuffs. She fell onto the sofa beside him.

He pulled her to him and kissed her on the ear.

'You work too hard,' he said.

She pulled out her hairclip and shook her hair loose.

'You know it's the management course this evening, don't you?' she said. 'I did tell you several times.'

He let go of her and reached for the remote again.

'Of course,' he said.

'Was there any post?'

She got up and went back up to the hall. He didn't reply. He heard her stockinged feet on the wooden steps, squeak, squeak, squeak. The sound of envelopes being opened, the drawer where they kept bills being opened and closed, the door of the kitchen cupboard where they put paper for recycling.

'Have there been any calls?' she shouted.

He cleared his throat.

'No.'

'None at all?'

He sighed quietly. 'Just my mum.'

'What did she want?'

'To talk about Christmas. I said I'd talk to you and get back to her.'

She came down the creaking stairs again, holding a piece of crispbread with low-fat cheese spread in one hand.

'We spent last Christmas with them,' she said. 'It's my parents' turn this year.'

He picked up the television guide from the coffee table, leafing through the film reviews.

'What about staying at home this year?' he said. 'We could have Christmas dinner here. Then both sets of parents could come.'

She chewed hungrily on the crispbread.

'And who'd do the cooking?'

'We could get caterers in,' he said.

She stopped by the sofa and looked down at him with crispbread crumbs in the corners of her mouth.

'Caterers?' she said. 'Your mum always makes pig's head brawn and my mum makes her own garlic sausages, and you think we should get caterers?'

He got up, suddenly annoyed.

'Okay, don't then,' he said, pushing past without looking at her.

'What's up with you?' she called to his back. 'Nothing's good enough any more! What's so wrong with our life?'

He stopped, halfway up the stairs, and looked at her. So beautiful. So tired. So far away from him.

'Let's just go to your parents,' he said.

She turned away and sat down at the far end of the sofa, changing channel.

His vision blurred and he felt a lump growing in his chest.

11

'Do you mind if I let in some fresh air?' Annika asked, walking over to the window.

'No!' the woman hissed, sinking back onto the bed.

Annika stopped at once, feeling foolish and clumsy, and shut the curtains again. The room was gloomy, grey and unhealthy, with a smell of fever and mucus. In one corner was a desk and chair, and she switched on the table-lamp. She pulled the chair over to the bed and took off her jacket. The woman really did look ill, someone ought to be looking after her.

'So what happened?' Annika asked.

The woman suddenly started to laugh. She curled into a foetal position and laughed hysterically until she started to cry. Annika felt uneasy, and kept her hands folded in her lap.

Another one who's just been discharged, she thought.

Then the woman fell silent, panting for breath and looking up at Annika. Her face was wet with tears and sweat.

'I come from Bijeljina,' she said quietly. 'Do you know Bijeljina?'

Annika shook her head.

'The war in Bosnia started there,' the woman said.

Annika waited in silence for her to go on. But she

didn't. She closed her eyes, her breathing grew heavier, and she looked like she was drifting off.

Annika cleared her throat hesitantly, looking uncertainly at the sick woman on the bed.

'Who are you?' she asked in a loud voice.

The woman started.

'Aida,' she said. 'My name is Aida Begovic.'

'What are you doing here?'

'I'm being followed.'

She was breathing quickly and shallowly again, apparently on the verge of losing consciousness. Annika's feeling of unease was growing stronger.

'Isn't there anyone to look after you?'

No answer. Should she ring for an ambulance?

Annika went over to the bed and leaned over the woman.

'Look, how are you, really? Can I call someone? Where do you live? Where have you come from?'

The response was breathless.

'Fredriksberg in Vaxholm. I can never go back there. He'd find me straight away.'

'Who would?'

She didn't answer, just lay there gasping for breath.

'What was it you wanted to tell me about Frihamnen?'

'I was there.'

Annika stared at the woman.

'What do you mean? Did you see them get killed?'

She suddenly remembered the article in the paper, the taxi-driver that Sjölander had found.

'It was you!' she said.

Aida Begovic from Bijeljina struggled to sit up in bed, piling the pillows behind her back.

'I'm supposed to be dead as well, but I got away.'

The woman's face was flushed, her hair matted with sweat. She had an ugly cut on her forehead, and a big bruise on her cheek. She looked at Annika with eyes that seemed bottomless. Annika sat down again, her mouth completely dry.

'What happened?'

'I ran and fell, and tried to hide. There was so much rubbish all along the quayside. Then I ran, and he shot at me, and I jumped in the water. It was so cold, that's how I got sick.'

'Who shot at you?'

She closed her eyes, hesitating.

'It could be dangerous for you to know,' she said. 'He's killed before.'

'How do you know that?' Annika asked.

Aida laughed tiredly, touching her fingers to her forehead.

'Let's just say I know him well.'

The usual story, Annika thought.

'Who were the dead men?'

Aida from Bijeljina opened her eyes.

'They aren't important,' she said.

Annika's uncertainty gave way to a sharp, clear anger.

'What do you mean, not important?' she said. 'Two young men have been shot in the head.'

The woman met her gaze.

'Do you know how many people died in Bosnia during the war?'

'That's hardly relevant now,' Annika said. 'We're talking about Frihamnen in Stockholm.'

'Do you think there's a difference?'

They stared at each other in silence. The woman's fevered eyes had seen too much, and Annika was first to look away.

'Maybe not,' she said. 'Why were they murdered?'

'What do you know?' Aida from Bijeljina asked.

'Not much more than it said in the paper. That the

men were probably Serbs, they were wearing Serbian clothes. No ID, no fingerprints. Interpol have already contacted Belgrade. The police are looking for you.'

'Officially?'

The question was terse and concise. Annika studied her carefully.

'I don't know,' she said. 'I think so. Why don't you contact the police yourself and ask?'

The woman looked at her through the veil of fever.

'You don't understand,' she said. 'You don't know my situation. I can't talk to the police, not at the moment. What do you know about the killer?'

'Someone from the criminal underworld, according to the police.'

'Motive?'

'Some sort of gang dispute, like we said in the paper. What exactly do you know about all this?'

Aida Begovic from Bijeljina closed her eyes and collected her thoughts.

'You can't tell anyone that you spoke to me.'

'Of course not,' Annika said. 'Your anonymity as a source is protected by law. No one representing any official body is allowed to try to find out who you are. That would be illegal.'

'You don't understand. It could be dangerous for you. You can't write about anything I've told you, because they'd work out that you know.'

Annika studied the woman, hesitated, and didn't respond. She didn't want to make any promises. The woman struggled up against the pillows again.

'Have you been there? Have you seen the lorries out by the sea?'

Annika nodded.

'One of them is missing,' Aida from Bijeljina said. 'A lorry full of cigarettes, not just under the floor but the whole thing. Fifty million cigarettes, Fifty million kronor.'

Annika gasped.

'There'll be more murders – the man who owns the shipment won't let the thieves get away with it.'

'Is he the one who's looking for you?'

The woman nodded.

'Why?'

She closed her eyes.

'I know too much.'

They sat in silence for a while, until there was a knock at the door. Aida's face drained of colour. The knock was repeated. A soft voice, dark and masculine, almost a whisper.

'Aida?'

'It's him,' the woman whispered. 'He'll shoot us both.' She looked like she was on the verge of passing out.

Annika had a sudden and intense feeling of giddiness. She got up and the room seemed to lurch, and she staggered slightly.

Another knock.

'Aida?'

'We're going to die,' the woman said hopelessly.

Annika saw her bow her head and pray.

No, Annika thought. *Not here, not now*.

'Come on,' she whispered, pulling the woman from the bed and dragging her into the bathroom, then throwing her clothes in after her. She pulled off her own top, held it in front of her breasts and opened the door.

'Yes?' she said in a tone of surprise.

The man outside the door was tall and handsome, dressed in black. He had one hand inside his jacket.

'Where's Aida?' he said with a trace of an accent.

'Who?' Annika said, feigning confusion. Her mouth was dry and her heartbeat was thudding in her head.

'Aida Begovic. I know she's here.'

Annika blinked in the light of the corridor, and pulled her top up under her chin.

'You must have the wrong room,' Annika said breathlessly. 'This is my room. If you don't mind, I'm not feeling too good. I'm having an early night.'

The man took a step forward, putting his left hand on the door in an attempt to open it. Annika put her foot against the door on the other side out of reflex. At that moment the door of the next room opened. A dozen or so slightly tipsy conference delegates from Telia's IT department rolled out into the corridor.

The man in black hesitated, and Annika took a deep breath and yelled, 'Get out of here! Leave me alone!'

She tried frantically to close the door. Some of the conference delegates stopped and looked round.

'Go away!' Annika shouted. 'Help me, he's trying to force his way in!'

Two of the men from Telia puffed out their chests and turned towards Annika.

'What's going on?' one of them asked.

'I'm sorry, darling,' the man said, letting go of the door. 'We'll talk later.'

He turned on his heel and walked quickly towards the entrance. Annika closed the door, feeling sick with fear.

Oh God, oh God, just let me live.

Her legs were shaking so much that she had to sit down on the floor. Her hands were trembling, and she felt like throwing up. The bathroom door opened.

'Has he gone?'

Annika nodded silently. Aida from Bijeljina let out a sob.

'You saved my life. How can I ever—'

'We have to get out of here,' Annika said. 'Both of us, right now.'

She stood up, turned off the desk-lamp and started to gather her things together in the darkness.

'Wait,' Aida said. 'We have to wait until he's gone.'

'He's going to hang around to keep an eye on us,' Annika said. 'Fuck. Fuck!'

She struggled to hold back tears. The woman staggered to the bed and sank onto it.

'No,' she said. 'He'll think he's been tricked. He'll have paid for the tip-off, and he'll want to get even.'

Annika took several deep breaths. *Calm, keep calm.*

'How could he know you were here?' she said. 'Have you told anyone?'

'He tracked me down yesterday as well, and he must have worked out that I wouldn't get far. He'll have people out looking for me. Can you see if he's gone?'

Annika wiped her eyes and peered behind the edge of the curtain. She could see the man standing in the car park with two other men. They all got into the car parked next to hers and drove off.

'They've gone,' Annika said, letting go of the curtain. 'Come on, we're leaving.'

She turned the lamp on again. She pulled on her jacket, dropped her pen in her bag and picked up her notepad from the floor. Her back felt sweaty and her hands were cold.

'No,' Aida said. 'I'm staying. He won't come back.'

Annika straightened up, feeling her face flush.

'How can you know that? He's dangerous! I'll drive you to the airport, or the station.'

The woman closed her eyes.

'You've seen him,' she said. 'You know he's looking for Aida from Bijeljina. He can't kill me here, not tonight. He never does anything if he thinks he could get caught. He'll get me tomorrow instead, or the day after.'

Annika sank onto the chair, putting her notepad on her lap.

'So you haven't got anywhere to hide?' she said.

Aida shook her head.

'And there's no one who could look after you?'

'I can't go to hospital.'

Annika swallowed, hesitating.

'There might be a way,' she said. 'There might be someone who can help you.'

The woman didn't answer.

Annika leafed through her notepad, but couldn't find what she was looking for.

'There's a foundation that helps people like you,' she said, hunting around in her bag. There, right at the bottom, was the card. 'Call this number, tonight.'

She wrote the Paradise Foundation's secret number on a scrap of paper and put it on the bedside table.

'What sort of foundation?' the woman asked.

Annika sat beside the sick woman and brushed her hair back, trying to look calm and collected.

'I don't know exactly how it works, but there's a chance that these people could help you. They wipe out people's pasts and help them disappear.'

There was a look of scepticism in the woman's eyes.

'What do you mean, disappear?'

Annika tried to smile.

'I don't really know. Call them tonight, and ask for Rebecka. Tell her I told you to call.'

She got up.

'Wait,' Aida said. 'I want to thank you.'

With a good deal of effort she dragged a large bag from under the bed. It was rectangular, with a handle and shoulder strap, and had a large metal lock that needed a key to open it.

'I want you to have this,' Aida said, holding out a

heavy gold chain to Annika, with two charms attached to it.

Annika backed away, sweating in her coat, eager to get away.

'I can't accept something like that,' she said.

Aida smiled, for the first time, sadly.

'We won't meet again,' she said. 'You'll embarrass me if you don't take my gift.'

Reluctantly Annika took the necklace, feeling how heavy and solid it was.

'Thank you,' she mumbled, putting it in her bag. 'Good luck.'

She turned and fled from the sick woman, leaving her sitting on the bed clutching her big bag.

The car park was empty. She hurried over the tarmac, with steps that seemed uncertain, and too timid. She glanced over her shoulder, but no one was watching as she climbed into the newspaper's car. She drove out onto the motorway, checked the mirror, turned off at the first exit and parked behind a petrol station. She waited, looking round constantly, then drove towards Stockholm by a circuitous route.

There was no one following her.

Once she had parked the car in the garage she sat for several minutes, leaning against the steering wheel, forcing her breathing to slow down.

It was a long time since she had been so frightened.

More than two years.

12

With an easy gesture, the tall man in black opened the door to the hotel room from the corridor, far out in the suburbs. He could tell by the smell that he was in the right place. It smelled of shit and fear. The darkness inside was fragmented by a streetlamp outside in the car park that threw angular shapes onto the ceiling. He closed the door behind him and it shut with a soft click. He walked further into the room, aiming for the bed. He turned on the light.

Empty.

The bedclothes were messy, there was a roll of toilet-paper on the bedside table, but otherwise the room looked fairly untouched.

Fury washed over him like a wave, leaving him feeling drained. He sank onto the bed, putting his hand on a pile of snot-soaked toilet-paper. There was a small box on the floor next to his feet. He picked it up and read the label.

An empty box of antibiotics, the text in Serbo-Croat.

It had to be hers, she must have been here.

He stood up and kicked the frame of the bed until it gave way.

Bitch! I'm going to find you.

He searched the whole room, inch by inch, drawer

by drawer, checking the wastepaper baskets, the cupboards, pulling out the desk and the mattress.

Nothing.

Then he pulled out a knife and systematically started to shred the bedclothes, the duvet, pillows, the divan mattress, the seat of the chair, the shower curtain, close to bursting from the pressure inside him.

He sat on the edge of the bath, resting his forehead against the cold blade of the knife.

She had been there, his source was reliable. So where the hell had she gone now? They'd be telling stories about him soon, the man who couldn't get hold of the bitch. He should have forced his way in when he was here before, but he'd been unlucky, those bloody guests in the corridor, and that Swedish cow.

He sat up straight.

The Swedish woman, who the hell was she? He had never seen her before. She spoke without an accent, and she must have known Aida. Where from? And what was she doing here? How was she involved?

Suddenly his mobile phone rang in his inside pocket. He flung his jacket open and pulled out the phone, his fingers stroking his gun in passing.

'Molim?'

Good news. Finally, some good news.

He left the room and slid away from the hotel, not seen by anyone.

Annika Bengtzon walked in without knocking, and slumped onto the old sofa without even noticing the smell.

'I've had a tip-off that I want to run past you as soon as possible. Would now be okay?'

She looked tired, almost ill.

'It doesn't look like I have much choice,' Anders Schyman said irritably.

She took a deep breath, and slowly exhaled.

'Sorry,' she said. 'I'm a bit wound up. I've just got back from a really nasty . . .'

She shrugged off her coat.

'Last night I went to see a woman called Rebecka. She runs a new organization, something called the Paradise Foundation. They help people who've been threatened to get a new life, mainly women and children. It sounded very exciting.'

'How do they help?'

'They erase them from every official register. She didn't want to tell me exactly how they do it before I'd got the green light for publication.'

Schyman was watching her. She was nervous.

'We can't give a guarantee like that until we know what the story's about, you know that,' he said. 'Any organization of that sort would have to be checked incredibly carefully before we ran a story about it. This Rebecka could be anyone, a fraudster, a blackmailer, a murderer, anything.'

She gave him a long look.

'Do you think I should find out? I mean, do you think I . . . ?' She fell silent. He realized what she was after.

'Meet her again and say that we're interested. But I don't want this to take time and effort away from your work here on the nightshift.'

She got up from the sofa and sat down in one of the chairs by his desk.

'You've got to get rid of that terrible sofa,' she said. 'Why don't you get someone to take it away?'

She put her notebook down on the desk. He hesitated for a moment, then decided to be honest with her.

'I know what you want. You want me to let you off the nightshift and let you be a reporter again.'

He leaned back, and finished the thought.

'And that isn't possible right now.'

'Why not?' she said quickly. 'I've been working nights for one year and three hundred and sixty-three days. I've been on a permanent contract since the court case. I've done my bit. I want to write. For real.'

He suddenly felt incredibly tired. *I want to. I'm going to. Why can't I?* Spoiled children, more than two hundred of them, all wanting to get their own way, all of them thinking that their articles or duties or pay-grade was the most important thing in the world. He couldn't re-allocate her now, not ahead of the looming reorganization.

'Trust me,' he said. 'Now is not the time.'

She looked at him carefully for several seconds, then nodded.

'I get it,' she said, and got up to leave, her coat and bag clasped to her chest in an untidy bundle.

Anders Schyman sighed as she closed the door.

The freshly polished floor shimmered, and the computer screens made the gloom vibrate. Ice-blue faces focusing all of their attention on the virtual world in front of them, keyboards sang, clickety clack, clickety clack, mice chased across screens, nibbling, copying, changing, deleting. Jansson was on the phone, hammering frantically at his keyboard. She dropped her things on the floor by the night-desk and went out to the toilets, where she ran warm water over her wrists. She felt frozen to the core.

She closed her eyes and saw the man in front of her, the handsome man in black with his hand inside his jacket, the murderer. She couldn't remember what she had said, what he had said, just her own awkward confusion and paralysing fear.

Why me? she thought. *Why is it always me?*

She dried her hands, looking at her miserable face in the mirror.

Grandma, she thought. *I can go and see Grandma tomorrow, sleep, relax, live.*

A vague sense of calm coursed through her hands, her body. The tightness in her chest eased slightly.

Paradise, she thought. *Maybe I should try to get to grips with the Paradise Foundation anyway. Perhaps I won't spend all my days off down in Lyckebo after all, perhaps I could do a bit of writing.*

She smiled to herself. The tip-off about the foundation might actually be a turning point. She would have to do some serious research, really work at it. Schyman would . . .

She suddenly felt extremely cold, and her chest felt tight again.

Schyman! What if he was right? What if Rebecka was bluffing, lying, making things up? She put her hand to her mouth and gasped. Damn. Aida from Bijeljina. She had already referred someone to Paradise . . .

The chill spread through her body.

Oh God, how could she have done something so stupid? Recommending an organization that she knew nothing about?

She went into one of the cubicles and sat down on the toilet, giddy and weak. Was there no end to her stupidity?

She took several deep breaths and tried to pull herself together.

What have I actually done? What choice did Aida Begovic have? If I hadn't been there, Aida would already be dead.

She went back to the basin and drank some water from the tap, then looked up at her flushed face in the mirror.

On the other hand, how could she be sure of that? Maybe Aida was lying as well – she could simply be mad. Maybe she spent her time cycling from Huddinge to Stockholm until she was exhausted, with no money to get home again. Maybe the handsome man in black was her brother, and just wanted to get her home to her family?

She shut her eyes again and leaned her head against the tiles, taking more deep breaths.

No one need ever know. No one would ever find out what she'd done. Aida was right. They would never meet again. If Paradise actually worked, she would disappear, for ever.

If it didn't, she would die.

There was one way to find out if Aida knew what she was talking about. Annika went back to her desk and dialled Q's number.

'I really don't have time for this tonight,' her police source said.

'Have you found the lorry?' she asked quickly.

A long, surprised silence.

'I know you're looking for it,' she said.

'How the hell do you know about the lorry?' he asked. 'We've only just been told that it's missing. We haven't even put out an alert.'

She breathed out. Aida hadn't been lying.

'I have my sources,' she said.

'You're getting more and more unreal,' Q said. 'Have you got second sight?'

She couldn't help laughing, a little too loudly.

'Seriously, though,' Q said, 'this isn't a game. Be careful who you talk to about this.'

Her laughter caught in her throat.

'What do you mean?'

'Anyone who knows about the missing lorry is in danger, including your source.'

She shut her eyes and gulped.

'I know.'

'Know what?'

'What do you know?'

He sighed quietly.

'This is a long way from over,' he said.

'There are going to be more murders,' Annika said in a low voice.

'We're trying to put a stop to it, but we're way behind them,' Q said.

'How much of this can I write?'

'We can let you have the lorry, or, to be more accurate, the trailer. You can write that you know it's gone missing, with a load of cigarettes of uncertain value.'

'Fifty million,' Annika said.

She could hear his breathing on the line.

'You know more than me, then, but I believe you.'

'Who were the two men?' she asked.

'We still don't know.'

'My source says they're not important. What do you think she meant by that?'

A few seconds of silence.

'So your source is female? You know we're looking for her? She was probably meant to be the third victim, we've found blood on the quayside not far from the site of the murders.'

Silence.

'Bengtzon, for fuck's sake, be careful.'

Then he hung up.

She sat there listening to the empty static of the line for several seconds with an indefinable sense of unease.

'What was all that about?' Jansson asked.

'Just checking something,' she said, and headed off towards the crime desk.

Sjölander was on the phone and looked up in annoyance. She perched on the edge of his desk, the way he always did on hers.

'The Frihamnen murders. The story's got a way to run yet. A trailer-load of smuggled cigarettes has gone missing, and the police are already waiting for the next murder.'

The head of crime nodded appreciatively.

'Good work,' he said. 'Are you writing it up yourself?'

'I'd rather not,' she said. 'But it's solid – I've got it from two sources. One of them's police.'

'Email me what you've got,' he said.

'Do you want a bit of background info on tobacco smugglings as well?'

He had already picked up his phone, and gave her the thumbs-up.

Tuesday 30 October

13

Annika was lying in bed, wide awake and staring at the grey, cracked ceiling. The daylight behind the white curtain suggested it was the middle of the day, bad weather. Unusually, she had slept well, and couldn't feel any aches or pains anywhere.

She rolled over onto her side, and her eye caught the card lying on her bedside table. Rebecka's number. The decision appeared out of nowhere, she just sat up in bed and dialled the number, impulsively, out of curiosity.

There was a ringing tone. It sounded just like any other phone. She waited expectantly.

'Paradise.'

The voice belonged to an older woman.

'Er, my name's Annika Bengtzon. I'd like to talk to Rebecka.'

'One moment . . .'

There was the usual sound of static as the phone was put down, and she heard footsteps, a toilet flushing. She listened hard. So far things at the Paradise Foundation sounded completely normal.

'Annika? Lovely to hear from you!'

The light voice, warm and relaxed.

Annika was suddenly eager, she had almost forgotten what it felt like.

'I'd like to see you again,' she said. 'When would suit you?'

'This week's difficult, we've got several new clients coming in. Next week looks pretty busy as well.'

Annika's heart sank. Damn.

'Why did you get in touch if you haven't got time to talk?' she said sullenly.

Silence again, the crackle of static.

'I'll be only too happy to meet you, when I've got time,' Rebecka said in an airy tone of voice, cool, neutral.

'And when will that be?'

'I've got a meeting in Stockholm at two o'clock. We could meet just before that. That's the only gap I've got.'

Annika looked at her alarm clock.

'What, today?'

'If that suits you.'

She lay down, holding the phone to her ear.

'Of course,' she said.

When they had hung up she didn't move, just lay there feeling content. For a moment light shimmered into the room again. She threw the covers aside, pulled on her jogging pants and hooded top and ran down to the shower in the building on the other side of the courtyard, clutching her soap and shampoo. The water was warm and soothing, and she washed her hair and dried herself thoroughly. The light had returned.

She ran back up the stairs, made some coffee and ate a yogurt, then brushed her teeth at the sink. She wiped up the water she had splashed on the floor.

There was a cold breeze from the broken window in the living room. She swept up the glass and plaster, dug out a large paper bag from the supermarket and taped it over the hole.

Soon, she thought. *Soon I'll know how Paradise works. And soon I'll be with Grandma in Lyckebo.*

106

Rebecka was wearing the same clothes as last time, neutral colours, linen or cotton. Her hair scraped back, blonde, a slightly strained set to her mouth.

Eva Perón, helping the poor and the needy, Annika thought.

'I haven't got long,' the woman said. 'Let's do this quickly.'

Annika decided that Rebecka seemed to have a fondness for hotel bars, as the woman waved over a waiter and ordered mineral water for them both.

'We'd got to the bit about erasing people,' Annika said, leaning back. Her hair was still damp and smelled of Wella shampoo. 'You help people to disappear. How does that work?'

Rebecka sighed and picked up a napkin.

'You'll have to excuse me,' she said, wiping her hands, 'but we've got a lot on at the moment. We've just got a new case that's quite complicated.'

Annika looked down at her notebook and tested her pen. *Aida from Bijeljina?* she thought to herself.

The waiter arrived with their water. His apron was clean. Rebecka waited for him to go, just like last time.

'Well, you have to bear in mind that these people are extremely frightened,' she said. 'Some of them are practically paralysed with fear. They can't go to the shops or the post office, they can't function as normal people.'

She shook her head at these tragic cases.

'It's awful. We have to help them with everything. Practical details like childcare, a new home, work, schools. Then there's psychiatric and social care as well, of course. A lot of them are seriously damaged people.'

Annika was taking notes and nodding. Yes, she understood, thinking of Aida again.

'So what do you do?' she asked.

Rebecka wiped a mark from her glass and took a sip of water.

'The client is able to get hold of their contact person twenty-four hours a day. It's absolutely vital that someone is available at all times, whenever they need help.'

Get to the point, Annika thought.

'Where do these people live? Do you have a large property somewhere?'

'Paradise has several properties around Sweden. We own them, in principle, or rent them through a dummy company so they can't be traced. Our clients stay in one of those for a while. Any treatment they receive during that time takes place without the doctor knowing their true identity. No official medical notes are taken. Our clients are given a reference number, and hospitals and medical centres can find out via Paradise which local health authority will pay the bill. Most of our clients usually don't seek help in their local area . . .'

Annika was taking notes. Yes, that all made sense.

'How long do you have a . . . client with you?'

'As long as necessary,' Rebecka said, her breathless little voice sounding very firm. 'There's no upper time limit.'

'But on average?'

The woman dabbed at her lips.

'If everything goes to plan, we're usually finished in three months.'

'And by then you'll have arranged a new home, medical help, and what else?'

The woman smiled. 'There's a lot that needs doing if you're going to set up a whole new life. Wages and child allowance, for instance. We have an arrangement with several banks. Our clients don't need to have an account based in the place where they live. Every time money needs to go in or out of the account, the bank contacts Paradise, which arranges the transactions using a reference number. The same thing applies with childcare, schools, clinics, national insurance, tax. Everything, really. A lot of them need legal assistance, and we sort that out for them as well.'

Annika carried on taking notes.

'So you organize new jobs, new homes, new child-care, schools, doctors, lawyers, and it's all managed through Paradise?'

Rebecka nodded.

'The person under threat disappears behind an impenetrable wall. Anyone trying to track down someone who's been erased will find only us, and that's where it stops.'

'What do these people live off while the process is going on? Surely they can't work?'

'No, of course not,' Rebecka said. 'A lot of them are on sickness benefit, others are on welfare. Often they have children, so they get child allowance and other benefits. And legal aid is often available for cases like custody disputes, for instance.'

Annika considered this.

'But if the people chasing them don't give up, what do you do then?' she asked. 'Can you help people to get new ID numbers?'

'We've carried out sixty successful erasures. None of our cases has needed to change their ID officially. It just hasn't been necessary.'

Annika finished what she was writing and lowered her pen. This all sounded quite incredible. She looked around the bar. Circular tables, lots of brass. A thick carpet, low lighting.

Where were the gaps in the story?

Annika shook her head.

'How can you be certain that everyone who comes to you is telling the truth? Couldn't they be criminals trying to get away from the police and the legal system?'

Rebecka shushed her as the waiter walked past.

'Could I have a new glass, please? This one's dirty.'

Turning back to Annika, she continued, 'I understand your question. But no private individual can turn to Paradise and ask to be erased. We only act at the request of the authorities. Our clients come to us via the police, social services, the public prosecutor's office, the foreign ministry, embassies, immigrant organizations and so on.'

Annika scratched her head. Okay . . .

'But if you're so secretive, how do you actually get your cases?'

The woman got her new glass, rattling with ice-cubes.

'Up until now our clients have reached us through contacts and recommendations. We've had cases from all over the country. As I said, the reason I contacted you is that we feel ready to expand our operation.'

The words hung in the air. Annika left them there for several seconds.

'Exactly how much do you charge for your services?' she asked.

Rebecka smiled.

'Nothing. The only payment we receive is from the social services, for administrative costs and any charges we incur during the process of erasing someone. We don't make any profit from our activities. We just cover our costs. Even if we're a non-profit organization with idealistic aims, we still have to charge for our work.'

Yes, she'd heard that one before.

'So exactly how much are we talking about?'

The porcelain woman bent down and took something out of her bag.

'Here's some information about our work. It's fairly informal, not very elegantly expressed, but the authorities we deal with already know us, one way or another, and already know how competent we are.'

Annika took the sheet of paper. At the top was a PO box address in Järfälla. There followed an outline of the services Rebecka had just described. At the bottom she read:

For information about costs please contact us at the address or phone number above.

'So what do they pay you?' Annika asked once more.

Rebecka was looking for something in her bag.

'Three thousand, five hundred kronor per day, per person. Which is a very low charge for looking after someone. Here, you can take a look at this as well,' she said, handing over another sheet of paper.

It contained roughly the same information, in a little more detail.

'Well,' Rebecka said. 'What do you think, are we worth writing about?'

Annika put the sheets of paper in her bag.

'I can't answer that now. First I have to talk to my bosses and find out if the paper is interested in covering this. Then I'll have to check what you've told me with some of the official authorities you deal with. Maybe you could let me have a few names?'

Rebecka considered this, folding her napkin.

'Well,' she said, 'I suppose I could. But you have to appreciate that this is all extremely sensitive, it really is top secret. No one will talk about us, unless I've told them it's okay. Which is why I'd rather get back to you with a list of names.'

'Of course,' Annika said. 'When that's done, I'll need to talk to some of your cases, someone who's been erased.'

111

The cool smile again.

'That might be trickier. You'll never find them.'

'Maybe you could ask them to call me?'

The petite woman nodded. 'Yes, that's one option. But they don't know our routines. We never let them find out how we work, that way they can't give themselves away.'

'I wasn't thinking of asking your clients about your working practices. I want to find a vulnerable woman who's prepared to say, "Paradise saved my life."'

Rebecka smiled broadly for the first time. Her teeth were small and white as pearls.

'I can probably arrange that,' she said. 'There are lots of women in that position. Was there anything else?'

Annika hesitated. 'Just one thing. What's your real motivation for doing this?'

Rebecka quickly crossed both her arms and legs, adopting the classic defensive posture.

'I don't want to talk about that.'

'Why not?' Annika said gently. 'Your organization is fairly unusual, there must have been something that prompted you to set it up?'

They sat in silence for a few moments. Rebecka's foot swung back and forth.

'I don't want you to write about this,' she eventually said. 'This is strictly private, between the two of us.'

Annika nodded.

The woman leaned forward, eyes wide open.

'As I said,' she whispered, 'I was personally threatened. It was an awful experience, absolutely awful. In the end I wasn't functioning at all, not sleeping, not eating.'

She looked over her shoulder, her gaze sweeping over the other customers in the bar, then leaned forward even closer.

'I decided to survive. That was how I began to construct this support network. Through my work I discovered loads of people in similar situations. And I decided to try to make a difference, to take responsibility in an area where official organizations weren't able to.'

'Who was threatening you?' Annika said.

Rebecka swallowed, her lower lip trembling.

'The Yugoslavian mafia,' she said. 'Have you ever heard of them?'

Annika blinked in confusion.

'What have you got to do with them?'

'Nothing!' Rebecka said hotly. 'It was all a big mis-understanding! It was dreadful. Dreadful!'

She got up suddenly.

'Excuse me,' she said, hurrying off to the toilet. On the table she left a little heap of crumpled napkins.

Annika sat looking in the direction Rebecka had disappeared in. What was this all about? Another tobacco thief?

She sighed and took a sip of the now lukewarm water, reading through her notes. Although she had written a lot, she knew there were gaps in the story, and she couldn't see what they were yet. And what did the Yugoslavian mafia have to do with it all?

The porcelain woman was taking her time. Annika was starting to get impatient, looking at her watch. Her train to Flen would be leaving soon. She paid the bill and had just put her jacket on when Rebecka came back, bright-eyed and carefree.

'I'm sorry,' the woman said with a smile. 'The memories are so painful.'

Annika looked at her, and decided she may as well get the question out of the way.

'Have you got anything to do with those missing cigarettes?' she asked, sounding slightly stressed.

Rebecka smiled and blinked innocently.

'Have you lost your cigarettes? I don't smoke.'

Annika sighed. 'Well, I won't be able to write anything without that list of contacts in official organizations,' she said. 'It's important that I get that as soon as possible.'

'Of course,' Rebecka said. 'I'll be in touch soon. If you don't mind, I'd prefer to leave before you, so that we're not seen together. Can you wait a few minutes?'

Mission Impossible, Annika thought. *The target has left the building.*

'Of course,' she said.

14

The rhythm of the train forced her into a sort of concentrated calm before they had even crossed the Årsta bridge. The Tanto district glided past on her left, big buildings with big picture windows facing the water. Then greenery: how small Stockholm was! The pine trees rushing past filled her field of vision with their dark winter greenery, swaying in time with the train.

Erasing people, she thought. Was that really possible? For an organization to be listed as representing people on official documents, contracts, any dealings with official bodies: was that even legal?

She took out her notebook and pen and started to make some notes.

If local councils really did pay for the services of the Paradise Foundation, then it had to be legal, she reasoned.

Then there was the money. How much did it cost to be erased?

She looked through her notes.

Three thousand, five hundred kronor per person, per day. Maybe that was a reasonable amount, she had no way of knowing.

She made a methodical list of the costs: five people working full time, earning maybe fifteen thousand per month, plus national insurance, that came to about one hundred thousand kronor per month. Plus property costs. Suppose they had ten houses, each one costing about ten thousand per month in rent or mortgage payments. Another hundred thousand kronor. What else? The local health authorities stood for healthcare costs. And local councils provided social security payments. National insurance covered sick pay, and legal aid paid for any legal costs.

So the total cost ought to be something like two hundred thousand kronor per month.

What about income?

Three thousand, five hundred per day for a month came to one hundred and five thousand kronor for one person.

If they help just one woman with one child each month, they're making a profit of ten thousand, she calculated.

She stared at her figures in surprise.

Did that really add up?

She went through the figures again.

Sixty cases at three thousand, five hundred per day, for three months, came to something like eighteen million.

Over the course of three years they'd built up costs of approximately seven million kronor, which meant a profit of almost twelve million.

This has to be wrong, she thought. *I'm only guessing at their costs. Maybe they're much higher, maybe there are things I have no idea about. Maybe they employ their own doctors and lawyers, with loads of contact personnel on standby up and down the country, all day, every day. That would be expensive.*

She put her things back in her bag, leaned back in her seat and let herself be gently rocked by the train.

The sounds were always the same, Anders Schyman thought. The scrape of chairs, a talk-show on the radio, CNN on low in the background, the rustle of paper, a cacophony of male voices rising and falling, short, heavily stressed sentences. Laughter, always laughter, hard and quick.

The smells, always coffee, a hint of foot-odour, aftershave. Lingering tobacco smoke on people's breath. Testosterone.

The management group met each Tuesday and Friday afternoon to go through long-term strategies and initiatives. They were all men, all over forty, they all had company cars and exactly the same dark blue jackets. He knew that they were known as the Blue Cock Parade.

They always met in editor-in-chief Torstensson's splendid corner office with its view of the Russian Embassy. They always had Danish pastries and biscuits. Jansson was always the last to turn up; he always spilled coffee on the carpet, never apologized and never wiped it up. Schyman sighed.

'Well, if we could . . .' Torstensson said, his eyes fluttering round the room. No one took any notice of him. Jansson drifted in, still half-asleep, his hair sticking out. He spilled coffee on the floor before taking a seat at the far end of the table. Sjölander was sitting next to him, talking into his mobile. Ingvar Johansson was leafing through a sheaf of printouts. Picture Pelle was standing there laughing at something the entertainment editor had said.

'Okay,' Schyman said. 'Sit down, so we can get out of here sometime soon.'

The chatter died away and someone switched off the radio. Sjölander ended his call, Jansson took a biscuit. Schyman himself remained standing.

'Well, with the benefit of hindsight, it was absolutely right to go hard on the hurricane,' Schyman said as the men settled into their seats. He held up a copy of Saturday's paper in one hand as he leafed through the rest of the papers with the other.

'We were best, from start to finish, and we deserved to be. We saw what was coming and we deployed our resources in a new way. All the different departments and teams worked together, and that gave us a strength that no one else could match.'

He put the papers down. No one said anything. This was more controversial than it seemed. Each of these men was lord of his own domain. No one wanted to relinquish power and influence to anyone else. In extreme circumstances it sometimes happened that these bosses sat on their own news in order to stop any of the others muscling in on it. If they collaborated, power was shifted further up the hierarchy, to the level of the assistant editorial manager that the editor-in-chief wanted to introduce.

He looked through the papers again, and sat down.

'Our coverage of the handicapped boy also seems to have been a success, the local authority is evidently re-thinking its decision and will now be giving him the help he's entitled to.'

There was a heavy silence. Only CNN and the air-conditioning carried on as usual. Anders Schyman knew that the others didn't like going through old papers. That was old news, and today was a new day. You had to push ahead to move upwards, that was their motto. The head-editor didn't agree. He believed that you had to learn from yesterday's mistakes in order to avoid to-morrow's, a fairly basic conclusion that they didn't seem to have grasped.

'What about our preparations for the Social Democrats'

conference?' Schyman asked, looking at the domestic editor.

'Well, we're well under way,' the suit said, leaning forward as he clutched some sheets of paper. 'Carl Wennergren has got a bloody good tip-off about one of the female ministers. It looks like she's paid for her own personal shopping with her government card. Nappies and chocolate.'

The men chortled. Typical, they could never be trusted to look after money! Nappies! And chocolate!

Schyman was looking at the other man with a neutral expression.

'I see,' he said. 'And what's the story?'

The laughter died away. The suit smiled uncertainly.

'Personal shopping,' he said. 'She paid for personal shopping with her government card.'

The others all nodded supportively, what a great story!

'Okay,' Schyman said. 'We'll have to go into this more closely. Where did the tip-off come from?'

Low-level muttering broke out. You didn't talk about that sort of thing. Schyman sighed.

'For fuck's sake,' he said. 'Surely you can see that someone's out to get her! Find out who it is. Maybe that's the real story – a power struggle within the Social Democrats, what they're prepared to do to damage each other in advance of the conference. Anything else? What about parliament?'

They carried on going through the work that was already underway within politics, entertainment, foreign news. They took notes and made comments, various positions were adopted, lines of attack were set down.

'What about Work and Money?'

The head of section enthusiastically proposed a new

119

series on the theme of financial funds – which ones were on the way up, which ones to avoid, which ones were ethical and which ones were good long-term investments. Headlines like *Be a Winner!* always sold well. The other men nodded, unanimous in their support of the idea. Every one of them had a considerable portfolio of their own to manage.

'Crime?'

Sjölander cleared his throat and sat up straight. He had been on the point of nodding off.

'Yes, well,' he said, 'we've got the double murder in Frihamnen, and the police reckon that's just the start of it. As you can see in today's paper, we're the only ones with the information about the missing cigarettes. Fifty million. They'll be killing each other in droves to get their hands on that lorry.'

They all nodded appreciatively, a good story.

'And we've got the privatizations in the public sector,' the editor-in-chief said, his voice higher than the others. 'Has anyone started to work on that?'

Schyman ignored him.

'Annika Bengtzon has something on the go, I'm not sure where it's going to lead. She's got information about some dodgy charitable foundation that does things social services can't handle any more, helping to hide vulnerable women and children.'

The Blue Cock Parade looked distinctly uncomfortable. What sort of story was that? A foundation, that sounded pretty vague.

'Annika Bengtzon turns up some good stories, but she's too fixated on this whole women and children angle,' Sjölander said.

They all nodded. Yes, it was bloody monotonous; there was nothing to be gained from stuff like that, no plaudits to be earned. It was just messy and tragic.

'Mind you, you have to bear in mind her background,' Sjölander said with a grin, and they all grinned back. Yes, they remembered.

Schyman looked at them in silence.

'Would it have been a better story if they'd been hiding vulnerable men?' he asked.

The men started shuffling their chairs, looking at their watches. Surely it was time for them to get out there and start producing something?

The meeting broke up, the radio was switched on, everyone got to work.

Anders Schyman went back to his office with the feeling of frustration that he almost always felt after planning meetings. The way that the editorial management of the paper categorized reality, their incestuously homogenous attitudes, their blinkered lack of self-criticism.

When he sat down to look through the latest news on the agency website, there was one overriding thought in his head: *How the hell is this going to turn out?*

15

Annika got off the bus outside the Konsum supermarket. The pavement was treacherously slippery. She hunched her shoulders and ignored the stares of passers-by. She could see people in loud ski-clothing from the corner of her eye, but turned her back on them. If they wanted to stare, that was up to them. She would carry on as usual. The road had been gritted, so she stepped onto it and headed towards the ironworks. The old industrial site pierced the heavy grey of the sky, and there was a smell of dirty slush. As usual, she tried to avoid seeing the huge blast-furnace by looking to the left instead, at the charming old workers' houses with their solid, red-painted timber walls. On her right was her old flat. She glanced at it: up to now it had stood empty.

It wasn't any more.

She stopped in the middle of the road, amazed.

There were curtains and plants in the window, along with a small lamp.

Someone was living in her kitchen, sleeping in her bedroom. Someone who was making an effort, watering plants, taking care of things. The empty windows had come back to life.

She was surprised at how relieved she felt, almost a physical reaction. Something lifted from her chest. The usual desire to just vanish faded away. For the first time since those terrible things had happened she felt a wave of affection towards this little community.

It wasn't all bad, she thought. *We had some good times as well. Maybe even love.*

She left the town behind her, emerging onto the road to Granhed. She quickened her pace, hoisting her bag higher on her shoulder. She looked up at the sky. There was a light wind brushing the tops of the pine trees, and soon it would be getting dark.

I wonder if there are trees on other planets, she thought.

The road was icy and uneven, she had to pick her way carefully. A few cars passed by, their dipped lights foggy in the gloom. She didn't recognize any of them.

All around her was silent. The crunch of her shoes, her own rhythmic breathing, the distant noise of a plane heading towards Arlanda. Her body felt light, carefree, her eyes roaming about her.

The forest had been hit badly by the storm. On the far side of the lake almost all the pine trees had been snapped off. Electricity and telephone poles had come down. The trees had succumbed in all manner of different ways, some lying with their roots upturned, others snapped off halfway up, or split down the middle. The road was littered with branches, and she had to pick her way across the remnants of a fallen birch.

How vulnerable we are, she thought. *How little we're really in control.*

The approach to Lyckebo hadn't been snow-ploughed. A car had passed by sometime earlier, and its tracks had thawed out and then frozen again into icy gullies. It made walking difficult, and her bag bounced on her hip.

The barrier marking the edge of the Harpsund Estate was open. The trees closed in around her. The darkness

123

was thicker, the storm had been less destructive here. The state could evidently afford to look after its forests better.

She passed the small stream, noting that its flow had formed an ice sculpture. There was the sound of trickling somewhere below. Animal tracks of all kinds criss-crossed each other, elk, deer, hares, wild boar. The ones that had been there a couple of days had melted into enormous footprints.

Annika emerged into the clearing surrounding the three red-painted buildings, the cottage, the woodshed and the barn. Everything was still. The tree-house to the left, the meadow sloping down towards the jetty. She stopped and pulled off her hat and gloves, letting the breeze from the lake blow through her hair. She shut her eyes and took a deep breath. The image of the cottage stayed on her retina like a black-and-white negative. Still, colourless, soundless. Gradually an indefinable anxiety began to take shape behind her eyes. Something was wrong, but what?

She opened her eyes wide, light flooded in, the scene was crystal-clear, and after a couple of seconds she knew.

No smoke from the chimney.

She dropped her bag on the ground and ran, her heartbeat thudding in her head. She tore open the door, to cold and darkness, the sour smell of fear.

'Grandma!'

A pair of legs were sticking out from under the gate-legged table, brown support stockings, one shoe fallen off.

'Grandma!'

She heaved the table out of the way, squashing her ring-finger as the tabletop folded down.

'Oh God, oh God!'

The old woman was lying on her side, and some blood had trickled from her mouth. Annika threw herself down beside her, taking her hand, ice-cold, stroking her hair, her eyes welling up, the adrenalin deafening her.

'Grandma, oh dear God, can you hear me? Hello? Grandma . . . ?'

Annika searched for a pulse on her wrist, couldn't find it, and tried her neck instead. Still nothing. Her hands were clumsy and clammy as she rolled the old woman over onto her back and leaned over to see if she could feel her a pulse. Thank God, she was breathing!

'Grandma?'

A groan, then faint muttering.

'Grandma!'

Her head fell to one side, the blood had dried onto her cheek. Her chin was hanging down. Another groan, whimpering.

'Hurts . . .' she said. 'Help me.'

'Grandma, it's me. Oh God, Grandma, you've had a fall, I'm going to help you . . .'

What to do? Annika thought, stroking the old woman's hair. Breathing, bleeding, shock. She had to keep her warm.

She dashed into the bedroom, where the old Gustavian-style bed was neatly made. With a single tug Annika pulled off the bedclothes, including the sheet and thin mattress, and rushed back to the kitchen. She lay the mattress on the floor, lifted her grandmother under her arms and kicked the mattress in under her, then moved her hips and legs. It wasn't exactly neat. Then she wrapped the sheets and blankets around her. She put her own woolly hat on the woman's head, her grey hair feeling rough against Annika's trembling fingers.

Ambulance, Annika thought.

'Wait here, Grandma,' she said. 'I'm going to get

help. I'll be right back.' And the woman whimpered in response.

She rushed out of the house, through the forest, past the stream and the barrier, across the road, ducking a drooping power cable, jumping over tussocks and fallen branches as she ran up the hill towards Lillsjötorp.

Dear God, please let old Gustav be home!

The old man was outside chopping wood. He was hard of hearing and didn't hear Annika approaching. She didn't bother to say hello, just rushed straight into the house.

Gustav's home-help was there, the slut that Sven used to mess around with, Ingela. She was doing the washing-up, and stared at Annika in astonishment.

'What the hell . . . ?'

Annika rushed over to the phone and dialled 90 000.

'You could at least close the door,' the slut said, annoyed, drying her hands on a towel and walking out into the hall.

'Emergency services. What's the nature of the emergency?' a woman's voice said at the other end of the line.

Annika started to sob.

'It's Grandma!' she howled.

'Can we take it from the beginning? What's happened?'

Annika closed her eyes and rubbed her forehead.

'Something's happened to my grandmother,' she said. 'I thought she was dead. She's in a cottage outside Granhed; you have to come and get her.'

'What have you done to your hand?' the slut said, aghast.

'Which Granhed?' the woman said.

Annika stammered out directions: turn off at Valla towards Hälleforsnäs, then Stöttastensvägen, past Granhed, first right after Hosjön.

126

'Has something happened to Sofia?' the slut said, wide-eyed.

Annika dropped the phone and left, running back the same way she had come. It was dark now and she stumbled several times. The little cottage had begun to melt into the dark forest behind it.

The woman hadn't moved, she was lying quite still, breathing calmly. Annika sat down, resting her grandmother's head in her lap, and cried.

'You're not going to die, do you hear? You're not leaving me now!'

Slowly she calmed down. It would be at least half an hour before the ambulance arrived. She wiped her nose with the back of her hand, and that was when she saw the blood. Her left ring-finger had been crushed when she let down the leaf of the table earlier. The blood had dried under her fingernails and was running down her wrist. And then she felt the pain. She gasped and felt the room sway. *What a baby!* She wrapped a dishcloth round the wound.

It would probably make sense to get some heat going in the kitchen.

She went over to the stove to light a fire, and put her hand on the iron. It was cool but not quite cold, there had evidently been no fire lit since early that morning. She crumpled a few sheets of newspaper, then added some kindling and bark. Her hand trembled as she lit the match, pain throbbing through her finger. Then she lit the paraffin lamp and put it in the window facing the lake.

She fetched a pillow and put it under her grandmother's head, then sat and looked at her old face. Sofia Katarina. The same name as the youngest child in the Kulla-Gulla children's books. Annika had always thought it a beautiful name. As a child she had imagined that Martha Sandwall-Bergström's books were really about her grandmother. Sofia Katarina. Sossatina.

Where the hell was the ambulance?

She looked round the kitchen. There was no sign of any coffee, sandwiches, porridge or lunch. Grandma must have collapsed early that morning, just after she had got up, lit the fire and made the bed. *Which makes eight hours*, Annika thought. *Eight hours. Is that too long? Can she still get better?*

The fire had taken, and she put a couple of logs in the stove. The heat spread out through the room, and the chill gave up without a fight. The house was used to warmth and light, love and harmony. But now things had changed.

Her grandmother moved her head and groaned. Annika's feeling of helplessness turned to burning rage.

Fucking bloody ambulance, where the hell is it?

16

The forest was thick, badly managed, not much better than a thicket. The track was muddy and rutted. Ratko swore as the rear left wheel spun in the mud. He stopped and put the engine into first gear, then carefully pressed the accelerator again. The big diesel engine throbbed, the wheel came free and he rumbled slowly onward. He ought to be there by now.

Yet another small tree had fallen over the track, and he was momentarily seized by a helpless rage. With a violent tug he pulled on the handbrake and got out to drag the tree away. He forced the trunk into the ditch, and stamped on it, before realizing that he had made it. The gash in the landscape where the lorry was parked was just a dozen or so metres away, the yellow cab visible through the naked branches of the trees. If that tree hadn't fallen there, he would never have found his way back again. Fate was working in his favour, but he brushed the thought away.

He stood there for a moment, his breath clouding around him.

There was no such thing as luck. He firmly believed that every man was responsible for his own success. The fact that they had found the lorry and the idiots who had stolen it wasn't luck, it was the result of decades of carefully cultivated contacts.

No one could escape Ratko – he always found them. These bastards thought they could get one over on him.

The sense of euphoria when the lorry had been found had quickly switched to impotent fury when they opened it. The cigarettes were gone. Someone had hidden them, but the men claimed that they didn't know who, or where.

Ratko clenched his teeth so hard it hurt.

There was only one reason why the men hadn't talked before their deaths. They didn't have the faintest idea where the goods had been taken.

He took off his gloves and lit a cigarette. Smoked it slowly, right down to the filter. Stubbed it out against the sole of his shoe and put the butt in his pocket. Nowadays they could get DNA from cigarette butts, from saliva. He would also have to remember to get rid of the shoes. He had enough crap to deal with already without the Swedish police at his heels as well.

He stood still and pulled on his gloves again. He had to admit that he was still a long way from his goal. He had had many reasons to get angry in his life, but this time it was different. He didn't know if he was the hunter or the prey. He could sense danger from several different directions. His superiors said they trusted him, that they knew he would put things right, but he was well aware that there was a limit to their patience. His work last night hadn't brought him any closer to the shipment, but it hadn't been entirely wasted. It had proved his initiative and willingness to act. Even so, he still wasn't sure. The woman was gone, and he had no idea where to. He still didn't understand her role in all this.

He got into the car and looked in the rear-view

mirror. Nothing. Just the bundles obstructing his view. He drove on about thirty metres, then turned in among the trees. The car bounced and rocked, but he was there now. He put the handbrake on, turned off the engine, but left the key in. He took the containers and got to work. Slowly and methodically he soaked the trailer and cab with petrol. The liquid splashed his hair and clothes. He put the containers away. He had to hurry, dusk fell quickly at this time of year. The fire would be more visible in the dark.

In the end only the bundles were left. He hoisted the first onto his shoulder, almost glad of the smell of petrol from his clothes. It really stank. When he tried to push the corpse into the driver's cab he dropped it on the ground and lost his grip. He kicked out with his steel-toed boots, making the flesh and bones judder and bounce, over and over again, until he was exhausted. He had to rest for a moment. The petrol on his clothes was making him dizzy. With a firm gesture he thrust the bundle into the passenger seat and went to fetch the other one. Suddenly he heard the sound of an engine in the distance. He froze mid-movement, tossed the bundle to the ground and threw himself into the bushes. He lay flat in the damp moss, wet through in just a few seconds.

The sound gradually died away and he got up on all fours, panting and wet, and brushed the twigs and leaves from his hair. It was a good job no one could see him.

He stood up, embarrassed, caught sight of the slumped corpse, and his fury returned. He yanked at it, kicking and punching it. Then he carried it to the driver's cab and forced it onto the floor on the driver's side. He worked quickly and methodically. He fetched the last two containers, one in each hand. He poured the liquid over the bodies, drenching them in petrol. He used the last little bit as a fuse, pouring it in a trail across the ground, in amongst the trees. He stopped and took several deep breaths, suddenly aware of how exhausted he was. After resting for a minute, he pulled off his clothes, including his underpants, and pulled out a gym bag containing a change of clothes. He dressed quickly, shivering in the raw air, rubbing his arms to get warm.

That was better. Now it was just the fireworks left.

He stared at the scene for a moment: the lorry, the bodies, the forest. He actually felt pretty pleased.

He sparked his Bic and put it to the ground, then turned and ran.

The ambulance bay was like a garage. The ambulance parked, and a swarm of hospital staff in fluttering coats with pens in the breast pockets appeared around them. They spoke to each other in calm voices, carrying out their tasks with efficient movements. The women all had freshly washed hair, the men were all clean-shaven. Annika's grandmother was rushed away in a flurry of health service polyester.

Annika climbed out of the ambulance, watching the crowd head towards the emergency room. A woman behind a glass screen directed her to the waiting room. It was full of whining children, restless parents, vacant-looking pensioners, and a noisy foreign family. Annika dug through her bag and found a phone-card. She headed off towards the public phone, apologizing as she pushed past the noisy family. Holding the receiver in her left hand, she leaned her forehead against the wall, taking a deep breath. She had no choice.

Her mother answered after the fourth ring, with a hint of irritation.

132

'It's Grandma,' Annika said. 'She's in a bad way. I found her in the cottage, she was almost dead.'

'What do you mean?' her mother said at the other end of the line. Then, to someone else in the room: 'No, not those glasses, the red ones . . .'

'Grandma's really ill!' Annika shouted. 'Are you even listening?'

'Ill?' Her mother's voice sounded surprised, not scared, not upset. Surprised.

'She was still alive in the ambulance, but they've taken her away and I don't know what's happening . . .' Annika started to cry quietly.

'Mum, can't you come?'

Her mother was silent, there was just a faint crackling on the line.

'And here we are, just about to have dinner. Where are you?'

'Kullbergska hospital.'

The noisy family was finally taken off elsewhere, and in the silence the sound of her mother hanging up echoed down the line.

A doctor fluttered towards her.

'Sofia Katarina's relative? Would you like to follow me?'

The man glided away through a glass door and vanished. Annika gulped and followed him. *Oh God, she's dead; he's going to tell me that she's dead. He's going to say you found her too late, why don't you look after your elderly relatives?*

The room was small, sad and windowless. The doctor introduced himself with a muttered name and a quick handshake, then clicked a pen and studied his notes. Annika swallowed.

'Is she dead?'

The doctor put his pen down and rubbed his eyes.

'We're going to do a neurological examination to try to work out what's gone wrong. Right now we're doing a number of tests: blood sugar, blood-count, blood pressure.'

'And?' Annika said.

'Her condition appears to be stable,' he said, meeting her gaze. 'She's not getting any worse, she's a little more awake, and we've reduced her high sugar-levels. But her reflexes are weak, and she's showing no response down one side. You probably noticed that one corner of her mouth was lower than the other.'

It was a statement rather than a question.

'What about the blood?' Annika said. 'Why was she bleeding from the mouth?'

The doctor stood up.

'She probably bit herself in the fall. What's that round your hand?'

'A dishcloth. I trapped my finger. Is she going to be all right?'

Annika stood up as well, as the doctor put his pen in his breast pocket.

'When we're done here we'll do a CT scan. It will be a while before we can say anything for certain.'

'A brain scan? What's wrong? Is she going to die?'

Annika's palms were wet with sweat.

'It's too early to—'

'*Is she dying?*'

Her voice was far too shrill, cracking, and the doctor recoiled.

'Something has happened in the left side of her brain, with the arteries. Either she's had an embolism in her brain, a cerebral thrombosis, or a cerebral haemorrhage. It's too early to say which.'

'What's the difference?'

The man put his hand on the door-handle.

134

'With a haemorrhage the symptoms strike suddenly and the patient often falls unconscious. Patients like that often have a history of high blood-pressure. You ought to get that hand seen to, and have a tetanus jab.'

He left the room with a crackle of static electricity as his coat brushed the plastic of the doorframe. Annika sat down again, her mouth half-open, unable to breathe properly.

This isn't happening, not to me, not now.

She sat there until a nurse came to sew up her finger and give her a tetanus shot, then put on a finger-guard. Then she went back to the waiting room, supporting herself against the glass-fibre panelling as she went. The sounds of the hospital seemed distant, and she felt panic bubbling close to the surface.

Her mother was standing in the waiting room, her old-fashioned mink coat open, way too tight across the shoulders. She was talking in a loud voice with the woman at reception. She settled onto the seat beside Annika without taking off her coat.

'Have they said anything?'

Annika sighed deeply, fighting back the tears. She held out her arms and gave her mother a hug.

'It's something to do with her brain. Oh, Mum, what if she dies?'

She was muttering into her mother's shoulder, making a mess of her fur coat.

'Where is she now?'

'They're doing scans.'

Her mother pulled free, patted Annika on the cheek, coughed, and wiped her forehead with her glove.

'Take your coat off, or you'll be far too hot,' Annika said.

'I know what you're thinking,' her mother said. 'You think this is my fault.'

Annika looked up at her mother, and could see that the anticipated criticism had given her a distanced look. Anger came like a flash of white lightning.

'Oh no you don't!' she said. 'Don't blame me for the fact that you're feeling guilty.'

Her mother fanned herself with her hand.

'I don't feel guilty, but you think I ought to.'

Annika had to move. She got up and went over to the reception desk.

'When will we hear anything about Sofia Katarina?'

'If you'd like to take a seat for the time being . . .' the woman said.

Her mother had slid her coat down off her shoulders.

'Do you know where the nearest place to smoke is?' she said, fingering her bag.

'Now that you happen to mention it,' Annika said, 'I do find it a bit odd that I was the one who found her, considering that I live over a hundred kilometres away and she's only three kilometres from you.'

She sat down a couple of chairs away, with her back to a radiator.

'So you're going to throw that at me as well,' her mother said.

Annika turned away, closing her eyes and letting the heat seep through her top. She leaned her head back, and the metal edge of the radiator scorched her neck. Her eyes were prickling with tears.

'Not now, Mum,' she whispered.

'Annika Bengtzon?'

It was a female doctor with a ponytail. Annika sat up and quickly wiped her eyes, looking down at the floor. The doctor sat down opposite her and leaned forward, she held a file in one hand.

'The scan showed exactly what we suspected,' she said. 'There's bleeding in the left side of the brain, in

136

the centre of the nervous system. That's why all the symptoms are on the right of her body, and why her sight doesn't seem to have been affected.'

'A stroke?' Annika's mother said breathlessly.

'Yes, a stroke.'

'Oh God,' her mother said flatly. 'Will she recover?'

'Some of the symptoms usually improve. But at her age, and after such a severe incident, I'm afraid we're looking at serious long-term consequences.'

'Is she going to be a vegetable?' Annika asked.

The doctor looked at her kindly.

'We don't know if the bleeding has affected her intellect. It might not have done. A lot will depend on rehabilitation – that's very important in cases like this.'

Annika bit her lip.

'Will she able to go back home again?'

'It's too early to say. Generally, though, most patients show more improvement if they are able to live at home, with a lot of help from social services, of course. The alternative is sheltered housing or long-term hospital care.'

'An institution?' Annika said. 'You don't mean Lövåsen?'

The doctor smiled. 'There's nothing wrong with Lövåsen. You shouldn't believe everything you read in the papers.'

'I wrote the articles,' Annika said.

'I haven't got anything against Lövåsen,' her mother said.

The doctor stood up.

'Well, she's been admitted to a ward now. Once they've got her temperature up a bit, you'll be able to see her. It'll be a little while yet.'

Annika and her mother nodded simultaneously.

17

Thomas crumpled up the hamburger wrapper and threw it in the bin. He must remember to empty it before he left, otherwise his room would stink of greasy food all week.

With a sigh he leaned back in his office chair and stared out of the window. The darkness outside was reflecting the room back at him, another civil servant in another world, a mirror image. The council building was silent; almost everyone had gone home. Soon the members of the social welfare board would start to gather in the conference room next door, but for the time being it was quiet. He felt peculiarly happy, free and at ease. He had blamed work when Eleonor had asked about dinner. It wasn't a lie, but it wasn't exactly the truth either. At this time of year he always had a lot of work, but it was no worse than usual. It had never stopped him getting home in time for dinner before. Dinner was their special time. Starter, main course, and Eleonor always had dessert. Always candles during the dark months of the year, always ironed napkins. He had appreciated it, and she loved it, often telling their friends about it. So romantic. So wonderful. Such a perfect couple, a match made in heaven.

No, he thought. *Not in heaven. In Perugia.*

He couldn't say exactly when boredom had started to creep in. The feeling of adult reality faded away and something else took its place, something that was more accurate. They weren't grown-ups, they were playing at being grown-up. They went sailing, held dinner parties, got involved in the community. Vaxholm was their world, its development and success their great interest and ambition. They were both born and raised here, had never lived anywhere else. No one could accuse them of not taking their share of responsibility, either socially or in terms of work.

But when it came to their own relationship, the sense of responsibility was badly diluted. They still behaved like a couple of teenagers who had just left home, playing romantic games and always having to worry about what their parents would think.

Thomas sighed. There it was again.

Parenthood.

Eleonor didn't want children. She loved the life they led, their shared existence, the dinners, holidays, her career, her portfolio of shares, their neighbours, the community groups, the boat.

'I don't have to reinforce my womanhood by having children,' she had said the last time they argued about it. 'It's my life. I do what I want with it. I want to have fun, meet people, have a good career, really invest in us, and the house.'

'We're ready to start.'

The administrative director was standing at his door, and Thomas blinked in confusion.

'Of course, I'll be right there.'

He quickly gathered his papers, slightly embarrassed. His mind had been elsewhere and he wondered how obvious it had been.

The eleven participants were seated around the table

and he sat down opposite the committee secretary at the chairman's end of the table. The heads of sections were seated next to each other and a couple of council officials were also present. The agenda contained some twenty points, and most of them didn't concern him. The budget would be discussed at a special two-day conference at the town hotel, so today he would only have to make a couple of short points and try to answer any urgent queries that the others had.

As the chairman opened the meeting he glanced through the agenda. There were all the usual subjects: childcare, personnel, help for the disabled, the home-help service. Half of them were old favourites that had been discussed umpteen times before and would hardly be decided that evening. His point about the galloping cost of mobility allowance was item number eight. With a little sigh he glanced down the page and took a sip of water. Item number seventeen was new: *Agreement with Paradise Foundation*.

What sort of revolutionary move was this? Did they really think they were in a position to enter into any new agreements, with the finances the way they were? He sighed as quietly as he could, and turned his attention to the participants instead.

The party demagogues, one Social Democrat and one from the right-wing Moderate Party, sat at their respective corners of the table, ready to jump in with arguments and objections. 'Individual freedom' would be the Moderate's catchphrase, and the Social Democrat would counter with 'solidarity'. Soon the politicians' desire for *something concrete* would pop up, with a demand to *follow it up at a later date*. And he would refer to figures and tables that wouldn't satisfy anyone.

Perugia, he thought. He's there right now, sitting on his hilltop in Umbria, lord of all he surveyed.

He smiled at the thought.

Odd that he should think of the city as male.

'Thomas?'

The chairman was looking at him encouragingly. He cleared his throat and leafed through his papers.

'We have to do something about mobility allowance,' he said. 'The cost looks likely to exceed budget by three hundred per cent over the current year. I don't see how we can put a stop to the increase: the legislation covering this issue offers little help, frankly. If access to the service is opened up, then demand will just keep growing.'

He ran through the numbers and charts, the consequences and alternatives. The chairman handed round a circular with new guidelines from the Association of Local Authorities: evidently they weren't alone in this problem. The Association may have drawn attention to the issue, but the tone of its central directive was as vague and pompous as ever. They soon ended up in a discussion of how to train staff in the new practices, and whether to send them on a course or bring in a consultant.

The Paradise Foundation, he thought. *Nice name.*

The meeting rumbled on. They got stuck debating another issue, the renovation of a playground, and he could feel his irritation rising. When they reached item number seventeen he leaned forward. One of the council officials, a female social worker with many years' experience, presented the item.

'This is a decision about whether or not to purchase, in principle, the services of a new organization,' she said. 'We have one urgent case that is already being dealt with by our committee for special cases, but we felt that we should raise this agreement with you before signing up to it.'

'What sort of foundation is this?' the Social Democrat demagogue asked suspiciously, and even at this point Thomas had a good idea how this was going to end. If the Social Democrat was against, the Moderate would be in favour.

The social worker hesitated, unwilling to go into the details because the minutes of the meeting were covered by freedom of information legislation.

'In general terms I can say that this organization works to protect people whose lives have been threatened,' she said. 'We've been through their methods and processes with their director, and in this particular instance we believe that they are offering a service that we need to pay for . . .'

They all read the agreement carefully, even though there wasn't a great deal to take in. Vaxholm Council would agree to pay for protection at a cost of three and a half thousand kronor per day until a satisfactory solution could be found for the client in question.

'So what exactly is this, then?' the Social Democrat went on. 'We already have arrangements with a number of different treatment centres and organizations. Do we really need another one?'

The social worker looked troubled.

'This is an entirely new and unique organization,' she said. 'The only purpose of the Paradise Foundation is to protect and help people, mainly women and children, whose lives have been threatened. Their clients are erased from all public registers, so that those threatening them will never be able to find them. Any trail would hit a brick wall, in the form of the foundation.'

They were all staring at her.

'Is that even legal?' asked a young woman, the recently elected Green Party representative. As usual, they ignored her.

'Why can't we sort this out ourselves, within the social services department?' the Moderate said.

The head of the family care unit, who was evidently aware of the case, spoke up.

'There's nothing unusual about this,' he said. 'You could say that it's a matter of attitude, and only an entirely independent organization has the flexibility to handle this. They are able to adapt to circumstances in a way that we as an official body simply can't. I think we should go ahead.'

'It's very expensive,' the Social Democrat pointed out.

'Welfare costs a lot of money, when are you going to understand that?' the Moderate countered, and with that they were off.

Thomas leaned back and studied the agreement. It really was extremely basic. There were no details about exactly what services would be offered, nothing about where the services would be provided, not even a registered company number. There was just a post office box in Järfälla.

As usual he wished that he had the power to say something, to raise concrete and fundamental objections against the proposal.

Naturally they would have to get references for the organization, and check with the council's legal experts that the foundation's activities were legally defensible. But how could they possibly agree to extra expenditure at a time like the present? And why the hell didn't they ask him if it was financially feasible to accept the proposal, seeing as he was the only one who had an overview of the finances? What the hell was he sitting there for if they weren't going to ask him? Maybe he was just there for decoration.

'Do we have to take a decision on this today?' the chairman asked.

143

Both the social worker and departmental head nodded.

The chairman sighed.

Something snapped inside him. For the first time in his seven years at the council Thomas raised his voice at a committee meeting.

'This is ridiculous!' he said angrily. 'How can you possibly agree to buy in a new service without working through the consequences? What sort of organization is this? A foundation, of all things! Christ! And look at this agreement – they haven't even got a registered company number. This whole thing stinks, if you ask me. Which, frankly, you ought to!'

They were all staring at him as if they'd seen a ghost. Only now did he realize that he was standing up and leaning across the table holding the agreement like a flag in his right hand above his head. His face was burning, and he had broken into a sweat. He let the agreement fall to the table, brushed his hair back and straightened his tie.

'Excuse me,' he said. 'I'm sorry, I . . .'

Bewildered, he sat down and started to leaf through his papers. The others stopped staring at him and looked down at the table in embarrassment. He wanted to die, for the floor to open up and swallow him.

The chairman took a deep breath.

'Well, if we put it to the vote . . .'

The proposal was passed by seven votes to four.

'I'm working on a fucking brilliant story.'

Sjölander and Ingvar Johansson looked up in irritation at the reporter who was disturbing them. The unhappy look on their faces quickly turned to smiles when they saw it was Carl Wennergren.

'Great, let's hear it,' Sjölander said.

The reporter sat down on the head of crime's desk.

'Those murders out in Frihamnen,' he said. 'I've got a brilliant tip-off.'

Both Sjölander and the head of crime dropped their feet to the floor and straightened up.

'What?' Ingvar Johansson wondered.

'I've just been talking to a cop,' Carl Wennergren said in a low voice. 'They think Ratko is behind it.'

The older men waited for their younger colleague to continue.

'Why?' Sjölander asked.

'You know,' Wennergren said, 'the mafia, Yugos, missing cigarettes. It stinks of Ratko.'

'Who did you talk to?'

'Someone in the crime unit.'

'Did you call him, or did he call you?'

The reporter raised his eyebrows in surprise.

'He called me. Why?'

Sjölander and Ingvar Johansson exchanged a quick glance.

'Okay,' the head of crime said. 'What did he want?'

'To tell me that Ratko's behind it, and that they're trying to find him. They want us to publish his name and picture.'

'So the police have issued an arrest warrant?'

The reporter frowned. 'He didn't say, just that they were looking for him.'

'Okay, this is good,' Ingvar Johansson said, making notes on a pad. 'This is what we do: Sjölander will pull together some background detail for Ratko, and you go round the Yugo bars and get a few quotes. We can get a front page out of this.'

'Right on!' Carl Wennergren said, and bounced off towards the picture desk.

The two older men watched him go.

'Did you know about this?' Ingvar Johansson asked.

Sjölander sighed and put his feet back up on the desk.

'The police have absolutely nothing to go on. The dead men were unknown to them, only just arrived from Serbia. There are no witnesses to the murders, no one who can talk. I don't know why, but the cops evidently want to smoke out Ratko.'

'Has he got anything to do with this?'

The head of crime laughed. 'Course he has; Ratko runs the whole Yugoslavian tobacco trade in Scandinavia. He might not be responsible for the killings, but he's bound to be involved somehow.'

The men sat absorbed in their own thoughts for a minute or so, then came to the same conclusion.

'So they're planting the story,' Ingvar Johansson said.

'Yep. I've never seen a more obvious case,' Sjölander agreed.

'Why?' the head of news wondered.

Sjölander shrugged. 'They've got nothing to go on, so they're trying to stir things up a bit. They're trying to either undermine Ratko's position or reinforce it. Not that it makes any difference to us. If some detective says that they're looking for Ratko, it's a done deal for us.'

They nodded to each other.

'So are you telling Jansson?' Sjölander asked.

Ingvar Johansson stood up and headed towards the night-desk.

18

A weak lamp was spreading a yellowish light in one corner. An ECG bleeped rhythmically and monotonously. Sofia Katarina lay hooked up to a drip and various monitors. Her body seemed to have shrunk and withered beneath the thin blanket, so still and small. Annika stroked her hair, struck by how incredibly old she looked. It was odd. She had never really thought of her grandmother as an old woman.

'Oh, just look at her,' her mother said. 'Look at her mouth.'

The right-hand corner of her mouth was drooping, and a thin dribble of saliva was running down her neck. Annika picked up a tissue and wiped it away.

'She's sleeping now,' the doctor said. 'But you can stay for a while.'

She left the room, the door hissing shut behind her.

They sat on either side of the bed, her mother still wearing her fur coat. The room was full of hospital noises, the hum of the ventilation, the electronic song of the equipment, faint footsteps in the corridor outside. Even so, the quiet was oppressive.

'Who would have thought it?' Annika's mother said. 'That something like this would happen today . . .' She began to sniff.

'Of course you couldn't have known,' Annika said. 'No one's blaming you.'

'She came in to do her shopping yesterday. I was on the till. She seemed so well, so cheerful.'

They sat in silence again as Annika's mother wept.

'We have to find her somewhere to live,' Annika said. 'She's not going to Lövåsen.'

'Well, I can't have her!' her mother said firmly, looking up.

'Neglect, the wrong medicines; I wrote a whole series of articles about how terrible things were at Lövåsen. Grandma can't go there.'

'That was a long time ago, it must be a lot better now.'

Her mother was dabbing at her face with a tissue. Annika stood up.

'Maybe we can find a private solution,' she said.

'Yes, well, she can't stay with me!'

Her mother straightened up and let the tissue fall. Annika looked at her, asthmatic from smoking, warm from her fur coat and hot flushes, with her thinning hair, accelerating weight-gain, stand-offish attitude and self-obsession. Before she had time to think she had gone over and taken her by the shoulders.

'Don't be so bloody childish,' she hissed. 'I meant proper private care. This isn't about you. Don't you get it? Just for once, you're not the centre of all this.'

The woman's mouth gaped open and her neck started to flare red.

'You, you . . .' she began, pushing Annika away and getting up.

The young woman looked at the older one and pre-empted her outburst.

'Go on,' she said, steeling herself. 'Say what you were thinking.'

Her mother clutched her fur together and took several quick steps towards her.

'You have no idea how much crap I've had to put up with because of you,' she whispered. 'What do you think these past few years have been like for me? Everyone staring at me? All the gossip? It's no surprise your sister moved away, she always looked up to you. I don't know how Leif has put up with it all, he's been on the point of walking out on me several times. You'd have liked that, wouldn't you? You never wanted me to find love, you've never liked Leif . . .'

The colour drained from Annika's face as her mother walked round her and backed away towards the door, pointing an accusing finger at her.

'Not to mention what it's done to Sofia!' she went on, louder now. 'She was so respected. Housekeeper at Harpsund, and to end her days as the grandmother of the woman who murdered . . .'

Annika couldn't breathe. 'Go to hell,' she managed to say in a gasp.

Her mother came close again, spit flying from her mouth.

'If you're such a brilliant journalist, you ought to be able to handle the truth!'

Suddenly she was back in the ironworks again, by the blast furnace, watching her cat's body flying through the air, and seeing the metal pipe lying there. She clutched her hands to her head with the memory and leaned forward, bent double.

'Go away,' she whispered. 'Get out of here, Mum. Now!'

Her mother pulled out a leather cigarette case and a green plastic lighter.

'Just sit there and think about everything you've done.'

Silence fell, and the darkness thickened. Annika was

149

struggling for air. Shock was sitting like a lump in her throat, making it hard to breathe.

She hates me, she thought. *My mum hates me. I've ruined her life.*

A wave of self-pity washed over her, pressing her to the ground.

What on earth have I done to the people I love? Oh God, what have I done?

Sofia Katarina's left hand was fumbling with the yellow hospital blanket.

'Barbro?' she muttered.

Annika looked up. *Grandma, oh, Grandma!* She rushed over to her and took hold of her cold, motionless right hand, forcing back her anxieties and trying to smile.

'Hello, Grandma; it's me, Annika.'

'Barbro?' her grandmother slurred, looking at her with clouded eyes.

Tears welled up, distorting her sight.

'No, it's me, Annika. Barbro's daughter.'

The old woman's gaze slipped away round the room, her left hand clutching and picking at the blanket.

'Am I in Lyckebo?'

Annika started to cry, breathing with her mouth open and letting her tears fall.

'No, Grandma, you got ill. You're in hospital.'

The old woman's eyes went back to Annika.

'Who are you?'

'Annika,' Annika whispered. 'I'm Annika.'

There was a flash of recognition behind the confusion.

'Of course you are,' Sofia Katarina said. 'My lovely girl.'

Annika wept, her head on the old woman's stomach,

as she held her hand. Finally she got up to go and blow her nose.

'You've been so ill, Grandma,' she said on her way round the bed. 'Now we have to make sure you get better as soon as possible.'

But her grandmother had fallen asleep again.

Wednesday 31 October

19

Aida took a deep breath. The hill in front of her seemed endless. The street was swaying as she staggered forward, sweat running behind her ears and down her neck. Would she never get there?

She sat down on the road, her legs in the ditch, and rested her head on her knees. She didn't feel the cold and wet; as long as she could just rest for a minute she'd be able to carry on again.

A car appeared over the brow of the hill and slowed down as it passed. She felt people staring at her back. She couldn't just sit here. In a nice place like this someone was bound to call the police before too long.

She got to her feet, and for a few moments saw nothing but blackness.

I have to find the house. Now.

She had gone no further than the next driveway when she saw the number. How ridiculous, she had been close to giving up just twenty metres from her goal. She tried to laugh. But she stumbled on a stone and almost fell, and felt like bursting into tears instead.

'Help me!' she muttered.

She eventually made her way to the steps and pulled herself up the railing and rang the doorbell. A solid front door, with two serious locks. A bell rang somewhere inside. Nothing happened. She rang again. And again. And again. She tried to peer in through the strip of brown glass beside the door, but saw only darkness and emptiness, not even any furniture.

She sank onto the steps and rested her head against the wall. She couldn't go on. Let him turn up. It didn't matter. Call the police. It couldn't get any worse.

'Aida?'

She could hardly summon the energy to look up.

'Oh, my dear, whatever's happened?'

She started to lose consciousness, and felt for the wall.

'Oh, but you're not well at all. Anders! Come and help me!'

Someone took hold of her and pulled her to her feet. An agitated woman's voice, a calmer male voice, it got warm and dark. She was inside the house.

'Put her on the sofa.'

Everything rolled and swayed as she was picked up and then put down. She could see the back of a sofa, brown, scratchy. A blanket was put over her, but she still felt frozen.

'She's really bad,' the woman said. 'She's got a raging temperature. We have to get a doctor.'

'We can't get a doctor, you know that,' the man said.

Aida was about to say something, to object – *no, no doctor, no hospital.*

The couple went into another room and she could hear them muttering. Maybe she fell asleep, because a moment later the man and woman were standing over her holding a cup of hot tea.

'We're assuming that you're Aida,' the woman said. 'My name's Mia, Maria Eriksson. This is my husband Anders. When did you start to get ill like this?'

She tried to answer.

'No doctor,' she whispered.

Mia nodded. 'Okay, no doctor. We understand. But you need medical attention, and we've got a solution.'

She shook her head.

'They're looking for me.'

Mia Eriksson stroked her forehead.

'We know. But there are ways we can help you without anyone finding out.'

She closed her eyes and breathed out.

'Am I in Paradise?' she whispered.

The answer came from far away, she was drifting off again.

'Yes,' the woman said. 'We're going to take care of you.'

She had slipped in and out of sleep all night. Sofia Katarina's feelings swung from confusion to fear, to sentimentality.

The physiotherapist gave a disappointing report after the short initial examination.

'She's badly impaired on her right side,' she said. 'It's going to need a lot of work.'

'What do you do to get movement back again?' Annika asked.

The woman smiled. 'The problem isn't in her limbs, it's in her head. No treatment can restore the function to dead nerve cells, so we have to make use of what's left. We need to activate the nerve cells that are still there but have been inactive. And we can do that with intensive physiotherapy.'

'When will she get better?'

'It can take up to six months before we see any results. The most important thing right now is to start her treatment as soon as possible and to make sure we stick to the programme.'

Annika gulped. 'What can I do?'

The physiotherapist took her hand and smiled. 'You're already doing the right thing, just by caring. Talk to her, try to engage her interest, sing old songs together. You'll notice that she likes talking about the old days. Try to encourage her.'

'But when will she be back to normal again?'

'Your grandmother will never be the same as she was before.'

Annika blinked and felt a great chasm opening up. She could feel herself starting to panic.

'What am I going to do? She's always been there for me.' Her voice was too shrill, too desperate.

'And now you have to be there for her.'

The physiotherapist patted her hand. Annika didn't notice her going.

'Grandma,' she said, stroking her hand. But the old woman was asleep.

The sounds of the day crept under the door and into the little grey room. Although Annika had slept fitfully and had woken up a lot, she felt wound up and restless, almost hyperactive.

She had to find somewhere where her grandmother could be properly rehabilitated. She was sure that Lövåsen wasn't the right place. She stood up and paced round and round the room. Her legs ached and her finger was extremely sore.

There had to be other alternatives, private care homes, sheltered housing, home-help.

Annika didn't see the door open, just felt the draught round her legs.

It was the woman doctor again, with Annika's fur-clad mother behind her.

'We have to talk about Sofia's future,' the doctor said, and Annika picked up her things and followed them out.

'I can't look after her myself,' her mother said as soon

as they had sat down in the doctor's office. 'I have to go out to work.'

'Barbro, you could get a carer's allowance if you looked after your mother,' the doctor said.

Annika's mother squirmed.

'I don't think I'm ready to give up my career yet.'

Something snapped. The lack of sleep, or love, or reason, flashed into Annika's mind. She stood up and shouted, 'You work part time as a cashier in a super-market, for fuck's sake! Why the hell is that stopping you from looking after Grandma?'

'Sit down,' the doctor said firmly.

'Bloody hell!' Annika yelled, still on her feet, her voice breaking, legs trembling. 'No one cares about Grandma! You want to shut her away in Lövåsen and throw away the key! I know what that place is like! I wrote about it! Neglect, staff shortages, wrong medication!'

The doctor stood up as well, walked round the table and over to Annika.

'Either you sit down,' she said calmly, 'or you leave.'

Annika rubbed her forehead, her legs gave way and she sank onto the chair. Her mother was nervously fingering the edge of her fur, trying to catch the doctor's eyes: *See what I have to put up with.*

'Lövåsen would be a good choice . . .'

'Like hell!'

'. . . if there were any vacancies there. Which there aren't. There's a long waiting list. It won't be long before Sofia's active medical treatment has been completed, but she'll still need care twenty-four hours a day, and an intensive and comprehensive rehabilitation programme. So we have to come up with other options quickly. Which is why I'm turning to you. Do you have any suggestions?'

Annika's mother licked her lips anxiously.

'Well,' she said, 'I don't know. You always think society will do its bit when things like this happen, that's what we pay our taxes for . . .'

Annika stared down at her hands, her face burning.

'Are there any vacancies anywhere else?' she asked.

'Possibly in Bettna,' the doctor said.

'But that's miles from Hälleforsnäs, and almost two hundred bloody kilometres from Stockholm,' Annika said, looking up. 'How are we going to visit her?'

'I'm not saying it's ideal—'

'What about Stockholm?' Annika said. 'Could she get a place in Stockholm? Then I could visit her every day.'

She was on her feet again, and the doctor waved her back down with her hand.

'That would be the last resort. We have to try to find a solution within the local health district.'

Her mother said nothing, just fingered the collar of her fur coat. Annika huddled on her chair, staring at the floor. The doctor looked at them in silence for a while, mother and daughter, the young woman in shock, the older one confused and worried.

'This has been a terrible experience for you,' she said, turning to Annika. 'You're probably going to feel ongoing effects from a trauma like this. You'll feel cold, burst into tears, feel depressed.'

Annika met the doctor's gaze.

'Great,' she said. 'So what do I do about that?'

The doctor sighed. 'Have a drink,' she said, standing up.

Annika stared at her. 'You're serious?'

The doctor smiled and held out her hand.

'It's a tried and tested cure in cases like this. I'm sure we'll meet again soon. If you like you can sit here for a while, but I'm afraid I have to do my rounds.'

She left the women in the little office, and the door

clicked shut behind her. Annika's mother cleared her throat.

'Did you talk to the physiotherapist?' she asked cautiously.

'Of course I did,' Annika said. 'I've been here all night.'

Barbro got up and went over to Annika and stroked her hair.

'We mustn't fight,' she whispered. 'We have to stick together now that Mum's ill.'

Annika sighed, hesitated, then wrapped her arms round her mother's solid waist and pressed her ear to her stomach. She could hear gurgling.

'No, we mustn't fight,' she whispered back.

'Go home and rest,' Barbro said, feeling in her pocket for some keys. 'I'll stay here with Sofia.'

Annika let go.

'Thanks,' she said, 'but I'd rather go back home to Stockholm and sleep there. I can be back here in no time, the express train only takes fifty-eight minutes.'

She gathered up her things and gave her mother a hug.

'You'll see, it'll all be fine,' Barbro said.

Annika went out into the hospital corridor, airless and cold.

Just as she had been warned, she got the shivers on the train. She had bought the papers and was sitting with them in front of her, but she couldn't bring herself to open them.

Drink, she thought. *Oh well.*

She had no intention of turning to drink. Her father used to do that, and that was quite enough for the whole family. He drank until he died, drunk in a ditch on the way to Granhed.

She shrank into her seat and pulled her jacket tighter

161

around her. It didn't help. The chill was coming from within, from her heart.

Everyone I love dies, she thought in a sudden attack of self-pity. *Dad, Sven, and now maybe Grandma.*

No, she thought after a moment. *Not Grandma. She'll get better again, even if she won't be the same as she was. We'll find somewhere where they can help get her back on her feet.*

She looked at the papers, but couldn't be bothered to read them. She leaned her head back instead, shut her eyes and tried to relax. It didn't work, her body kept twitching and shaking.

She sighed and reached for the paper and went straight to pages six and seven, where they always put the heaviest news stories. A large picture of a man, grainy, on the very limits of what was printable, stared out at her from the page. After a moment she recognized him. *Where's Aida? Aida Begovic. I know she's here.*

The headline was just as big and heavy as the man outside the hotel room door had been the day before yesterday.

Leader of the Tobacco Mafia, it said, and under the picture:

His name is Ratko, he arrived in Sweden in the 1970s, and has previous convictions for bank robbery and kidnapping. Today he is wanted for war crimes in the former Yugoslavia. Swedish police believe he is the mastermind behind organized tobacco smuggling in Sweden.

She closed the paper. Her teeth were chattering, and her injured finger with its three stitches ached. She felt sick again.

20

Anders Schyman slammed the paper down on the desk in front of Ingvar Johansson.

'Explain this to me!' he said.

The man on the grainy picture looked sightlessly up at the two men. The head of news glanced up from his computer screen.

'What do you mean?'

'My room. Now.'

Sjölander was already there, standing in the little pile of dust where the sofa had been. Schyman sat down heavily on his chair, and it creaked under his weight. Ingvar Johansson closed the door.

'Who took the decision to print Ratko's name and picture?'

The two men standing in front of the head-editor exchanged a glance.

'I go home after the handover, I can't really speculate about what—' Ingvar Johansson began, but Schyman cut him off.

'Bollocks,' he said. 'I know a story that's been handed over from daytime when I see one. And I've already spoken to Jansson and Torstensson. The editor-in-chief wasn't informed about the decision to publish at all, and Jansson was surprised and said the whole package was passed on from the dayshift. Sit down.'

Sjölander and Ingvar Johansson sat down in unison on the chairs on the other side of the desk. No one spoke.

'This is unacceptable,' Schyman said when the silence had become oppressive. 'Any decision to publish the name of anyone who hasn't been found guilty of a crime must be taken by the publisher, who is legally responsible for everything we publish. Now, surely that can't be too much of a bloody surprise to either of you.'

Sjölander was looking down at the floor. Ingvar Johansson squirmed.

'We've identified him before. The fact that he's a gangster is hardly new.'

Anders Schyman let out a deep sigh. 'We aren't just saying he's a gangster. We're linking him to the double murder in Frihamnen, and indirectly identifying him as the murderer. I've spoken to the lawyers – if Ratko decides to sue then we don't have a leg to stand on, not to mention what the press ombudsman would have to say.'

'He won't sue,' Ingvar Johansson said confidently. 'He'll see this as an advertisement for his work. Anyway, we tried to get hold of him for a comment. Carl Wennergren was out talking to people in the Yugo bars last night—'

Anders Schyman slammed his hand down on the table, making the other two men jump.

'I'm perfectly well aware of that,' he roared. 'That isn't what I'm talking about. I'm talking about way too many people in this damn newsroom taking unilateral decisions about what we publish! The pair of you have no authority to take this sort of decision! The legally responsible publisher decides! How fucking difficult is that to understand?'

Sjölander went red, while Ingvar Johansson went pale.

Anders Schyman watched their reactions and knew that he finally had their attention. He forced himself to calm down, and concentrated on lowering his voice to its normal level.

'I presume you have more to say than the material that made it into the paper,' he said. 'What have we got?'

Finally he managed to hold the discussion that ought to have taken place precisely twenty-four hours earlier.

'The police have found the spent cartridges, and one bullet,' Sjölander said. 'The ammunition is extremely unusual, 30.06 calibre, American, Federal, the Trophy Bond brand. The cases are nickel-plated, shiny, they look like little toadstools. Almost all other cases are brass.'

Schyman was taking notes. Sjölander relaxed slightly.

'The bullet was found burrowed into the tarmac between the silos,' he went on. 'It's impossible to draw any conclusions about where the killer was standing, seeing as the bullet crashed around in the bloke's head and changed direction several times. The cases were found at the back of an empty warehouse.'

'The gun?' Schyman wondered.

Sjölander sighed. 'It's possible the police know, but they haven't said anything to me,' he said. 'But they've drawn a number of other conclusions. For instance, that the killer was extremely fussy about his choice of equipment. These things are lethal, the sort of thing you use to bring down big game.'

'Perhaps that isn't so odd,' Schyman said. 'If you really want to kill someone, it makes sense to do it properly.'

Sjölander was starting to warm up, and was leaning over the desk.

'That's what's so weird,' he said. 'Why did he shoot the victims in the head? A shot to the chest or back would have killed them in a couple of seconds. There's something odd about this killer. He's driven by something more than just wanting to kill quickly and efficiently. Ego, hate, revenge. Why take the trouble to make the perfect shot when pretty much anything would have done the job?'

'Why isn't any of this in today's paper?' Schyman asked.

Sjölander leaned back again. 'It could sabotage the investigation.'

'And identifying Ratko as the murderer, what sort of effect does that have on the investigation?' the head-editor wondered.

Silence again.

'We have to talk about things like this,' Schyman said. 'It's bloody important for the stability of the paper in the future. Who tipped you off about Ratko?'

Ingvar Johansson cleared his throat.

'We've got a source in Crime who said we could publish his picture. The cops are convinced he's involved in this somehow, and they wanted to put the wind up him.'

'And you volunteered your services?' Anders Schyman said quietly. 'You risked the credibility of this paper, and decided to take on the role of editor-in-chief just so you could do what the police wanted? Get out of here. Now!'

He turned away from the two men and clicked to open the news agency website instead. From the corner of his eye he saw them quickly disappear out into the newsroom.

He breathed out, slightly uncertain about the way the discussion had gone. One thing was certain: it was high time for him to act.

His outburst at the committee meeting had sat like a
lead weight on his chest all night, and showed no signs of
disappearing. Thomas ran a hand down to smooth the
front of his jacket, paused for a moment, then knocked
on the door of the head of social services. She was in.

'I'll get straight to the point,' he said. 'There's no
excuse for my behaviour yesterday, but I feel I owe you
an explanation.'

'Sit down,' she said.

He sank onto the chair and took a few quick breaths.

'I'm not feeling too well,' he said. 'I'm off kilter.
Things have been a bit tough lately.'

The head of social services looked at the young man
in silence. When he didn't continue she finally asked
quietly, 'Is it Eleonor?'

She was on the periphery of their circle of friends. She
had been to dinner with them maybe ten times or so.

'No, not at all,' Thomas said quickly. 'It's me. I . . .
I'm questioning everything. Is this all there is? Is this as
much fun as it's ever going to get?'

The woman behind the desk smiled sadly.

'Midlife crisis,' she diagnosed. 'But it's a bit early,
isn't it? How old are you?'

'Thirty-three.'

She sighed. 'Your outburst yesterday was indefensible,
but I think we should draw a line under it now. I daresay
you won't do it again.'

He shook his head, stood up and left. Outside the
door he stopped, thought for a moment, then went to
see the official who had raised the matter of the Paradise
Foundation.

'I'm busy,' she said brusquely, evidently still angry
about the previous day.

He tried to smile disarmingly.

'Yes, I understand,' he said. 'I just want to apologize for yesterday. It was extremely unprofessional of me to behave like that.'

The official jerked her neck and made a note of something.

'Apology accepted,' she said stiffly.

He widened his smile.

'Great. There are a couple of things I was wondering about all this. The registration number of the organization, for instance.'

'I haven't got it.'

He looked at her for so long that she started to blush. Evidently she didn't know anything about the foundation.

'I can find out,' she said.

'That would probably be best,' he said.

Silence again.

'What exactly is this all about?' he said eventually.

She looked up at him, an annoyed look on her face.

'I can't tell you, you know that.'

He sighed. 'Come on. We're all working towards the same goal. Do you really think I'm going to talk?'

The woman hesitated for a moment, then pushed her notes aside.

'It's an extremely serious case,' she said. 'A young woman, a refugee from Bosnia, is being pursued by a man. He's threatened to kill her. We only got the case yesterday, and it's urgent. It really is a matter of life or death.'

Thomas looked straight at her.

'How do we know it's true?'

The woman swallowed, and her eyes seemed to glaze over slightly.

'You should have seen her, so young, so beautiful . . . and so brutalized. She had scars all over her body, several bullet wounds, marks from knife-wounds, and a deep gash to her head; half her face was swollen with bruises. Two of her toes had been shot off. On Saturday the man tried to kill her again, and she only survived by leaping into the water, catching pneumonia in the process. The police can't protect her.'

'But this Paradise Foundation can?'

The woman was talking quickly now, discreetly wiping her eyes. She was only human, after all.

'It's a truly fantastic organization. They've worked out a way of erasing people so that their location isn't given away in any official registers. All contact with the outside world is channelled through the foundation. They offer help twenty-four hours a day – doctors, psychologists, lawyers, as well as help with housing, schools, work and nurseries. Believe me, buying in the services of this organization is a good deal for the council.'

Thomas squirmed.

'So, where exactly is Paradise? In Järfälla?'

The woman leaned forward.

'That's the whole point,' she said. 'No one knows where Paradise is. Everyone who works there has been erased. Their phone lines are connected to military exchanges in other provinces. The protection they offer really is watertight. We've never come across anything like it before, it really is quite remarkable.'

Thomas looked down at the floor.

'So all this secrecy means that no one can check out what they do either?'

'Sometimes you just have to trust people,' the woman said.

21

The flat was cold; the paper bag Annika had taped over the broken window did nothing to keep the heat in. Exhaustion hit her the moment she dropped her bag on the hall floor. She let her outdoor clothes fall in a heap and crept into her unmade bed, falling asleep with her clothes on.

Suddenly the presenters from *Studio Six* were standing in front of her. Their hostile scrutiny always brought the same cramp to her stomach.

'I didn't mean it!' she shouted.

The men came closer.

'How can you think it was my fault?' she yelled.

The men tried to shoot her. Their guns thundered inside her head.

'I didn't do it, I just found her! She was lying on the floor when I arrived! Help!'

She woke up with a start, out of breath. Barely an hour had passed. She took several deep breaths. Then she started to cry uncontrollably. She lay there for a long time until the sobbing gradually subsided.

Oh Grandma, good God, what on earth are we going to do? Who's going to look after you?

Annika sat up and tried to pull herself together. Someone had to take charge of this, and it was her turn to shoulder the responsibility.

She reached for the phonebook and called the local council, to see if there were any vacancies at any care homes in Stockholm. She was told to contact the authorities in her local district, to discuss suitable accommodation with a care assessor.

If she wanted to, she could find information online or at the local citizens' advice office at number 87 Hantverkargatan. She jotted down the address on an old newspaper, thanked the woman, then sighed. She went out into the kitchen and tried to eat a little yogurt, turning on the television. She realized she smelled of sweat and squeezed her clothes into the wash-basket, filled the sink with cold water and washed under her arms.

Why did I come home? Why didn't I stay at Grandma's?

She sat down on the sofa in the living room, leaned her head on her hands and made up her mind to be honest with herself.

She couldn't bear being in that hospital. She wanted to get back to something she was on the verge of finding again, something she had once had but somehow lost. There was something here in Stockholm, something in her work on the *Evening Post*, in this flat, something that ought to be enticing and vibrant, not making her feel ambivalent, or numb.

She got up abruptly and found her notebook in her bag. She dialled the number to Paradise without further reflection.

This time Rebecka Björkstig herself answered.

'I've been thinking about a few things,' Annika said.

'Aren't you going to have your article ready soon?' The woman sounded rather stressed.

Annika pulled her legs up beneath her and rested her head on her left hand.

171

'There are a couple of details I'm missing,' she said. 'I hope we can get it finished as soon as possible. My grandmother's ill.'

Rebecka's voice was full of sympathy when she replied.

'Oh, I am sorry. Of course, I'll help you in any way that I can. What do you need to know?'

Annika straightened her back and looked through her notebook.

'The number of employees. How many people work for Paradise?'

'We've got five full-time employees.'

'Doctors, lawyers, social workers, psychologists?'

'No, not at all.' Rebecka sounded amused. 'Things like that are provided by the authorities, local councils, the legal aid committee and so on.'

Annika brushed her hair back.

'The contact staff on call twenty-four hours a day, who are they?'

'Our employees, of course. They're highly qualified.'

'And what do they earn, per month?'

Now Rebecka sounded rather indignant.

'They earn fourteen thousand kronor per month. They don't do this to get rich, but because it's in a good cause.'

Annika leafed through her notebook, glancing at what she had written before.

'And how many properties do you have?'

Rebecka hesitated. 'Why do you ask?'

'To get an overall idea of your organization.'

'We don't really own any properties, we rent them as we need them,' Rebecka said, after a short pause.

'And the money,' Annika said. 'If you ever make a profit, what happens to it?'

There was a long silence, and Annika began to wonder if the woman had hung up.

'The small profits we make have been put back into the foundation, and used to build up our work. I'm not sure I like what you're insinuating here,' Rebecka Björkstig said.

'One last question,' Annika said. 'I was wondering if you've sent that list of people in official bodies that I could talk to?'

'This is a secure line,' the woman said quietly. 'I can be honest with you. Any money that's left over goes towards building up an exit route for our really difficult cases. For some time now we've had the resources to help clients who can no longer remain in Sweden at all. Using our contacts we can organize public-sector employment and housing in other countries. We can also help to arrange healthcare and counselling, as well as work and language courses.'

Annika dropped her feet to the floor, scribbling notes. This was strong stuff.

'But how does that work?'

The woman sounded very happy. 'The strategies are already in place, and we've tested them on two cases with great success.'

Annika was astonished.

'Two cases that have been given new lives in other countries? Without changing their identities? Just with help from Paradise?'

'Two whole families, that's right. Neither we nor anyone else has the power to change anyone's official ID numbers. Only the government can do that. As far as that list goes, I've already put it together for you. Just tell me where to fax it, and you'll have it within the next fifteen minutes.'

Annika gave her the fax number of the crime desk at the paper.

'I'll call back to let you know that I've got it,' she said.

'That would be good. Speak to you soon.'

They hung up. The silence was back, less threatening, the boundaries clearer. She had a task, a responsibility, a job that needed her.

The runner speeded up, his feet drumming on the ground. His pulse-rate increased, but not his breathing. It just got deeper, harder. Good! He was in fine form, gliding over the ground even though it was rough territory. Undergrowth, fallen trees, uneven ground. He glanced at the map, 1:15,000 scale, based on aerial pictures and comprehensive surveys on the ground that he often helped out with himself. Full-colour, produced by the Swedish Orienteering Society. This was on the edge of his usual stamping-ground, but a good place to train in slightly more challenging terrain.

He practised changing direction as he ran, holding his compass in his right hand and the map in his left, not slowing down, even though he had decided to identify all the marked symbols: rocks, ridges, bends in the path. That was why he didn't see the tree-root. It sent him flying, and he fell headfirst among the young trees. His forehead hit the ground, and he blacked out for a few seconds. When he came to his senses he felt the pain in his foot. Blast! Only one more race left this season, and this had to happen! Typical!

He groaned and sat up, feeling his ankle. Maybe it wasn't too serious. He tried moving his foot. No, nothing broken, probably just a sprain. Carefully he got up and put some weight on the foot. Ouch! He would have to take it slowly and try to get back to the car the shortest way possible. He studied the map to find the quickest route.

A few minutes before he had passed a muddy forest track that followed the base of one of the ridges. On the map he could see that it led to the main road, and from there he would be able to get a lift back to his own car. With a deep sigh he put the map and compass away inside his jacket and limped off.

A hundred metres or so along the muddy track he caught sight of some badly scorched birch trees in the forest. He stopped in surprise. A forest fire, after all this rain? Then came the smell, acrid and metallic.

He checked that the map and compass were hanging inside his jacket, then stepped off the track. He took it very slowly, following some tyre tracks through the trees, down towards a narrow ravine. At the edge of the forest he stopped, perplexed.

In front of him was a warped metal skeleton, the burned-out remains of what must have been a big articulated lorry. How on earth had it ended up here? And how had it managed to burn out so completely?

Carefully he limped towards the wreckage, his shoes blackened by the soot on the ground. It got warmer as he approached, so it couldn't have been long since the fire.

The ground near the cab was covered in fine glass that crunched beneath his feet. The remains of the doors were hanging off, and he walked up and looked inside the cab.

There was something on the floor, and something on the passenger seat, shapeless and soot-covered. He leaned over and prodded the thing closest to him. Something gave way. He pulled off his glove and brushed the soot away. When he saw the teeth grinning back at him he realized what he was looking at.

22

The crime team's fax machine was on the desk of their researcher, Eva-Britt Qvist. Eva-Britt provided a number of functions to the department – checking records and searching archives, cataloguing court reports and doing other research. She wasn't at her desk. Annika looked through the little pile of faxes that had come in during the day: a communiqué from Stockholm Police press department, some information from the National Prosecutor's office, a court judgment from a narcotics case—

'What are you doing in my things?'

The thick-set woman came storming over from the cafeteria with an angry frown on her face. Annika backed away.

'I'm waiting for a fax,' she said. 'I was just checking to see if it had arrived.'

'Why are you giving out my number? This is the crime desk fax.'

Eva-Britt Qvist grabbed the papers from Annika's hands and gathered up those still on the desk. Annika stared at her in astonishment. They had hardly ever spoken before; Eva-Britt Qvist worked days and Annika nights.

'Sorry,' she said, surprised. 'I usually give out this

number at night if I need a fax. I didn't know I was doing anything wrong.'

The researcher fixed her eyes on Annika.

'And you never fill out the form.'

Hostility was firing out of her like little arrows.

'Of course I do!' Annika said, annoyed. 'Most recently on my last shift! What's this all about? It's not your private bloody fax, is it? Have I had my list of contacts from the Paradise Foundation or not?'

'What's all this, girls?'

Anders Schyman was standing behind them.

'Girls?' Annika said, spinning round. 'I suppose you think that's funny?'

The head-editor laughed.

'I knew it would wind you up. What's going on?'

'Rebecka Björkstig is sending me a fax so I can finish off that series of articles about the Paradise Foundation, but Eva-Britt isn't happy about me giving out her fax number.'

Annika realized that she was upset, and was ashamed at her lack of self-control.

'It hasn't arrived yet,' the researcher said.

Schyman turned to Eva-Britt Qvist.

'Do you think you could keep an eye out for it, please?' Schyman said calmly and slowly. 'It's part of an important new investigation for the paper.'

'This is supposed to be the crime desk,' Eva-Britt Qvist said.

'And this is a crime story,' Schyman said. 'Look, it's high time to stop these divides – we need to work together. Annika, come with me, I'd like an update on how the story's going.'

Annika followed the head-editor to his office, focusing on his broad back ahead of her.

The sofa was gone.

'I followed your advice,' Schyman said. 'From now on all my visitors will have to sit on the floor. Please, sit down!'

He gestured toward the dusty corner, as she sank onto a chair instead.

'I think it's falling into place now,' she said, rubbing her forehead. 'Rebecka Björkstig has promised to send me the last bit of information I need, and I've had an explanation of where the money goes.'

Schyman looked up.

'The money? They take payment for this?'

Annika looked through a large notepad she had pulled out of her bag.

'Any profits go towards building up a means of escape for people who can't stay in Sweden,' she read from her notes. 'Paradise has contacts who can arrange public-sector work and housing in other countries. They've managed to get two cases through so far, two families. No one had to change their identity. Only the government can change a person's ID number – Paradise can't, nor any other organization. But that hasn't been necessary for Paradise's clients.'

She looked up at the head-editor and tried to smile.

'It's not bad, is it?'

Anders Schyman was looking at her calmly.

'This doesn't make sense,' he said.

She looked down at the desk without responding.

'Arranging public-sector work in other countries?' he said. 'That sounds like a pretty tall story. Has she got any evidence to back up her claim?'

Annika looked through her notes without looking up.

'Two cases,' she said. 'Two entire families.'

'Have you spoken to them?'

She gulped and crossed her legs, aware that she was adopting a defensive posture.

'Rebecka seems to know what she's talking about.'

Schyman tapped a pen thoughtfully on the desktop.

'Really? The government can't decide whether to give someone a new ID number. That can only be done by the Tax Office, at the request of the National Police Board.'

Everything went quiet, and Annika could feel the blood draining from her face.

'Is that true?'

He nodded. Annika straightened up and leafed frantically through her notes.

'But she said the government, I'm sure she did.'

'I believe you,' Schyman said. 'But I don't believe this Paradise woman.'

She slumped back in the chair and closed her notes.

'So I've done all this work for nothing.'

Anders Schyman stood up.

'On the contrary,' he said. 'This is where the work really begins. If this organization really does exist, then it's a great story, no matter if this woman is lying or not. So tell me, what exactly has she said?'

She gave him an outline of how Paradise worked, how it erased people, about the unexplained threats made against Rebecka in the past, something to do with the Yugoslavian mafia, and finally her own thoughts about where the money went.

Schyman walked round the desk, nodding, then sat down again.

'You've made good progress,' he said, 'but we really need that list of contacts. If this is all a bluff, we need help from someone working for a public organization in order to get our hands on all the information about this foundation.'

'Or,' Annika said, 'we get hold of one of the women who has been through the organization. Or someone who works there.'

179

'If those women really exist,' Schyman said. 'And if there are any employees.'

The list hadn't arrived. There was nothing wrong with the fax. More than two hours had passed since she had spoken to Rebecka.

Annika sat down at Berit Hamrin's desk and dialled the number. The secret, unlisted number. The ringtone echoed down the line, and she hung up and dialled again. No answer. No answer-machine. No connection to another line.

'Can you tell me if that list turns up?' she called to Eva-Britt Qvist.

The researcher was on the phone and pretended not to hear.

Annika went onto the internet and signed in to the national address register, which held the records of everyone with a Swedish ID number. She typed in 'Björkstig Rebecka'. The computer thought for a moment, then spat out its answer.

One hit: *personal details protected*.

Nothing more. Nothing at all.

Annika stared at the screen. *What the hell?*

Hindered by the bandage on her finger, she typed in her own details, 'Bengtzon Annika Stockholm'. And after a moment there she was: ID number, address, the most recent change in the records two years ago. She clicked onto her personal history, and found her old address on Tattarbacken in Hälleforsnäs. There was nothing wrong with the website.

She started again and typed in 'Björkstig Rebecka woman' one more time, and got the same result.

Personal details protected.

So she really had managed to erase herself.

Annika stared at the screen. One of her nightly tasks

180

was to track down pictures of people, usually passport photos. And for that she needed a date of birth and an ID number, and in order to find those she used this website. She must have carried out close to a thousand searches on here since she started working nights, but she had never come up with this result before. She clicked to get a printout, paused, then typed in 'Aida Begovic'. Eight results. One of the women lived at Fredriksbergsvägen in Vaxholm. That had to be her Aida. She printed that page as well and sat back in Berit's chair.

'Still no list?'

Eva-Britt Qvist shook her head. Annika called Paradise again. No answer. She slammed the phone down. *Damn.*

So what was she going to do now? Her finger ached. Go back to the hospital? Try to find a care home in Stockholm? Go home and do some cleaning?

She searched through her papers, and dug out the folder about foundations registered with the Tax Office that she had ordered from the archive.

She read that since 1 January 1996 foundations had been governed by legislation covering their establishment, management, accounting, supervision and registration, etc. She skimmed the text. There were various different sorts of foundations, evidently, which affected how much tax they paid. Those that were recognized as working 'for the public benefit' paid less, she read. It wasn't enough to have a nice document of establishment in order to avoid tax; their activities had to match their words.

She put the folder down. What on earth was she doing? This was rubbish, so why was she wasting her time on it? It was all meaningless.

But, she suddenly realized, it did mean that some-where there had to be a document of establishment for the Paradise Foundation. And there had to be accountants and auditors involved. They must have to pay some sort of tax. They couldn't have managed to erase the records of that as well.

She picked up the information sheets Rebecka had given her and looked at the PO box number in the top corner. She called Järfälla post office and asked who was paying to use that particular PO box.

'I can't tell you that,' a slightly stressed clerk said.

'But there must be a street address linked to every PO box, mustn't there?' Annika said. 'I'm trying to find out who's using box 259.'

'That's confidential information,' the woman said. 'Only government agencies can ask for that sort of detail.'

Annika thought hard for several seconds.

'Maybe I'm from a government agency,' she said. 'You can't know, because I didn't introduce myself and you haven't asked.'

There were a few seconds of silence.

'I have to check with Disa,' the woman said.

'Who?' Annika wondered.

'The Disa system, the post office intranet. It holds the details of what information we're allowed to divulge. One moment . . .'

The moment lasted several minutes.

The woman's voice was even cooler when she returned.

'Since the Post Office became a registered company, all dealings between us and our customers are confidential. We can give out information if the police suspect a crime punishable by more than two years in prison has been committed. But not otherwise.'

Annika thanked her and hung up. She took a restless walk around the newsroom. People were talking, shouting, laughing, phones were ringing, computer screens flickering.

Someone from a government agency, she had to get hold of someone from a government agency who knew something about all this. Seeing as she didn't know the details of a single case, she would have to try her luck. She went back to Berit's desk, took out the phonebook and called Stockholm City Council.

'Which district is it?'

She picked her own, Kungsholmen, and found herself in a queue. After twelve minutes of deafening silence she hung up.

What about Järfälla, then?

The social services department took calls between 8.30 and 9.30, and on Thursdays between 17.00 and 17.30.

She groaned. It was hopeless ringing round at random. Even if she did manage to find someone who happened to know something, they weren't going to talk to her. Any cases of this nature would be confidential. She needed a way in, somewhere that she knew the local council was already involved.

She fetched a cup of coffee, blowing on it as she walked back to the desk. She passed a group of women sitting and laughing together, and looked down at the floor without saying hello. She got the impression that the voices got quieter as she passed by, that the conversation stalled, that they were talking about her.

Paranoia, she thought, but wasn't convinced.

She put the plastic cup down on Berit's desk, spilling some as she did so, and tried to concentrate on her work. There was no point approaching social workers – they always started to panic before you even began to ask questions, and they never gave a straight answer, even when the subject was in the public domain.

Where else could she get hold of information about Paradise?

She burned her tongue on the coffee as it dawned on her.

Invoices! Of course!

There would have to be a mass of information on Paradise's invoices, registration numbers, address, bank account details and so on. Someone in the finance office of a local council ought to be able to find out information about tax, regulations and accountants.

She looked through the list of councils in the phonebook. Which one should she choose?

She put the phonebook down and looked at the printouts from the address register instead. Rebecka's local council was hidden, but Aida was listed as a resident of Vaxholm.

Vaxholm.

Annika had never been there, just knew that it was on the coast, somewhere north of the city.

It's a long shot, she thought. It's not even certain that Aida actually tried to contact Paradise. Or that her local council was involved yet. Maybe it was too soon.

On the other hand, it was a possibility. She dialled the number, waiting an age for the call to be picked up. Her thoughts wandered, she ought to phone and see how her grandmother was. When the receptionist finally answered, she briefly forgot who she had called. She asked to speak to the finance officer of the social services department. The number was engaged, and there were already calls waiting: could she call back?

She hung up, pulled on her coat, put her notebook in her bag and headed off to see if she could borrow one of the paper's cars.

'No list?'

Eva-Britt Qvist didn't respond.

23

The afternoon traffic on the E18 out towards Roslagen was notoriously heavy. She sat in a jam at Bergshamra for quarter of an hour before the queue started moving again.

It was good to be behind the wheel. She drove too fast, overtaking, the car was quick. She reached the centre of Vaxholm sooner than she had expected. Neat bunting hanging over a cobbled street lined with ornate buildings. A bank, a florist, a supermarket. Annika realized that she didn't have a map.

The town hall, she thought. *The main square.* It could hardly be that complicated.

She carried on until she reached the shore, turned right at a mini-roundabout and found herself in the car park for the ferry. A long queue of cars was waiting for the dirty yellow ferry out to Rindö.

She turned left. Östra Ekuddsgatan. She peered up at the row of expensive villas lining the shore, each one fronting onto the water.

Millionaires' row, she thought. *La crème de la crème.*

The car glided slowly up a steep slope of sand-blown tarmac. Each house was surrounded by gates and fences.

'God, how dull,' she said aloud, then realized she was back where she had started. She drove back down the street with the bunting and this time turned left instead of right at the roundabout. She eventually came to a police station on a small square. Ahead of her was a large, ochre-coloured building with a little Russian onion-dome at the top. The double doors were painted to look like marble, as were the streetlamps flanking it. On a small letterbox she read: VAXHOLM TOWN COUNCIL.

The weather wasn't getting any better. The greyness had burrowed into Thomas's head, and he felt like crying. The narrow street outside his window looked like a mud-filled ditch. Piles of paper and overdue work were threatening to overwhelm him, and the bastard telephone wouldn't stop ringing. He stared at the shrieking machine.

I'm not going to answer, he thought. *It'll only be another nursery thinking that they've still got some money left from this year's budget.*

He grabbed the receiver.

'Hello, this is reception. There's a reporter here who wants to talk to someone in charge of social service budgets and contracts, so I thought maybe you could . . .'

Oh, God, would it never end?

'I'm not a politician. Send her to one of the councillors.'

The receptionist disappeared, then came back, sounding sharper this time.

'She doesn't want to talk to a politician, she just wants a bit of . . . what did you say you wanted to ask about?'

He leaned his head on his hand and groaned. *Give me strength!*

There was muttering in the background.

'Can't I just talk to him myself?' he heard someone say, then a new voice came on the line.

'What's this about?' he asked abruptly, feeling tired.

'Well, my name's Annika Bengtzon, I'm a journalist.

186

I was wondering if I could possibly come up and ask a few quick questions about how you deal with contracts and external services in the council?'

Why me? he thought.

'I haven't got time,' he said.

'Why not?' she asked quickly. 'Burned out?'

He burst out laughing, what a question.

'You haven't got an appointment,' he said, 'and I've got an awful lot to do at the moment.'

'It'll take fifteen minutes,' the journalist said. 'You don't have to move, I'll come up to your office.'

He sighed quietly. 'To be honest—'

'I'm already at reception. It won't take long. Please.'

The last word was almost a plea.

He rubbed his eyes, feeling how tired they were. It would take more effort just to get rid of her.

'Okay, come up.'

She was skinny, her hair was a mess, she looked a bit manic, and the shadows under her eyes were too heavy for her to be described as pretty.

'I'm really sorry to barge in like this,' she said, stuffing her big bag under the chair in his office. She threw her jacket and scarf on the back of the chair, one arm of the jacket falling to the floor. She held out her hand with a smile. Thomas shook it, realizing that his hand was clammy. He wasn't used to the media.

'Just tell me if I'm going too far,' the woman said. 'I realize that social services is a very sensitive area.'

She settled onto the chair, her eyes fixed on his, concentrating hard, her pen at the ready.

He cleared his throat.

'What have you done to your hand?'

She didn't look away.

'I trapped my finger. Have you ever heard of a foundation called Paradise?'

187

His reaction was physical. He jerked.

'What the hell do you know about that?'

The woman had noted his reaction, he could tell from the look of satisfaction on her face.

'I know a bit,' she said. 'Not enough. I was thinking that maybe you knew more than me.'

'All details of the social services department's work are confidential,' he said tersely.

'No they aren't,' the journalist said, sounding almost amused. 'There's a lot that's public. I don't know how it all works, and that's what I wanted to ask you about.'

He was confused. How the hell was he supposed to handle this? He couldn't say anything about the case in question – the woman from Bosnia. He wasn't even supposed to know about her. And he certainly didn't want the press publishing anything about Vaxholm Council buying in expensive services from some peculiar foundation.

'I can't help you,' he said curtly, standing up.

'She's lying,' the journalist said quietly. 'The manager of the Paradise Foundation is a liar. Did you know that?'

He stopped, and she looked him in the eye. She was leaning forward, her legs crossed. Large breasts.

He sat down again and looked down at his desk.

'I don't know what you're talking about. I'm sorry, but I can't help you. If you'll excuse me, I've got a lot . . .'

She was leafing through a large, scruffy notepad, making no effort to get up.

'Would you mind if I asked you some general questions about the purchase of services of this sort?'

'As I said, I really don't—'

'How has the outsourcing of public services affected the work of the council?'

She looked him deep in the eyes, focusing on him, expecting an answer. He swallowed and cleared his throat again.

'After the decentralization that followed the changes in social services legislation in nineteen eighty-two, there was a lot more number-crunching. Every single playgroup, care home, everything – they all had their own individual budget. Now, after privatization, there aren't so many details. Each point of service exists as a single cost in the budget.'

She was listening expressionlessly, her pen hadn't moved.

'What does that mean in normal language?'

He felt the blood rise to his face, annoyed at being corrected like that. He decided not to let it show.

'In some ways things have got easier,' he said. 'Now councils just have to pay out one lump sum, then the service providers do what they want with the money.'

She was making notes now, and he fell silent.

'So what do you do?' she asked. 'What's your title?'

'I'm a senior accountant with responsibility for social service finances and planning, I manage and plan the budget. I'm in charge of contract work within the council, I'm responsible for financial management, and I respond to the needs and requests of staff in the various services. I'm in charge of quarterly reporting and the annual accounts . . . Usually I'm looking after three years simultaneously, the previous, current and forthcoming years . . .'

'That's amazing,' the woman said. 'Do you always talk like that?'

Thomas lost his train of thought, surprised.

'It took a bloody long time to learn how to do it,' he said.

She laughed, showing her even, white teeth.

'So how have people reacted to the new arrangements?' she asked. 'Do they like the new set-up?'

She changed position, her breasts moving under her top. He looked down at the desk again.

'It's mixed,' he said. 'The heads of the various departments have lost a lot of their influence, which hasn't been popular. They can't go in and micro-manage any more, the way they used to when childcare and care homes were run by the council. But, on the other hand, they've got a lot less responsibility.'

He was surprised at how open he was being. She was making notes without looking up. Strong, attractive hands.

'People have the right to their opinions,' he went on. 'Even council staff have a political attitude to the changes, different ideologies and so on.'

'Can you explain exactly what you do, and why?' she said.

He nodded, and did so. He had to explain certain things several times, with different words and phrases. She didn't seem terribly well educated, but was quick to grasp the facts. He explained his role in the social services management team, which, apart from him, consisted of the director of social services, and the heads of the different sections: childcare, schools, care of the elderly, families . . . They discussed the decision-making process, the way the social services committee took its decisions, the fact that the head of department was always present at such meetings, and usually the financial manager and the council staff presenting the different proposals, as well as the section heads on occasion.

'So who has the real power?' she asked.

He looked at her from the corner of his eye. Narrow thighs, tight trousers.

'It depends on the nature of the proposal,' he replied. 'A lot of decisions are taken by staff on the ground. Others end up with the committee. Some go all the way up to council meetings themselves, or even government departments, before a decision can be taken.'

She reflected for a moment, tapping her forehead with her pen.

'If you received a proposal from an entirely new organization,' she said, looking at him hard, 'a foundation, for instance, that wanted to help people in trouble. Who would take the decision to buy in that service?'

Suddenly he realized where all of this line of questioning had been leading. For some reason he wasn't annoyed.

'The initial decision to purchase a service of this sort would probably be taken by the committee,' he said slowly. 'But once the basic decision had been taken, individual cases would be dealt with by individual council officers.'

'Do you get many proposals of that nature? From foundations and other private businesses?'

'Not really,' he said. 'Usually it's the council that asks for bids when various activities are being put out to tender.'

She looked through her notes.

'So if Vaxholm Council decided to employ the services of a foundation of that sort, you would know about it?'

Thomas let out a deep sigh. 'Yes.'

'So has such a decision been taken?'

He sighed again. 'Yes. The social services committee took the decision to buy in the services of the Paradise Foundation at a meeting yesterday evening. The minutes haven't been written up yet, but the committee's acceptance of the agreement will appear there, under item number seventeen. And the minutes are in the public domain. That's the only reason I'm telling you about it,' he said.

The young woman was quick to blush.

'What do you know about the woman in the case, Aida Begovic from Bijeljina?'

He stopped, suddenly annoyed.

'What exactly do you want?' he snapped. 'You turn up here and ask a load of nonsense, then you insinuate that—'

'Calm down,' Annika said sharply. 'I think we might be able to help each other.'

He lost his train of thought, and realized that he was standing up, annoyed, the blood burning in his face. His fists were clenched. What the hell was he doing? *Christ, get a grip!*

He said down abruptly, and his hair flopped forward. He pushed it back with both hands.

'Sorry,' he said. 'God, I'm sorry, I didn't mean to flare up like that . . .'

Her face broke into a broad smile.

'Great,' she said. 'I'm not the only one who gets aggressive.'

He stared at her, at the hair that wouldn't stay in place, and those eyes that seemed to see right through him.

He looked down again.

'What do you really want?'

She turned serious, finally sounding sincere.

'I'm stuck,' she said. 'I'm trying to look into this organization, and it isn't going very well. According to Rebecka Björkstig's own figures, Paradise ought to have pulled in more than eighteen million over the past three years, and if my guess is correct their outgoings are somewhere around seven million. I don't know exactly what sort of foundation Paradise is, so I can't work out what tax laws are applicable, but it still doesn't feel right.'

'Do you know if they do what they say?' he asked.

She shook her head, looking honestly concerned.

'Nope. I've met Rebecka, and I've met Aida, but I don't know if they really help people.'

'Rebecka, she's in charge?'

The journalist nodded. 'At least that's what she says, and I believe her. You haven't met her? She seems credible, but I know that she's lied about one thing, or at least been misleading. She doesn't know as much as she makes out, and when you question her she avoids giving direct answers. What exactly do you know?'

He paused, but only for a second.

'Practically nothing. No one seems to know anything. The committee took the decision yesterday, even though the information it had was extremely sketchy. I haven't even got a registration number for the organization.'

'But you can find that out?'

He nodded.

'Does it check out, from a purely legal perspective?'

'We put that question to our lawyers this morning.'

Annika Bengtzon gave him a long, hard look.

'What do you know about these charitable foundations in general? Why do you think Rebecka Björkstig would have chosen that form of business model?'

He leaned forward.

'A foundation has no owners or members. The rules are much less restrictive than for limited companies or partnerships.'

Annika was taking notes.

'What else?'

'As far as I know, foundations are sometimes used as a way of salting away money after bankruptcy. They can also be used for various forms of deception,

193

which is where the lack of official supervision comes in handy.'

The woman looked up.

'Why isn't there any supervision?'

'When a foundation is registered, the people representing it don't have to volunteer their ID numbers. Sometimes they've turned out to be completely fictional individuals.'

She nodded, and scratched her head thoughtfully.

'So on the one hand, it makes everything even murkier. Rebecka could have set up the foundation simply to get her hands on other people's money. But on the other hand, if the organization really does work the way she says, a foundation would be the best way of setting it up.'

They sat in silence for a few moments. Thomas realized that the rest of the town hall had gone quiet, and looked at his watch.

'Bloody hell,' he said, 'is it really that late?'

She smiled. 'Time flies when you're having fun.'

'I have to go,' he said, standing up quickly.

Annika gathered her things and put them in her bag. She pulled on her jacket and scarf, then shook his hand.

'Thanks for letting me take up so much of your time.'

Firm gaze, straight back. Not too tall. And those breasts. He realized his hand was getting clammy again.

'I'm going to do some more work on this,' she said, keeping hold of his hand after shaking it. 'I'm just wondering,' she said, 'if I do find out something, do you want to know about it?'

He gulped – his throat was dry – and nodded.

She smiled.

'Good. And if you find out anything, will you tell me about it?'

He let go of her hand.

'We'll have to see . . .'

'Well, bye for now.'

A moment later she was gone. He stared at the closed door and heard her footsteps disappear down the corridor. He went round to the chair she had been sitting in and sat down. The seat was still warm. From the heat of her groin.

He stood up quickly, pulled out a file and started to look at the department's personnel budget, but the numbers danced in front of his eyes. Irritated, he shut the file and went over to the window. The picturesque signs in the shops below grinned at him, *Among Cobs and Skerries, Vaxholm Tea & Spice Traders.*

He ought to go home. Eleonor would have their meal ready.

24

The traffic heading towards Stockholm was considerably lighter than the queue heading in the other direction. Annika stared out through the windscreen as the monotony of Swedish suburbs enveloped the car. As soon as she left the centre of Vaxholm behind her all sense of the picturesque vanished and large blocks of council housing took over. *This could be Flen*, she thought. A sign to her left pointed to Fredriksberg, where Aida had lived. She slowed down, wondering for a moment about turning off and going to look at her address, but decided not to.

Over the radio came a warning of icy roads.

At least I'm still alive, she thought. *I get to play along for a bit longer.*

She tried to peer up at the sky, but the clouds were solid. No stars in sight. No one could see her from space.

She drove back slowly, getting overtaken this time instead of the other way round. She felt a calmness in her stomach, even though her grandmother sat like a small core of sorrow deep within.

The landscape as she headed back towards Stockholm was astonishingly bland. The 274 could easily have been the road between Hälleforsnäs and Katrineholm. She retuned the radio and found a station that was running a Boney M marathon.

There was rain in the air by the time she reached Arninge and turned onto the E18, but it just hung there, not actually falling. She listened to the thud of German disco all the way back to the paper's offices in Marieberg.

The caretakers had gone, so she left the car key on the desk and walked home towards Hantverkargatan, through Rålambshov Park and along Norr Mälarstrand. It was bitterly cold, the darkness broken by streetlamps and neon signs, but still somehow thick and oppressive. Her thoughts went back to her grandmother. Whatever were they going to do?

The anxiety in the pit of her stomach started to grow again.

She was frozen by the time she got home, her teeth chattering. The telephone rang, and she ran to answer it in her muddy shoes.

Grandma! Oh God, something's happened to Grandma!

Ashamed of having felt so calm, guilty about the fact that she shouldn't have been at home.

'I'm going to stop at the Thai takeaway on the way home and get stir-fried chicken with cashew nuts,' Anne said. 'Can I get you some?'

Annika sank onto the floor.

'Yes, please.'

Anne Snapphane turned up half an hour later with two foil containers in a bag.

'Fuck, it's cold,' she said as she took off her boots. 'Raw air like this plays havoc with your airways. I can feel I'm coming down with bronchitis.'

Anne had an unfailing tendency towards hypochondria.

'Put some thick socks on. If your feet are warm, you'll be fine, as Grandma always says,' Annika said, and burst into tears.

'My goodness, what's the matter?'

Anne went over and sat beside Annika on the sofa, waiting. Annika cried, and felt the lump in her stomach heat up, soften, and gradually dissolve.

'It's Grandma,' she said. 'She's had a stroke and she's in hospital in Katrineholm. She's never going to be right again.'

'Oh, shit,' Anne said sympathetically. 'So what's going to happen to her now?'

Annika blew her nose on a tissue and wiped her cheeks. She took a deep breath.

'No one knows. There's no room for her anywhere, and no one has time to look after her, and she needs loads of support and physiotherapy. I suppose I'll have to give up work and look after her here.'

Anne leaned her head to one side.

'Three floors up, with no lift, no toilet, and no hot water?'

Annika formulated the thoughts that had been bubbling inside her all day.

'I suppose I'll have to move to a flat in Katrineholm. It's not the end of the world. Anyway, what am I really doing up here? Sitting in that office rewriting other reporters' work for a crap paper with a dreadful reputation. Is that supposed to be more important that looking after the only person you love?'

Anne didn't answer, letting Annika get it all out. She went and fetched glasses and cutlery from the kitchen. Annika turned on the television, and they sat and watched the news as they ate their stir-fried chicken straight out of the cartons. The stock exchange had gone up again. More violence in Mitrovica. The Social

Democrats ahead of their conference.

'Are you serious about giving it all up?' Anne Snapphane asked, leaning back in the sofa, too full to move.

Annika rubbed her forehead and sighed.

'If it comes to it. I don't want to give up work, but what else can I do if there are no other options?'

'Winning the martyrdom world cup won't make anyone happy,' Anne said. 'You've got a responsibility to yourself as well, you can't make the whole of your life dependent on someone else. Do you want some wine?'

'The doctor told me to have a drink,' Annika said. 'White, preferably.'

'What do you think I brought? Red wine makes my face puff up. God, it's cold in here, have you got the window open?'

Anne got up and went out into the kitchen.

'The wind broke the glass,' Annika called after her.

Anne came back with the wine, and they each sat under a blanket and drank chardonnay from a winebox.

'So what about everything else?' she asked.

Annika sighed, closed her eyes and leaned her head back on the sofa.

'I had a fight with Mum. She really doesn't like me. I always knew, but it still feels crap to hear it.'

She felt the pain run through her body. The feeling of not being loved had its own unique ache.

Anne Snapphane looked sceptical.

'I don't know anyone who gets on with their mother.'

Annika shook her head, realized that she was capable of smiling, and looked down at her wineglass.

'I really don't think she likes me. And if I'm honest, I don't think I like her either. Do we have to?'

Anne thought for a moment.

199

'Not really. It depends on how the mother behaves. If she deserves it, you love her, if you feel like it, but there shouldn't be any pressure. But,' she held a finger in the air, 'you have a duty to love your children, always. That's one responsibility you can never escape from.'

'She doesn't think I deserve to be loved,' Annika said.

Anne Snapphane shrugged. 'She's wrong. That just proves she's an idiot. Okay, I want to hear about something fun now. Hasn't anything nice happened?'

The pressure eased, and Annika breathed out with a smile.

'I'm working on a good story at work. A really dodgy foundation that wipes out the pasts of people who've been threatened.'

Anne Snapphane took a sip of wine and raised her eyebrows. Annika went on.

'I met a bloke who works for a local council today who's had dealings with this foundation. If I handle this carefully I could be in there.'

'Was he cute?'

Anne Snapphane emptied her glass and poured some more wine.

'He had the personality of a lump of wood,' Annika said. 'He kept coming out with all this official crap. I tried to get him to relax, talking round the subject, but nothing really worked. I don't think he'd ever met a journalist before, he was so twitchy . . .'

'Oh,' Anne said, fiddling with her glass, 'he was probably too busy looking at your tits.'

Annika stared at her friend.

'You're crazy,' she said. 'A council finance officer?'

'So? He's got a penis, hasn't he? And what was he doing in Frihamnen?'

Annika groaned, put down her glass and stood up.

'You're not listening. Frihamnen was the day before yesterday. He's in Vaxholm. Do you want some water?'

She got a jug and two fresh glasses. Per, the smiley blonde, had finished the weather forecast and the next programme started: a group of middle-aged women with pretensions to cultural relevance discussing something completely meaningless. Annika switched it off.

'How are things on *Sofa Talk*?'

It was Anne's turn to groan.

'Michelle Carlsson, the new girl, wants to be on screen the whole time. She does pieces to camera in every one of her items, and refuses to cut them out. Now she's suggesting that we should have a panel of women to discuss different things, sex and so on, and of course she'd be part of that.'

'Has she said so?' Annika said. 'That she wants to be part of that?'

Anne Snapphane groaned again.

'Not in so many words, but that's the only reason she ever suggests anything.'

'Isn't it a good thing that someone wants to be on screen?' Annika said. 'I'd refuse point blank. I'd rather die.'

'Most people are the exact opposite,' Anne Snapphane said. 'They'd step over a dead body if it got them on television.'

25

The television discussion was about the meaning of art, a question that always seemed relevant.

'So let me ask the panel,' the presenter said, 'what does the concept of art mean to you?'

The first panellist rotated her right hand as she spoke. 'It's a never-ending conversation.'

'Good art is socially conscious, it involves taking risks, it's got real substance, and it has the power to affect people profoundly,' said the second panellist, gesturing with her left hand.

'Serious artists reflect the age they live in. Personally, I think it's a good thing if it leads to a discussion, and this debate shows that art is important,' the third one said, raising her eyebrows.

'But does that mean that art is always important merely because it sparks debate?' the presenter asked.

'There are limits to that,' the third one explained, 'and those limits differ from case to case. If you see the creative minds behind the work, you tend to know how serious they are. But we mustn't allow ourselves to become complacent in our opinions. Conceptual art, where the ideas behind the work in question are the very point of it, is . . .'

Thomas got up from the sofa.

'I'm going to get a beer, do you want one?'

Eleonor didn't answer, the frown on her face indicating that she didn't want to be disturbed. He went up the stairs with the cultural debate ringing in his ears.

'. . . contemporary art has always been a little difficult. Who knows, perhaps Giotto di Bondone's modernization of religious painting led contemporary onlookers to mutter and complain . . .'

He went to the fridge. No cold beer. He sighed, went to the pantry and found an unchilled can. He looked round for the evening papers but couldn't see them.

'Aren't you going to watch?' Eleonor called.

He sat on one of the kitchen chairs for a few seconds, took a long swig of beer, the bubbles going up his nose. He sighed and went downstairs again.

'Feminism has had a serious influence on the debate about literature, and the construction of literary history,' the presenter was saying. 'But has it also affected literature itself? And, if so, in what ways?'

Thomas sat down on the sofa. The woman who attempted to answer the question looked like a pear. She was the publisher of a literary journal, and was so full of shit that Thomas couldn't help laughing.

'. . . female writers were favoured,' the pear said, 'by the fact that they were identified in a particular way. I remember the response of the Danish author—'

'Talk about taking yourself too seriously!' he exclaimed.

'Shh, I'm trying to listen.'

He got up from the sofa and went back to the kitchen.

'Thomas, what's the matter?' Eleonor called after him.

He groaned silently, hunting through his briefcase for the evening papers.

'Nothing.'

There they were. He pulled them out, slightly crumpled, but they would soon be yesterday's news.

'Aren't you going to watch the debate? We're going to be talking about it at the cultural association on Saturday.'

He didn't answer, and began to read the *Evening Post*. That was where she worked. He hadn't recognized her, so she probably didn't write those articles with the little portrait of the writer under them.

'Thomas!'

'What?'

'There's no need to shout at me. Have we got any spare videos? I want to record this!'

He put down the paper, shutting his eyes tight.

'Thomas?'

'I don't know! Bloody hell! Leave me alone!'

He picked up the paper demonstratively again. A large man in dark clothes stared out at him from the pages, the head of some mafia gang. He could hear Eleonor looking through the videos downstairs, and knew what was coming next. She'd start shouting and hitting the machine, demanding that he come and sort it out.

'Thomas!'

He threw the paper aside and took the stairs in three strides.

'Yes,' he said. 'Here I am. Tell me what the hell it is you want from me so I can go back upstairs and read my fucking paper in peace!'

She stared at him as if he were a ghost.

'What's wrong with you? Your face is bright red. I just need some help with the video, is that too much to ask?'

'You could learn to press the button yourself.'

'Oh, stop it,' she said uncertainly. 'I'm missing the debate!'

'A group of pretentious middle-class hags mastur-bating in front of each other on television. No, you wouldn't want to miss that, would you?'

She was staring at him, mouth open wide.

'You're not serious,' she said. 'Sweden would sink into a cultural abyss if it weren't for these women! They represent and formulate our culture for us, the social image we have of contemporary culture!'

He looked at her, so neatly formulated, so well pre-sented.

He turned on his heel, took his coat and walked out.

As soon as Aida opened her eyes she knew the fever had gone. Her thoughts were clear and pure, all her pain was gone. She was thirsty.

The woman from that morning was sitting on a stool beside her.

'Would you like something to drink?'

She nodded and the woman gave her a glass of apple juice. Her hand was trembling as she took the glass, she was still very weak.

'How are you feeling?'

She swallowed and nodded, looking round. A hospital room, something uncomfortable in her right arm, a drip. She was undressed.

'Much better, thanks.'

The woman got up from her stool and leaned over her.

'My name's Mia,' the woman said. 'I'm going to help you. We're going to get out of here this evening, so try to get as much rest as you can. Do you want anything to eat? Are you hungry?'

Aida shook her head.

'What's this?' she asked, holding up her right arm.

'Intravenous antibiotics,' Mia said. 'You had a serious

lung infection, both sides. You'll be on antibiotics for ten days, but only pills.'

Aida closed her eyes and rubbed her forehead with her left hand.

'Where am I?' she whispered.

'A hospital, a long way from Stockholm,' Mia said. 'My husband and I drove you here.'

'Am I safe?'

'Completely. The doctors are old friends of mine. There's no record of you being here, and we'll take your notes with us when we leave. The man looking for you will never find you here.'

She looked up.

'So you know . . . ?'

'Rebecka told me,' Mia said, leaning over her again. 'Aida,' she whispered, 'don't trust Rebecka.'

PART TWO

No one is free from guilt.

Not even I can escape the consequences of my actions.

Feelings of guilt, however, are not distributed correctly. There is no divine justice when the burden is shared out. The person who ought to feel the most guilt usually manages to avoid it, leaving an inhumanly heavy burden to be carried by those with the greatest degree of empathy. I'm not prepared to go along with that.

I know what I have done, and I have no intention of meekly accepting the role that is being forced upon me. On the contrary. I intend to carry on using all the tools at my disposal until I have reached my goal. Violence has become part of me, it is destroying me, but I have accepted my own destruction.

My guilt sits deeper, it has filled the part of my soul that I still have control over. I can never put it right, I can never come to terms with my own mistake.

I can never have absolution. My betrayal is as great as death.

I have tried to learn to live with it. That isn't possible, because the very idea contains a paradox.

I am alive, and that is the source of my guilt.

There is only one way to put that right.

Thursday 1 November

26

It was snowing. The flakes were sticking to her jacket, and turning Annika's hair and front white. On the ground it quickly dissolved into a paste of salt and water. Annika trod in a puddle and discovered that her shoes leaked.

The city council's district office was on her street, at the far end near Fridhemsplan, in the Tegeltraven block. She caught her reflection in its plate-glass windows; she looked like a snowman. Behind the glass was a small display showing plans for a new hotel next to Rålambshov Park, by the slip-road onto the Essinge motorway, and inviting comments on the plan.

She rang the bell and was let into the office. There were brochures and leaflets everywhere. She picked up anything she could find that dealt with sheltered housing and care of the elderly. As she left she noticed there was a funeral parlour next door.

Despite the snow, the air was clear and clean. All sound seemed muffled, as though wrapped in cotton-wool. She took the time to listen properly, to breathe, to feel things. She had slept well, her thoughts were clear, calm.

There was a way through this. Everything would work out.

She walked slowly up the stairs towards her flat, looking down at the steps as she went. Which is why she didn't see the woman waiting outside her door.

'Are you Annika Bengtzon?'

She gasped, stumbled, almost falling back down the stairs.

'Who are you?'

The woman walked towards her, holding out her hand.

'My name's Maria Eriksson. I'm sorry, I didn't mean to scare you.'

Annika had a faint sense of tunnel vision, and she was ready to run.

'What do you want? And how did you find me?'

The woman smiled rather sadly.

'You're in the phonebook, along with your address. There's something I'd like to talk to you about.'

'What?' Annika felt a flash of irritation.

'I'd rather not say anything out here on the stairs.'

Annika gulped. She didn't want this, not now. She wanted to sit on her sofa, under a blanket, with a mug of tea, looking through the leaflets about care of the elderly. She wanted to find a solution, to find peace. Whatever this woman wanted to talk to her about, it wasn't her problem, and she was determined to keep it that way.

'I haven't got time,' Annika said. 'My grandmother's ill, and I have to find someone who can help her recover from a stroke.'

'That is very important,' the woman said solemnly.

She showed no sign of moving from Annika's door.

Irritation turned to anger, then suddenly to fear. This woman wasn't going to give up, and she was the sort who commanded respect.

Aida, Annika thought, backing away.

'Who sent you?'

'No one,' Maria Eriksson said. 'I'm here of my own accord. It's about the Paradise Foundation.'

Annika stared at the woman, who looked back at her calmly. She was still suspicious.

'I don't know what you're talking about,' she said.

The woman suddenly looked desperate.

'Don't trust Rebecka!' she said.

Curiosity got the better of her and Annika no longer wanted to get away. This really was her problem, a problem she had chosen.

'You'd better come in,' she said, going over to the door and unlocking it. She hung her wet clothes over the radiator in the bedroom, shut the door and pulled off her trousers and socks. She got some fresh clothes from the wardrobe, dried her hair with a towel and went out into the kitchen to put some water on to boil.

'Would you like coffee, Maria? Or tea?'

'Call me Mia. Nothing for me, thanks.'

The woman was sitting on the sofa in the living room. Annika prepared a large pot of lemon tea and carried it through on a tray.

Maria Eriksson was focused, but tense.

'You've met Rebecka Björkstig, haven't you?' she said.

Annika nodded and poured herself a cup of tea.

'Are you sure you don't want any?'

The woman didn't seem to hear her.

'Rebecka's going round saying that you're writing a big article for the *Evening Post* about how wonderful the organization is. Is that true?'

Annika stirred her tea, a growing sense of unease nagging at her stomach, somewhere just behind her curiosity.

'I can't tell you anything about what the paper might or might not print.'

Suddenly the stranger on her sofa began to cry. Annika put her cup down, unsure of what to do.

'Please, don't write anything until you know what it's really like,' Maria Eriksson said. 'Wait until you've got all the facts.'

'Of course I will,' Annika said. 'But it's a very difficult organization to research. It's so secretive that I've had to get all my information through Rebecka.'

'That isn't her name.'

Annika dropped the teaspoon in her cup, speechless.

'She was called something else until very recently, I know that much,' Maria Eriksson continued, pulling out a tissue and wiping her eyes. 'I don't know what, Agneta something, I think.'

'How do you know that?' Annika asked.

Maria blew her nose.

'Rebecka says I've been erased,' she said.

Annika looked at the young woman on her sofa, so real, so tangible. Erased!

'So it works?' she asked.

The woman put the tissue back in her bag.

'No,' she said. 'I don't think it works at all. That's the problem.'

'But you were erased?'

Maria laughed. 'My personal details have been protected for several years now,' she said. 'I haven't been listed on any official registers for ages, but that's nothing to do with Rebecka or Paradise. I sorted out my own protection for myself and my family. The problem is that it wasn't enough, which is why I turned to Paradise.'

'So you're inside the organization now?'

'My case hasn't been completed yet, social services in my home town haven't accepted the terms of the agreement,' Maria Eriksson replied. 'So I'm not really inside yet, but standing on the threshold like this has given me a better idea of what's really going on.'

Annika reached for her cup, blew on the tea and tried to sort out her thoughts: fear, scepticism, excitement, surprise. The woman was so real, all blonde and serious – presentable – with penetrating eyes. But was she telling the truth?

She felt confusion getting the better of her.

'How long have you been in contact with Paradise?'

'Five weeks.'

'And your case hasn't been processed yet?'

Maria Eriksson sighed. 'Social services are still working out whether they're willing to pay for us to be set up abroad.'

'Via Paradise?'

The woman nodded.

'Rebecka wants six million to help us move abroad. Our case is crystal clear, really. The Court of Appeal said we won't be able to live a normal life in Sweden. I'll show you the documentation.'

Annika put her hand to her forehead.

'I have to make notes. Is that okay?'

'Of course.'

She went out into the hall. Her bag was wet, and she tipped its contents onto the floor: a little box of sweets, tampons, a crumpled train ticket, notepad and pen, and a chunky gold chain.

The gold chain. Annika picked it up, her gift from Aida. She'd forgotten all about it.

She quickly put everything apart from the pad and pen back in the bag.

'So what sort of threats were made against you?' she asked as she settled back onto the sofa.

Maria Eriksson smiled weakly.

'Maybe I will have some tea after all, it looks good.

215

Thanks. It's the usual story. I fell in love with the wrong man. I thought you'd probably ask, so I brought proof.'

She pulled out a file of papers.

'These are copies. You can keep them if you like, but I'd appreciate it if you could keep them in a safe place.'

'Tell me about it,' Annika said, taking the file.

'He tried to strangle me,' Maria Eriksson said, putting some sugar in her tea. 'Threatened me with a knife. Abuse. Rape. Attempted to kidnap our daughter. Damaged the house. Everything you can imagine, really. Arson. I could go on. But no one really cares.'

She took a cautious sip. Annika felt her old rage bubbling up again.

'I know what it's like,' she said. 'Why didn't the police do anything?'

Maria smiled again.

'My parents still live in my old hometown,' she said. 'He'd kill them if I talked.'

'How do you know he isn't bluffing?'

'He tried to run my father over.'

'I'll go through your papers properly later,' Annika said, putting them on the floor.

She couldn't think of anything to say. She was planning to look through the documentation properly, but imagined that it would merely confirm what Maria had just told her. She believed this woman. There was something genuine about her. Maybe it was fear.

They sat in silence for a few minutes, the only sound the chink of china.

'So is there an actual organization?' Annika asked.

Maria Eriksson nodded. 'Rebecka takes the money, but that's practically all she does. As far as I understand it, no one has ever been "erased". All that happens is

216

that Rebecka requests that her clients' details are made confidential by the local council registrar.'

'How do you mean?' Annika asked.

Maria settled back in the sofa.

'There are two different ways to protect people who have been threatened. The simplest is to conceal the person's ID number, address and family relationships on all official registers. All that shows up in any search is the fact that the person's details are confidential.'

Annika nodded: Rebecka's record on the database.

'That's fairly unusual, isn't it?'

'Less than ten thousand people in the whole of Sweden,' Maria Eriksson said. 'The decision has to be taken by the head of the local tax authority where you're registered. And in order for that to happen, there has to be a credible threat against you.'

'And that's what you've got?'

'No, my family and I have a more serious level of protection. In cases like ours, only the head of the local tax office knows your current place of residence. The level of proof required to get that sort of protection is far greater than when you just have your details concealed on the main register – it's roughly the same as the police would need to issue a restraining order.'

'And how many people have got that level of protection?'

'Less than a hundred,' Maria said.

So you really had been erased, properly.

'Are there any other ways?'

'Well, of course you can change your name and ID number. But that can only happen through the National Police Committee, which then asks the Tax Office to issue a new ID number.'

She knows what she's talking about, Annika thought.

'Have you changed identity?'

Maria hesitated, then nodded.

'I've had several names, and I had a new ID number for a while. I went from being a Virgo to Aries!'

They both laughed.

'So what else does Rebecka do?'

Maria Eriksson grew serious once more.

'What has she told you she does?'

Annika emptied her cup. She had to make a decision. Either she trusted this woman or she threw her out. She picked the first option.

'Sixty cases in three years,' she said. 'Two whole families installed in new lives abroad; five full-time employees on a salary of fourteen thousand kronor a month; all contact with the outside world conducted via a reference number through Paradise; contact staff available twenty-four hours a day; telephone numbers via non-local exchanges; properties throughout Sweden; the possibility to arrange public-sector jobs in other countries; full medical care; legal assistance. Total care, basically.'

Maria sighed and nodded.

'That's pretty much what she usually tells people. I'm surprised she told you about the foreign placements, she usually keeps that one quiet.'

'She tried to, as long as she could.'

'Okay,' Maria said. 'The five employees are her, her brother, her sister and her parents. They get a salary, but they don't do any work. In fact, no work gets done at all at the Paradise Foundation. Her mother answers the phone sometimes, that's all.'

They fell silent.

'What about the properties?'

Maria laughed. 'They have a run-down house in Järfälla, which is where we're living. That's where the phone is. It rings every now and then when Rebecka

218

gets a new case. Some poor, desperate soul is out there, calling and calling, and no one answers . . .'

Annika shook her head.

'So it's all lies?'

Maria Eriksson blinked, tears in her eyes.

'I don't know,' she said. 'I don't know what's happened to the others.'

'The others?'

The woman leaned forward and whispered, 'The others who come to Paradise, I don't know what happens to them! They arrive, they pass through, and they vanish!'

'They don't live in the house?'

Maria Eriksson laughed. 'No, that's just us, we rent a room from her, unofficially. She's convinced she's going to make a fortune from us, because we've got such an open-and-shut case, so that's why she's letting us live there. But I've figured out the way she works. If our social services department pays out the money, she'll take it and disappear. We won't see a penny.'

She leaned her head in her hands.

'And to think I believed her! Out of the frying-pan, into the fire!'

Annika suddenly remembered the council official out in Vaxholm the day before, Thomas.

'You have to tell your council about it,' she said.

The woman pulled out a fresh tissue.

'I know. We have to find somewhere else to live first, my husband's trying to sort out a cottage for us. As soon as we've got the go-ahead, we'll escape from Paradise, and that's when I'm planning to tell the council. I can't say anything as long as I'm living in a house owned by the foundation.'

'How long do you think that will be?'

'A couple of days, the weekend at the latest.'

Annika thought for a moment.

'This threat against Rebecka, has she ever spoken to you about it?'

Maria sighed. 'Rebecka reckons she was being pursued by the mafia, I've no idea why. It sounds a bit far-fetched, in my opinion. What could she have done to them?'

Annika shrugged. 'Do you know what happens to all the money?'

Maria shook her head.

'I never go into the office. She keeps the paperwork in a room on the ground floor and the door's always locked. But she gets a good salary, I found a payslip in the bin last week.'

Annika straightened up. A payslip . . . That meant bank account details, ID numbers, loads of information.

'Have you got it with you?'

'Yes, I think so . . .'

She hunted through her handbag and pulled out a crumpled piece of paper, stained with coffee-grounds.

'It's a bit messy,' she said apologetically as Annika took it.

It was all there. Bank account, ID number, address, tax code, everything apart from the Paradise Foundation's registration number. She was certainly well paid, fifty-five thousand kronor a month.

'She's got an account with Swedbank,' Maria said. 'The address is the same as Paradise's, the PO box in Järfälla.'

'What's the street address?' Annika asked.

Maria told her.

27

As usual, the eleven o'clock meeting dwelled too little on what had happened the previous day, and too much on what was going to happen in the future. The editors' visions of tomorrow's paper were often complete fantasies, extremely partial predictions about people spilling the beans, confessing or denying scandals, talking about whatever sorrow, pain, anger, maltreatment or injustice had befallen them. Catastrophes were made out to be worse than they were, the private lives of celebrities embellished beyond belief. The consequences of new political developments were simplified, with the general public always categorized as 'winners' or 'losers'.

Anders Schyman sighed. So this was what the newspaper business had become. Over-enthusiastic section-heads were certainly not confined to the *Evening Post* alone. The same thing was happening in Swedish Television, where he had worked for so long, although the signs were different. Future plans always assumed the best possible outcome. For the *Evening Post*, this would be a television celebrity breaking their leg on some reality show; for a current affairs programme on television it would be a politician stammering and messing up. At the moment Ingvar Johansson was outlining how he wanted to follow up the successful campaign about the handicapped boy and their victory over his local council. Flowers and a cake, but no champagne, a big picture with the kid in the middle and his whole family hugging him and celebrating. Something for the centrefold, with the headline, *The Evening Post Made the Difference!*

'Do we know if the family is happy with this?' Schyman asked.

'No,' Ingvar Johansson admitted, 'but our reporter will sort that out. It's Carl Wennergren – he's a safe pair of hands.'

The others nodded confidently.

'The story of the Frihamnen murders is getting bigger,' Sjölander said. 'Some old boy who likes orienteering – in the upper age bracket, I'd guess – found the lorry carrying the load of missing cigarettes yesterday. It was completely burned out, in some ravine on the boundary of Östergötland, Södermanland and Närke.'

'Maybe someone was a bit careless with a cigarette-end,' Picture Pelle said, to a scattering of laughter.

'There were two bodies in the cab,' Sjölander went on without smiling. The forensic examination isn't complete yet, but the police are pretty wound up about it. It looks like the victims were tortured before they died. Virtually every bone in their bodies was broken. The officer I spoke to said he'd never seen anything that bad before.'

There was silence in the room. The air-conditioning hummed.

'How much are they making public?' Schyman asked.

Sjölander leafed through his notes.

'The lorry was discovered in a remote piece of woodland just north of Hävla, in Finspång. There's evidently some sort of old forestry track leading to the clearing where it was found. They've got some useful

222

evidence, including a set of extremely unusual wheel-tracks. From some sort of winter tyre that doesn't need studs. Wide, American, only used on a few makes of car, mainly those big 4x4s, like Range Rovers or the bigger Toyota Land Cruisers. The police have removed the wreckage now, which sounds like it was a hell of a job. They're asking people to come forward if they saw anything unusual.'

'How did they get the lorry into the ravine in the first place?' Ingvar Johansson wondered.

Sjölander sighed. 'Well, they must have driven it there, on a day when the ground was properly frozen. The landowner is furious, they mowed down hundreds of saplings getting the lorry down the track.'

'So who did it?' Schyman wondered.

'The Yugoslavian mafia,' Sjölander said. 'No question. And we haven't seen the end of this yet. The dead men in the cab can't have talked, or they'd have had at least a couple of unbroken bones. The people who own that shipment of fags are going to carry on killing people until they find it. Things are looking bleak for anyone who knows anything at all about any of this.'

'So what else have we got on the Yugoslavian mafia?' Schyman asked. 'The sort of thing we can't actually publish, I mean.'

'Well, the Serbian government are believed to be behind all this,' Sjölander said, 'but no one's ever managed to prove it. Because these operations are so incredibly well-funded, there's a general suspicion that the state has at the very least sanctioned them. That's one reason why no one's in any position to grass on the whole operation: no one has the whole picture. Anyone who knows most of the facts is either in or close to the government in Belgrade, or is high up in the police or military.'

'So how dangerous is it to go poking about in all this?' Schyman asked.

Sjölander hesitated. 'It shouldn't be too bad. Writing about the killings is fairly harmless. They're prepared for that. You have to remember that this is a business, and for the people involved it's just another day in the office. But you don't try to trick them. You don't try to steal their property, and it's best not to know anyone who does.'

The meeting slid onto other subjects, but Anders Schyman wasn't paying complete attention. They had seldom had this sort of discussion. He felt a warm sense of satisfaction and relief. He had been anxious after the previous day's confrontation, but now he was sure.

He had won.

The end-of-month finances in October and November were always a nightmare. The council committee's budget was agreed in October, and the full council's in November. Well, if he was honest, it was usually a few days into December. And then every children's playgroup in the district would phone and ask if it was true that they still had a few thousand left of this year's allocation. He was still working to finalize the figures for the last complete quarter.

Despite all this, he was having trouble concentrating. He was genuinely concerned at his recent outbursts. That journalist had asked yesterday if he was burned out, and he'd thought about that several times since then. But there was really no good reason for him to be having a breakdown. He was only doing the same things he had been doing for the past seven years, living in the same house with the same wife, working in the same place.

It was something else. He hardly dared formulate the

thought even to himself, because he knew it would have serious consequences. But the truth was that he wanted something more from life. There, he'd acknowledged it. He wanted to move on; he knew this job inside out now. He wanted to live in the city, he wanted to be able to go to the cinema and theatre without a month of planning, he wanted to be able to walk home through streets full of tall buildings and Indian restaurants and people he didn't know.

The previous evening he had spent hours walking round Vaxholm, up and down the streets. He felt that he knew the location of every single rock and stone now. He had sat for a while in a tacky restaurant, drinking a couple of beers, but had left when a group of noisy customers rolled in for last orders. It was past midnight when he got home. He had hoped that Eleonor would still be awake so they could talk, but she was fast asleep, the latest issue of *Modern Times* on the bedside table.

The telephone rang again. He resisted the urge to rip the cable from the wall.

'Yes?' he snarled.

'Thomas Samuelsson? It's Annika Bengtzon, from the *Evening Post* – we met yesterday. I've found out several things about the Paradise Foundation. Have you managed to get the registration number yet?'

He groaned.

'I've actually had other things to do,' he said.

'Great,' she said. 'Good to know you're doing your job. In that case, maybe you've already found out that Rebecka Björkstig used to have a different name, that the foundation is based in a rundown house in Järfälla, that it doesn't have any employees, and it doesn't actually do anything apart from raking in payments?'

He struggled to find an answer.

'Is that all true?'

The journalist sighed at the other end of the line.

'It looks like it. I'm not one hundred per cent sure yet, but I've got hold of Rebecka's ID number, and I'm going to check her out with the National Enforcement Service in Sollentuna. I'm catching the train out there in fifteen minutes. If you're interested in what I've found out, you could meet me there.'

He looked at the time. He'd have to cancel three meetings.

'I don't know if I've got time,' he said.

'Your choice,' the reporter said. 'If you decide to come, bring Paradise's registration number with you.' And she hung up.

Thomas closed the file in front of him and headed off to see the social worker in charge of the Bosnian woman's case. She had a visitor, a young man with a shaved head who was fingering his acne nervously. Thomas went in anyway.

'I need Paradise's number,' he said.

The woman behind the desk tried to maintain her composure.

'I'm very busy,' she said, stressing each word heavily. 'Please, leave us alone.'

'No,' Thomas said. 'I need that number. Now!'

The social worker's face turned red.

'Okay, you really have to—'

'At once!' Thomas roared.

She stood up, alarmed, and pulled out a file that she opened and held out to him.

'Top right,' she said tersely.

'Let me know as soon as you get an invoice,' Thomas said. 'Sorry to intrude.'

He took the file and left. He wrote the number on a

Post-it note, put it in his wallet, pulled on his coat and walked out. He didn't have his car at work, so he would have to walk home and fetch it.

'I'll be out for the rest of the day,' he called to the receptionist on his way out.

28

As Thomas was walking up Östra Ekuddsgatan it occurred to him that he didn't know how to find the Enforcement Service in Sollentuna. He had to go into the house and look it up in the phonebook. Tingsvägen 7; where the hell was that? He tore the relevant page out of the map section of the Yellow Pages and ran out to the car.

The traffic grew heavier as soon as he hit the E18. The 262 was at a complete standstill at Edsberg because of an accident, and he hit the steering wheel in frustration. Eventually he reached the centre of Sollentuna. The Enforcement Service was just behind the big exhibition centre, in a yellowish building shared with the police and other official bodies. He pulled up in a reserved parking spot and took the lift up to the sixth floor.

She was already there, sitting at a table in the waiting room with a heap of computer printouts in front of her, her hair sticking out like it had dried without being brushed. She gestured absent-mindedly at the seat beside her.

'Look at this,' she said. 'If this ID number is right, then our friend hasn't paid a single bill in the past five years. Probably longer, but those debts are no longer in the system. They'd have been microfiched by now.'

He stared at the piles of paper.

'What is all this?'

Annika Bengtzon stood up.

'Rebecka Björkstig's records in the Enforcement Service's files. One hundred and seven. Do you want coffee?'

He nodded and pulled off his coat and scarf.

'Please, with milk.'

He sat down and started looking through the print-outs at random. There was no indication of whose debts they listed, all they said was 'personal information blocked'. But the debts themselves were not blocked, they were catalogued in long columns, public, private, from public bodies, individual companies, sole traders. Unpaid tax demands. Parking fines. Driving penalties. Unpaid invoices from Ikea, car rental companies, travel agents. Bank loans, unpaid Co-op card accounts, Visa, home shopping, Eurocard . . .'

Christ! He carried on through the pile.

. . . unpaid student loans, unpaid television licence, a loan from a private individual called Andersson, debts on a rented television from Thorns . . .

'There's no milk,' she said, putting a brown plastic cup down on the printout he had just read. The white bandage was gone from her finger, replaced with a plaster.

'Bloody hell,' he said. 'When did you find out about all this?'

She sat down beside him with a sigh.

'This morning. A source gave me an ID number that is almost certainly Rebecka's. I can't be sure it's hers, seeing as her details are hidden on open-access records, but for the time being I'm assuming the details are correct. She's only thirty years old, but she hasn't wasted any time getting herself into debt. The receptionist is

229

checking the Patent and Registration Office, to see whether she's ever been declared bankrupt. Have you got the official registration number?'

He took out his wallet and gave her the Post-it note.

'I'll be right back,' she said.

He sipped his coffee, weak enough for the lack of milk not to bother him. He tried to order his thoughts. What exactly did this mean? The fact that this woman was useless at paying bills wasn't really relevant. It didn't mean she wasn't any good at erasing other people's details. But the sheer quantity, the apparently consistent strategy of never paying for anything, seemed to give a good clue as to what to expect next.

He finished the coffee and threw the cup in the bin, then carried on looking through the printouts.

. . . debts with American Express, quick-fix loans from Finax, unpaid speeding fines, insurance bills, electricity bills, road tax . . .

Most debts ended up written off, or paid back through salary deductions, asset seizures or bankruptcy.

Where on earth had Annika Bengtzon got to?

He went out of the room. As he turned the corner to go to the reception desk he bumped right into her. He could feel her breasts against him.

'Shit,' she said, stumbling and dropping a bundle of papers on the floor.

He caught her and put her back on her feet. And blushed.

'Sorry,' he said. 'It was my fault.'

She bent down and started to gather up the papers.

'Wait till you see this,' she said. 'She's managed to work her way through pretty much every form of bankruptcy. She's been declared personally bankrupt twice in four years, as well as limited company bankruptcy, corporate bankruptcy, limited partnership bankruptcy. The Paradise Foundation has huge debts, for cars, televisions, two properties that have never had a penny paid off their mortgages . . .'

She went ahead of him back into the room.

'The question is, what does all this mean?' she said, sitting down. 'It doesn't necessarily mean that Rebecka Björkstig is a crook, but it doesn't exactly make a good impression.'

He stared at her. It was exactly the same thought that had struck him a few minutes ago. He sat down beside her and picked up the printout from the Patent and Registration Office, and checked the dates of the debts and bankruptcies, when Rebecka's new businesses had been registered, and when they had stopped trading.

'There's a pattern here, isn't there?' he said. 'Look, she sets up a company, buys loads of stuff, takes out big loans, then goes bankrupt. Over and over again. Then she declares individual bankruptcy, again. But eventually that doesn't work any more. No one will lend her a penny. So instead she sets up a foundation. And it can't be traced back to her. It's listed as being set up by entirely different people, if they even exist at all.'

Annika followed his finger as it moved from one entry to another.

'Then she could go on another spending spree,' she said, holding up the list of Paradise's debts. 'Look, she started missing loan repayments four months ago.'

'It's quite likely that the foundation is no older than that,' Thomas said.

'So much for three years' experience and sixty cases,' Annika said.

They sat silently beside one another, reading and checking. Then the reporter stood up and gathered together the documents.

'I have to talk to the Enforcement Service officer

again before he goes home. Have you got time to come along?'

He looked at his watch. His third meeting should have just started.

'Yes, no problem.'

They walked down a long corridor, a dark blue carpet sucking up sound and dust. Annika Bengtzon walked ahead of him towards a door at the far end.

'Hello,' she said as she walked in, 'it's me again. This is Thomas Samuelsson, finance officer with Vaxholm Council.'

The inspector had a set of files open in front of him.

'Did you find what you were looking for?' he asked.

Annika sighed. 'That, and plenty more besides. I don't suppose you remember ever coming across the name Rebecka Björkstig?'

He shook his head. 'It doesn't ring any bells.'

'What about this?' she said, passing him the list of the Paradise Foundation's debts. The man put his glasses on and glanced down the page.

'Yes,' he said, putting his finger halfway down the page. 'I remember this one. I spoke to the car-dealership that owns these cars last week, they sounded desperate. They can't get hold of the person who leased the cars, and they hadn't taken any sort of deposit.'

'How could they let the cars go without a deposit?' Thomas asked.

The enforcement officer looked at him over his glasses.

'They said the woman seemed trustworthy.' He turned to Annika. 'Do you know where the person behind the Paradise Foundation might be found?'

'No,' she said honestly. 'I know the address of one of their properties, but she doesn't live there. But that information ought to be held by the mortgage-broker who lent her the money to buy the place.'

Annika Bengtzon held out the printouts.

'What conclusions can you draw from debts like these?'

The inspector sighed. 'People are having trouble coping,' he said. 'We keep getting more work, with fewer and fewer staff. But this lady hasn't just become poor overnight, she hasn't fallen behind with her repayments. She's notorious, a pathological bad debtor.'

'You recognize the type?' Annika asked.

The man sighed again. They thanked him and went out into the corridor.

'Okay, I've had enough of this for today,' Annika said as they headed towards the reception desk, yawning and stretching her arms above her head. 'I've got to get home and call my grandmother.'

Thomas looked at her, soft hair, clear skin.

'Already?'

She smiled.

'Time flies,' she said. 'Do you want your own set of printouts?'

She went over to the receptionist. He stood where he was, his brain empty and his cock throbbing.

'Can I drive you somewhere?' he called after her.

'Thanks!'

He went to the toilet, washed his hands and face, tried to relax.

She was waiting for him by the entrance, holding his copies in a plastic bag.

'Wow,' he said. 'You're pretty efficient!'

'I'm not,' she said. 'But my new friend is.'

He was confused.

'Who?'

'The receptionist! Where's your car?'

29

It was a fairly new Toyota Corolla, green, well-polished, with an alarm and central locking, bleep bleep. He had parked in someone else's space and found an angry note on the windscreen. He pulled it off, crumpled it up and threw it in a bin three metres away with perfect aim. His hair flopped forward and he pushed it back with an unconscious gesture. Dark grey overcoat, expensive suit, tie.

Annika was looking at him from the corner of her eye. He had broad shoulders, and moved quickly and smoothly. She hadn't noticed the way he moved: she'd only seen him behind a desk or sitting down. She hadn't realized he was quite so defined, so purposeful.

Former athlete, she thought. *Lots of money. Not afraid of the space he takes up.*

He threw his briefcase in the back seat.

'It's open,' he said.

She sat in the passenger seat and cast a quick glance behind. No child-seats, in spite of the wedding ring. She squeezed her bag in by her feet. He started the car and the heater hummed into action.

'Where do you live?'

'In the middle of town. Hantverkargatan.'

He put his hand behind her head as he reversed

from the parking spot. Annika felt her mouth getting dry.

'The Klarastrand motorway is always terrible at this time of the afternoon,' she said. 'The best bet is probably to go via Hornsberg . . .'

They sat in silence beside each other, and she discovered a new feeling, a different sort of silence. He had narrow, strong hands, changed gear a lot, drove quite fast. His hair didn't want to stay back, it kept falling forward, light and shiny.

'Have you lived on Kungsholmen long?' he asked, glancing at her. There was something in the way he looked at her; she saw it, could feel it.

'Two years,' she said, looking straight ahead, feeling her cheeks getting warm. 'A three-room, top-floor flat in a back courtyard.'

'Was it expensive?' he asked.

She started to laugh. In his world you bought your home, you didn't rent.

'The building's condemned,' she said. 'No central heating, no hot water, no lift, and no toilet.'

He glanced at her again.

'Seriously?'

She laughed again, feeling hot inside.

'But you do have television?'

'Oh, yes,' she said. 'But no cable.'

'Did you see the cultural discussion on Two last night?'

She looked at him carefully. Why did his voice suddenly sound sharper?

'I saw a few minutes,' she said slowly. 'To be honest, I turned it off. I don't know why, but there's something about those women that always makes them sound so bloody confident about everything. They think anything that isn't pretentious cultural elitism is crap. I don't have time for that sort of attitude, that they're somehow better than the rest of us.'

He nodded enthusiastically.

'Did you see the one from the literary journal? She really did talk a load of bullshit.'

'What, the pear-shaped one? I heard her more than all the rest.'

They laughed again.

'So you don't belong to any cultural associations?' he asked, glancing back at her, his hair over his eyes once more.

'I go to watch Djurgården play ice hockey,' she said, 'if that counts as culture.'

He turned his head to look at her.

'You like ice hockey?'

She looked down at her hands.

'I spent years watching outdoor hockey, every week. Fun, but really cold. Ice hockey's better – at least you're not freezing there. It's easy enough to get tickets for league matches, the Globe only gets really packed for the final play-offs.'

'Did you see the finals this spring?' he asked.

'I was in the crowd shouting in the stalls,' she said, raising her right fist and beating it on the car-roof: 'Hardy Nilsson's Iron Stoves!'

He laughed, laughter that faded away into a lingering melancholy. She looked at him, surprised at the silence.

'Are you a Djurgården fan?'

He was overtaking an airport bus.

'I played hockey until I was eighteen, in Österskär,' he said. 'I gave up when I fell out with the coach. And I suppose I wanted to concentrate on my studies.'

His face was in sharp profile against the car window. Annika swallowed, turned and looked out of her own window instead. She could feel her cheeks burning, and a tickling sensation between her legs. The Karolinska hospital flew by up on their right, and she had a vague sense of panic: they would soon be there, he would soon be gone, maybe she'd never talk to him again.'

'How long have you lived in Vaxholm?' she asked, slightly breathless.

'Forever,' he said.

She turned to look at him. Was she imagining it, or did his mouth have a rather bitter turn to it?

'Fed up?' she asked.

He took a quick glance at her, hesitating.

'What do you mean?'

She looked straight ahead.

'Vaxholm doesn't exactly seem very rock 'n' roll,' she said. 'It reminds me a bit of where I grew up, Hälleforsnäs.'

'Not much rock 'n' roll there either?'

She took a chance.

'Are you married?'

'For twelve years now.'

She looked at his profile again.

'You must have been children.'

He laughed. 'That was certainly suggested. Is this where you want to get out?'

She swallowed. *Shit.*

'Yes, this is fine.'

He stopped the car abruptly, looking in the mirror. Annika realized he was checking the bus behind them. She got out of the car, pulled out her bag, then leaned in again.

'Thanks for the lift.'

But he was no longer looking at her, his thoughts were somewhere else entirely.

'Don't mention it.'

*   *   *

237

There was a click and a crackle as the nurse wheeled the phone into her grandmother's room.

'Hello?' Annika said.

Static on the line.

'Grandma?'

'No, this is Barbro.'

Not 'Mum'. Barbro.

'How is she?'

'Not so good. She's sleeping now.'

Silence. Distance. An intense desire to build bridges.

'I've got some information about care homes in Stockholm,' Annika said. 'There are several on Kungsholmen—'

'That won't be necessary,' her mother said firmly, her voice harsh, unwilling to accept any new bridges. 'This has to be sorted out in this health district. I've spoken to . . . someone today, and that's what he said.'

A new wave of feelings. Unfairness. Irritation. Resignation.

'Have you spoken to a care manager? Mum! I told you I wanted to be there for that!'

'Yes, and now you're up in Stockholm. This has to be sorted out now.'

'I'm coming down tomorrow. I've just got to deal with something in the morning, then I'll be there.'

'No, there's no need. Birgitta was here today. We'll be fine, don't worry about it.'

She shut her eyes, her hand on her forehead, struggling against the pain of being left out, against the unfairness of it all, holding back on her rage. When she spoke, her voice sounded muffled.

'See you tomorrow.'

238

Friday 2 November

30

Thomas tore off the plastic covering his suit in a single movement, caught his finger on the sharp hook of the hanger and swore. Bastard dry-cleaner's! Eleonor was sighing over the state of a pair of laddered nylon tights.

'Seventy-nine kronor,' she said, tossing them into the wastepaper basket near the bed.

'Can't you get cheaper ones?' Thomas wondered, sucking his finger so that he didn't drip blood everywhere.

'Not with *shape up*,' his wife said, opening a new packet. 'You haven't forgotten that Nils and Ulrica are coming tonight?'

He turned away and went into the bathroom for a plaster. He stared at himself for a few seconds in the mirror: the swept-back hair, shirt and tie, cufflinks. He put a small plaster on his finger and went back to the bedroom. Eleonor was pulling on a new pair of tights, struggling to get them over her hips. He swallowed.

'Do we have to have guests tonight?' he said. 'I'd like us to have a proper talk instead. We've got a lot to sort out.'

'Not now, Thomas,' his wife said, forcing herself into the tights.

He walked round her and embraced her from behind, one bra cup in each hand, and blew on her neck.

'We could spend the evening together, just the two of us,' he muttered. 'Drink some wine, watch a film, just talk.'

She pulled his hands away and went over to the wardrobe, put on a white blouse and pulled out a hanger holding a black skirt.

'We've been planning this dinner all week. Nils and I want to run through some of the details for our new project. You know we can't talk about it at the bank.'

He looked at her. He knew her so well, it had always been obvious she was going to object.

'Eleonor,' he said, 'I really don't want to. I'm tired and pretty fed up with everything at the moment, and I really think we need to talk to each other.'

She was still pretending not to hear what he was saying, and walked over to him without looking him in the eye.

'Can you fasten this? Thanks.'

He took the necklace and fastened it round her neck. He let his hands slide down her shoulders and held her tight.

'I'm serious,' he said. 'If you're going to have dinner with your work colleagues again tonight, then I won't come home. I'll go and get some dinner in Stockholm instead.'

She pulled free and marched back to the wardrobe, pulled out a pair of pumps and stuffed them in a bag. When she looked up at him her hair had fallen out of place and her face was burning, two red spots blazing on her cheeks.

'Pull yourself together,' she said. 'You can't just come and go as you please in this house, you know that. There are two of us here, and we share certain responsibilities.'

'Exactly,' Thomas said heatedly. 'There are two of us, so how come you have the power and I get all the responsibility?'

Eleonor pulled on her jacket and went out into the hall.

'That's really unfair,' she said shortly.

Thomas stood where he was in the bedroom, their bedroom, her parents' bedroom.

Damn it, he wasn't just going to let this go.

'Stop being so damn superior all the time,' he shouted, rushing after her. He caught up with her in the hall and grabbed her arm.

'Let go of me,' she yelled, pulling free of his grasp. 'Are you mad?'

He was breathing fast, hair over his eyes.

'I think we should move,' he said. 'I don't want to live in this house any more.'

She stared at him, more scared than angry.

'You don't know what you want,' she said, trying to move away.

'Yes, I do,' he said hotly. 'I know exactly what I want! I want us to buy a flat in Stockholm, or a villa in Äppelviken or Stocksund. You'd like that!'

He went up to her again and hugged her, breathing in her perfume through her hair.

'I want a new job, maybe with the county council or the association of local authorities, or some firm of consultants, maybe even a government department. I know that you want to stay here, but it's suffocating me. Eleonor, this is killing me . . .'

She pushed him away, wounded, close to tears.

'You look down on me because I'm happy here. You think I'm complacent, that I haven't got any ambition.'

He pushed his hair back with both hands.

'No,' he said, 'quite the opposite, I envy you! I wish

I felt the same contentment as you, I wish I was happy with what we've got!'

She dabbed at the corners of her eyes, her voice restrained.

'You're so childish and spoiled that you want to throw away everything we have, everything we've worked for all these years!'

She turned round, heading for the front door, and he shouted at her Armani-clad back.

'No! I don't want to throw anything away, I want to move on! We can live in the centre of Stockholm, I can get a new job. You can commute to start with, and maybe you might want to find a new job one day . . .'

She reached for her coat, and he could see that her hands were shaking as she fastened the buttons.

'My life is here. I love this town. Why don't you get a new job and start commuting instead, if you really want to do something different?'

He stopped, amazed that her idea had never occurred to him before.

Of course he could get a new job, somewhere else. He didn't need to move. He could commute, maybe get a little overnight flat in Stockholm.

The door closed behind her with a well-oiled click. Loneliness descended like a dusty blanket, heavy and suffocating.

Christ, what on earth was he playing at?

The sound of the phone ringing forced its way into Annika's brain. Her eyes felt full of grit. She picked it up without lifting her head from the pillow.

'Something terrible has happened!' The voice was a shrill screech.

Annika sat up instantly, her heart hammering in her throat.

'Grandma? Has something happened to Grandma?'

'This is Mia, Mia Eriksson. A woman's gone missing. She said she was going to go to the council and tell them everything, and Rebecka was furious!'

Annika rubbed her forehead and sank back onto the pillows. Her panic subsided, it was nothing, it would all be all right.

'So what's happened?'

'There was a huge row here last night, and I wanted to ring and tell you, I thought you should know.'

Annika could feel her irritation building.

'How does this concern me?'

'The woman said she knew you, that you were the one who recommended Paradise to her. Her name's Aida Begovic, she's from Bijeljina in Bosnia.'

Annika closed her eyes. She could feel her face getting hotter. *This isn't happening, this isn't happening.*

'What's happened to Aida?' she managed to say, her cheeks blazing.

'She said she was going to tell her local council that Rebecka has been deceiving them, and Rebecka started screaming at her, telling her to think really carefully, because Rebecka knew exactly who was trying to track her down. That was last night, and now Aida's gone!'

Mia started crying. Annika shook her head in an attempt to get her thoughts in order.

'Hang on,' she said, 'let's look at this calmly. Maybe it isn't that serious. Perhaps Aida has just gone shopping or something.'

'You don't know Rebecka,' Maria Eriksson said breathlessly. 'She's said things like this before, in confidence. That she'd kill anyone who betrayed her.'

Annika felt a cold knot in her stomach.

'That's just talk,' she said. 'Rebecka's full of crap, but she isn't a killer. Take care not to get paranoid.'

'She's got a gun,' Mia said. 'I've seen it, a pistol.'

Annika was getting really cross now, sitting up in bed again.

'She just trying to frighten you, don't you get it? She wants to make sure that no one finds out what she's doing.'

Maria Eriksson wasn't convinced.

'We're leaving, today. I'm never going to set foot in this house again.'

'Where are you going?'

The woman hesitated. 'Away, we're going away. We've got hold of a cottage in the middle of the forest.'

Annika had read through Maria Eriksson's papers the evening before, and could well understand why she never gave away where she was.

They sat in silence for a few moments at either end of the line.

'I'm going to carry on looking into Paradise,' Annika promised.

'Don't trust Rebecka,' Mia said.

Annika sighed. 'Good luck.'

'Don't write anything you can't prove for certain,' Maria Eriksson said.

The silence crept up on her after she'd hung up. The curtains swayed, the shadows danced. Paradise didn't want to let go of her.

The post hit the hall floor with a thud. She got up, happy to have a reason to get out of bed, picked up the envelopes and took them with her to open as she sat on the toilet. A gas bill. An offer from a book-club. An invitation to a school reunion.

'I'd sooner die,' she muttered, and stuffed everything apart from the bill in the empty box for sanitary towels.

She had to get to the paper.

31

Eva-Britt Qvist was at her desk, sorting piles of paper.

'Have I had any sort of list through?'

The secretary looked up at Annika.

'Your sources don't seem very reliable,' she said.

Annika bit her tongue and smiled instead.

'Maybe you could put it in my pigeon-hole if it does show up?'

She turned away without waiting for an answer. *Sit and guard your bloody fax-machine, you stupid woman.* She settled down at her desk and logged into the online national address database.

'You do know that every search you do on there costs money?' Eva-Britt Qvist called from her desk.

Annika got up and went over to the secretary again, resting her hands on the piles of paper and leaning towards the woman.

'Do you suppose that I'm here just to annoy you?' she asked. 'Who knows, maybe I'm here because I want to do my job, just like you?'

Eva-Britt Qvist leaned back, blinking uncomprehendingly, insulted.

'That search database is my responsibility, I was just reminding you.'

'You're not responsible for the budget, are you? I thought that was Sjölander.'

The woman's round cheeks started to blush.

'I'm actually rather busy,' she said. 'I have to make a call.'

Annika went back to her computer, clenching her hands tight to stop them shaking. Why did that woman always have to have the last word? How come she could never be that polished?

She sat down, her back to the secretary, pulled out her notes, shut her eyes and tried to concentrate. Where to start?

She went into the search screen and tried Rebecka again. *Personal details protected.*

She sighed heavily. Why was she bothering?

She decided to try a different search, and typed in Rebecka's ID number instead. After a few moments thought, the same result: *personal details protected.*

She tried a search of archived records instead, typing in Rebecka's ID number again. This time: *Nordin, Ingrid Agneta.*

Annika stared at the information. *What the . . . ?*

She checked the number, and performed the search again.

Same result.

Ingrid Agneta Nordin, listed at Kungsvägen in Sollentuna. The most recent amendment had been made some six months ago. Annika went back to the first search screen and typed in the new name. Ha!

Annika stared.

It worked. Information appeared on screen, with a further reference back to a previous record, three years before.

She quickly logged out, grabbed the phone and rang the enforcement officer from the day before.

'I was wondering if the name Ingrid Agneta Nordin means anything to you?' she said.

The man thought, and Annika held her breath.

'Yes,' he said, 'here in Sollentuna, is that right? I had a lot to do with a woman with that name for a couple of years.'

She breathed out. *Yes!*

'She's changed her name and is now called Rebecka Björkstig, but there's another historical record for her in the national database that I can't get at. Would you be able to see if the information is recorded on your system?'

She heard the inspector shuffling some papers.

'What sort of information?'

'Maybe nothing more than an old address,' Annika said. 'But it might even be another, earlier alias.'

The man made a note of Rebecka's ID number.

'And when would this have happened?'

'Three and a half years ago.'

He was gone for five minutes.

'You're right,' he said, 'she had a different name before. She used to be Eva Ingrid Charlotta Andersson, resident in Märsta.'

Annika closed her eyes. *Bull's-eye!*

Anders Schyman closed the door behind him and looked round his dusty little room. He sat down behind the desk and gazed out at the newsroom through the glass walls. Annika Bengtzon bounced past his aquarium, full of energy, towards the cafeteria. He'd try to grab her on her way back, to check if she'd made any progress.

The management meeting that day had made the horizon a bit clearer. The editor-in-chief, Torstensson, had made up his mind to come clean and had told them about his job offer at the EU. The party wanted him to look after their policy on freedom of information down in Brussels. There was a note of quiet pride in his voice as he told them, and Schyman could guess why. Torstensson didn't actually have any personal attachment to the *Evening Post*. His appointment had been political, and Schyman doubted if he had ever read the paper regularly before he was made editor-in-chief.

In spite of his fine title, Torstensson had never been particularly comfortable in his role. He never quite got to grips with what the paper was actually doing. Whenever he appeared on television he managed to let slip his ignorance every time he opened his mouth, in sentences full of politically correct jargon.

Anders Schyman had been wondering why the EU appointment had arisen at this particular time. As far as he understood it, there was no desperate need in Brussels for yet another lobbyist in matters of freedom of information. His guess was that the board had grown tired of the red figures in the accounts and had been trying to find a way to avoid the media storm that any public execution of the editor-in-chief would have provoked. Presumably pressure had been brought to bear on the party leadership, and they had managed to conjure up a nice little job a long way away.

The question was, what was going to happen next? Would Torstensson actually get the job, would he accept it, and would he have time to force though his reorganization before he went? And who would his successor be? A twinge of nervousness ran through his gut, and he forced it away.

Annika Bengtzon came back into view, holding a plastic cup. Schyman got up, opened the door and called her in.

'How are you getting on with Paradise?'

The young woman sat down on the other side of the desk.

'You really should ask someone to hoover in here. It's going okay. I've dug up a load of information about our dear friend, Eva Perón herself.'

The head-editor blinked and Annika Bengtzon waved her hands.

'Rebecka Björkstig,' she said, 'aka Ingrid Agneta Nordin or Eva Ingrid Charlotta Andersson. She has one hundred and seven personal debts registered with the Enforcement Service, and twenty or so just for Paradise. She's been declared bankrupt in pretty much every way possible at least once. I've got a source who says that Paradise does nothing beyond taking payments, but I don't have categorical proof of that yet.'

Schyman was making notes. He wasn't surprised.

'If this checks out, she sounds like the archetypal financial crook.'

Annika nodded enthusiastically. 'Yep. I've called the police in the districts whatever-her-name-was used to live in. I got hold of one officer who spent six months trying to find her. Evita is suspected of criminal activity in connection with all of her bankruptcies.'

Schyman looked at the young reporter thoughtfully. She was a demon at ferreting out information. You could see that she thought this was fun.

'So what are we going to do with this? When do you think you'll be able to start writing?'

Annika Bengtzon was looking through her notebook.

'I've got the skeleton of the article, but I still need to flesh it out. I've spoken to a woman who was inside the organization recently, and I know another one as well. I've got hold of a council official out in Vaxholm who's prepared to talk, and I'm thinking of taking a trip out to that address in Järfälla. I need to get a better grasp of what they actually do – or rather, what they don't do. And, of course, I have to try to get hold of Rebecka again, and ask her to explain why she's been lying.'

He nodded, this all sounded reasonable.

'We should probably count on some sort of chain reaction,' she said. 'Once we start printing the details, other people will come forward wanting to tell their own stories.'

'That isn't something we can plan for,' he said.

'No,' Annika said, 'but we have to be prepared to listen to their information when it comes.'

'Then there are the councils that have paid out money to her,' he said. 'They might well be interested in pressing charges against her.'

'Police investigations, court cases, prison . . .' Annika said.

He smiled at the young woman.

'Great,' he said. 'This sounds like a plan.'

'I'm going to write up my notes,' she said, 'then I'm going to take the weekend off and go down to see my grandmother. She's had a stroke . . .'

Annika Bengtzon got up and hoisted her bag onto her shoulder.

'You really do need to hoover in here; you'll end up with asthma.'

The sludge on the pavement had frozen solid, making it hard to walk. The sun was shining, a cold white November light that made things shimmer.

Annika lifted her face to feel the oblique rays. It had taken longer than expected to write up her notes, and the sun was already low in the sky.

She sighed. She hadn't told Anders Schyman everything. She hadn't told him that she had persuaded a woman to approach Paradise, that Rebecka had threatened to kill her, and that the woman was now missing.

If any of that was true.

She shook her unease away and jumped on the number 62 bus. She got off at Tegelbacken and walked the short distance to the Central Station. The next train for Katrineholm would be leaving in thirty-five minutes, so she bought a sandwich and sat down with her back to the main hall. The noise hung like a fog behind her, and she let her thoughts wander.

Rebecka Agneta Charlotta, dangerous and evasive.

Thomas Samuelsson, rich and handsome.

She ought to tell him what she had found out, about Rebecka's other identities, and suspected criminal activity. She finished the sandwich, picked up her things and headed for the public phones.

The finance officer had left for the day, did she want to leave a message?

Left for the day, home to his wife.

'No thanks, no message.'

32

Her grandmother had changed rooms. The electronic apparatus was no longer so intrusive, but otherwise it looked much the same. She was awake when Annika arrived.

'Sorry I couldn't come sooner,' Annika said, pulling off her outdoor clothes and dropping them in a heap in the corner, then going over to the old woman.

Sofia Katarina looked up at her, slightly confused.

'Barbro?'

'No, it's Annika, Barbro's daughter.'

The old woman tried to smile.

'My darling,' she said, her voice broken and panting. She spoke in a whisper, the words slurred, her eyes hazy.

Annika felt her chest tighten, and tears hung like a veil over her eyes.

'Have you and Mum worked out where you're going to live?' she asked.

Her grandmother's eyes fluttered round the room, unseeing, or seeing sights from long ago.

'Live? We lived in Hästskon,' she said. 'We got a room with the stove right in the middle of the wall . . .'

Annika took the old woman's paralysed hand in hers, gently stroking her fingers. She could feel hope draining away.

'Has anyone been to evaluate your needs? Do you know if they've managed to find a home for you to go to?'

'We had just the one room,' her grandmother said breathlessly. 'Mother had fifteen saucepans, she cooked all the food on the stove by the wall, and she took in washing, ten öre for a handkerchief, fifteen for overalls . . .'

Annika nervously licked her lips, unsure how to respond, what to say. She stroked the old woman's arm. Then her grandmother fell silent, her chest rising and falling, quickly, shallowly, her eyes hunting through her memories.

'The fire alarm woke us up, Mother and me,' she whispered. 'It was still dark out, and it rang and rang, the whole foundry was on fire. We ran out, it was warm outside, I was only wearing my nightgown. It burned so high, the flames were up in the sky, it burned and burned . . .'

Annika knew what her grandmother was talking about: the big fire at the ironworks, the night of 21 August 1934. Sofia Katarina had been fifteen years old.

'We helped, Mother and me, we fetched papers from the office, important papers for the business. Father stood in line, passing water from the river. The fire-engine came from Flen, then it started to rain . . .'

'I know,' Annika said quietly. 'You helped to save Hälleforsnäs.'

Her grandmother nodded.

'When it was light they brought the pump from Eskilstuna, Arvid was helping, too. He got a job at the works right after he finished school. Twenty-one öre an hour, ten kronor and ten öre a week, and the first thing he bought was a bicycle.'

She tried to smile, but one side of her mouth wouldn't move.

'He used to give me rides on the bike, all the way past Fjellskäfte to the big church in Floda. "That's where we're going to be married," he said, but that didn't happen, it was the church in Mellösa in the end . . .'

Annika lowered her head, patting the old hand, and let her tears flow. She had never met her grandfather. He died the autumn before she was born, his lungs ruined. Throughout her childhood he was in the background like a soot-smeared ghost, always dirty after work, always full of stories and pranks. She grew up with tales of her Granddad Arvid, they lived on long after his death, forming an image of him that she would never be able to compare with reality. Annika looked into her grandmother's confused face, watching her see Arvid anew, as a young man, on his bicycle.

'Do you miss Arvid?' she asked.

Her grandmother's eyes cleared and she looked at Annika.

'I miss the young man,' she said, 'the strong, healthy Arvid, not the miserable drunk.'

Annika jerked. This was the first time she had heard that her grandfather drank.

'He could drink his own money away, but he never got at mine, my wages kept both me and the girl, and put food on the table for him . . .'

Suddenly her grandmother started to cry. Tears ran down the sides of her face, towards her ears. Annika wiped them with a tissue.

'It was hard for Barbro,' Sofia Katarina muttered. 'She had to spend so much time alone as a child. I couldn't always take her to work, there were ministers and presidents and members of parliament, and you couldn't have a little girl running around. It wasn't good, it left her with a sadness that will never die.'

Her grandmother laid her healthy hand over Annika's and looked into her eyes.

'Don't be too hard on Barbro,' she whispered. 'You're much stronger than her.'

Annika blinked away her tears and tried to smile.

'I won't,' she said. 'We're going to stay friends, and you're going to get better.'

Her grandmother closed her eyes for a minute, resting. Then she opened them again.

'Annika,' she muttered. 'I loved you most of all. That was probably wrong of me, to love one more than the others.'

'That's what made me so strong,' Annika whispered.

In the silence that followed she realized that her grandmother had fallen asleep again.

The snow-laden branches formed a tunnel through the winter night. The car carrying Maria Eriksson, her husband and their children rolled slowly along the icy roads. The north wind howled at the windscreen, throwing cascades of snow at them, around them.

'We need to stop for petrol,' Anders said.

The woman sitting beside him didn't respond, just stared out at the forest, endless, impenetrable. She knew what lay ahead. Another frozen, draughty wooden cottage with a woodstove that smoked and rats under the floor. Another kitchen with no running water, with mismatched crockery and scorched pans. An outside toilet. She thought she had left all that behind, that Paradise would provide a solution.

'I know what you're thinking,' Anders said, putting a hand over hers. 'It will soon be over.'

They reached a small settlement, with a closed

newsagent's, a pizza parlour, a petrol station with automated pumps.

'Have you got any notes?' she asked.

He nodded and got out. She hesitated for a moment, but decided to stretch her legs. They had been driving for ages, the children had fallen asleep on the back seat a long while ago. She got out into the ice-cold air. This really was Norrland. She took a walk round the little garage, wondering whether to do a pee in the shadows behind the building but deciding against it. She put her hands in her pockets, felt the cold metal, and stiffened.

She pulled out the objects, two keys for tumbler locks, one skeleton key, and a plastic Mickey Mouse key-ring. Rebecka would be furious.

Oh well, never mind. They'd never see her again. She walked over to the rubbish bin beside the pump to throw the keys away.

'Mia, are you ready?' her husband asked. 'The kids have woken up.'

She stopped. Why throw them away? She thought for a moment, and remembered the words: *I'm going to carry on looking into Paradise.* She turned to her husband.

'Have we got an envelope anywhere?'

He was about to close the car door, and paused.

'What, out here? Why?'

'The inspection documents from the cottage, are they still in the glove compartment? Give me the envelope, and the kids' chewing gum.'

Her husband sighed and gave her what she asked for. She quickly put the keys in the used envelope, then put a piece of gum in her mouth and chewed furiously for thirty seconds. Then she sealed the envelope with the gum, and pulled a pen from her inside pocket.

'And my purse,' she said.

She stuck four stamps to the top right corner, and wrote the name and address, *Hantverkargatan 32, third floor.* In the bottom left she wrote:

> The keys to Paradise.
> Best wishes, Mia

'Are you done?' he asked.

'I just need to post this,' she said, and walked over to the yellow post box.

Saturday 3 November

33

He heard the demonstration before he saw it, a rumble of voices shouting in rhythm. Cars ground to a halt, people looked confused, there was a certain degree of chaos. His senses pricked; it would soon be time. He looked round, glancing at the buildings – glass and steel, bricks and mortar – until his eyes settled on the triangular pattern of the large paved area on the level below him. She would be there. Sooner or later she would show up. He just had to be there first, to make sure he had the upper hand. He shivered in the cold; God, this country was freezing.

Now he could see the procession, six women at the front holding a banner and a picture of their imprisoned leader. Behind them came a sea of people, mostly men, but also some women and children, thousands of people protesting about something. He stamped his feet on the ground, freezing in his thin jacket. Some young men set fire to a Turkish flag below him, it burned quickly and then the men seemed to lose interest in the protest.

People were streaming into the pedestrianized area of Sergels torg, covering up the triangular paving. Now he could hear what they were shouting. *Turkish terrorists, Turkish terrorists.* Flags, banners, large photographs all fluttering in the wind. A sort of improvised platform was set up, and a loudspeaker was conjured out of nowhere. A Swedish man, presumably a politician, began to speak.

'The PKK has fought a military campaign,' he declared. 'This has led to an abuse of democracy and terrorist actions that are indefensible. But this has happened in a state of war, because of the offensive Turkish attacks . . .'

Now or never.

He began to make his way quickly and discreetly through the crowd, putting his hand inside his jacket to feel the gun, a Beretta 92, 9 mm ammunition, fifteen bullets in the magazine and one in the chamber. And a silencer.

He kept to the wall, under the roadway, slightly hunched.

'Oi, mate, got any speed?'

He waved away the druggie in front of him, wondering if he would need the telescopic sight, but decided against it. He had a better view without it.

Suddenly he saw her. Twenty metres away, with her back to him. She was being driven slowly forward by the demonstrators, away from him. *Perfect.*

He speeded up, weaving between pushchairs and banners, saw her pause and look round. Adrenalin was singing in his veins, a song he recognized.

When he was a metre behind her he pulled out the gun, took the last step, yanked her arm up behind her back and put the barrel to her neck, under her hair.

'That's enough,' he whispered. 'You lose.'

All sound vanished, the people around them were mouthing their slogans, time had stopped. The woman stood stock-still, frozen to the spot, not breathing.

'I know it was you,' he snarled, the words echoing in his head.

He took another step closer, staring at her hair, it was glinting almost blue. He wished he could see her face. The gun rested perfectly in the nape of her neck.

'Bijeljina,' he whispered. 'Do you remember Bijeljina?'

Suddenly the pressure against the gun was gone. The woman pulled her arm free and was pushing quickly through the sea of people. It took a moment before he threw himself after her, almost tumbling over a pushchair. He caught up with her again, adrenalin pumping, grabbed her arm and twisted it back once more, she struggled, prepared this time, she had a gun in her hand. People were shoving them and they were forced backwards, as he smashed her fingers with the barrel of his pistol. She dropped the gun, and a woman stared at them in horror. He tried to smile, then managed to get the pistol to the back of her head again, he could see her mouth moving and leaned forward.

'What did you say?'

'You can never win,' she whispered. 'I've destroyed your life.'

He looked at her from the side, meeting her gaze.

She was smiling.

Something snapped in his head, and his trousers. He squeezed the trigger and she slumped softly in his arms, eyes open wide. He laid her on the ground, put the gun back inside his top, and registered the first surprised glances from the corner of his eye. Sound returned. *Turkish terrorists.* He walked quickly towards the underground station, pulling off his jacket and gloves as soon as he was through the doors, and dropped them into a rubbish bin. He headed for the next exit to the street.

The car slid up the moment he emerged beside Åhléns department store. He got into the back seat, shut the door, his whole body trembling. The driver pulled away, running an amber light, turning right into Klara Norra Kyrkogata. They wouldn't have long before roadblocks were set up. At Olof Palmes gata they turned left, then sharp right up Dalagatan, accelerating hard until they reached Vanadisvägen. They pulled into the courtyard, down into the garage, and stopped. There was no one about.

'Did it go okay?' the driver asked.

He opened the door and climbed out, lit a cigarette, and slammed the door shut.

'Get rid of the car,' he said as he headed towards the lifts.

He had to change his clothes before the stench made him faint.

It had been a quiet night. Annika had slept on a camp bed beside her grandmother, fast asleep, not waking once. In the morning the old woman had slept on, and they had to wake her for breakfast. After eating she fell asleep again.

Annika showered and turned her underwear inside out. Then she sat and watched her grandmother for a long time, looking at her peaceful face, the waves of wrinkles, the faint down on her cheeks. Her mouth was drooping, and Annika occasionally leaned over to wipe the saliva.

She went for several restless walks along the corridor. She called her mother but got no answer, then her sister. No reply there either. She drank some coffee. Then a plastic cup of warm rosehip soup from a machine in the corridor.

You have to look after the people you love.

At lunchtime Annika tried to feed her grandmother again, but the old woman said she wasn't hungry.

The afternoon dragged past. She managed to find some

newspapers, but was too anxious to read. The *Evening Post* was leading with a story by Carl Wennergren. He had managed to find a receipt that proved that a female government minister had paid for a bar of chocolate with her government charge card.

God, Annika thought, *talk about a planted story*. Someone thought the minister was getting too powerful, that she was too young, too attractive, too smart. A nice little scandal to shift the focus of attention away from the main story of the Social Democrats' conference: who was going to be elected the new general secretary, and thus the next big name for the future.

She put the paper down, went out and sat in the dayroom. She switched on the television and found a programme in Turkish. *I don't have to live in Stockholm*, she thought. *I could live in Istanbul and work in a hotel. Or I could live in Katrineholm and look after Grandma.*

She stopped at that thought, letting it settle in.

Why not? What reason did she have for not letting the most important person in her life determine her future?

Her work. Her career, everything she believed in and had struggled for in journalism. Her friends, although they would still be there if she moved, of course. Her home, her flat, although if she was honest that wouldn't be much of a loss.

Suddenly she started to cry. She felt consumed with loss, a longing for the way she had felt when she first moved in. She remembered how the light had flooded in through the rooms, bringing the walls and ceilings to life. The peace and quiet, the desire to carry on. She had managed to achieve everything, and where had it got her?

An old boy on a zimmer frame and two noisy women came into the dayroom. Annika quickly wiped her tears.

'Are you watching this?' one of the women asked nonchalantly.

Annika shook her head, got up and walked out. The women took over the room.

'There's an afternoon concert on at five o'clock, you'd like to watch that, wouldn't you, Dad?'

The corridor outside was gloomy, the neon lights in the ceiling were off and daylight crept in through open doorways, reflecting off the waxed floor. She walked slowly towards her grandmother's room, feeling tight across her chest again. Her sadness lingered, memories of moments when she had been able to breathe freely and easily, hot summer days, happy times with Sven. She leaned her head against the door to her grandmother's room, desperate for love, for a sense of belonging. She swallowed and felt in her back pocket where she kept her change. She went over to the little phone-booth just outside the ward and looked up the number in the phonebook, his home number. Östra Ekuddsgatan. She dialled seven digits, paused before the eighth, but finally pressed it. The ringing tone, once, twice, three times.

'Samuelsson.'

A woman. They had the same surname.

'Hello?'

Had she taken his name, or he hers?

'Is anyone there? Hello?'

She hung up without speaking, the mistake weighing heavily on her. She went back and checked on Grandma. She was sleeping, so Annika went back to the dayroom, which was empty now. She tried to breathe, tried to read.

It will all be all right. Everything will be fine.

34

'Who was it?' Thomas asked.

He was standing with his back to her, and when she didn't reply he looked over his shoulder. Eleonor had a curious, cautious look on her face.

'There was no one there. Are you expecting a call?'

He turned away again, focusing on the kitchen knife.

'No, should I be?'

'It's just a bit odd that they didn't say anything.'

'Must have been a wrong number,' Thomas said, chopping the last of the onion. 'Can you get the oil?'

She passed him the bottle. Corn oil, it didn't burn so easily. Thomas poured some in the pan, a thin, slippery trickle.

'We should have had a gas oven,' Eleonor said. 'It's much better for stir-fries. Maybe we could get a gas one put in when we re-do the kitchen, what do you think?'

'This one's fine,' Thomas said, stirring the onions roughly.

Eleonor came over and stood beside him, kissed him on the cheek.

'You're so good in the kitchen,' she said.

He didn't reply, just tipped in the chopped chicken breasts and started to stir again. He poured in the fish sauce, struck as usual by its vaguely sexual smell, then added chilli paste, ready-chopped coriander and fresh basil.

'Can you open the coconut milk?'

Eleonor passed him the tin, already opened.

'There,' Thomas said, as it began to simmer.

'The rice is ready,' Eleonor said.

He turned towards his wife, looking down at her smooth, unmade-up face. She looked her best like this. He put down the spatula, took a step towards her and wrapped his arms round her. She responded by stroking his shoulders and kissing his neck.

'Sorry,' she muttered.

'I'm the one who should apologize.'

His reply came as a whisper in her hair.

'You've been unhappy for so long,' she said quietly, kissing him on the lips.

He tasted her lips, salty, slightly dry, and he felt a wave of desire, felt himself getting hard.

'Let's go to bed,' she said.

He followed her towards the bedroom, but she stopped at the bathroom door.

'You go ahead,' she said.

He knew what she was going to do, apply a little lubricant to make things easier. He walked slowly over to the bed, removed the bedspread and took off his clothes. She came in and stood behind him, taking hold of his hips and rubbing his buttocks against her crotch. He sank onto his knees by the bed and she walked round him and sat down in front of him, one leg on each side of him, then leaned back. He stared down at her crotch, shiny with lubricant, stroked her with his fingers, finding her clitoris. He massaged it gently and slowly until she began to whimper. His cock was standing up like a javelin, and he pulled her towards it and inserted himself. She gasped. He pressed forward, very gently, and the warm depths closed around him, pulling him in, making him groan. Her body came to life beneath him, around him, stroking and caressing. He pulled out, still slowly, and rubbed his cock over her clitoris until she leaned her head back and screamed. Then he pressed forward, hard and deep, pushing in rhythmically until he felt her contractions. He let himself go, caught up in her swell.

'Oh darling,' she said, 'that was wonderful.'

He collapsed on top of her, his head between her breasts.

'Goodness, the chicken was ready ages ago,' she said. 'Have you got the tissues?'

The sensation of sinking through the bed meant he couldn't answer. She wriggled out from under him and he saw her take the tissues from the bedside table and wipe her crotch.

'I'll go and turn off the stove,' she said.

He crawled up onto the bed and dozed off immediately. He woke again a minute or so later, his feet were cold and he'd grazed his knees. He staggered to his feet, pulled on his dressing-gown and went out into the kitchen.

'I've laid the table down here,' she said.

He went to the bathroom, then went down to the recreation room. There was wine, salad and two place settings on the coffee table. He sat down and she followed him with the pan of chicken and a trivet. She crept up beside him on the sofa and kissed him on the forehead.

'Sex makes me so hungry,' she said.

They ate and drank in silence.

'I've been behaving like an idiot,' he said eventually.

She looked down at her glass of wine, a punchy Australian chardonnay.

271

'You've just been a bit low,' she said. 'It happens to us all sometimes.'

'I don't know what got into me,' he said. 'Nothing felt fun any more.'

'That's bound to happen if you work as hard as we do. We have to take care not to get burned out.'

He blinked, hearing the journalist's voice asking if he was burned out. He cleared his throat, put his arm round her, and, leaning back, picked up the remote with the other hand. The news had just started. A row had broken out in advance of the Social Democrats' conference, and he picked up that it was something to do with personal purchases made with a government charge card. A forest fire in the Philippines was threatening a city. A Kurdish woman had been killed during a demonstration in Sergels torg.

'Do you want to listen to some music?' she said, getting up from the sofa.

He muttered something as he tried to hear what had happened. Shot in the head, in the middle of a mass of people. How was that possible?

'Bach or Mozart?'

He forced himself not to sigh out loud.

'I don't mind,' he said. 'You choose.'

Sunday 4 November

35

Annika hated Sundays. They seemed endless. Everyone was busy doing stupid things, filling up the time with pointless rubbish. The whole of society seemed to be constructed around meaningless niceties, like picnics, going to museums, playing with children, having barbecues. Everyday life, with its ability to stifle anxiety, was shut off, unplugged. Her only good excuse for not joining in was to blame her job; she had to rest, sleep, relax so she would be able to carry on working the nightshift.

Thank goodness she was back on her normal shifts again that evening.

Her mother and sister Birgitta had appeared on the ward after lunch. The three of them sat and talked to their grandmother. Annika was starting to see a pattern: Arvid, the works, her parents, mostly her mother, the younger sister who had died. After an hour or so the old woman was tired and fell asleep. They went down to the cafeteria but of course it was closed. Sunday, day of rest. They bought some little packs of biscuits and coffee from the automated machines.

'This isn't a good environment for her,' Annika said. 'Grandma needs proper rehabilitation, the sooner the better.'

'What are we supposed to do, then,' Birgitta said, 'when there aren't any places? Have you thought about that?'

Annika looked at her younger sister, surprised at the aggression and distance in her voice.

She on Mum's side, Annika thought. *She doesn't like me either.*

'Well, yes,' Annika said, 'I have thought about it. Maybe I could take care of her.'

'You?' her mother said scornfully. 'And how would that work, in your awful old-fashioned flat? I don't know how you put up with it.'

Suddenly she felt like crying, unable to carry on. She stood up, put on her coat, hoisted her bag onto her shoulder, then looked at her mother.

'Don't make any decisions without talking to me first,' she said.

She turned to her sister.

'See you.'

She turned and walked out of the hospital, into the car park. The sun was shining weakly, there was snow on the ground, and her shoes crunched. It was cold. She wrapped her scarf round her head, breathing deeply through her mouth. She wasn't far from tears.

The station. She had to get home. Away.

Sjölander was sitting on Jansson's desk drinking coffee when she appeared in the newsroom. It was already dark, reality was manageable, the room was still quiet, buoyant, almost deserted. Her shift didn't start for another couple of hours, but she didn't want to be alone any longer. The train had ground to a halt outside Södertälje because of signalling problems. She had imagined that the only place they still had those was on the green line of the underground. She had made her way to the paper directly from the Central Station.

'So what have we got?' Jansson said, typing away at his keyboard, writing notes and memos straight into the computer.

'Quite a lot,' Sjölander said, putting his notes down on the desk.

'How much can we make public?' Jansson wondered without looking away from the screen.

'Almost everything,' Sjölander said.

'What's this about?' Annika asked as she sat down, took out her notebook and pen and switched on her computer. 'The Kurdish woman at the demonstration?'

'Yes,' Jansson said. 'A bloody awful story. Five thousand witnesses and not a single one of them saw anything.'

'The police have found the killer's clothes,' Sjölander said, 'brown gloves, dark-green cotton jacket. The gloves were bought in Åhléns just before the attack, and they're full of fingerprints. So far they've identified eighteen, most of them from different people. The jacket is clean from a forensic point of view, apart from evidence from the actual shot, a few traces of powder on the sleeve.'

'So they managed to find his laundry basket, or what?' Jansson said.

'Rubbish bin. The clothes were found in a bin at T-Centralen underground station.'

Annika leaned back, her head starting to slip into the old routine, welcome, familiar.

'And no one saw anything?' she said.

'Well,' Sjölander said, 'about a hundred people have described a man in dark clothing who might have been Swedish, or Turkish, or Arabic, or maybe Finnish. Evidently he spoke to the victim first, then shot her and laid her down on the ground before running off towards the underground. His things were found just inside the entrance. There are witnesses who say they saw him taking his clothes off, among them a security guard. He was wearing light-coloured clothes underneath. But then there are various versions of where he went next. Straight out again, according to the security guard. Down towards the platforms, according to a group of teenagers. Back out into the square, according to a mother with a pram. She was almost knocked over by him. Either way, he vanished.'

'That's pretty damn audacious,' Jansson said. 'Among so many people.'

'That probably made it easier, the crowd helped to conceal him. It's incredibly cold-blooded.' Sjölander sounded almost impressed.

'What else do we know? Weapon?'

Sjölander leafed through his notes.

'Silencer, obviously. So we're talking about a pistol or revolver. I've got details of the bullet, but we can't use that. The ammunition was soft pointed. The woman was shot in the neck, and a fully jacketed bullet would have gone right through her head and blown her face off. A real mess, in other words. This one stopped behind her nose, but by then it had already mashed up her brain. She looked intact from the front, people evidently thought she'd just fallen over to start with.'

Annika shuddered. This one was nasty. She yawned: the first night back always felt longer than usual.

'Do we know her name?'

'Yes, they've released a name. She didn't have any relatives here, she was a refugee, from Kosovo, I think. Apparently no living relatives there either, from what I've got here. Ah, she was from Bosnia, some place called Bije . . . how do you pronounce this? Bijeljina? Her name was Aida. Aida Begovic.'

278

The newsroom shrank around Annika, her field of vision reduced to a tunnel. All colour drained away, all sound seemed to reach her at the bottom of a deep well. She stood up.

'What the hell?' Jansson said, and she heard his voice from far away, saw his face in front of her, the floor tilted. Voices in the distance, 'Annika, what the hell? Are you ill? Sit down, for fuck's sake, you're pale as hell . . .'

Someone sat her down on an office chair, pushed her head between her knees to help her breathe.

She stared at the underneath of the chair, the mechanism for raising and lowering the seat, and shut her eyes, hard, and held her breath.

Aida, Aida from Bijeljina was dead, and she was responsible.

I've done it again, she thought. *I've killed someone else.*

'Annika, for fuck's sake, what's wrong?'

She sat up, her hair falling over her face. The whole building seemed to be swaying.

'I don't feel well,' she said, her voice someone else's. 'I have to go home.'

'I'll get you a taxi,' Jansson said.

36

Darkness. She couldn't be bothered to turn on the lights. She sat in her sofa staring at the curtains. They were swaying gently, forming dancing shadows.

Aida was dead. A man had killed her. The man in the dark suit had found her. How?

Rebecka, of course. Aida had sworn to uncover the deception surrounding the Paradise Foundation. Rebecka had got her revenge by betraying Aida to the man who was trying to find her, by telling him where she was.

What a bitch. What a fucking murderous bitch.

And she was the one who had led Aida into the trap. Causing another person's death.

The pressure on her chest increased, hardened. Soon, she would fall apart.

She reached for the telephone; she had to call someone, had to talk to someone. Anne Snapphane was home.

'What's happened?' Anne said. 'Are you ill?'

'The girl who was shot in Sergels torg,' Annika said. 'I knew her. It's my fault she's dead.'

'What are you talking about?'

Annika pulled up her legs and wrapped her arms

round her knees, rocking back and forth on her scratchy sofa, crying into the phone.

'I lured her into Paradise, and they betrayed her. And now she's dead.'

'Hang on,' Anne Snapphane said. 'The girl was murdered, wasn't she? Shot in the head? So how is that your fault?'

Annika took several deep breaths and her sobbing subsided.

'Paradise isn't real. The woman who runs it is a fraud. Aida, the girl, said she was going to reveal the truth. That's why she's dead.'

'Okay,' Anne said. 'Let's take this from the start. Tell me the whole story.'

Annika took a deep breath and told her everything, how Rebecka had called, wanting to publicize her work, their meeting at the out-of-the-way hotel, the way the organization was set up, the second meeting, how she couldn't get what Rebecka said about the money to add up, the threat from the Yugoslavian mafia, Rebecka's imaginative story about contacts abroad, how she'd tracked down Rebecka's debts and previous identities, the bankruptcies, and the crimes she was suspected of. Then Aida, the threat hanging over her, the man who tried to get into the hotel room, how she had given Aida the phone number for Paradise and encouraged her to seek help there. Then Mia's appearance outside her flat, her story, the desperate call from Mia telling her that Aida had vanished, and that Rebecka had made threats against her.

'And you think all this is your fault?' Anne Snapphane said.

Annika gulped. 'Well, it is.'

'Oh please!' Anne sighed. 'You can't take responsibility

for everything that happens on the planet. I know you want to make the world a better place, but there are limits, you know. And you've gone way beyond them. You sound exhausted. Your grandmother's ill, don't you see how much that's taken it out of you, worrying about her? You're so considerate about other people, so try to be a bit kinder to yourself.'

Annika didn't reply, just sat there in her gloomy flat and absorbed her friend's words.

'It can't possibly be your fault this woman got a bullet in the head,' Anne went on. 'She'd already landed herself well and truly in the shit, hadn't she? You tried to help her, and, okay, so maybe that didn't go too well. But we're talking about intent here. Why did you give Aida the number to Paradise? Because you wanted to help her. Come on, Annika. This isn't your fault. Not at all. Can't you see that?'

Annika started to cry again, thin tears of relief.

'But she's dead. I liked her.'

'Of course you're allowed to mourn her. You tried to help her and she still died. It's fucking awful, but it wasn't your fault.'

'No,' Annika whispered. 'It wasn't my fault.'

'Are you okay?' Anne asked. 'Do you want me to come over? I've got a kilo of pic 'n' mix I could bring with me.'

Annika smiled.

'No,' she said. 'You don't have to do that.'

'Okay,' Anne said. 'You obviously don't give a damn about me. Imagine what I'm going to look like once I've eaten the whole bag on my own. By the way, they might be putting me on screen as a presenter.'

'You?! How come?'

'Don't sound so shocked! The presenter of *Sofa Talk* has been lured to another channel. Bad transfer of the season, if you ask me. So we need a new presenter, fast as fuck, and it's between me and the bimbos' revenge, Michelle Carlsson, you know . . . God, I get palpitations whenever I think about it. I'm going to have to eat some sweets.'

The darkness was friendlier when she hung up, the curtains breathing in an irregular, abstract rhythm.

Not her fault. It was awful, but there was nothing she could do about it now. It was too late. Too late for Aida from Bijeljina.

She undressed in the dark, leaving her clothes in a heap on the sofa.

She slept without dreaming.

Monday 5 November

37

Annika woke up to the sound of someone repeatedly ringing the doorbell. She stumbled to her feet, confused, and wrapped the duvet around her as she went out to see who it was.

'This is no good,' the postman said.

He was holding up a plastic bag containing what looked like rubbish.

Annika blinked at him bleary-eyed, rubbing one eye.

'What?' she said.

'Tell your friends to use proper materials from now on. We haven't got time to waste fixing envelopes that burst open like this.'

'Is that for me?' she asked suspiciously.

'Are you Annika Bengtzon? In that case, yes.'

He held the bag out to her, as well as a small bundle of window envelopes. All bills. What a brilliant start to the morning.

'Thanks,' Annika muttered, closing the door.

She let the duvet fall to the floor behind the door and looked at the bag: what the hell was this? She held it up to the light to see better. A torn envelope, some old chewing-gum and a key-ring? She tore open the plastic bag, walked naked into the living room and tipped the contents onto the coffee table. She checked the envelope

287

cautiously, and it was certainly addressed to her. The writing was legible but rushed, and whoever had written it evidently hadn't had an even surface to lean on. There was something written in the bottom corner:

The keys to Paradise.
Best wishes, Mia

She sat on the sofa. *The keys to Paradise*. She picked up the envelope, it had already been used before, and it was sent in a hurry. She looked at the postmark. Somewhere in Norrland.

Of course. Mia no longer needed them. They must be the keys to the house in Järfälla. She had the address somewhere, Mia had told her and she had made a note of it. She went and got her bag, emptied the contents: tampons, sweets, notepad, pen, gold chain . . .

She stopped. The gold chain. She sat on the floor and picked it up. Aida's gold chain, the two charms, one lily, one heart. Aida's gift to her for saving her life.

And she died anyway, Annika thought, *but it wasn't my fault. I did what I could.*

She put the chain over her head, round her neck. The metal was cold and heavy. She put everything apart from the notepad back in her bag. She took that with her back into the living room and looked up the address. The corner of the page was missing, where she had copied the address and given it to that council official, Thomas Samuelsson. Thomas, the former hockey player, married. To his wife, Mrs Samuelsson.

She got the Yellow Pages and looked up the map covering Järfälla.

The phone rang, making her jump.

'How are you feeling? Jansson said you got ill yesterday and had to go home.' It was Anders Schyman.

'Better,' she said, hesitantly.

'What happened? Did you faint?'

'Sort of,' she said.

'You've been looking tired lately,' the head-editor said. 'Maybe you've been putting in too much work on that foundation.'

'But I haven't—' she began.

'Listen to me,' Schyman interrupted. 'Take the rest of this run of shifts off sick, then we'll see how you feel. Don't think about Paradise at all, just concentrate on getting better. And how was it – was it your mother who wasn't well?'

'Grandmother.'

'Look after her, and we'll see you when your next run of shifts begins. Does that sound reasonable?'

She felt a warm feeling inside when they had hung up. People did care. She sighed, leaning back in the sofa. The unexpected time off didn't feel threatening and gloomy, but rather pleasant.

She went into the bedroom and pulled on her jogging pants. She knew what she was going to do today, but she needed to shower first.

He would have to be careful. He had to make sure that the people he trusted and intended to rely on in future didn't hit the wall. They would be no use to him as burned-out vegetables. Annika Bengtzon had to hold it together for a while longer.

Anders Schyman took a deep breath. His room smelled of cleaning detergent. Throwing out the sofa and requesting that his aquarium be thoroughly cleaned over the weekend had been a stroke of genius.

Feeling comfortable and in control, he leaned back and opened the newspaper. His mood gradually deteriorated as he read through it. The first news pages dealt with the

289

astonishing murder in Sergels torg, the young woman who had been shot in the head during a demonstration. The article was illustrated by a large, fuzzy picture of the woman. She was young and beautiful. Publishing the victim's name and picture wasn't controversial, but the macabre details of her death were described far too elaborately. Readers really didn't need to be told that the soft-pointed bullet had destroyed her brain and stopped just behind her nose. Schyman sighed. Well, perhaps this was a small point really.

The next double-page spread covered the looming crisis in government. The week-long Social Democratic conference was due to start on Thursday, and there was a full-blown power struggle underway. Carl Wennergren was continuing to dig around in the female minister's overdue childcare payments, and was getting perilously close to going beyond what was journalistically and ethically defensible. The paper still hadn't got to grips with the fundamental issue: why this minister's position was under attack at this particular time. It was well-known that she was the election nomination committee's preferred candidate for the position of general secretary of the party, and thus likely to be the next prime minister, which meant that many of the overlooked middle-aged men were sharpening their knives. He wanted this to be covered in the paper, an analysis of how these powerful men were reacting, and of what they were prepared to do to protect their position. The other nominations hadn't yet been leaked, even though it was known that three members would be stepping down from the party's executive committee, its powerful elite. He had a feeling that these names would be controversial, and that it would be an eventful conference. There was talk that the former Minister for Foreign Trade, Christer Lundgren, who had been forced to resign after the *Studio Six* scandal, was on his way back. Schyman doubted this, the scandal had been too big, there were still too many unexplored aspects to it, too much potentially explosive material under the surface. But it was quite likely that the Minister for Culture, Karina Björnlund, would be appointed to the executive committee, which, if you asked him, was in itself a scandal. She had proposed, in all seriousness, that the state should appoint and replace the editors-in-chief and legally recognized publishers of all of Sweden's media companies. Yet she was still in her job, and he knew why. Annika Bengtzon had told him two years ago.

The rest of the paper was fairly thin. New share tips, how to become a winner. He sighed. In the middle there was an interview with a television personality who was about to move from one channel to another. There didn't seem to be any conflict behind the move, just more money. Schyman sighed again. Nothing of any significance had been produced over the past week, nothing that could help to shore up the Monday edition until reality and the working week rolled into action.

Oh well, what the hell. The printers had done their job, the paper was out in time. Sometimes you just had to be grateful for the little things.

The pizza sat like a brick of cheese in Thomas's gut, making him feel sick. After lunch he took the evening papers with him and escaped to his room, skipping coffee.

In the middle of his desk lay the invoice from the Paradise Foundation, for protection of their mutual client in November, December and January. Three hundred and twenty-two thousand kronor. He knew there wasn't that much money left in the budget. They'd have to postpone the refurbishment of a nursery with a serious damp problem in order to pay this fraudster her money.

The social worker had presented him with the invoice as he was on his way out to lunch with his colleagues.

'This has just arrived by fax,' she said, eyes and voice equally cold. She still hadn't forgiven him for showing her up in front of a client.

He had thanked her, more embarrassed than he wanted to admit.

Now he was staring at the invoice, as he ran through the various things they could cut in order to keep the budget together.

What the hell, he thought, letting the various ideas drop. *This isn't my problem. The committee agreed to this crap; it's up to them to clean up the mess.*

He sighed, leaned back and picked up the *Evening Post*. In the middle he found a long interview with some female television presenter who was leaving her job. *How incredibly interesting*, he thought, and quickly turned back to the news pages. There was a picture of the victim from Sergels torg on Saturday, the Kurdish woman who had been killed during the demonstration. She looked so young. He glanced down at the caption.

Aida Begovic from Bosnia.

His brain stopped working for several seconds. Then he cast the paper aside and picked up the invoice from Paradise. It was dated today, 5 November.

This is impossible, he thought. Opening his bottom drawer, he pulled out all his notes and documents relating to the case. He leafed through them until he found the one he was looking for.

Aida Begovic from Bijeljina, Bosnia.

He was so angry he stopped breathing for a moment, his vision turning red. That fucking . . . She had the nerve to demand payment for a woman who had just been murdered.

He scattered the papers on his desk. He knew he had a note of the address somewhere. It fluttered out when he shook the photocopies from the Enforcement Service in Sollentuna, a torn-off corner from Annika Bengtzon's notebook. Putting the invoice and the address in his inside pocket, he pulled on his coat and walked out.

38

Annika got off the train in Jakobsberg, clutching page eighteen of the Yellow Pages map section in her hand. There was a cold, sharp wind blowing, the sort that cut into your skin. She was surrounded by brown, brutalist 1960s buildings, the adult education centre, a hairdresser's, Jakobsberg Church. She checked the map and saw that she needed to head north-west. She found a tunnel under the Viksjö road, stopped at Emil's Fast Food and wolfed down a hamburger.

When she emerged from the kiosk she was struck by the full force of her nerves. The taste of the greasy food sat in her mouth, the hamburger was churning in her stomach, and she had indigestion. She was probably on her way to making herself guilty of breaking and entering.

She looked up at the buildings, colourless and blurred in the haze.

I don't have to do this, she thought. *I'm off sick. Paradise can wait.*

She paused, staring up at the buildings.

I could always go and take a look, she thought. *I don't have to go in just because I have a look from the road.*

Relieved that she had postponed the decision, she

headed off towards the residential area that was evidently called Olovslund. The houses were all different, built in various styles and decades: buildings from the late nineteenth century, a big old farmhouse, some housing blocks from the thirties, modern buildings with cladding and brown-stained wood. The area had grown up along the side of a steep hill, and a lot of the street-names gave a straightforward description of their geographical position. Others were named after seasons or months.

I wonder how much people keep an eye out for each other in places like this, she thought. *Not much,* was her guess.

She reached the right road and started walking slowly up it. Loose gravel chippings covering the tarmac, scruffy ditches, the key-ring jangling and burning in her pocket.

The house was almost at the top of the hill, on the north side of the road. She stood to one side at the bottom of the drive and looked cautiously up at it. The sloping plot was overgrown, the year's leaves brown and rotting in between the patches of snow. Some large boulders blocked the view. The house itself was from the 1940s, maybe early 1950s. Two storeys, pale, greyish-brown plaster that had probably once been white but which was now starting to crumble. No curtains, no lights anywhere. The windows looked like gaps in a row of bad teeth.

Her heart was thudding, her breathing shallow in the cold. She looked round. There were no lights in any of the adjacent buildings, and no one in sight.

Swedish suburbs on a weekday afternoon look post-apocalyptic, she thought, weighing the keys in her hand.

Mia Eriksson rented a room in this building, and she

had already paid for the rest of the month. Mia had told her the address and given her the keys, which was tantamount to inviting her to go inside.

She took a deep breath and walked up the drive. The path was icy and uneven from previous walkers and neglected snow-clearing. She glanced over her shoulder, but no one was watching, no one was wondering what she was doing there. She went quickly up the steps, checking that the keys were in her pocket. She listened at the door, but couldn't hear anything. She rang the bell, unleashing a terrible cacophony inside the house. If someone answered she'd think of something – ask for directions or if they were interested in buying the *Big Issue*. She rang again. No response. She studied the door, solid, 1940s, two tumbler locks. She pulled out the keys, weighing them in her hand. She tried one key in the top lock. It didn't fit. Her upper lip started to sweat, what if this was a trap? She changed keys with trembling fingers. Click. She breathed out, changed keys, bottom lock, click click, then the skeleton key, clunk. The door slid open with a creak. She went in, her heartbeat thudding in her ears, and pulled the door shut behind her. She was in a dark hall, and blinked to get used to the gloom, too scared to turn on the lights.

She stood where she was, just inside the door, for a long time, waiting for the darkness to retreat, and for her heart to calm down. There was a rather bad smell, damp and mildew, and it was pretty cold. She wiped her feet on a threadbare little mat, not wanting to leave any footprints behind as evidence.

The hall was empty, no furniture. There were several doors. She opened the first one on the left. Behind it a staircase led upstairs, thin daylight falling from a window far above. She closed it silently and opened the next. A cleaning cupboard under the stairs.

Suddenly she heard a car on the road outside and froze, her heart seemed to stop.

The door, she thought. *I have to lock it again, otherwise they'll know someone's here straight away.*

She ran back to the door and locked it, all three locks, with trembling hands. She breathed out, and felt sweat running from under her arms. She listened for sounds from the road, but couldn't hear anything. She crept back to the cupboard. When she opened it again a key fell out of the lock and clattered onto the floor. The noise echoed through the empty house. *Shit!* She quickly replaced the key, listened, heard nothing, went to the next door, opposite the front door. The kitchen, not modernized since the house was built, low worktops and a rusty draining board. Two windows, one to the north, one west. An old table with a patterned laminate top and four mismatched chairs. A coffee machine. She went over and opened the top drawer: some cutlery and a carving knife. The second one: empty. The third: empty. She went through the kitchen cupboards and found a few saucepans, a cast-iron frying-pan, a colander. In the pantry were a packet of quick-cook macaroni and two tins of tomatoes. She stopped and looked around her. The kitchen was fairly clean, probably thanks to Mia.

In the east wall there was a sliding door, pulled shut. Annika went over to it and tugged the shiny handle. Locked. She pulled again with both hands, in vain. She fingered the lock, the key must be very small, none of the ones she had would fit. She went back out to the hall and tried the last door, and found herself in a well-lit room containing a sofa, a low table, and an open fire in one corner. The floor was linoleum, patterned to look like wood. On the left was another door, which ought to lead to the room behind the kitchen. She went over and tried it. Locked. She tried her keys but they didn't fit.

297

The office, Annika thought. This was the room Mia was never able to get into.

She was on her way back to the kitchen to try to find a key to the locked room when she heard the top tumbler lock click.

The blood ran from her head down to her feet, and she stood glued to the hall floor as the first lock opened. When the second began to turn she suddenly managed to move her feet again and flew over to the door hiding the stairs to the first floor. She pulled it open, slid through and closed it quietly behind her, then padded quickly and silently up the stairs. She found herself on a landing, with the same wood-effect lino floor, four doors. She tore one of them open and went into a bedroom, and threw herself under the bed furthest from the door. *Oh God, help, forgive me all the stupid things I've done . . .*

The floor under the bed was incredibly dusty and she put her hand over her nose and mouth to filter the air a little and stop herself sneezing. She heard noises in the room below her, a tap running; she must be above the kitchen. She was starting to breathe heavily and quickly, deeply.

No, she thought. *Not a panic attack. Not now.*

Her breathing had other ideas, however, and she was starting to hyperventilate. She wriggled onto her back, searching through her pockets for something to breathe into. She found her gloves and put one over her nose and mouth, breathing, breathing, breathing until the attack had passed and she was left lying there quietly, completely exhausted. She stared up at the sixty-year-old bed-frame, strips of beige fabric holding the dusty steel springs together.

She turned her face to the wall, putting her ear to the floor. She could hear raised voices, a man and a woman. The man was aggressive, and the woman sounded hysterical. She recognized one of the voices. Rebecka Agneta Charlotta Evita.

'This was my case!' the woman said. 'My big case! What a traitor! Social services are about to pay up and she runs out on me. Bitch!'

She's talking about Mia, Annika thought. Then came the sound of something breaking, she guessed it was the coffee machine. The man muttered something, she couldn't hear what, and then there was a terrible noise right in her ear. She flew up, hitting her head on the bedsprings. *What the fuck?* The noise stopped and she lay down again, touched her forehead and found she was bleeding. Then it started again: the doorbell. It was mounted in the kitchen, just below the ceiling.

In the silence that followed she heard voices muttering, more surprised than upset, more scared than aggressive.

'. . . no, I'm not expecting anyone . . .'

'. . . might have come back . . .'

There were steps across the floor downstairs, as Annika tried to concentrate her hearing, ignoring the trickle of blood into her eyebrow.

A man, it was definitely a male voice at the door. They were discussing something, and eventually their voices grew more heated. The front door closed and they went back into the kitchen.

'If you think I'm going to pay this invoice, you're mad,' said one of the men, and Annika gasped.

Thomas Samuelsson.

The woman's voice seeped through the floor, cool and scornful.

'We have an agreement, and I suggest you follow it.'

'This woman's dead, for God's sake!'

The council official sounded extremely angry.

'She ran away from here,' Rebecka Evita said. 'It was her choice. It doesn't absolve you from your duty to pay.'

Thomas Samuelsson lowered his voice and Annika had trouble hearing the rest of the conversation.

'I'm going to report you to the police, you're nothing but a fraud,' she thought she heard him say. 'I know all about your debts and your bankruptcies, so don't expect to see any money from Vaxholm Council anytime soon.'

Chaos ensued. The other man shouted something, Thomas Samuelsson replied, the woman screamed, there were thuds, splintering wood, yelling and shrieking, the whole house seemed to shake.

Then Rebecka yelling: 'Lock him up.'.

There was a more distant thud, muffled cries, and the rhythmic sound of someone being punched.

'What the hell do we do now?' the man said.

'Shut him up,' the woman shouted.

Fists, thud, thud, thud, furious shouting – 'Let me go, you fucking crooks!' – then steps across the floor, a smaller thud, then silence.

'Is he dead?' It was Rebecka asking.

Annika held her breath.

'No,' the man said. 'He'll be all right.'

She shut her eyes and breathed out.

'Why did you have to hit him so hard? Idiot! He can't stay here!'

'We'll have to get the car,' the man said.

'Well, I'm not going to carry him out!'

'Oh, stop whining, for God's sake! All I'm saying is—'

The front door closed with a slam and the voices stopped.

39

Annika lay there in the silence, dusty and hot. A feather came floating down through the springs and landed on her nose. Time stood still, as she lay there, breathing softly and silently.

They're coming back. They'll soon be back again, this time with a car. Then they're going to take Thomas Samuelsson away, and then it will be too late.

This last thought echoed round her head. Too late, too late. Too late for Aida from Bijeljina, too late for Thomas from Vaxholm.

She blew the feather away and crept out, covered in dust. She sneezed, then crawled over to the window and looked out. Rebecka and the man were on their way down the hill, past a car that Annika recognized as Thomas Samuelsson's green Toyota Corolla.

She sat on the floor, her head empty of thoughts. What should she do? She had no idea how long Rebecka and the man were likely to be gone. It would probably be best to lie here and wait, let them collect the council official and then creep out once it was dark.

She looked out again, it was already getting darker. No Rebecka. If she was going to do anything but wait, she would have to act fast.

She sat down again, closed her eyes, hesitating.

If only she wasn't such a coward. If only she wasn't so weak. If only she had a bit more time.

Bloody coward, she thought. *You have no idea how much time you've got. Maybe you've got time to get him out of here if you get going now.*

She got up and crept onto the landing again, down the stairs, breathless with nerves, and looked round. The cast-iron frying-pan was lying in the middle of the floor. But what had they done with him?

A faint groan from the cupboard under the stairs made her spin round. The key was in the lock, and she ran over and turned it.

The man tumbled out, falling into her, and she caught him and slumped to her knees. His head landed in her lap, he was bleeding from a deep wound on his hairline, his pale blond hair brown with blood. She loosened his tie and he groaned.

Tears of fury came to her eyes. Cold-blooded murderers! First Aida, now Thomas. When would they stop?

'Listen,' she said, patting him gently on the cheek. 'We have to get out of here.'

She tried to get him to his feet, but she lost her grip and he slid to the floor.

'Thomas!' she said. 'Thomas Samuelsson from Vaxholm, where are your car-keys?'

He groaned in response, rolling onto his back and adjusting his head on the threadbare little mat.

She hunted through his coat-pockets, soft material, clumsy hands, there they were. She went into the room with the sofa to see if Rebecka was on her way back, but there was no one in sight.

As she was on her way back out, she saw that the door to the locked room was now open. She stood hesitating for a moment. She ought to get out of there immediately. She ought to see what was in there.

'Fuck, what happened?'

The voice in the hall was thick and confused. She ran out to him.

'They hit you over the head ,' she said. 'We're getting out of here, but I just need to check something first.'

Thomas Samuelsson tried to stand up but collapsed again.

'Sit here for a minute, I'll be right back,' she said.

She ran back to the unlocked room, opened the door wide, prepared to memorize whatever she saw in there.

Disappointment.

She didn't know what she'd been expecting, but it wasn't this. A desk. A telephone. A bookcase containing a mass of files and some piles of paper. She listened, heard nothing, and opened the first file, which bore the word, *Erasures*.

Empty.

The next one: *Follow-up*.

Empty.

The next one, invoices to various local councils. Twenty or so. Österåker Council, your ref. Helga Axelsson, our ref. Rebecka Björkstig. Nacka Council, your ref. Martin Huselius . . . All of them for large amounts, at least a hundred thousand kronor. She ran through the files in the top shelf, with titles like 'Rehabilitation', 'Protected Properties', 'Foreign Placements'.

All empty.

The heaps of loose papers contained personal information, court judgments, references, forms from the social services. The private documents relating to various threatened individuals.

She turned her back on the bookcase and looked round the room. She had to go. Had she missed anything?

The desk. She rushed over and pulled at the drawers. All locked.

Okay, she thought, *sod this*.

Thomas Samuelsson was sitting up, leaning back against the wall with his head between his knees.

'Are you still with us?' she asked nervously.

'Almost dead,' he muttered.

She undid the three locks, then knelt down beside him.

'Thomas,' she said, gulping, 'they might come back at any moment. We have to get out of here. Can you walk?'

He shook his head, his hair like a curtain, flecked with brown.

'Put your arm round my shoulders and I'll try to drag you out. Come on.'

He did as she said. He was heavier than she had expected, and her knees buckled under his weight. She got him over to the door, kicked it open, it was almost dark now. She sat him down on the steps, where he swayed alarmingly. Her hands were shaking so much that she dropped the keys, which fell down into the grass. She almost burst into tears. Fuck it, maybe she shouldn't bother locking up? She listened for noise from the road. No cars. She dodged past the unsteady Thomas, got the keys, then climbed over him again. She suddenly remembered the door of the cleaning cupboard and ran in and locked it again, then closed the front door and locked all three locks. She heaved the man up onto her shoulders and dragged him off towards the Toyota. She opened the car with a cheery bleep and tipped him into the passenger seat, then ran round the car and got in. She had to hold the key steady with both hands as she put it in the ignition. Thank God, it started first time. She revved the engine, put it into first gear and headed away over the brow of the hill.

The last thing she saw in the rear-view mirror was a car further down the hill, on its way up behind them.

She drove straight on, panicking, on the verge of breathing too fast, too deep again. The road came to an end and she swung sharp right. Thomas Samuelsson slid towards her and she shoved him upright.

Fuck it, how was she going to get out of here? Which way was Stockholm?

She headed down the hill, there had to be a main road somewhere, one of the big ones. Which one would it be out here, the Mälaren road?

She glanced in the rear-view mirror, and saw a few headlights of other cars, but nothing that seemed to be following her. She looked ahead again, and only just saw the red light in time. A main road! The Viksjö road! She turned right, away from the house, away from Rebecka, then soon realized that she was driving in a large circle as she passed another large main road. That one had to be the Järfälla road. Suddenly she recognized where she was. The Factory Outlet in Barkarby! She could hear Anne Snapphane's excited voice in her head: *Today is Outlet Day*! They used to go on raids there every spring and autumn, buying up leather jackets and trainers and bits of crazy designer clothing for stupidly low prices. She knew her way home from here. She swung onto the E18 and thundered towards Stockholm in the fast lane.

The man beside her suddenly began to throw up. He was violently sick over his coat and trousers, hitting his head on the dashboard.

'Shit,' Annika said. 'Do you need help?'

He groaned and threw up again. Annika drove on, searching frantically for a slip-road. She felt trapped, unable to do anything.

Thomas was sitting with his head against the glove compartment, his hands over his head.

'What the hell happened?' he asked dully.

'Rebecka and her friend,' Annika said. 'They knocked you out.'

He glanced quickly up at her.

'You!' he said. 'What are you doing here?'

She was staring ahead, the traffic was getting thicker.

'I was listening when they locked you up under the stairs. When they left to get their car I let you out. You've got concussion, you need to see a doctor. I'm driving you to Sankt Göran's.'

'No,' he protested feebly. 'I'm okay. Just a bit of a headache, that's all.'

'Rubbish,' she said. 'You might have a haemorrhage up there. And you really don't want one of those.'

She got a bit lost in the tangle of roads when they joined the E4, but finally emerged onto the motorway by Järva krog. She headed across Hornsberg towards the Accident and Emergency entrance, and parked the car. Her hands were steady as she pulled the key from the ignition, her relief at having escaped purely physical.

It was completely dark now, and a yellow streetlamp made everything look brown.

'I can't go in like this,' Thomas muttered, gesturing towards his vomit-stained coat.

'We'll throw it in the boot,' Annika said, getting out of the car and going round to his side to open the door.

'Come on,' she said, 'get out. I'll help you.'

He got to his feet. He really had been very sick.

'Let's get this off you,' Annika said, pulling his coat off. He swayed alarmingly as she helped him.

'Where did you appear from?' he asked, looking at her like she was a ghost.

'We'll deal with that later,' she said. 'Let's go in.'

She lifted one of his arms over her shoulders, took a firm grip of his waist and steered him towards the entrance. Inside, there was the same sort of woman behind the same sort of glass screen as in Katrineholm.

'My trousers,' he said. 'I've got sick on them.'

'We'll wash it off in the toilet,' she said. 'Hello, Thomas Samuelsson, he's had a blow to the head and was unconscious for several minutes, he's got a headache and has been sick. He's a bit confused and his memory's not great.'

'You're in luck,' the woman said. 'We're not too busy at the moment, you can go through at once. Date of birth?'

'My trousers,' Thomas whispered.

'Great,' Annika said. 'He just needs to go to the toilet . . .'

40

She sat in the waiting room, but the examination was soon over. There was nothing seriously wrong with him. He had none of the clinical symptoms of brain damage, and would soon be back to normal. The doctor came with him out into the waiting room.

'How long do I have to rest?' Thomas asked.

The doctor smiled.

'Oh, not at all. Getting back to your normal routine can only be beneficial. It stops symptoms like headaches and tiredness getting a grip.'

They went out to the car again, both of them exhausted but relieved.

'I'll drive you home,' Thomas said, going towards the driver's door.

'Not on your life,' Annika said. 'You're not doing any more driving today. I'll drive you home.'

His answer came before he could stop it.

'I don't want to go home.'

She turned towards him, her face registering no surprise. She was looking at him in a way that he couldn't decipher, apparently weighing up the options.

'Okay,' she finally said. 'Then we'll go to mine. You need a bit of time before you get back behind the wheel.'

He didn't protest, just got into the passenger seat and

fastened his seatbelt. It struck him that he never usually sat there. Eleonor never drove his car, but of course she had the BMW.

They set off towards Fridhemsplan. Thomas sat looking through the windscreen in silence. So many twinkling lights, so many nameless people. There were so many different ways of living, life could be so incredibly different.

'Does your head really hurt?' Annika asked.

He look at her, and smiled.

'Quite a lot.'

For once, there were parking spaces near her house.

'They're cleaning the streets tonight. If you're here after midnight you get a four hundred kronor fine.'

He held her shoulders as she helped him upstairs. She was strong, considering she was so slight. He could feel her breast under his arm.

The flat was entirely white, the wooden floor worn into soft undulations.

'The building's from the eighteen eighties,' she said as she took off her coat. 'The owner went bankrupt after the property crash in the early nineties, and all his plans for renovations ground to a halt. Would you like some coffee?'

He felt his damp trousers, wondering if they smelled.

'Yes please. Or some wine, if you've got any?'

She stopped and thought, standing tall, clear-eyed.

'I think I've got an old wine-box somewhere, white, but maybe you shouldn't have alcohol yet, what do you think?'

He smiled, slightly confused, and pushed his hair back. He had five stitches along his hairline. He felt his tie and adjusted his jacket.

'It probably won't do any harm,' he said. 'Getting back to normal can only be a good thing, you know.'

She vanished into the kitchen, leaving him standing in the living room, slightly unsteady, uncertain. He looked round slowly: what a strange room. Blank white walls, transparent white curtains, a sofa, a table, television, telephone. The rest of the large room was empty. A broken windowpane had been patched up with a paper bag, and the draught was making the fabric sway. The floor was grey, matt, silky smooth.

'Sit down if you want,' she said, carrying a tray containing a glass, two mugs, the wine-box and a cafetière. She moved easily and nimbly, laying the table with quick little movements. A heavy gold chain hung down towards her breasts.

He sat down. The sofa wasn't particularly comfortable.

'Do you like living here?'

She sat down beside him, poured herself some coffee and wine for him, then sighed.

'Sort of,' she said. 'Sometimes.'

She picked up her mug and looked down at the liquid.

'I used to like it,' she said quietly. 'When I moved in I thought it was great living here. Everything was so light, it was like floating on air somehow. Then . . . well, things changed. Not the flat, but other stuff in my life . . .'

She fell silent and drank some coffee. He tasted the wine, which was surprisingly decent.

'What about you?' she said, looking up at him. 'Are you happy?'

He was about to smile, but gave up the idea.

'Not really,' he said. 'I'm fed up with my life.'

He took a large sip of wine, surprised at his own honesty. She just nodded, didn't ask why.

'What were you doing out in Järfälla?' she asked.

He shut his eyes and thought, his head throbbing.

'The invoice,' he said. 'Have I still got it?'

'What invoice?'

'From Paradise, I had it in my hand when I went in. Three hundred and twenty-two thousand kronor, secure accommodation for our mutual client for three months. We got it by fax this morning, even though the woman in question is already dead. Bloody crooks!'

'I didn't see any invoice,' she said. 'Mind you, I didn't look in the cupboard under the stairs. Have you checked your pockets?'

He tried the outer pockets of his jacket, nothing, then the inside pocket, and found a folded sheet of paper which he pulled out.

'Here it is! Thank God!'

He studied the numbers for a moment, then let the paper drop and looked at Annika.

'What happened, exactly?' he said. 'Where did you appear from?'

She got up and went towards the kitchen.

'I think I'll have some wine as well.'

She came back with another glass.

'Well,' she said, 'I tried to call you. I found out quite a bit more about our friend Rebecka Björkstig. She's had several different aliases, and is suspected of serious fraud in all her bankruptcies.'

She poured herself a glass of wine, then refilled his glass.

'I got a set of keys in the post this morning. I was in touch with a woman who was on the periphery of Paradise, she'd been living in the house in Olovslund. She and her family moved out on Friday, and she posted the keys to me from some place up in the middle of Norrland. I headed out to Järfälla at once.'

He looked at her, aware that he was gawping.

311

'So you let yourself in with the keys? Wasn't there anyone there?'

She shook her head. 'No, but they turned up fairly soon afterwards. I hid upstairs. Then you arrived, and there was a huge commotion. They must have hit you on the head with something pretty heavy. Rebecka and the bloke disappeared to fetch a car, so I dragged you out to your Toyota and we drove away.'

He felt his forehead, trying to gather his thoughts.

'So you were already there when I arrived?'

'Yep.'

'And you got me out of the cupboard and drove me away?'

'That's right. And I locked the cupboard and the front door after us. I wish I could have seen the look on their faces when they came back to get you!'

She grinned happily. He stared at her for several seconds, then burst out laughing.

'You locked the cupboard? And the front door?'

'Yes, every lock!'

They were both laughing, harder and harder. He started to roar with laughter, and she was practically shrieking.

'God, that's good!' he exclaimed.

'They must have thought you'd dematerialized!'

He calmed down, although the laughter was still bubbling away underneath.

'That I'd what?'

She smiled. 'Dematerialized, dissolved, been digitized. It'll be the only way to travel in the future. You dematerialize and send yourself over the net, quickly and pollution-free. Imagine when we start going into space, it'll be a huge help.'

He was staring at her. What the hell was she going on about?

'There ought to be somewhere between ten and a hundred thousand planets with our level of civilization or higher, in the Milky Way alone,' she said. 'Scientists reckon life can develop much more easily than we used to think. Maybe it just isn't that complicated. If the right conditions exist, maybe there's life developing everywhere, all the time. The only requirement is water.'

Thomas laughed in surprise.

'What a head fuck. How did you come across that?'

'I wonder what they look like,' she said. 'Imagine the day we finally meet them! Bloody brilliant! Think of all the new food we get to try. I'm so sick of carrots and potatoes. All the new vegetables! All the spices! There ought to be so many new planets out there, and I'm so tired of this one!'

She fell silent. Their laughter had died away.

'Why?' he asked.

She looked into his eyes, suddenly serious.

'I could ask you the same thing.'

He sighed silently, drank the rest of his wine, feeling more drunk than he ought to.

'I don't like my life any more,' he said.

Somehow it felt obvious to tell her, he knew she would understand, that she wouldn't judge him. He looked at her: tired, a bit too skinny, her strong hands resting in her lap.

'I love my wife,' he said. 'We have a nice house, more than enough money, a large social circle, I do a job I've chosen, working on things I enjoy. But somehow . . .'

He fell silent, hesitated, sighed, touched his tie, then pulled it over his head, folded it up and put it beside him on the sofa.

'We want different things from life,' he said. 'She wants her career at the bank, to be on the board

313

eventually. She's starting to feel the pressure, she'll be forty this spring.'

They sat in silence for a while.

'How did you meet?' Annika asked.

He sighed, smiled, and realized with irritation that there were tears in his eyes.

'She was the sister of one of the boys in the hockey team, quite a bit older than us. She used to drive us to matches sometimes. Attractive. Cool. Driving licence.'

He laughed to shrug off his sentimentality.

'Your secret fantasy?' she wondered, and he blushed.

'You could say that. I used to think about her sometimes before I fell asleep. Once, when I was round at Jerker's, I saw her come out of the bathroom in her bra and pants. She looked great. I masturbated like an idiot that night.'

They both laughed.

'So how did you get together?'

He looked down into his empty wineglass. He really shouldn't drink any more, but poured the last of the wine-box into his glass.

'The summer after I turned seventeen, a whole group of us were planning to go inter-railing. We were all supposed to get summer jobs to earn a bit of money, then we'd set off in the second half of July. Well, you can imagine how it turned out . . .'

She smiled. 'No one got a job.'

'Apart from me, of course,' Thomas said. 'My parents own the Ica supermarket in Vaxholm, so there was no way I could get away with not working. I used to be in charge of the deli counter. I always worked during school holidays and at weekends anyway, so by the middle of July I was rolling in money.'

'But had no one to go with,' Annika said.

'And Mum wouldn't let me go on my own,' Thomas

said. 'I was desperate. I went around slamming doors, I stopped talking to my friends and my parents. Then a miracle happened.'

She picked up his tie and unfolded it.

'Eleonor's boyfriend, a horrible posh git, dumped her just before they were due to go on holiday to Greece. Eleonor tore up the tickets and threw them in his face. She decided to go inter-railing instead, something her ex would have really looked down on. But she didn't want to go on her own.'

Annika had put his tie on, and gave a salute.

'You ended up as her escort.'

He pulled the tie and Annika pretended he was strangling her. They laughed, then sat in silence for a few minutes. She took the tie off again.

'What happened?'

Thomas drank some more wine.

'Eleonor wasn't particularly keen to start with. She said we could go to Greece together, then we'd see how things were going. In Munich we got on the wrong train and ended up in Rome. It was forty degrees when we got there. While I was off getting some water a gang of kids showed up and mugged Eleonor. When I got back she was furious with me, with Italy, with everything. I was ashamed I hadn't been able to protect her. We found a grotty room near the station that I paid for, then we got very, very drunk. We were staggering round the streets, each of us clutching a bottle of Chianti. Eleonor was yelling and fooling around, clinging to me, or anyone else for that matter. I tried to join in as best I could. Things were going okay until we got to the Piazza Navona. Eleonor got it into her head that she wanted to bathe in the fountain, just like Anita Ekberg.'

'Wrong fountain, though,' Annika said.

Thomas nodded.

'Yes, and the wrong time to try it as well. There were seven thousand drunk Italian football supporters in the piazza, and when Eleonor's T-shirt got wet it turned transparent. They literally tried to tear her clothes off, she was about to get raped in the fountain.'

Annika smiled and saluted again.

'But you came to her rescue this time.'

'I started shouting like the chef in *Lady and the Tramp* – *sacramento idioto*, and all that – then I pulled her out of the fountain and dragged her back to the hotel.'

'And that's when it happened?'

'Sadly not,' Thomas said. 'Eleonor spent the night throwing up. The next day her face was sickly green. We spent the morning reporting the mugging to the police, then the afternoon at the Swedish Embassy organizing a replacement passport for her. That evening we stood by the A1 autostrada and hitchhiked north, homewards. We stood there for hours, it was ridiculously hot, and we were standing there with exhaust fumes all round us. Eventually we got a lift from a fat little man in a red car. He was just as hungover as Eleonor and couldn't speak a word of anything but Italian. He pulled in at the first service area we got to, and waved us into the bar with him. He ordered three glasses of something red and sticky, and emptied the contents of his in a single go. As he slammed the glass down on the counter he looked at us expectantly, gesturing wildly and shouting, '*Prego, prego.*' We were terrified he was going to throw us out of the car, so we drank it and we set off again. The same thing happened at every service area. Three glasses, down in one, slam, on the counter. Soon we were singing away in the car. Darkness fell, and late that evening we arrived at a quite magnificent city, at the top of a big hill. Perugia, the man said, and got us a room with his friend the baker. Our room was up in the eaves over the shop and had rose-patterned wallpaper. And that's where we got together. It was my first time.'

He fell quiet, as his memories flickered round the room. Annika swallowed hard, feeling closeness and distance at the same time, moments of pain and longing.

'Last spring we went on a wine-tasting holiday in Tuscany,' he said. 'One day we took an excursion to Umbria. It was so odd going back to Perugia, because the city has always meant something very special to us. That was where we got together. We've been together every day since then.'

He fell silent once more.

'What happened?' Annika asked.

'We didn't recognize anything. Our Perugia was a quiet mediaeval city, a beautiful theatre-set on top of a hill. The real Perugia was a sprawling, vibrant, messy university city. I thought it was fantastic. Perugia was like our relationship, something that started as a teenage fantasy but had developed into a sprawling, vibrant, intellectual union. I wanted us to stay there, but Eleonor was horrified. She felt disappointed and betrayed. She didn't find a vibrant marriage in Perugia, she just lost her dream instead.'

They sat in silence for a while.

'Why didn't you recognize anything?'

He sighed. 'Probably because we'd never been there before. The man in the red car was so drunk that he could easily have got the wrong city. Or else we mis-understood him. We could have been in any one of a whole load of Umbrian hill-towns. Assisi, Terni, Spoleto. Who knows.'

41

She watched him struggle with his memories, leaning forward, elbows on his knees, his unruly hair still stained with blood. She had to suppress an impulse to brush it to one side. He really was very sweet.

'Are you hungry?' she said.

He looked at her, seemingly confused for a moment.

'Yes, actually,' he said.

'I'm a demon at tagliatelle and ready-made sauce,' she said. 'Will that do?'

He nodded indulgently.

She went out into the kitchen, glancing out of the window. Someone was sitting on the toilet in the hospitality flat opposite. She got out the tagliatelle and a jar of Italian sauce, and put some water on to boil. He came and stood in the doorway, leaning against the doorframe.

'Still a bit groggy?' she asked.

'It's probably the wine,' he said. 'This is a great kitchen. And a gas cooker!'

'Original, nineteen thirty-five,' she said.

'Where's the toilet?'

'Half a flight down. Put your shoes on, the floor's filthy.'

She laid the table, wondering about napkins, then

318

stopped and thought about what she was doing. Napkins? And when exactly did she last use napkins? So why would she use them now? To impress him, to pretend she was someone else?

She was tipping the pasta into a colander when he came back in, she heard him take off his shoes and clear his throat. When he came into the kitchen his face looked less pale.

'Interesting bathroom arrangements,' he said. 'How long did you say you've lived here?'

'Two years. More or less. Do you want a napkin?'

He sat at the table.

'Yes please, if you've got one.'

She handed him a bright yellow paper napkin from last Easter. He unfolded it and put it on his lap, as if it were the most natural thing in the world. She left hers folded up next to her plate.

'Good pasta,' he said.

'You don't have to say that,' she said.

They ate hungrily in silence. Glanced at each other, smiled. Their knees bumped under the little kitchen table.

'Let me do the washing-up,' he said.

'There's no hot water,' Annika said. 'I'll do it later.'

They left the dishes to their fate and went back to the living room, a new silence between them, a tingling in her stomach. They stood either side of the coffee table.

'What about you?' he said. 'You've never married?'

She sank onto the sofa again.

'I was engaged once,' she said.

He sat down beside her, the distance between them electrified.

'Why didn't you get married?' he asked, interested, friendly.

She took a deep breath and tried to smile. Such an

319

innocent question, so normal. Why didn't she get married? She struggled to find the right words.

'Because . . .'

She cleared her throat, ran a finger along the edge of the table. How to find a normal answer to such a normal question?

'Was it that bad? Did he leave you?'

His voice was so friendly, so sympathetic, that something snapped inside her and she started to cry, crouching over. She could sense his surprise, uncertainty, bewilderment, but could do nothing about it.

He'll leave now, she thought. *He's going to disappear for good. Maybe it's just as well.*

'But,' he said, 'what on earth's the matter?'

'Sorry,' she sobbed. 'Sorry, I didn't mean . . .'

He patted her tentatively on the back and gave her hair a gentle stroke.

'Annika, whatever is it? Tell me . . .'

She tried to calm down, to breathe. She let the snot run onto her knees.

'I can't,' she said. 'I just can't.'

He took hold of her shoulders and turned her towards him, and she instinctively tried to hide her tear-swollen face.

'I'm so drunk,' she muttered.

'What happened to your fiancé?'

She wouldn't look up.

'I can't tell you,' she said. 'You'd hate me.'

'Hate you? Why would I do that?'

She looked up at him, realizing that her nose was red and her eyelashes stuck together. He looked worried, concerned, his eyes sparkling blue. He cared. He genuinely wanted to know. She looked down again, breathing quickly through her mouth. She hesitated, then hesitated some more, then finally jumped.

320

'I killed him,' she whispered towards the floor.

The silence that followed was large and heavy, and she felt him stiffen beside her.

'Why?' he said quietly.

'He used to beat me up. He was strangling me. I had to leave him, otherwise I would have died. When I finished it he cut my cat open with a knife. He was going to kill me as well. I hit him, and he fell into a disused blast furnace . . .'

She was staring hard at the floor.

'And he died?'

His voice different now, muffled.

She nodded, tears running down her cheeks.

'If I could change just one thing in my life it would be that day, that blow.'

'Was there a trial?' His voice sounded distanced. Retreating.

She nodded again. 'Causing another person's death. A supervision order. I had to have therapy for a year, my probation officer thought I needed it. It was pointless. The counsellor was just weird. I haven't felt up to much since then.'

She fell silent, closed her eyes, waiting for him to get up and leave. He did. She hid her face in her hands, waiting for the sound of the front door closing, for the abyss to open up, for the despair, the emptiness, the loneliness, *oh God, help me . . .*

Instead she felt his hand on her hair.

'Here,' he said, handing her a yellow Easter napkin. 'Blow your nose.'

And he sat down beside her again.

'To be honest,' he said, 'it probably isn't a bad idea to kill them every now and then.'

She looked up quickly, he was smiling sadly.

'I work in social services,' he said. 'I've spent seven

years there, and there isn't much I haven't seen. Your case isn't that unusual.'

She blinked.

'Women in your position can have a terrible time afterwards,' he said. 'I don't think you should feel guilty. It was self-defence, after all. It's just a shame that you had to meet a bastard like that. How old were you when you got together?'

'Seventeen years, four months and six days,' she said.

He stroked her cheek.

'Poor Annika,' he said. 'You deserve better.'

Then she was in his arms, her cheek against his chest, feeling his heart beat, his arms round her head. She put her arms round his waist and held him, so big and warm.

'How did you cope?' he whispered into her hair.

She closed her eyes, listening to his heart, alive, thudding.

'Chaos,' she said to his chest, 'to start with every-thing was just chaotic. I couldn't speak, couldn't think, couldn't eat. I really couldn't feel anything, everything was . . . white, somehow. Then it hit, all of it at once. I thought I was falling apart, nothing seemed to work. I didn't dare sleep, the nightmares were terrible, and in the end I was admitted to hospital for a few days. That was when my parole officer forced me to have therapy . . .'

He was stroking her hair and back.

'Who was looking after you?'

He sounded careful now, considerate.

'My grandmother,' she said. 'I spent the whole of the first year at Grandma's, as soon as they let me go. I walked a lot in the forest, I talked a lot, cried a lot. Grandma was always there, she was incredible. Every-thing faded away, but there was nothing left afterwards.

Just a cold, empty space. Everything seemed meaningless.'

He was rocking her gently, breathing into her hair.

'How are you now?'

She swallowed.

'Grandma's ill, it's awful. She's had a stroke. I'm thinking of asking for unpaid leave from work so I can look after her. It's the least I can do.'

'But how are *you*?' he said.

She screwed her eyes shut to stop herself from crying.

'Okay, sort of,' she whispered. 'I still have trouble eating, but it's getting better. If it wasn't for Grandma, things would be pretty all right. I'm glad I've met you.'

She heard the words as she said them, and his hand stopped stroking her.

'Are you?' he asked.

She nodded against his chest. He let go of her and looked at her, into her dark eyes, understanding their depth, seeing their sadness. She met his gaze, stroked him on the cheek, and kissed him. He hesitated for a moment, then responded, kissing her, licking her, sucking on her lips.

She pulled off her top and her breasts rolled out, the gold chain dancing. No bra. He stared at them, fascinated. They were so big, he put his hand on one of them, so warm, so soft. She pulled his jacket off, undid his shirt, revealing his smooth chest, broad, not much hair. She kissed his shoulder, biting him until he groaned. He kissed her neck, his tongue playing along the line of her chin until he reached her earlobe. He nibbled at it, sucking, licking, as her hands slid over his back, her nails tracing circles, lightly, gently. Then they stopped and looked into each other's eyes, seeing the emotion, their mutual desire, and gave themselves up to it. They pulled off the rest of their clothes, hands tongues lips everywhere, breasts, stomachs, genitals, arms, feet . . .

He lay back on the sofa, his feet dangling over the end, and she sat on top of him, gliding over him, surrounding him. His cock slid in all the way, filling her up, filling a space she had almost forgotten existed. He felt her heat, pressure, pulse, wanted to slide into action, but she said 'Wait.'

They looked into each other's eyes, into each other's lust, sucked into each other. Suddenly he felt dizzy, a feeling of complete, uncompromising ecstasy. He shut his eyes, leaned his head back and groaned. She started to ride him, slowly, he wanted her to speed up but she held him back. He was panting and groaning, crying out, on the edge of exploding.

She looked at him, matching his lust, letting his cock slide in so slowly that his soul slid in before it, deep inside, as deep as possible, again and again and again, then relenting. She felt the wave come, felt the dampness running down her thighs. His body stiffened, every muscle tensing as his seed pumped into her. She collapsed on top of him and he put his arms round her, still inside her, and stroked her hair. Only now did he realize how sweaty they were, slippery and shiny. She was lying with her nose against his collarbone, breathing in his scent, strong, slightly bitter.

'I think I love you,' she whispered, looking up at him. He kissed her, and they started to move again, gently, carefully, then faster, harder.

42

He woke up freezing. One foot had gone to sleep, her leg was resting on it. Her breathing was slow and heavy; he realized she was fast asleep.

'Annika,' he whispered, stroking her hair. 'Annika, I have to get up.'

She woke with a start, looked at him in surprise, then smiled.

'Hello,' she whispered.

'Hello,' he said, kissing her on the forehead. 'I have to get up.'

She lay there for a moment.

'Of course,' she said, getting up stiffly and pulling him up from the sofa.

They stood facing each other, naked and sweaty, she half a head shorter than him, and kissed. She wrapped her arms round his neck and reached up on tiptoe. He felt her breasts against his ribs, so incredibly soft.

'I have to go home,' he whispered.

'Of course,' she said again, 'but not yet. Let's sleep for a bit.'

Taking him by the hand, she led him to her bedroom. The bed, a mattress with no headboard, was unmade. She sank down, pulling him with her.

They made love again.

*   *   *

The heavy building looked dark and foreboding. Ratko stared up at the brick façade, seeing the streetlamps reflected in the windows, his mouth dry.

Why had they called him here, in the middle of the night? Something funny was going on.

Cars rushed behind him as he slowly went past the main entrance, turned the corner and saw the delegation's car park, one space for the consul, one for the ambassador. He went up to the door and knocked, quickly and gently.

The fat man opened the door.

'You're late,' he said, turning his back on him and swaying off into the building.

Ratko followed the fat man up the steps to the large room, the waiting room, and immediately found himself back in Belgrade: Eastern-bloc green walls, grey plastic chairs. The hatch ahead of him, the glass wall to the left. He could just make out light coming from the consul's office.

'Why am I here?' he asked.

The fat man pointed to the door next to the glass wall.

'Sit down and wait,' he said.

He walked through the room, round the table and chairs, passing the narrow corridor with the fat man's desk, and walked into the reception room. Nothing had changed, still the same chairs against the wall, the sofa, the bookcases, the map of pre-partition Yugoslavia. He considered sitting down, but stayed on his feet. The previous occasions he had been here had almost always been under more congenial circumstances, or had at least been amicable. This time was different. He couldn't sit down, because then he would be at a disadvantage when his superiors entered the room.

326

On the table were marks left by bottles, Slivovits, and he suddenly realized how thirsty he was. A good, clean vodka, no ice. He gulped and licked his lips.

Where the hell were they? What were they up to? They had his balls in a vice, and he didn't like the feeling.

He took a few steps, glancing out into the corridor. There were several men, none of whom he had ever seen before, all in similar suits, brown, ill-fitting. *What the hell?* He retreated quickly into the room, sweat breaking out on his forehead. He knew who they were – RDB people from Belgrade – but why were they there? Because of him?

'You can go in to the consul now.'

Out into the corridor again, past the fat man, into the next room, ignored by the unknown men.

'Ratko,' the consul said. 'There's a plane leaving for Skopje via Vienna at seven o'clock tomorrow morning. You'll be met at the airport by our people. You leave at once.'

He stared at the bald little man who was now looking at some papers on his desk. What on earth was happening?

'Why?'

'We've had bad news from The Hague.'

The threat sank in: *Bloody hell, the war crimes tribunal.*

'They're going to announce that you're officially wanted at twelve o'clock tomorrow.'

He gulped, feeling his sweat burn. All those men, what did they have to do with it?

The consul gathered his papers together into a neat bundle against the edge of the desk, then stood up and walked round the desk.

'We've sorted new documents for you,' he said. 'Our visitors have been busy working on them all evening.

You have to sign here, and we need a photograph, then it's done.'

His brain rolled slowly into action.

'But all arrest warrants are confidential until they're announced publicly,' he said. 'How can you know?'

The consul stopped in front of him, a head shorter, his eyes giving nothing away. He didn't enjoy doing this.

'We know,' he said simply. 'As soon as you get your new passport, you have to leave the country, tonight. You're flying from Oslo, Gardemoen.'

He wanted to sit down, drink vodka, let it sink in. He wouldn't be safe by lunchtime tomorrow, because he'd be in the air between Vienna and Macedonia, and then Skopje was several hours from Belgrade.

'If you get there in time, of course you won't be able to leave Serbia for the foreseeable future,' the consul said. 'I assume you have no unfinished business here.'

He gulped, staring at the consul.

'Your new passport is Norwegian. Your name is Runar Aakre. We hope it will hold up long enough for you to get home.'

The men in the room went up to him on a given signal. They each had their own task, and they were in a hurry.

Tuesday 6 November

43

The house was dark, squatting threateningly on the edge of the sea. Thomas swallowed hard, knowing that she would be awake. Somewhere in the darkness Eleonor was sitting and waiting. He had never gone missing like this before, not once in sixteen years.

He closed the car door carefully and the bleep of the central locking echoed around the houses. He took three deep breaths, shut his eyes, and tried to work out how he was feeling.

The young woman he had left asleep in bed was still inside him, warm, all-consuming. Fuck, he'd never felt like this before. This was real. She was amazing, so real, so alive.

Annika.

Her name had thudded within him all the way from the centre of the city out to Vaxholm. His decision had developed in the speed and darkness, but really it was obvious.

He would be honest. He would explain everything, tell it exactly how it was. Their marriage was dead, Eleonor had to realize that. He wanted to live with her, the other woman, have a new life, another existence. He didn't want a divorce because of Annika, she had just provided the catalyst for him to act.

He walked towards the house, relieved at being able to put his decision into action. The frozen ground crunched under his feet.

It wasn't going to be easy, but Eleonor would get over it. She could keep the house. He didn't want it. But she probably ought to buy him out, seeing as the increase in value wasn't hers alone.

She was standing inside the door, in her pink dressing-gown, eyes red from crying, face white with fury.

'Where have you been?'

He put his briefcase down on the hall floor, hung his coat up and turned on the light. She screamed.

'What have you done? What's happened?'

She rushed up to him and put her fingers to the stitches in his forehead. He flinched and caught her hand.

'It hurts,' he said.

She hugged him, pulling him to her, and started to cry. She looked up at him and stroked his hair.

'Oh, I've been so worried. What on earth happened? What have you done?'

He avoided looking at her and pushed her away, didn't want to feel her body, the harsh outline of her bra under the dressing-gown.

'I have to go to bed,' he said. 'I'm shattered.'

He walked round her towards the bedroom, but she grabbed his arm and pulled him back.

'Tell me!' she screamed, tears streaming down her face. 'What's happened? Did you have an accident?'

He looked at her, on the brink of falling apart, her hair a mess, her face streaked with tears. He struggled to find the right words, but failed, and just stood there, paralysed.

She took a step closer, her lips drained of colour.

'Don't you realize how worried I've been?' she whispered. 'What if I'd lost you, what would I have done?'

She closed her eyes and started crying helplessly. He stared at her, had never seen her this cut up, his wife, the woman he had promised to love until he died.

'If anything had happened to you it would have killed me,' she said, opening her eyes and staring into his.

The full force of his conscience woke up, threatening to smother him. God, what had he done? Was he mad?

He pulled her to him and held her tight, stroking her hair as she sobbed into his shirt, crying just like . . .

'Sorry,' he whispered. 'I've been . . . sitting in Accident and Emergency all night.'

She pulled away and looked up at him.

'Why didn't you call?'

He pulled her to him again, unable to look her in the eye.

'I couldn't,' he said. 'I was in an examination room all night, you know, X-rays and all that . . .'

'But what happened?'

Suddenly he caught the smell of sex, a smell from his own body that should never have been there. He gulped, stroked her back, the rough velvet of the dressing-gown.

'Put some coffee on,' he said, 'I have to have a shower. Then I'll tell you. It's a long story.'

They let go of each other, looked into each other's eyes, he forced himself to hold her gaze, made himself smile.

'Don't worry,' he said, kissing her on the forehead. 'I love you.'

She kissed him on the chin, let go of him and went into the kitchen. He walked into the bathroom, pressed all his clothes deep into the laundry basket, got in the shower and stood under the hot water. She was all over his body, in every pore, he could smell the scent of her everywhere, it rose up with the steam and filled the whole of the bathroom. He felt her hard little body under him, her soft breasts, her wild hair. He closed his eyes and saw her bottomless brown eyes, and felt his penis rising again. He turned on the cold tap and scrubbed his groin with shampoo.

He felt despair growing, as indecision got the better of him.

A planning meeting. Another one. Christ, he seemed to do nothing but sit in meetings all day. How the hell were you supposed to produce a paper when everyone just spent all their time babbling?

Anders Schyman strained to suppress his bad mood. Having to be the responsible, sensitive, incisive boss the whole time was starting to get on his nerves.

On the other hand, he was used to running a kindergarten. And having to think about the way things looked from the outside. What was sucking up all his energy was something else, something new.

The power struggle.

This was something he wasn't used to. Every job, every post he had had up to now he had had because people wanted him to be there. He had been offered positions of influence without a struggle, he had been given the power without having to trample over anyone in the process.

He looked out over the newsroom. The day's work had begun. Reporters were making calls; editors tapping away at their keyboards, checking, evaluating, their mice chasing around, making changes and corrections. Soon he would walk the forty-five steps to the editor-in-chief's airy corner office, a man of influence. As he passed by conversations would pause, people would sharpen up, straighten their backs.

So what were men of influence prepared to do to hold on to their power?

He could see them gathering from the corner of his eye, their blue-jacketed forms heading for the management rooms, the cherished corridor with its views, its spacious offices. He followed them and, as he entered the room, the others sat down, expectant, silent.

'Let's make a start,' he said, looking at Sjölander. 'Crime. Where are we going with this story about the Yugoslavian mafia? Did that Bosnian woman who was murdered in Sergels torg have anything to do with it?'

Everyone looked from him to Sjölander, who straightened up.

'Possibly,' the head of crime said. 'The two bodies found in the burned-out lorry have been identified. Two young men from a refugee centre in Upplands Väsby, north of Stockholm. Nineteen and twenty years old. They'd been missing for a while, the police and the staff at the centre thought they'd gone into hiding to avoid being repatriated. But apparently not. One of them was identified by his dental records, he'd actually seen a dentist since he arrived here. They're not a hundred per cent sure about the other one yet, but everything suggests that it's the missing friend of the first man. The police believe there may be a link between them and the woman in Sergels torg.'

'How come?' Schyman said. 'Were they from Bosnia as well?'

'No,' Sjölander said. 'They were Kosovan Albanians. But Aida, the dead woman, was in the same refugee centre. A long time before, admittedly, but the staff say she used to call in and visit. So she could have met them there.'

The head-editor leaned back.

'So what does this tell us?' he said. 'What sort of story is this, exactly?'

They all looked at him, silent, expectant, uncertain.

He looked around at the Blue Cock Parade, the writers, the heads of entertainment, social affairs, sport, pictures, the op-ed editor, Torstensson.

'We've had five murders in just over a week,' he said. 'They've all been pretty remarkable. First the two young men in Frihamnen, shot in the head from a distance with a powerful hunting rifle. Then those poor bastards in the lorry, tortured to death, their bones broken one by one. And the woman in Sergels torg, executed by a shot to the neck in front of five thousand witnesses. What does that tell us?'

They all stared at him.

'Power,' he said. 'This is a power struggle. For money, maybe, or influence, political or criminal: power over life and death. I don't think we've seen the last of this yet. Sjölander, I want us to go big on this.'

They all nodded. They all agreed with him, he noted.

Power. He was on his way to getting a firm hold of it.

44

The ceiling above her swayed, shimmering in the gloom. She lay there for a second, wondering where she was, enjoying the sense of intoxication, of total bliss, before she realized what was wrong.

Annika sat bolt upright in bed, her hand feeling the pillow beside her to confirm that he wasn't there. A stab of emptiness, sharp and cold.

He had gone. Gone home to his wife called Eleonor, Eleonor Samuelsson.

She got up quickly to see if he had left her a note, a few words about their night together, or a promise to call her. She looked in the kitchen, the hall, the living room, she tore at the bedclothes to see if he had put anything on the pillow, a note that had slipped down somewhere, she pulled the bed out, checked underneath.

Nothing.

She tried to work out what she felt: happiness, disappointment, emptiness, belief, intoxication.

She lay down among the sheets and duvet and stared up at the ceiling again.

Bliss. She had never known bliss before, not like this. With Sven there had always been a dark undertone to their love, a demand to live up to expectations, to pretend to be happy.

This was different. Warm, easy, strange, fantastic.

She lay on her side, pulled up her legs, his semen still sticky between her thighs. She pulled the duvet over her, inhaling his scent.

Thomas Samuelsson, local council bureaucrat.

She laughed out loud, letting the bubbling feeling tingle all over her.

Thomas Samuelsson, with his glossy hair and broad chest, a mouth that could kiss and lick and suck and bite.

She curled into a little ball, rocking gently, humming quietly.

She knew. She was absolutely certain. She wanted him. Thomas Samuelsson, the local council bureaucrat.

She sat up and grabbed the phone.

'Thomas Samuelsson is off sick today,' the receptionist at Vaxholm Council told her. 'He was attacked. We're all very concerned.'

Annika smiled to herself, aware that there was nothing too much wrong with him. She said thank you and hung up. She sat with the phone in her hand for a few seconds, hesitating. Then she dialled the number, his home number, eight digits. She waited with her heart thudding as the phone at the other end rang, soon he would be with her again, soon, soon, soon. She smiled, feeling the temperature rise.

'Samuelsson.'

She was home. Eleonor hadn't gone to the bank, she was there with him.

'Hello? Who is this? Why are you doing this?'

Annika slowly put the phone down, her mouth dry. *Shit, shit, shit.* The tingle of desire died away and loneliness welled up instead.

She could see them together, the well-defined man and the vague outline of the woman, love's young dream. She swallowed hard, as failure gnawed at her. She pulled on her tracksuit and walked up and down a few times, then went down to the toilet. Then went into the kitchen and made coffee, then sat in the living room with her notes and the phone.

Thomas Samuelsson and his wife. Shit, shit, shit.

She called Anne Snapphane, but she wasn't home. Her mother: no answer. The ward at Kullbergska hospital: her grandmother was sleeping.

'I'll be there later,' she told the nurse.

Then she dialled Berit Hamrin's direct number: no answer. She tried Anders Schyman. The phone rang. She was about to put the phone down when he picked up, slightly out of breath.

'Busy?' she asked.

'I've just got out from a planning meeting,' he said. 'How are you?'

She felt a pang of conscience, she was supposed to be ill.

'Not too bad,' she said. 'I was out in Järfälla yesterday, checking Paradise's address. It was an interesting experience.'

She could hear the sound of furniture being moved, then a loud sigh.

'I told you not to think about that.'

'I felt okay,' she said, 'so I went for a walk. The information I got from my source seems to check out. I went through their office, but couldn't find any trace of activity beyond the actual invoices. They're good at demanding payment. All the other files were empty—'

'Hang on,' the head-editor interrupted. 'Rebecka let you into her office?'

She closed her eyes, and clenched her teeth for a moment.

'Not exactly,' she said. 'But I didn't break in, if I can put it like that. I was invited, I had keys.'

'From Rebecka?'

'From her tenant. And while I was there Rebecka turned up with some bloke, her brother, maybe . . .'

'And you just happened to be in their property?'

Annika stood up, suddenly irritated.

'Listen,' she said. 'I was hiding, and while I was there Thomas Samuelsson arrived, the council official from Vaxholm. He was furious about an invoice Rebecka had faxed that morning because the client she was demanding payment for looking after was already dead!'

There was silence on the line. Annika felt Thomas Samuelsson's name echoing in the silence, that her voice had sounded different when she said his name, had become oddly round and warm.

'Go on,' Schyman said. 'What happened?'

She cleared her throat.

'They knocked him unconscious and locked him in a cupboard and went to get a car. I let him out and took him to hospital.'

'Christ, so they're violent? Annika, you're not to go out there any more, do you hear?'

She scratched her forehead, feeling the mark left by the bedsprings the day before, hesitating. She decided not to mention Aida.

'Okay,' she said.

'We have to run this story soon,' Schyman said. 'What else do you need before you can start writing?'

Annika thought for a moment.

'Comments from people, interviews with lawyers, social workers . . . Their activities need to be placed in a broader context. It'll take a bit of time. And Rebecka has to have the chance to answer the criticism against her.'

'This council bloke, will he talk?'

'Thomas Samuelsson?' Her voice soft again. 'He might.'

'Have you got any others contacts in local authorities?'

She shut her eyes and thought.

'I saw a few invoices, which probably isn't exactly legal, but I managed to see some of the names given as references. Helga, Helga Axelsson, I think it was, in . . . Österåker. And someone in Nacka, Martin something . . . I think it ended in -elius, there can't be many of them there. I didn't have time to go through the others, it was all a bit of a rush.'

'You know this could count as breaking and entering?' Schyman said. Annika couldn't work out if he was pleased or annoyed.

'Yes,' Annika said. 'If I get caught. I let myself in with a key and didn't leave any trace that I'd been there.'

'Were you wearing gloves?'

She didn't answer. She hadn't been wearing gloves, and she was in the police database.

'I don't think Rebecka's likely to call the police,' she said.

'Do you need help with the research?' the head-editor asked.

Not from Eva-Britt Qvist, thank you very much, she thought.

'I'd be happy to work with Berit Hamrin,' she said.

'I'll ask Berit to call you,' he said.

'Okay.'

Silence. She could almost hear him thinking at the other end.

'Right, this is what we're going to do,' Anders Schyman said. 'I'm going to get you off your next run of nightshifts. You're to take it easy for the rest of this week, then come into work on Monday. You'll be working days until this is finished. Does that sound okay?'

Annika shut her eyes, letting out a deep breath. Her smile came from deep inside.

'Great.'

She practically flew down to the station, her feet scarcely touching the ground. She didn't even notice the biting wind. She had made it, she had got what she wanted! They were going to let her be a reporter again, she was sure of it. She'd be able to conduct interviews, write articles, investigate corruption and scandals, put forward the views of normal people, defend people in trouble.

On the train she had the choice of staring at a luggage rack or out at the brown and green fir trees rushing past. She closed her eyes as the train rattled on.

Tho-mas Tho-mas, Tho-mas Tho-mas, Tho-mas Tho-mas.

Her happiness was losing its sheen and she was starting to feel annoyed and insulted. He hadn't phoned. He hadn't left a note. He had left her sleeping in her bed without a word. Had he looked at her before he left? Had he stroked her cheek? What had he been thinking, feeling? Shame and regret? Bliss and delirious happiness?

Not knowing was physically painful, it burned in her chest, making her hands tremble. She clenched her teeth and stared out of the window.

Grand-ma Grand-ma, Grand-ma Grand-ma, Grand-ma Grand-ma.

Stability and love – where would she have been without them? The old woman was her still, calm centre, her anchor in a reality that never seemed to stop spinning.

She ought to do everything she could, it was the very least she could do, but she felt that she just couldn't, didn't want to. The realization made her feel ashamed, and she huddled into the corner of her seat, suddenly freezing.

She had finally made it, after all. Her studies, the years of slog on the local paper, all those nightshifts. Now it was time to reap the rewards. Was she really going to give all that up to take on something that should be society's responsibility? But was it actually society's? How much were we really obliged to do for one another?

The train rattled, snow smeared the window. By the time she got out in Katrineholm the weather was terrible. The storm hit her in the face like a sharp broom. She felt a growing sense of injustice and anger. Why here, why now?

She stumbled on, across the square in front of the station and off towards Trädgårdsgatan. The wind was against her, and it was soon treacherously slippery. The low pressure made the darkness more dense, sounds seemed muffled. Cars glided past, their headlights struggling to cope, winter tyres crunching. The hospital finally appeared up on the right, square and grey. She stumbled towards the entrance, where she leaned against the wall to catch her breath. Two young women were on their way out. They were both pregnant, dressed in colourful raincoats.

Annika turned away, pretending she hadn't seen them.

I'd rather die than live in this town.

She walked slowly up to the ward, seeing the long hours unfurling ahead of her, with her grandmother's stuttering attempts to remember the past, the hard bunk that she would be sleeping on tonight.

The corridor lay deserted in flickering, blue-tinted fluorescent light. She caught part of a conversation from the nurses' office, but went past without announcing her presence. Some of the doors were open, she could hear old people rattling and coughing. Her grandmother's door was closed, and when she pushed it open she was met by a cool draught. The room was dark, and the old woman was lying in her bed. She went in and lit the lamp beside the bed, lighting up the yellow blanket.

She smiled and raised her hand to stroke the old woman on the cheek.

'Grandma?'

She was lying on her back. Annika looked at her sunken face and knew at once, instantly, immediately. Too still, too pale, too relaxed. She let her hand touch her skin anyway, cold, grey. The stab of awareness hit her chest, then her brain, then her lungs. And she screamed, and screamed and screamed until the nurses came, until a doctor came. Screamed and screamed.

'Save her, you have to save her, heart massage, electric shocks, a respirator. Something, anything . . .'

The doctor with the ponytail came over to her, serious, backlit.

'Annika,' she said, 'Sofia Katarina is dead.'

'No!' Annika screamed. 'No!'

She backed away, something toppled over, she couldn't see what, chaos . . .

'Annika—'

'You've got to bring her back, do something, operate . . .'

'She died in her sleep, peacefully. She was very ill, Annika; maybe this was for the best . . .'

Annika stopped and stared hard at the doctor, her field of vision reduced to a narrow tunnel.

'Are you mad? Best? You didn't look after her, you

344

let her just lie here and die, you neglected her. I'll report you for this, you bastards . . .'

She had to get out, headed for the door, but there were people in the way. She turned and collided with a nurse, and the doctor took hold of her shoulders.

'Annika, calm down, you're hysterical. We were here with Sofia Katarina an hour ago, and she was sleeping peacefully then.'

Annika pulled free.

'She can't be dead, she's in hospital. Why didn't you look after her? Why did you let her lie there and die, you bastards, you bastards . . . ?'

Someone took hold of her and she lashed out, screaming. They wanted to take her away from her grandmother, they wanted to do more damage; she wouldn't let them.

'Let me be, let me stay with her, you let her die, let me look after her . . .'

Faces flashed past, she didn't want to see them, she threw herself backwards as they shouted at her, *Annika!* She roared in response, refused to listen, refused to hear.

'Murderers!' she screamed. 'You left her to die!'

They forced her onto a trolley and held her down. Now they were going to start on her as well. She screamed and struggled to get free.

'A tranquillizer,' the voices said, 'give her some Oxazepam . . .'

All of sudden she ran out of energy, slumping back on the trolley. She felt her grief suffocating her, light vanished, she couldn't scream any more, she felt frozen, couldn't breathe. She fought for air, breathing, breathing, and someone else screamed, *She's hyperventilating, get a bag.* And then mist. Mist. Darkness.

45

Her mother was sitting beside her. Her mink coat was tossed over the next chair along. Annika was lying on the hard camp bed in her grandmother's hospital room, she'd been drugged, the room had slid away, sinking and swaying. She looked up at the window, it was completely black outside.

I don't know what time it is, she thought.

Her grandmother was still lying in her bed, motionless and white. Two candles were burning, one on each side of the bed, forming two golden circles in the darkness.

Annika sat up. Her mother was crying.

'I didn't get here in time,' Barbro sobbed. 'They called, but Mum was already dead when I got here. She died in her sleep, peacefully, they said.'

Annika felt the room sway, a force-nine gale. Her mouth was dry.

'They can't know that,' she said. 'I found her. There shouldn't be any candles here.'

Annika got up, set off across the floor, stumbling, lurching, trying to get to Grandma, wanting to get rid of the candles, of death, wanting to shake life back into her.

Her mother stood up and took hold of her.

'Sit down. Don't spoil this. Let's say goodbye to her in a calm and respectful way.'

She led Annika back to the bed.

'It was for the best,' her mother said, drying her eyes. 'Sofia would never have got back to normal again. She was so fond of walking in the forest, imagine her just lying here like a vegetable. She wouldn't have wanted that.'

Annika was sitting on the bunk, having trouble staying upright. Her mother seemed to be rising and falling, swaying from side to side.

'They killed her,' Annika said.

'Don't talk rubbish,' her mother said. 'She had another stroke, the doctors said, probably in the same place. There was nothing they could have done.'

Annika looked at her grandmother, her love, her strength, her still point, so small, so white, so thin. Soon she would be gone for ever. Now she was alone.

'How am I going to manage?' she whispered.

Her mother got up and went over to the dead woman, stopped and looked down at the old face.

'She had so many different sides,' Barbro said. 'She could be unfair and judgemental, but now that she's gone we have to try to forget that. We have to remember the good times.'

Annika tried to find something to say, but couldn't even find any thoughts, and didn't feel like squeezing out any platitudes. She couldn't join in her mother's act. She sat in silence, staring at her hands. She remembered the feeling of cold skin, the dead face. She buried her hands in the warmth of her armpits.

'She had her faults,' Barbro said, 'but we all do. I wanted a mother who cared, who looked after me. Like all the other girls had when I was little.'

Annika didn't respond, was trying not to hear. Her

mother carried on, mainly to herself. 'But you always love your mother anyway; your mother is always the person closest to you, come what may.'

'Grandma was closest to me,' Annika whispered, feeling her tears overflow and trickle down her cheeks. She did nothing to stop them, letting them fall, letting the pain sink in.

Her mother looked over at her, distant, her eyes dark.

'How typical of you to say something like that at a time like this,' she said.

Leaving the dead woman, she went over to Annika, red-eyed, thin-lipped.

'Mum always hid you behind her back,' Barbro whispered. 'Well, she can't do that any more.'

Annika shut her eyes, feeling her mother come even closer.

'All these years she favoured you over Birgitta, and you just soaked it up. How do you think that made your little sister feel? Well?'

Annika hid her face in her hands.

'Birgitta had you,' she said.

'And you didn't, you mean? Have you ever wondered why that might have been? Maybe it was to do with you as a person? Look at me when I'm talking to you!'

Annika looked up, blinking. Her mother was standing in front of her, above her. Her eyes were dark, her face twisted, full of pain and derision.

'You've always ruined things for everyone else,' Barbro whispered. 'You're like a bad-luck charm, there's something wrong with you, you've done nothing but spread misery around you since the day you were born.'

Annika gasped and backed away on the bed.

'Mum,' she said, 'you don't know what you're saying.'

Her mother leaned forward.

'We would have been a happy family,' she said, 'if it hadn't been for you.'

The door opened and the doctor came in, turning on the lamp in the ceiling.

'Excuse me,' she said. 'Would you rather I came back later?'

Annika's mother straightened up, her eyes staring into Annika's.

'No,' she said, 'don't worry. I was just leaving.'

She picked up her handbag and coat, then held out her hand and thanked the doctor, muttered something, took a last glance at the dead woman, then walked out of the room.

Annika was left sitting there open-mouthed. Her tears veiled the room. She felt crushed, had she really heard right? Had her mother really said those words, those never spoken but always present, forbidden words that defined and held the key to her childhood?

'How are you feeling?' the doctor asked, sitting down beside her on the bunk.

Annika lowered her head, panting for air.

'I'm going to write you a sick-note for the rest of the month,' the doctor went on. 'I'll give you a prescription as well – twenty-five doses of Oxazepam. You can't overdose on them, but don't take them with alcohol, that can make them dangerous.'

Annika put her hands over her face, trying to stop herself shaking. The doctor sat in silence for a while.

'Were you very close to your grandmother?' she asked.

Annika nodded.

'This has been a terrible shock for you,' she said. 'Well, two really. You found her at home as well, didn't you?'

She nodded again.

'All bereaved people go through the same stages, to

349

a greater or lesser extent,' the doctor said. 'The first is shock, and that's where you are now. Then there's often a period of aggression, followed by denial, then finally acceptance. You have to be gentle with yourself now, you're quite likely to feel very depressed for a while, and you may well have trouble eating and sleeping. That's perfectly normal, and it will pass. But if it gets too hard, you have to get help. Take the tablets if it gets bad. You can always call someone here at the hospital if you want to talk. You can get an appointment with a counsellor if you want, too.'

Annika shook her head. 'No counselling,' she said.

The doctor stroked her back.

'Just let us know. We need to move Sofia Katarina now. Do you need any help getting somewhere?'

'Sofia Katarina,' Annika whispered. 'I was named after her. My middle name's Sofia.'

'Annika Sofia,' the doctor said. 'Well, try to look after yourself now.'

Annika looked up at her, standing so close yet sounding so far away.

She didn't answer.

PART THREE

Shame is the most forbidden feeling of all

We can talk about everything apart from what we are most ashamed of. Other feelings, even difficult ones, can be shared and aired, but never shame. That is in its nature. Shame is our biggest secret, a punishment in itself.

There is no mercy for shame. Everything else can be forgiven: violence, evil, injustice, guilt, but for the most shameful crimes there is no absolution. It is not granted to shame.

In my case shame and guilt coincide. This is quite usual, but not inevitable. I was guilty of betrayal. Everything I have done in recent years has been an attempt to assuage my weakness. For this reason, the sense of guilt can still be a creative force, it pushes you towards action, towards revenge.

I cannot deal with my shame. It is destroying me, together with violence. It is not growing, it is not shrinking, it sits like a cancer in the depths of my consciousness.

Biding its time.

Hollowing me out.

Monday 3 December

46

The man in dark clothing jumped noiselessly onto the station platform. His knees absorbed most of the shock, and the rubber soles of his shoes the rest. He breathed out and looked round. He was the only person getting off here. He turned and quickly closed the door – he didn't want anyone to notice his departure.

The air was fresh and cold, he felt triumphant.

Ratko was back in Sweden. Everything had gone exactly as he had planned. It was all a matter of will-power, of relentless ambition, never compromising. They thought they knew where they had him, that he was under their control.

Like hell.

The conductor opened a door further along the platform and he moved quietly and not too quickly towards the station building, just someone taking a nocturnal walk along the platform in Nässjö, a restless soul.

He glanced at the time: 03.48. The train was almost on schedule.

As he reached the corner of the station building he cast a quick glance over his shoulder. The conductor had his back to him, hadn't noticed him. But why should he have?

He turned to face the sleeping town, as the Norwegian citizen, Runar Aakre, slept on in his compartment on the way to Stockholm.

He walked over to the esplanade, he hadn't been here for a long time. He was starting to feel worried, what if something had gone wrong? He mustn't take anything for granted, anything could have happened to the car – it might have been stolen, the engine might have frozen, the battery might be flat.

Well, imagining that things are worse than they are is the last thing I need right now, he thought crossly.

He cut across the main square, already freezing. It was going to be a long, cold walk.

Outside the Cultural Centre on Rådhusgatan he came across a cluster of bicycles. He quickly went through them and found an unlocked woman's bike. It would be even colder, but much faster. He pedalled quickly northwards, heading towards the main road to Jönköping.

It was terrible, the wind was against him, it was dark, he was already gasping for breath.

Soon, he thought. *Soon I'll be there*.

The journey had been trying. The false passport burned in his pocket. He had been nervous at every border crossing, almost twitchy. He knew why.

He no longer had the whole picture. Power had been taken from him. They had let him keep the nightclub, but the rest of his privileges were gone. Things like that get noticed straight away in a city like Belgrade. He lost all respect, his wife wanted a divorce. Not even his reputation as a war hero helped any longer, because people thought he was past it, that he hadn't done his duty in Kosovo, and for his superiors he was simply the man who had managed to lose goods worth fifty million. The workers in the factories making pirated cigarettes went unpaid. The whole organization lost momentum. Now everyone was forced to work twice as hard to make up for the loss, his loss. What were ten years of forgotten ethnic cleansing compared to that?

He pedalled on, Christ, what a lot of hills there were – he'd forgotten that, how hilly and wet and crap it was.

They had expected him to give up, that the arrest warrant from The Hague would make him crawl away into hiding in some hideous suburb, go to football once a week, spend the rest of his life drinking Slivo. *Like fuck!*

He was his own boss now, in charge of his own destiny. He could do whatever he wanted.

His treacherous whore of a wife was welcome to her new life, wondering who the hell was going to pay for her clothes and drink in the future.

The journey back to Belgrade a month ago had gone as planned. No one had queried his passport, and people had been waiting for him in Skopje as he had been told they would. The drive to Belgrade had been as mind-numbingly boring as usual, but Slivo helped it go quicker. They were all fairly drunk when they arrived, and no one remembered to ask him to hand back the passport.

After that he was out in the cold. His superiors no longer contacted him. If he wanted bodyguards he'd have to pay for them himself.

Bitterness gnawed away at him, and he pedalled harder.

They were weak, he thought. They didn't realize what it was like out in the field. They didn't know how to survive in enemy territory.

He caught his breath as the bike coasted down a hill, and the sharp wind gave him back his sense of triumph.

He'd fooled them! Just set off without them having any idea where he'd gone. He'd vanished into thin air.

Runar Aakre, the Red Cross worker, had hired a car in Belgrade for a trip to Hungary, and at the border he had explained in English that he had to get to Szeged to sort something out, it would only take a few hours. He had all his papers ready, his green card, international insurance. The border guards had checked him out, searching through the car with a torch. Beside him on the passenger seat he had a copy of *Verdens gang*, the Norwegian evening paper, twenty-five days old, but they couldn't see that. He'd saved it from the airport outside Oslo, aware even then that it would come in handy.

They had waved him through.

Of course he didn't stop in Szeged but carried on to Budapest, where he slept in the back seat for a few hours before abandoning the car in a car park outside a big furniture store.

His tickets had been waiting for him in a PO box in the city centre. He had bought them over the phone from a bar, using a clean credit card and giving the PO box as his address. He had used it before.

The wind was picking up, hitting him from the side now. The wheels were slipping in the slush, and he was panting again. Well, he shouldn't let the cold worry him. Soon he would never have to bother with it ever again. His new activities would be based in places where it never snowed. He just had to pull it all together, the funding, customers, partners.

Naturally it was stupid to leave Belgrade when The Hague was after him. No one imagined he would even try. They all assumed he would sit and rot away in his suburban hell. But it was perfectly possible to travel about unnoticed in western Europe, as long as you stuck to intercity trains. The old milk-trains were no good, but trains for businessmen racing between capital cities scarcely even slowed down for the borders. He had to

358

get back up to Sweden, and he had to meet his friend in the east.

The train journey had been nerve-racking but uneventful. Vienna, Munich, Copenhagen. He had arrived at Limhamn the previous evening with four hundred homeward-bound Swedes, all dragging trolleys loaded with crates of beer. He was carrying a couple himself in order to blend into the crowd, and had sung along with a drunk local as they went through passport control.

The night train to Stockholm left at 22.07, precisely on time. He slept like a stone until 03.30.

He had reached the little village of Äng. He pedalled on, quickly and silently, not wanting to be seen. The whole place was sleeping.

Then he turned off to the right, in among the trees, up the hill. The tree-trunks closed around him, making him invisible again. The road was worse, harder to cycle on, he fell twice. Eventually he saw the track leading off to the left and stopped, suddenly aware how worn out he was. His legs were trembling from the exertion, his hands looked like they had frostbite, and he realized his nose was streaming. He rested for a moment, leaning over the bike and panting for breath. Then he threw the bastard contraption in among the trees to rust, and walked with long strides up the hard, dry snow towards the garage.

There, the rust-red gable. His heartbeat quickened. What if something had gone wrong, what would he do then?

He fumbled with trembling fingers along the back wall, imagining that it was gone and getting close to panicking. But it was still there, the key was where he had left it.

He strode round and unlocked the doors, forcing them open. He had to use his shoulder to push aside the thin layer of snow outside. He stopped and looked at the car. It wasn't much to boast about, a two-door Fiat Uno from 1987. He fished out the tax-disc he had taken from a truck in Malmö. The registration number didn't match, but no one would notice unless they looked closely.

Okay, this was it.

He walked round the car, felt the top of the right front wheel and found the keys. He unlocked, got in, turned the key.

The engine turned over, whined, coughed, died.

He swallowed nervously.

He turned it again, it coughed, caught, and started. He breathed out, all of a sudden aware that he was sweating in spite of the cold. He revved the engine a few times inside the garage, letting the engine and the oil warm up.

While the car was slowly thawing out, he leaned over and opened the glove compartment, searching for the little brass key. It, too, was still there.

He closed his eyes and relaxed, feeling himself getting calmer.

The money was still safe. It was in a safety deposit box in the cellar of the SEB bank in Stockholm's Gamla stan. He'd never planned to use it for his own purposes, it had been put aside for unexpected expenses incurred by the tobacco business. But they only had themselves to blame. They had left him out in the cold, so they would have to pay.

He couldn't understand why they had cut him off so completely. That bastard missing shipment may have been worth a lot of money, but that didn't explain the total severance of ties by his superiors. Even an arrest warrant from the war crimes tribunal wouldn't normally have that sort of consequence. There were plenty of men suspected of war crimes who enjoyed a perfectly good reputation in Serbia.

This was something else. He couldn't put his finger on what. Maybe someone was actively trying to get rid of him, someone who wanted to get their hands on his power and influence.

They can never replace me, he thought. *No one else has my experience, my contacts.*

He revved again, the engine roared, the car was starting to get warm.

Apart from the money, he had several other items of unfinished business in Stockholm. The shipment may be long gone, but he didn't like leaving loose ends.

Slowly he let the car roll out into the night.

47

Advent stars were hanging crookedly in the windows of the hospitality flat opposite. A woman from the construction firm had been clambering around in there on Friday, trying to get it sorted out. Annika stared at the straw stars as they swayed gently in the heat rising from the radiators. She was amazed at the human capacity for wasting time and energy on pointless things like Christmas decorations.

She went and lay down again, staring at the wall, concentrating on the pattern showing through the thin layer of whitewash. The rest of the building was deserted, apart from the unemployed rock-musician on the ground floor. She closed her eyes, feeling the bass-line throb in the walls.

This can't go on, she thought. *I can't go on like this.*

She rolled over onto her back and stared up at the ceiling, watching the cobwebs sway in the breeze from the broken window in the living room. She followed the cracks with her eyes, seeing the butterfly in the pattern, then the car and the skull. With the insistent hum of loneliness in her left ear, she rolled onto her side again and put the pillow over her head. It didn't help, she couldn't escape, ever, she could never hide. Despair washed over her and she huddled up into a tight little ball. Her head fell back and she heard the sound coming, her own sound, uncontrollable sobbing. She recognized it, wasn't remotely alarmed, just let it rip into her; she knew it would end, because her body couldn't keep it up for ever.

Afterwards she felt tired and thirsty, sore from the exertion. The backache was worst, it never seemed to improve, and the constant tension in her gut. She lay there for a while, panting, heavy, her tears drying on her cheeks.

I wonder what the neighbours think. They probably think I'm going mad.

She got up, dizzy, and felt her way along the walls to the kitchen. The straw stars swayed. The tap dripped. The fridge was empty.

She sat down at the kitchen table, collapsing with her arms out across the cold tabletop, her head in her hands, staring at Grandma's brass candelabra. It had been a wedding present when Sofia Katarina and Arvid got married, it had stood on the dresser in Lyckebo all these years.

Annika closed her eyes. Grandma was gone. She had almost no recollection of the funeral, just her despair, tears, helplessness. There had been a lot of people there, staring, whispering, reproachful glances.

Ashes to ashes, dust to dust . . .

She got up and went over to the sofa in the living room. A cloud of dust flew up as she sat down. She looked at the phone. Birgitta had called after the funeral, to ask why she had been so mean to their mother.

'Aren't you ever going to stop?' Annika had screamed. 'How long are you going to punish me just because somebody loved me? When will you be happy? When I'm dead?'

'You're mad,' Birgitta had said. 'What everyone says is true. Poor you.'

Grandma had very few possessions, but what little there was naturally led to arguments. Annika had asked for the candelabra. She didn't care about anything else.

She pulled up her legs and rocked gently back and forth. The window with its paper-bag covering rose and fell.

Thomas hadn't called. Not once. That night had never happened, that intoxicating feeling was a memory of a dream. She cried, silently, over the love that never was, rocking and rocking. Monday 5 November, that was their day, their night, it had vanished twenty-eight days ago. She was a month older. It was twenty-seven days since Grandma died, and she was now twenty-seven days more lonely. She wondered how long she would keep count, a year since Grandma died, two years, seven years since she was left alone.

The ache in her stomach never seemed to go, the ache in her back nagged at her. She stopped rocking and stared at the table. The flat had swallowed her, she had been inside it for four weeks, alone almost all of the time. The doctor in Katrineholm had given her a sick-note for the rest of the year. Anne Snapphane had come up a couple of times a week, bringing food, a video and a ghetto blaster.

'It belongs to the production company,' she had explained. 'I've borrowed it.'

The silence and emptiness now had competition from rented videos and Jim Steinman and Andrew Lloyd-Webber on the stereo.

She had wanted him. She had had him for one night, twenty-eight days ago. Soon she would no longer be able to remember it.

Her gut ached, a familiar feeling, her period had

started. She groaned and went into the bedroom to find a tampon.

The box was empty. She stood there holding it, thinking. Did she have any tampons anywhere else?

She went into the hall and pulled out her bag. The seals of the tampons had broken, and they were dusty and dirty. She sat down on the floor, suddenly dizzy, feeling sick. She checked her underwear.

Nothing. No period.

Twenty-eight days ago.

She gasped as a huge thought slowly took root. She picked up her pocket diary. Today was Oscar and Ossian's name-day, the moon was waning, Christmas Eve was on a Monday this year.

She counted, trying to work it out. When? The weekend of the 20th, 21st October? She couldn't remember.

What if . . . ?

Her head felt empty. She stared at the diary, and her hand went to her stomach unconsciously, just below her navel.

It couldn't be true.

'Are you free?'

Anders Schyman looked up. Sjölander and Berit Hamrin were standing in the doorway. He gestured to them to come in.

'We're ready to run the Paradise story,' the head of crime said. 'Berit's been through everything Annika Bengtzon put together and added the last details. It's quite a story.'

Anders Schyman leaned back. Berit Hamrin put a bundle of papers on the desk.

'These are the suggested articles,' she said. 'You can take a proper look later. I've kept the woman in charge, Rebecka Björkstig, anonymous. Sjölander thinks we should go public with her name and picture, but I thought maybe we could discuss that once I've been through this with you.'

The head-editor waited as she arranged the articles into different piles.

'First there's the actual story,' she said. 'The details that Annika put together seem to be completely correct. There was a bit of fuss with the authorities in Nacka and Österåker, but since that bloke in Vaxholm decided to tell us everything he knew, the others agreed to talk.'

She picked up the first article and looked through it.

'So, the first day's articles,' she said: 'revelations about the Paradise Foundation, Rebecka's version of the story, proof of all the lies.'

'Who have we got quotes from?' Schyman asked.

'Mainly the bloke in Vaxholm, he's been extremely helpful. Thomas Samuelsson, finance officer for social services there. He's the one who comes out of this as the hero, if you like. He was beaten up and knocked unconscious when he tried to discuss an invoice with Rebecka.'

'Yes,' Schyman said, 'Annika told me about that. Has he reported it to the police?'

'Yep. Then there are people at the other authorities, they want to stay anonymous but are willing to confirm that Paradise didn't do what it was supposed to.'

'How much did they pay out?'

'One of them 955,000 kronor, and the other 1,274,000, split into two different payments. Vaxholm refused to pay, their client was already dead when the invoice arrived.'

The head-editor whistled.

'You know this part of the story pretty well already,' Berit said. 'It's the rest we're not so sure about.'

Berit picked up another article.

'Rebecka Björkstig may be guilty of conspiracy to murder,' she said.

Schyman's jaw dropped.

'What the hell . . . ?'

Berit handed him the article.

'The woman who was killed in Sergels torg about a month ago, you remember? She was one of Paradise's clients.'

'Seriously?' Schyman said.

The reporter nodded.

'The woman, Aida Begovic, was threatening to uncover the fraud to her local council. Rebecka made a threat against her, which was, in itself, nothing unusual. It looks as though she'd done it before. All the women who turned to the foundation realized pretty quickly that they weren't going to get any help. And obviously a lot of them were angry and upset about it. The people involved in the cases from Österåker and Nacka both said they were going to tell their social workers.'

'How did they end up with Paradise?' Schyman wondered.

'In both cases it started when they met Rebecka together with someone from their social services department. They were all told the same wonderful story, and the really odd thing is that they all fell for it. Once the first payment had been received, the clients were taken out to Paradise's property in Järfälla. At that point Rebecka would get hold of all their documentation, read through it and check that she had all the details, then she drove them out.'

'The clients?'

Berit nodded, her lips pursed.

'One of the cases we're featuring consisted of a single mother and her two children, and the other a woman with three children. Rebecka threatened her: "I know who's after you, and if you breathe a word to your council I'll make sure he knows where you are."'

'Bloody hell,' Schyman said.

'And Aida died,' Sjölander said. 'There's a witness who says that Rebecka made threats against her, and the next day she was dead.'

'What do the police say?'

Berit picked up the third article.

'I've just spoken to them. Their financial crimes unit has been after Rebecka for some time, but this new information means that she's now under suspicion for a lot more criminal activity, all of it more serious. The police want to get hold of her as soon as possible, so we have to publish quickly.'

'Okay,' Schyman said. 'The first day we have the organization itself, the bluffs and threats. What have we got on day two?'

Berit looked through the articles.

'The threatened women's stories. Annika wrote the main piece before she went off sick, about a woman called Maria Eriksson. I've got the two other cases and their stories. But we'll have to be prepared for more people contacting us once we've started printing the first articles.'

Schyman made some notes.

'Good, let's make sure we're ready. Day three?'

'Reactions,' Berit said. 'I've got a few already, from a professor of criminal law, a doctor of social psychology, and the head of the National Organization of Women's Shelters. I'm working on a response from the police, and I'm going to try the Minister for Health and Social Affairs and the Justice Minister. We can probably count on several other local authorities reporting cases to the police.'

'What does she have to say for herself?' Schyman said.

'Rebecka Björkstig says that everything we've got is nothing but vicious slander. She can't understand why anyone would want to say such awful things about her. Her organization is still at a very early stage, admittedly, but any suggestion that she's lying or has threatened anyone is a complete falsehood.'

'And we can prove that isn't the case?' Schyman said. 'Is she threatening to sue if we publish anything?'

The reporter sighed. 'Oh, yes. She's given a figure for the amount she wants in damages as well: thirty million.'

Anders Schyman smiled.

'She can't sue us if we don't print her name or picture. If she can't be identified, then no public damage has occurred.'

'I think we should publish her name and picture anyway,' Sjölander said. 'She needs to find out what it's like to end up in the shit.'

Schyman looked at the head of crime with a neutral expression.

'And when did this newspaper become an instrument of punishment?' he wondered. 'Rebecka Björkstig isn't a well-known public figure. Naturally, we'll describe what she's done and the way she keeps changing her identity, we'll lift the lid on her murky finances and unsettling threats. But the story doesn't get any better if you know exactly what her name is, at least not yet.'

'It's just weak not to publish everything you've got,' Sjölander said. 'Why should we pay the bitch any consideration?'

Anders Schyman leaned forward.

'Because we work *for* the truth,' he said, 'not *against* the criminal. Because we have an ethical and public responsibility, because we have the power and the duty to define reality for people living in this society. We are not supposed to use our power to crush any specific individuals, whether they be politicians, criminals or celebrities. Ending up in the paper doesn't mean the same as ending up in the shit.'

Sjölander's cheeks flushed slightly and Anders Schyman realized there was no great danger here. Sjölander was good at being reprimanded. He'd already worked that out.

'Okay,' he said. 'It's your decision.'

The head-editor leaned back again.

'No,' he said, 'it isn't. It's Torstensson.'

The three of them looked at each other for a moment, then burst out laughing simultaneously. Torstensson, what a joke.

'Anything else?' Schyman asked.

'Well,' Sjölander said with a sigh, 'it's all a bit too quiet. It's been a while since anything happened. We're wondering about dragging out the Palme murder again. Nils Langeby has had a new tip-off.'

The head-editor frowned.

'Keep a close eye on Langeby's tip-offs, I don't trust them. What happened with that story about the Yugoslavian mafia out in Frihamnen?'

'It ran into the sand. The bloke they suspected, Ratko, has probably fled the country.'

'So did he actually do it?'

The head of crime shuffled on his chair, remembering his earlier categorical statements.

'Not sure,' he said. 'Ratko may never have been convicted of murder, but he's a really nasty character. Bank robberies, threats, beatings, and, more than anything else, he's acted as a heavy. His speciality was scaring the life out of people, getting them to talk. He sticks a sub-machine gun in someone's mouth, and they usually talk.'

'And then there are the war crimes,' Berit reminded him.

'It must have become pretty hard for him to move between countries,' Anders Schyman said.

The man's arrest warrant had been issued by the war crimes tribunal in The Hague at lunchtime on Tuesday 6 November: he was suspected of crimes against humanity during the early phase of hostilities in Bosnia.

'He'll probably end up drinking himself to death in some Belgrade suburb,' Sjölander said.

Schyman sighed. 'What about the woman in Sergels torg? Are they any closer to catching her killer?'

Berit and Sjölander shook their heads.

'She's being buried tomorrow,' Berit said. 'Bloody awful story.'

'Okay,' Schyman said. 'I'll go through the article – if you don't hear anything from me, then you've got a green light.'

48

Annika was leafing through an old copy of *Parenthood* from two years ago. She'd read three issues of *Amelia*, two leaflets about Aids, and yesterday's *Metro*. She didn't want to go home, didn't want to be alone. She said she'd rather sit in the waiting room until the result came through. The midwives looked at her a bit strangely, but didn't say anything.

Time seemed to exist outside her, as if she were looking on as it swept past. She couldn't imagine what her reaction to the result was going to be.

Once she had thought she was pregnant with Sven. It was towards the end of their relationship, when she was already looking for a way out. She'd been terribly worried: a child would have been a disaster. The test result had been negative, but she still hadn't felt relieved. To this day she couldn't understand the disappointment she had felt, the sense of emptiness.

'Annika Bengtzon?'

Her heart leaped into her throat and she gulped. She got up and followed the white coat over to a desk further inside the maternity clinic.

'The result is positive,' the woman said slowly and carefully. 'It means that you're pregnant. When did you last have your period?'

Her head lurched. *Pregnant, with child, bloody hell, a child . . .*

'I can't remember, around the twentieth of October, I think.'

Her mouth was dry.

The nurse fiddled with a small electronic gadget.

'That means you're in the seventh week of pregnancy. We count from the first day of the last period. So it's still very early days. Are you thinking of going through with the pregnancy?'

The floor swayed and she held on to the counter.

'I . . . I don't know.'

'If you decide to terminate the pregnancy, it's better to do it sooner rather than later. If you want to keep the baby we should book you an appointment to see a midwife here at the clinic. It usually takes about an hour. The same midwife would follow you right through your pregnancy. You live on Kungsholmen?'

'There's no doubt at all?' Annika said. 'That I'm pregnant, I mean? It couldn't be a mistake?'

The woman smiled. 'You're pregnant. Guaranteed.'

Annika turned away and headed towards the door. Her back was aching like hell. What if she had a miscarriage?

'A miscarriage,' she said, turning back towards the counter again. 'How common is that?'

'Fairly common,' the midwife said. 'The risk is greatest up to twelve weeks. But we'll talk about all that at your first appointment, if you decide to keep the baby. Phone and let us know when you've made up your mind.'

She went out into the stairwell and walked down the wide staircase of the old Serafimer Lasarettet hospital. These days it was her local health centre. Her general practitioner. The maternity clinic for her and her child.

Her child.

Her stomach seemed to lurch and jolt as her feet hit the steps.

As long as I don't miscarry. As long as nothing happens to the baby.

She gasped. Bloody hell, she was going to have a baby, with Thomas. A feeling of happiness overwhelmed her, from the inside out. A baby! A little baby, a reason to live!

She walked over to the wall, leaned against it and wept, tears of relief, light and gentle.

A baby, her little baby.

She walked out into the dusk, it had never got properly light today. The clouds drifted in dark-grey veils across the sky. It would soon be snowing again. She walked home carefully, not wanting to slip over, not wanting to harm the baby.

Up in the flat it was pretty cold, and she turned the radiators on. She lit all the lamps, then sat on the sofa with the phone in her lap.

She ought to call at once, before he went home from work. She didn't want to get hold of Eleonor again. Her heart was thudding, what on earth was she going to say?

I'm pregnant.

We're going to have a baby.

You're going to be a dad.

She shut her eyes, took several deep breaths, trying to slow her heartbeat, then dialled the number.

Her voice sounded shaky when she asked the receptionist to put her through to him. The noise in her head increased and her hands were shaking.

'Thomas Samuelsson,' he said.

She couldn't breathe, couldn't speak.

'Hello?' he said, sounding annoyed.

'Hello,' she said, in the smallest voice in the world. 'It's me.'

Her heart was racing and she was panting for breath. He didn't say anything.

'Annika Bengtzon,' she said. 'It's me, Annika.'

'Don't call me here,' he said, his voice short, restrained.

She gasped.

'What do you mean?'

'Please,' he said, 'just leave me alone. Don't call this number again, please.'

The click as he hung up echoed round her head as the conversation abruptly ended, leaving her listening to emptiness on the line, and the emptiness she herself was feeling.

She put the phone down, her hands shaking so hard that she had trouble replacing it properly. Her palms were dripping. She began to cry. Oh God, he didn't want her, he didn't want their child. *Oh God, help . . .*

The phone rang furiously in her lap, and the shock jolted her out of her misery. He was phoning back, at least he was phoning back.

She grabbed the receiver.

'Annika? Hi, it's Berit at the paper. I thought I should let you know that we're running your piece on the Paradise Foundation tomorrow . . . What's the matter?'

She was sobbing down the phone, so hard that she was making it wet.

'But whatever's happened, you poor thing?' Berit said anxiously.

She took a deep breath, forcing herself to stop crying.

'Nothing,' she said, wiping her nose with the back of her hand. 'I'm just a bit low. Sorry.'

'Don't apologize; I know how close you were to your grandmother. I just wanted to let you know that we're publishing your articles.'

Annika put her hand over her nose and mouth to hide the sound of her sobbing.

'Great,' she said. 'That's good.'

'The worst thing is what happened to Aida. I can't stop thinking about it,' Berit said. 'Her funeral's tomorrow, poor woman. She had no relatives, no one's asked for the body, so it'll just be a short service up at the Northern Cemetery—'

'Sorry, Berit, but I've got to go,' Annika said.

'Hang on,' her colleague said. 'How are you really? Do you need any help?'

'No, no,' Annika said, 'everything's fine.'

'You promise to call if you need to talk?'

'Of course,' she said quietly.

She put the phone down again, heavy, hot.

He didn't want her. He didn't want their child.

There didn't seem to be a single free parking space on the whole of Kungsholmen. Thomas had been driving round for twenty minutes in vain. Not that it mattered. He wasn't here for an appointment, he was just driving round aimlessly. Scheelegatan, right onto Hantverkargatan, slowly past number 32, up the hill, into Bergsgatan, past the police headquarters, down along Kungsholmsgatan, and back where he started.

He'd done the right thing, the only decent thing. Eleonor was his wife, and he believed in the vows he had made, in trust, responsibility.

Even so, hearing her voice on the phone today . . . He had lost his grip, and reacted in a way he wouldn't have believed, so physical, so hard. Carrying on with work was impossible. He had hurried out of the Town Hall, jogging down to the water. It was windy, starting to snow, he could hear her voice, remember her body.

376

Oh God, what had he done? Why was his memory so remorseless, so reliable?

He had stood in the wind until his hair and coat were wet with spray and snow, consumed by a sad little voice. Then he had walked slowly towards his empty house, Eleonor was off on her management course. He had got in the car and headed into the city, without reflection, not wanting to think, just driving.

I'm going to get a bite to eat, he told himself. *I'm going to sit in a bar with the evening papers and a beer.*

A bar on Kungsholmen.

He wasn't going to contact her. He would keep his distance. He just wanted to see how it could be, what that life would feel like, what sort of people he might see, what sort of food he would be able to get.

What he had done to Eleonor was unforgivable. His shame had burned on his face for the whole of the first week, he'd had to make a real effort to act normal, walk normally, make love normally. Eleonor hadn't noticed anything, or had she?

He had dreamed of Annika at night to start with, but recently her memory had started to fade, until today. He hit the steering wheel with his palm. Damn it, why did she have to phone? Why couldn't she just leave him alone? It was hard enough as it was.

All of a sudden he realized he was on the verge of bursting into tears. He clenched his teeth, and accelerated up the street. He really did need some food. He turned into Agnegatan and parked illegally. What the hell . . .

He locked the car with a bleep. This was her block. He stood and looked up at the crumbling façade. It should have been renovated twenty years ago.

Maybe she was home. Maybe she was up in her flat

on the third floor, her white, flowing rooms, maybe reading a book, watching television.

The thought made his mouth go dry, his pulse race.

A lamp was shining dully in the passageway to the courtyard. The gate was open, the way was clear. As easy as that. He slowly walked towards the building, seeing the things she saw every day, the graffiti on the wall, the crumbling plaster.

What if she came out? He halted abruptly, she mustn't see him. He stopped at the end of the passageway and looked up.

Two windows lit up, the one on the right with a paper bag in its frame, her flat. She was home.

Then he saw her. She walked past the window, picking something up from the window sill, the one on the left. For a moment he saw her as a black silhouette against the light room, her hair, her slender body, her graceful hands, then she turned away again and the light went out.

Maybe she was on her way out.

He turned on his heel and ran back to his car, jumped in and drove off without properly taking off the handbrake. Only then did he realize that his pulse was racing.

He was never going to see her again.

Tuesday 4 December

49

Annika tried to avoid looking at the billboard. It seemed an even brighter yellow than usual, screaming out, the headline loud enough to threaten a new world war: '*Evening Post* Exclusive: the Paradise that Betrayed Vulnerable Women!'

She hurried past, didn't want to take it in, clutching her coat tighter, her purse in her hand. She was freezing. She jogged up the steps into the shop. The man behind the counter hadn't unwrapped the papers yet, and she tore at the plastic to get a copy.

On the front page was a picture of a woman, taken with a hidden camera from a distance. Probably Rebecka, but her hair and face were pixellated. Annika squinted her eyes, and the picture became clearer but the woman was still unidentifiable.

She weighed the paper in her hand, how light it was, how little all her effort really meant. She folded it up and put it in her basket, she'd read it properly when she got home. She went and got some yogurt and bread, cheese and sausages, paid, put the paper under her arm and walked out. It was clear and cold, the sun was on its way up over the horizon. She hurried back along Hantverkargatan, slipping, her heart thudding, she couldn't help it. Paradise was still her story, after all.

She put the bag of groceries down on the hall floor, took out the paper and went and sat on the sofa. She looked at the front page again. It referred readers to pages 6, 7, 8, 9, 10 and 11. The hairs on the back of her neck were standing up. Talk about going for broke.

She quickly leafed past the editorial and culture pages. The first double-page spread was about the organization, Rebecka's story about how Paradise worked. There were more hidden camera shots of Rebecka and several other people, probably her family. Annika thought she could make out the Paradise building in Olovslund in the background, but the pictures could really have been taken anywhere. She read the articles carefully. They were written by Berit, but based entirely on her original material. The articles had a double byline, both her and Berit's names.

She looked at her own name for a long while, trying to work out what she felt. Pride, maybe. Some fear, too, because this would have consequences. A certain distance, as well – she didn't feel close enough to absorb it all properly.

She sighed and turned the page. And gasped.

Thomas Samuelsson stared out at her from a black-and-white photograph on page eight. It was taken in his office in the Town Hall in Vaxholm, she recognized the bookcase behind him. The headline announced that he had uncovered the scam. Berit's text made mincemeat of Rebecka's arguments, uncovering her lies, debts, changes of identity. Thomas Samuelsson appeared as the hero who had crushed the criminal organization. He had a scar on his forehead, and the caption explained that the finance officer had been beaten up and knocked unconscious when he tried to stop an attempt at extortion. Several other officials were quoted, anonymously, but they confirmed that Paradise was a scam. They had paid very large amounts of money to Rebecka, in total more than two million kronor.

She gave up reading, unable to carry on, just wanted to stare at the picture, at him. He looked serious, determined, his hair had fallen forward. His jacket was done up, his tie perfectly knotted, his hand resting on his desk, his strong, warm hand.

Something caught in her throat, oh God, he was so handsome, she had almost forgotten what he looked like, tears ran from her eyes as she wept over the newspaper.

'We're going to have a baby,' she whispered to the picture. 'A little boy. I know it's a boy, but you don't want us. You want your beautifully knotted tie and your job in finance and your expensive villa on the coast.'

She ran her finger over the picture, following the line of his chin and stroking his hair.

I can't give birth to him if you don't want him.

She pushed the paper away and cried helplessly. When she was too exhausted to cry any more, she picked up the phone and rang Södermalm hospital. She got an appointment that same morning.

Ratko was out in good time. He had checked the area thoroughly the day before, walking around with a rake and pretending to tend to the graves. No one had paid him any attention in his dark, anonymous clothing. His Fiat Uno was parked on Banvaktsvägen, next to a large hole in the fence. He guessed it had been made by cyclists so they had a short-cut through the cemetery. In the boot of the car was a sports bag holding a tennis racket and some sports gear. Beneath them lay the money and his heavier weaponry.

He felt nervous and uncertain. He wondered if he was starting to go mad, to lose his grip?

He walked towards the main entrance on Linvävar-vägen. The headstones here were older and bigger, most of them from the first decade of the twentieth century, men with titles, surrounded by their families. The place tried to give an impression of peace and tranquillity, which was difficult with a motorway thundering past just fifty metres away. He leaned on his rake and looked out at the wintry scene, with its clipped box hedges and huge, naked oak trees, its knotted pines and black wrought iron railings. It was certainly different from the war graves in Bosnia. He leaned against the fence, sighing, remembering his time in the UDBA, the Yugoslavian security service, in the 1970s, all the opposition politicians they had shut up, Germany, Italy, Spain, the bank robberies, the years in prison.

Never again, he thought, sighing, freezing.

He walked slowly towards the North Chapel, as big as a church, newly restored, its brown-glazed roof-tiles glittering in the sun. The building sat on a hill at the far end of the cemetery, and behind it a vast pale-blue ghetto of housing blocks rose up, Hagalundsgatan, Blåkulla. He skirted round a clump of trees and emerged at the flat western corner, section 14E. He stopped at the edge of the trees and looked at the hole, Aida's final resting-place. A leafless hedge separated her grave from the road. On the other side lay a petrol station and a drive-through McDonald's. He turned away, taking his rake with him, and headed off towards the Jewish section.

The funeral service was due to start at two o'clock that afternoon – he had phoned to check – and that was still several hours away. Was he barking up the wrong tree here? Was he imagining things? Had he finally managed to conjure up some ghosts of his own? Had his superiors' reaction really been anything more than might have been expected? And what could any of it possibly have to do with Aida from Bijeljina?

To be honest, he didn't care. The only thing that interested him was his own future. He wanted to know what arena he was playing in, what the conditions were, he wanted to be able to identify his enemies. Aida could help him to do that posthumously.

He lit a cigarette. Inhaled deeply several times, feeling the air fill his lungs and send nicotine to his brain. This wretched country really was cold.

If everything went the way it should, he would never have to come here again. He could leave this fucking country behind him, with his laundry washed, hanging up and dry.

'Thomas! You're in the paper!'

The social worker who had been in charge of Aida Begovic's case came bouncing out of her office in what could loosely be described as a jog. Her cheeks were red and her forehead shiny, she had a silly grin on her face and was eagerly waving the early edition of the *Evening Post*.

Thomas forced himself to smile back.

'I know,' he said.

'It says here that you—'

'I know!'

He went into his room, shutting the door hard behind him. He couldn't bear it. He sank onto his chair and leaned his head in his hands. This morning he had hardly been able to drag himself to work. The council had passed the budget, the quarterly reports were finished, he had succeeded, they were ready in time. And now it was time to start again, for the eighth successive year. And each time there was less money, larger costs, staff cuts, the people affected going to the press, angry, desperate, sad, resigned. The number of long-term sick went up, the resources for their rehabilitation went down.

He sighed and stretched, and his eyes fell on the open newspaper, and her name. He had read the articles in advance, but hadn't been aware that she had written them. Another woman had called him, an older reporter, Berit Hamrin. Why hadn't Annika called?

Irritated, he brushed the thought aside. He didn't want her to call. He smoothed out the paper in front of him. The picture of him was awful, his hair was over his face, he looked a mess. He read the articles again, Annika's articles, he recognized her information, she really had told him everything, she had been honest.

There was a knock at his door and he instinctively folded the paper and put it in the top drawer of his desk.

'Can I come in?'

It was his boss. He swallowed.

'Of course. Sit down.'

The woman looked at him thoughtfully as she walked over to the chair on the other side of his desk, the chair where Annika had sat. He felt a shiver of anxiety. He had talked about the articles with her, what he was going to say and not say. She hadn't read the articles, but there shouldn't be anything that she was unhappy with.

'I know you've been having a tough time,' his boss said, 'but I want you to know that we truly appreciate what you do here.'

She sounded friendly, serious. She was looking directly at him. He lowered his gaze to stare at a document on his desk.

'I'm extremely happy with your work here. I know you've had a bit of a rough time lately, but I hope things will get better now that work on the budget is complete. If you ever feel the need to talk to anyone, you can always come to me.'

He looked up at her, unable to conceal his surprise. It was her turn to look away.

'I just wanted you to know that,' she said, getting up.

Thomas stood up as well, muttering his thanks.

When the woman had shut the door behind her he sank back onto his chair, astonished. *What was all that about?*

That moment the phone rang, making him jump.

'Thomas Samuelsson?'

It was one of the directors of the Swedish Association of Local Authorities. Christ, what did they want with him? He stretched out automatically behind the desk.

'You probably don't remember me, but we met at the social work seminar on Långholmen last year.'

He remembered the conference, a dull affair that had dragged on for three days. The director, however, had passed him by completely.

'Your name has cropped up in conversation here a few times since then, and then we saw you in today's paper and realized that you're exactly the right man for us.'

Thomas cleared his throat and made a vaguely curious noise.

'We're looking for a project manager to lead an investigation into the differences in the social payments made by the various local authorities. It doesn't have to be a full-time commitment. If you wanted to do it part time, we estimate that it would take approximately a year. Are you interested?'

He closed his eyes, speechless, and pushed his hair back. He was overwhelmed. Working in the middle of the city, managing an investigation. Bloody hell, this was exactly what he'd dreamed of.

'Yes, yes I am,' he managed to say. 'It sounds like a very interesting, and very worthwhile, project.'

He tried to stop himself sounding too enthusiastic.

'I'd be happy to discuss terms and conditions,' he said, slightly more subdued.

'Excellent! Can you come in on Thursday?'

When he had hung up he stared into space for a minute. The job offer was tingling through him like a spring stream. What an opportunity! His smile burst out from deep inside. This explained his boss's peculiar visit, she must have had a call about this beforehand.

They had seen his name in the paper.

He opened his desk drawer and pulled it out again, read her name, breathed out.

He would forget her. It would all get better. He just had to stay focused.

He had made the right decision.

50

Annika gasped involuntarily for breath: the bluish gel was ice-cold as it landed on her stomach. The woman in the white coat was fiddling with a large spatula at the end of a long lead as Annika looked on, wide-eyed.

'The gel is so we get a good image on the ultrasound,' the doctor said.

Annika was lying on a pale-green couch. The woman sitting beside her placed the spatula in the gunk on her stomach and started moving it around. She gasped for breath again, God, it was cold. Then the spatula headed south, towards her crotch. The edge of her underwear got sticky blue gel on it. The doctor turned a dial next to a small grey television-screen, and white lines wriggled like worms across the screen. Then she stopped.

'There,' she said, pointing.

Annika struggled to sit up and stared at the screen. There was a little white ring in the top-right corner.

'There's the pregnancy,' the woman said, twisting the dial.

Annika was looking in disbelief at the object as it shifted position, turned round, appeared to swim.

Her child. Thomas's child. She gulped.

'I want an abortion,' she said.

The gynaecologist removed the spatula from her

stomach, the picture died, the little swimming bubble vanished. The nurse passed Annika a length of coarse green crêpe paper to wipe her stomach with.

'I'd like to take a quick look as well,' the doctor said, handing the spatula to the nurse to be cleaned. 'Could you move over to this chair, please?'

Her voice was efficient, in a friendly but disinterested way. Annika stiffened.

'Do I really need an . . . examination?' she asked.

'We're already behind schedule,' the nurse said quietly.

The doctor sighed.

'Please, sit up here.'

Annika pulled off her trousers and underwear and obediently pulled herself onto the gynaecologist's chair, the torture instrument, and the doctor took up position between her legs, pulling on a pair of gloves.

'Can you just slide down a bit more. A bit more. More! And relax.'

Annika took a deep breath and closed her eyes as the doctor pushed her fingers into her vagina.

'Relax, or it'll hurt.'

She clenched her eyes tight shut as the doctor squeezed and felt her stomach, one hand outside, the other inside. Pain. Nausea.

'You have a backwards womb,' she said. 'It's unusual, but it's not dangerous.'

She pulled off her gloves. Annika heard a squelching noise and felt embarrassed.

'Okay, you can get dressed. Then come through to see me.'

The doctor threw the gloves in a bin and walked quickly into the next room. Annika tried clumsily to get her legs down from a position slightly above her ears, feeling exposed and disgusting. There was something sticky between her legs, but she didn't dare ask for something to wipe it off with. She quickly pulled on her pants and jeans. The whole bottom half of her stomach felt sticky. She followed the nurse into the next room.

'You're in week seven of your pregnancy,' the doctor said. 'You said you wanted an abortion?'

Annika nodded, swallowed hard, cleared her throat, sat down.

'You can see a counsellor, if you'd like to?'

She shook her head. Her hands felt too big and she hid them between her thighs.

'Well, then. We can book you in for Friday, the seventh of December. Is that okay for you?'

No, she thought. *Now! Friday's three days away, I can't do it, I just can't. I can't have the baby inside me for another three days, I don't want to feel the weight, I don't want to feel sick, or have swelling breasts and another life beating inside me.*

'So, shall we say the seventh?' the doctor repeated, looking at her over the top of her glasses.

Annika nodded.

'Get here at seven in the morning. You mustn't have anything to eat or drink after midnight, because you'll be given a mild sedative. First we need to dilate your cervix, then you'll be sedated. We'll be using a method known as vacuum aspiration, which means that the cervix is dilated and the contents of the uterus removed by suction. It takes about fifteen minutes, and you'll be able to go home that afternoon. Afterwards you shouldn't have intercourse for two weeks, because of the risk of infection. Any questions?'

Fifteen minutes, contents sucked out.

No, no questions.

'Well then, we'll see you back here on Friday.'

And then she was out in the long, grey corridor again. She bumped into a young woman on her way into the examination room, they avoided looking at each other, and she heard the doctor saying hello. Her sea-sickness had returned, along with the nausea, the backache. She had to get out.

The number 48 bus rocked and swayed. Annika was on the point of throwing up all over the floor. She staggered off at Kungsholmstorg and made her way quickly to number 32 Hantverkargatan. She stood for a minute in the courtyard, trying not to be sick, before struggling up the stairs to her flat.

The bag of groceries was still sitting in the hall where she had left it, but she didn't care. She sank onto the sofa and stared into space.

A little bubble, a little white ring.

She knew it was a boy, a little blond boy, just like Thomas. She shut her eyes, cried, tore the cartoon page out of the paper and blew her nose on it. She turned to the articles about Paradise again and read through the text on the last double-page spread. Rebecka was wanted by the police, suspected of conspiracy to murder. She had made threats against a client, Aida Begovic, who had been killed in Sergels torg the following day. The young woman was being buried at two o'clock that afternoon.

She let the paper fall, failure gnawing at her. She leaned forward, her stomach ached, the little bubble was swimming around, her heart-rate increased, as she rocked and rocked. She heard Berit's voice from the phone-call yesterday: *she had no relatives, no one's asked for the body, so it'll just be a short service up at the* Northern Cemetery . . .

No one should be that abandoned, Annika thought. *Everyone deserves to have someone say goodbye to them.*

She shut her eyes and leaned back in the sofa.

Three more days with the baby inside her.

She looked at her watch. If she set off now, she would just make it to Aida's funeral.

There were people sitting inside.

Annika stopped in the doorway, suddenly unsure, and looked around discreetly. Several women and a young man sitting on the bench at the back turned to look at her.

At the front was a small coffin, shiny and white, with three red roses on the lid.

She gulped, feeling sick and nervous, and took a few steps, pulling off her jacket and settling onto an empty bench towards the back. She had forgotten to bring any flowers, and her hands suddenly felt very empty.

The silence was oppressive, the light gentle. It streamed in through the leaded windows under the dome, forming coloured fragments on the walls and floor. The sun struck the walls, making the yellow paint glow.

There was a sound of low muttering and Annika tried to glance at her fellow mourners without anyone noticing. Most were women, about half looked Swedish, the others presumably from the former Yugoslavia. There were maybe twelve, fourteen of them in total, and they were all carrying flowers.

Her surprise over their presence drifted into annoyance.

Where were they all when Aida needed help? It was all very well showing up now that it was too late.

The bell began to ring somewhere above her head. The solemn, ominous sound filtered down to the scantly populated benches, running through her body like an electric current. She felt tears start to well up.

The bell died away, leaving an echoing silence. There were sniffs and coughs, the sound of prayer-books rustling. Someone switched on a CD-player and she recognized the first notes of Mozart's Requiem. Her tears took over as the music filled her, the slow opening bars composed by the dying Wolfgang Amadeus.

The music faded, and a man in a dark grey suit, the officiating minister, went over and stood behind the coffin. He talked, probably about life and death, platitudes. After a minute or so she shut her eyes, hearing his words but letting them flow over her like music. Sunset is the most beautiful time of day, heaven is a place of boundless love, then music again. Ulf Lundell's *Öppna landskap*, with its line about being happiest in open landscapes. Which made her cross again.

What fucking open landscapes? Sergels torg may just about qualify as an open bloody landscape, but it seemed pretty unlikely that Aida was happiest there. Who the hell chose this music?

Annika wiped her tears, still annoyed. Everyone seemed to be crying. She looked at the minister, at his dutifully bowed head in the front row. What did he know about Aida? He didn't have a single personal thing to say about her, because he'd never even met her.

She closed her eyes and tried to remember Aida. She could see her in front of her, ill, scared, hunted.

Who were you? Annika thought. *Why did you die?*

The man in the suit was talking again, melodically, a poem by Edith Södergran. Then one of the women in the front row stood up and sang, alone, in a clear, pure voice. Annika couldn't understand a word. Serbo-Croat. The notes took flight, swirling round the roof, alive and growing. The sorrow rising within the chapel was suddenly completely genuine, tortuous and grief-stricken: why, why?

Annika was sobbing into her hands, her sadness heavy in her chest, tangible and guilty.

We're doing this for our own sakes, she thought, not for Aida's. She wouldn't have given a damn.

Then a hymn she recognized, that they had played at Grandma's funeral. *Beautiful is the earth, Beautiful is God's heaven, Let us go to Paradise singing.* She bowed her head and clenched her lips together.

Silence filled the room and she felt she couldn't breathe. The church-bells started to toll again, it was over. Aida was on her way out, erased. Suddenly she wanted to protest, stop the men who were going over to pick up the coffin, who were carrying it past her on their shoulders, scarcely a metre from her. *I'm not finished with her! I have to know!* Annika stood up, feeling sick, and waited until the other mourners had passed her, aware that they were stealing glances at her, then walked out last of all.

The cold hit her, clear and fresh. The sunlight was making the snow sparkle. The men were putting the coffin on a trolley. She watched as the other mourners gathered on the steps and along the path, wiping their noses, muttering.

They all knew Aida. They all had some sort of relationship to her. They all know more than me.

She walked slowly over to a woman who was standing several steps below her.

'Excuse me,' Annika said, introducing herself. 'I don't really know anyone here. How did you know Aida?'

The woman gave her a friendly smile and wiped her eyes with a tissue.

'I'm the manager of the refugee centre where Aida lived when she first arrived in Sweden.'

They shook hands. They both took a deep breath, smiling awkwardly.

'I'm a journalist,' Annika said. 'I came because I thought Aida was so isolated.'

The manager nodded.

'She was very isolated. A lot of people tried to get close to her, but she was a very difficult person to reach. I think she chose her own isolation.'

Annika swallowed hard. It was bloody easy to blame Aida for that, especially now she was dead.

'What about everyone here?' Annika said. 'If she didn't really have any friends, who are these people?'

The woman looked at her in surprise.

'They're refugees from the centre. They got to know Aida there, she used to come and visit sometimes. I recognize her neighbour in Vaxholm, and the representatives from the Bosnian Cultural Association. The singer was from there; wasn't it beautiful?'

'Couldn't anyone have helped her?' Annika asked. 'Did she really have no one to turn to?'

The manager looked at Annika sadly.

'You didn't know her terribly well, did you?'

The men had finished putting the coffin on the trolley and it started its slow journey to the grave. The woman headed over towards the others and Annika went with her.

'That's true,' Annika said quietly. 'I didn't know her well. I met her a few days before she died. When did she arrive in Sweden?'

The manager looked at Annika over her shoulder, hesitating.

'Towards the end of the war,' she whispered. 'She had several gunshot wounds, bits of shrapnel everywhere, she was in a terrible state. Flashbacks, the shakes, night sweats, and a very shaky grasp on reality. She was drinking a lot. We did all we could to help her – doctors, counsellors, psychologists. I don't think it made much difference. Aida was carrying some terrible demons within her.'

Annika opened her eyes wide.

'What do you mean?'

Another woman came over to the manager and whispered something, and they went over to one of the women from the refugee centre who was collapsing into floods of tears. Annika looked around in confusion, slipped on a patch of ice and came close to falling. She was feeling sick. The trolley crunched over the cold ground. The coffin slid away among the trees, in among the shadows, out of reach. She suppressed an urge to run after it and bang on the lid.

What demons were you carrying? What did they do to you?

51

The grave was disquieting, lost in darkness and cold. Why did they always dig so deep? Annika leaned forward cautiously and stared into the ground, seeing her own shadow disappear in the depths. She quickly stepped back.

The coffin was resting beside the grave on some planks. The mourners had gathered round, all of them red-eyed. The minister was talking again, and Annika was so cold she was shaking, eager to get away. Aida wasn't in the coffin, Aida wasn't there, Aida had already slid away among her demons and secrets.

From the corner of her eye she saw something heading towards them, two large black cars, tinted glass, blue number-plates. They braked and stopped, and the engines cut out. Annika looked on in surprise.

Suddenly all the doors opened at once, and five, six, seven men got out. The minister stopped talking, all the mourners looked at each other in confusion. The men in the cars were wearing grey coats, looking round, staring intently at the mourners.

Then an old man detached himself from the group. Annika stared at him, open-mouthed. He was wearing military uniform, his walk was heavy and stooped, his face closed, his eyes focused on the coffin. His uniform was lavishly decorated, and he was holding a small paper bag in his hand. The other mourners made way for him. Annika was standing on the other side of the grave and watched, astonished, as the old man fell to his knees, took off his cap and began to mutter incomprehensibly. His hair was grey and thin, a bald patch glinting underneath. He knelt there praying for a long while, breathing heavily.

Annika couldn't stop staring, listening intently to his broken voice.

Finally he got up with an effort, put one hand in the bag and pulled out something that he scattered on the coffin. Soil! A handful of soil!

The muttering grew louder. Annika listened, entranced. Another handful of soil, more words, sad, heavy, measured, a third handful, and the words faded away. The man put the bag back in his pocket and brushed his hands.

You know all about Aida, Annika thought. You *know what her demons were.*

She rushed round the grave. The man was walking away, back to the cars and the other men. She grabbed hold of one of his sleeves.

'Please, sir!'

He stopped, surprised, and looked at her over his shoulder.

'Who are you?' she asked in English. 'How did you know Aida?'

The man stared at her, tried to pull free of her grasp.

'I'm a journalist,' Annika said. 'I met Aida a few days before she died. Who are you?'

The men in dark-grey coats were suddenly all around them, between her and the officer. They seemed upset, asked the man something, the same thing several times. The old man waved them off with his hand, turned his back on her and they glided off towards the cars, a mass of grey. They got inside, the cars started up and rolled off through the trees.

Annika stared after them, sweating and pale.

She had understood one word the man had muttered at the grave, just one. He had repeated it several times, she was sure of that.

Bijeljina.

The women took a step closer to the grave, one by one, said something and laid their flowers on the coffin. Annika felt panic rising, she had no flowers, she had nothing to say, apart from sorry: sorry I let you down, sorry I lured you towards your death.

She turned away, stumbled, had to get away, couldn't stay by the grave.

The old man must have been very close to Aida, maybe he was her father.

What if, she suddenly thought, *what if he knew what I did?*

I really was trying to help, she told herself. *I meant well.*

She walked towards the bus-stop, weaving slightly from guilt and shame. She felt ill, and wondered if she was going to be sick.

She had gone a couple of hundred metres beyond the gap in the fence when someone put their hand over her mouth.

Her first thought was that the men in the grey coats had come back to get her. The old soldier wanted to set things straight.

'I have a pistol aimed at your spine,' the man snarled. 'Now start walking.'

Annika stood frozen to the pavement, with Ratko at her shoulder.

He thrust a hand up into her hair and yanked her head back.

'Forward!'

I'm going to die, she thought. *I'm going to die.*

'Walk, for fuck's sake, bitch!'

She shut her eyes, breathless with terror, and started to stumble slowly along the street. She could feel the man breathing at her neck. He stank. After ten metres or so he stopped.

'Into the car,' he said.

She looked round, her neck stiff, her scalp stinging. *Which car?*

He hit her across the face and she felt something warm trickle from her mouth. Suddenly her head was completely clear, she knew what this was, she was used to being beaten up, she could handle this.

'And if I refuse?' she said, as she felt her lip swelling already.

He hit her again.

'Then I'll shoot you on the spot,' he said.

She stared up into his face, red with cold, shadowed with tiredness. She felt her breathing speed up, faster, shallower. Her vision started to flicker, she couldn't, she wouldn't.

'Okay,' she said.

Something happened to the man, he pulled out a rope, pressed her against the car closest to them, a small blue car. He twisted her arms behind her and tied her hands together. Then pressed the cold barrel of a pistol to the nape of her neck.

'You know what happened to Aida.'

She shut her eyes, then her defence mechanism kicked in. She felt nothing, turned everything inwards, shut off.

Have to do what he says.

'Now get in, for fuck's sake.'

401

Ratko tore the door of the blue car open and she tumbled into the back seat, petrified. She saw the man go round the car, start it up, drive off. She stared at the back of his head, it was red, he had dandruff on the dark shoulders of his jacket. She felt shut off from reality, as if there was a perspex screen between her and the rest of the world. She looked out at the houses rushing past, no people, no one who cared.

'I've got the gun in my lap,' Ratko said. 'I'll shoot you if you try anything.'

The sun was going down, the day was red and cold. Blåkulla swirled past. The Solna road, cars, people, no one she could call out to, no one who could help. She was stuck in the back seat of a dirty little car, sitting on her hands. They were aching. She tried to move to take the weight off them.

The man at the wheel spun round, glancing at her over his shoulder.

'Sit still, for fuck's sake.'

She froze mid-gesture.

'I'm very uncomfortable.'

'Shut up!'

The northern link road towards Norrtull, Sveaplan, Cedersdalsgatan. The traffic rushed around her, thousands of people, yet still so alone, always alone.

She shut her eyes, seeing Aida's coffin in front of her, the old man bent over, hearing his muttering.

Maybe it's my turn now.

They ground to a halt in a traffic-jam at Roslagstull, and she could see right into the car next to them, a mother and a small child. She stared at the woman, trying to catch her eye. Eventually the woman realized she was being watched and turned to look at her. Annika opened her eyes wide and silently mouthed the words: *Help! Help me!*

The woman quickly looked away.

No! she thought. *Look at me! Help me!*

'Help!' she screamed, banging her head against the window. 'Help me! Help me!'

The blows echoed through her head, and she soon felt dizzy. The window was hard and cold.

Ratko stiffened but didn't move, just kept the car moving in the queue heading for the Roslagen road.

Annika took a deep breath and screamed as loudly as she could: 'He's kidnapped me, help me! Help!'

The other cars glided past her, one by one, passing her at just a metre's distance, but a thousand years away. She was alone. She yelled and shrieked, thrashing against the roof, making herself sweaty, giddy, hoarse. She threw herself against the window, screaming, bashing her head against the glass. A man in a new Volvo caught her eye, looking at her in concern. Ratko turned to the man, shrugged and smiled. The man smiled back at Ratko.

Annika stopped. She was panting for breath, staring derision in the face.

There was no point. The people around her were too busy with their own lives. How were they supposed to deal with a screaming madwoman in another car?

She fell quiet, her head aching from all the blows, and started to cry. Ratko said nothing. They emerged from Roslagstull, drove past the Museum of Natural History. They turned off at Albano. Annika let her tears fall. *It's over now. Who would have guessed it would end like this?*

The car headed along a load of narrow roads, she caught sight of signs saying Björnnäsvägen, Fiskartorpsvägen, woods, trees.

Finally the car stopped. Annika stared ahead of her. In front of them was an old shack. Ratko walked round the car and got something out of the boot, then opened the passenger door and slid the front seat forward.

'Get out,' he said.

She did as he said. Her throat was sore.

'What do you want with me?' she asked hoarsely.

'Inside the shack,' the man said.

He gave her a shove and she stumbled off, feeling sick, ready to faint.

It was dark inside the wooden shack. The last of the daylight failed to seep through the gaps between the planks, leaving the logs and cobwebs in darkness and shadow.

Ratko pushed her down onto a chopping block in one corner. Annika felt terror rising up her spine, the walls were swaying and lurching. He tied a rope around the block and bound her feet. Then he leaned forward and snarled in her ear, his voice harsh and low.

'I ask the questions,' he said, 'and you answer. There's no point acting tough, everyone talks sooner or later. You'll save yourself a lot of pain if you answer sooner.'

She was breathing quickly, feeling panic rising. Ratko grabbed his sports bag and rummaged around the bottom, pulling out a sub-machine gun. He stood in front of her, stretching himself up to his full height, the gun right in front of her face.

'The shipment,' he said. 'Where is it?'

She gulped, took a deep breath, then another, then gulped again.

'The shipment!' he screamed. 'Where the fuck is it?'

She started to shake all over. She closed her eyes, losing the ability to talk.

'*Where?*'

She felt the barrel of the gun pressed against her forehead, and started crying with panic.

'I don't know!' she stammered. 'I only met Aida once!'

He pulled the gun away and hit her hard in the face.

'Don't talk crap,' he said, grabbing her necklace. 'You've got Aida's gold necklace.'

She trembled, tears running down her cheeks and onto her neck.

'She gave it to me,' she whispered.

She sat quietly, unable to think, paralysed by fear. The man let go of the necklace and said nothing for a while. She could feel him staring at her.

'Who are you?' he asked in a low voice.

She took a deep breath.

'I'm . . . a journalist. Aida called the paper where I work. She needed help. I met her in a hotel room. Then you turned up and . . . I tricked you. Then I gave Aida a number to call, to some people who could help her to—'

'Why did you trick me?'

The question tore her breathless explanation apart.

'I wanted to save Aida,' she whispered.

She felt the man move, and his face appeared right in front of her.

'Who was the man at the funeral?' he asked, his eyes flaring.

Annika stared at him blankly.

'Who?'

'The officer,' he shouted, 'you stupid fucking bitch! Who the fuck was the officer?'

She closed her eyes tight, feeling his saliva on her face.

'I don't know,' she whispered, her eyes screwed shut.

'So what the hell were you doing talking to him?'

She gasped for breath.

'That's . . . that's just what I asked him, who he was . . . how he knew Aida.'

'What did he say?'

She was trembling, didn't reply.

'*What did he say?*'

'I don't know,' Annika sobbed. 'He said the word Bijeljina when he was standing by the grave, Bijeljina, Bijeljina, I'm sure that's what he said . . .'

It was several seconds before she realized that Ratko had gone quiet.

'Bijeljina?' he said suspiciously. 'Her hometown?'

Annika gulped and nodded. 'I think so.'

'What else?'

'I don't understand Serbo-Croat.'

'What did the guard-dogs say?'

She looked up at him in surprise.

'What dogs?'

He waved the gun in front of her face.

'The security, the RDB officers from the embassy, the grey-coats! What did they say?'

She searched her memory.

'I don't know! Nothing I could understand.'

'I don't care if you didn't understand! What did they say?'

He put the barrel of the gun to her forehead again and she slumped, shut her eyes, panting for breath.

'If you can't talk,' Ratko said, 'you don't need your jaw, do you?'

He moved the gun to her mouth, knocking against her teeth, and she felt the taste of metal, cold, darkness seeping through her brain. She lurched.

'What did the guard-dogs say? Are you going to tell me or not?'

Darkness, cold; did she have her eyes shut or had the day died completely?

'For the last time, what did the guards say to the officer? Are you going to tell me?'

She nodded, slowly, the barrel moved, hitting her teeth again; she could breathe again, wanted to throw up.

406

'They said something several times,' she whispered. 'Porut . . . something. Porutsch . . . porutschn . . .'

'Porutschnick?' Ratko asked breathlessly.

'Maybe,' she whispered.

'What else? What else did they say?'

'I don't know . . .'

The gun pressed against her lips again.

'Mii,' she said. 'Miisch . . . miischitch.'

'Miischitch?'

The gun was removed and she nodded.

'That was it. They said miischitch.'

52

Ratko stared at the pathetic woman before him, feeling triumph physically rising in his trousers once more. Victory! Now he knew, he understood, the pattern resolved itself before his eyes in the dark shack.

Porutschnick Müschitch.

He quickly packed away his things and put the gun back in the bag. He left the rope, it was sold in iron-mongers all over Sweden and carried no fingerprints.

'I'll always know where to find you,' he said, his usual line to informants who talked. 'If you ever breathe a word about what happened here today, I'll kill you. Understand?'

She didn't appear to hear him. She was sitting slumped with her head between her knees.

'Understand?' he screamed in her ear. 'I'll kill you if you talk, get it?'

Her whole body was shaking, and he suddenly felt that he had had enough. He glanced at his watch, it was time to go.

'One word and you're dead. I'll put this gun in your mouth and splatter your brain halfway across Djurgården, okay?'

He opened the door, taking a last look at her. She wouldn't talk. And even if she did, so what? If they ever managed to get hold of him, there were far worse things than this to charge him with.

He went out into the winter night, letting go of the door behind him, breathing out.

Porutschnick Miischitch. Or Porucnik Misic, to be more accurate.

It had actually worked! He could hardly believe his luck.

He opened the back of the car, took the gun out of the sports bag and hid it under a filthy blanket in the boot.

Luck? he thought with a snort. *Skill! Start the interrogation with something you don't give a damn about, then, once they're softened up, you move onto what you really want to know.*

He got in the car and tossed the bag on the passenger seat. The car started obediently. He turned round and drove off towards Frihamnen.

Colonel Misic, a legend with the KOS, the Yugoslav Army's counter-espionage unit. A man who had survived all the purges, and a man who had Milosevic's ear.

Ratko turned the heater up. Soon he would be free of this cold for ever.

He didn't know how, but the man had obviously been close to Aida. When and why didn't bother him, he wasn't remotely interested in their relationship, but now he had his answer. He knew what had gone wrong in his own case, why he had been stripped of power.

Aida had had a protector, and she must have managed to get a message to him before she died.

He shrugged, and loosened his shoulders, he was tense and stiff. Aida Begovic from Bijeljina didn't matter any more, she could rot in her grave by that petrol station in Solna.

He turned off from Tegeluddsvägen, heading for the harbour. He saw the signs for Tallinn, Klaipeda, Riga,

St Petersburg. He found a space for the car, reserved, but who cared? He took out the sports bag containing his sports gear and cash. The wind from the Baltic hit him square in the face and he let out a deep breath.

The area between the various warehouses was bathed in the golden yellow of the floodlights. He could see the container park at the far end, near the sea.

This was where it started, he thought. *Or rather, this was where it ended*.

He glanced at his watch.

It was time.

As if from miles away, she heard a car start up and disappear. She could still taste metal in her mouth. She was leaning forward. It was getting cold, quiet, dark.

She was freezing. Her body felt numb, her thoughts paralysed. She was still sitting on the chopping block, on the verge of falling asleep, on the point of tumbling off. The cold grew harsher, she felt more and more drowsy.

How easy. How nice it would be to just drift off.

She untangled her feet from the block of wood, the rope wasn't tight, and lay down on the earth floor. Uncomfortable. She lay with her cheek to the floor, feeling her hands getting cold and numb. The insistent sound of loneliness started to buzz, rising and falling in her left ear.

Soon, she thought. Soon it'll be over. Soon it'll be quiet.

The thought made the sound vanish.

It would soon be over.

The realization brought her back to her senses. The ground beneath her cheek was frozen and gritty, and smelled bad. She was lying on one arm, and it had gone numb below the elbow.

She groaned.

If she lay here in the dark it would soon be very quiet indeed.

She tried to get up, leaning against the chopping block. The cold was going right through her jeans, and her senses were starting to give up.

What if he came back?

The thought made her breathe faster, then she calmed down again.

She started to cry again from exhaustion.

I want to go home, she thought. *I want to go home. I've got sausages for tea.*

She cried for a while, racked with sobbing and the cold.

I have to get out of here.

She struggled to her feet, the rope scratching her wrists. It wasn't particularly tight; she twisted her hands for a couple of minutes, then managed to free her left hand and the rope fell away. She stood there in the solid darkness, searching for any chinks of light that could tell her where the door was. Nothing.

What if he'd locked it?

She stumbled over to the wall and felt her way along the planks, getting splinters in her fingers. Then the wall gave way and the door slid open. The wind took it, a chill blast from the sea. Outside she glimpsed trees and a narrow track.

God, where am I?

She leaned against the doorpost, shut her eyes, rubbed her forehead.

They had driven along Roslagsvägen, and turned off the motorway just before the university. So she was somewhere in Norra Djurgården, not far from Stora Skuggan. She rubbed her eyes. They were dry and red.

The 56 bus, she thought. That runs from Stora Skuggan to Kungsholmen.

411

She stumbled out; she could just make out a road at the end of the slope. She stopped and looked up at the sky. Down to the right it was brighter, the horizon shimmering yellowish pink.

That's not the sun, she thought. *It's the city.* And she started walking.

Wednesday 5 December

53

The eleven o'clock meeting began ten minutes late, as usual. Anders Schyman could feel himself getting annoyed. He was struck once again by a thought that had occurred to him with increasing regularity recently.

When I'm in charge, I'm going to make sure we stick to schedule.

He had just sat down and got the Blue Cock Parade to shut up. The lead columnist and the heads of entertainment, social affairs, sport and pictures were sitting waiting when Torstensson knocked on the door.

Schyman raised his eyebrows, the editor-in-chief was rarely present at the daily run-through and planning meeting.

'Welcome,' the head-editor said, a little too sarcastically. 'We've just started.'

Torstensson looked around, bewildered, for a free chair.

'In the corner,' Schyman said, pointing.

The editor-in-chief cleared his throat and remained standing.

'I've got something important to tell you,' he said, his voice slightly too shrill.

Anders Schyman made no attempt to get up and offer his place at the end of the long table.

'Please, take a seat,' he said, gesturing to the spare seat at the far end of the table once more.

Torstensson slunk off, scraped his chair, sat down. The silence was deafening as they all stared at the little man. He cleared his throat again.

'My position in Brussels has been postponed indefinitely,' he said. 'The party secretary has just informed me that the question of freedom of information is no longer a priority. As a result, there's no longer any question of me leaving the paper for the time being.'

He fell silent, bitterness hanging in the air. The lead columnist made a sympathetic noise. The others glanced at the head-editor.

Anders Schyman was sitting still, glued to his chair, not a thought in his head. He hadn't made any contingency plans for this. The possibility that the party would withdraw the editor-in-chief's exit strategy hadn't occurred to him.

'I see,' he said, his voice neutral. 'So, shall we get going?'

They started shuffling through their papers, looking at print-outs and pictures. There was contented murmuring, unhappy grumbling. Torstensson remained in his seat, empty-handed.

'Pelle,' Schyman said, 'can you hold up the pictures we've got of our fraudster?'

The picture editor held up several shots that had been taken in Järfälla that morning. They showed Rebecka Björkstig in handcuffs alongside three policemen, heading towards a police car.

'Torstensson,' Anders Schyman said, 'what do you think about going public with her identity now?'

The editor-in-chief blinked. 'Sorry?'

'Printing her name and picture,' the head-editor said. 'Do you think we should risk being sued for defamation of character in the case of Rebecka Björkstig?'

'Why?' Torstensson said, bewildered.

I'm a bad man, Anders Schyman thought. *I'm perfectly aware of how little the editor-in-chief knows, and I'm making a laughing stock of him.*

'We can't run it on the front page tomorrow anyway,' Schyman said amiably, 'so what do you think, Torstensson?'

'Why can't we run it on the front page?' the editor-in-chief asked.

Schyman allowed the silence to speak for itself, letting the full situation filter into the brains of the Blue Cock Parade. They all knew why you couldn't run the same story on the front page for three days in a row. Sales always went down on the third day, no matter how good the story was. Changing the front page on day three was fairly elementary stuff. And they all knew, apart from the editor-in-chief.

'It's a damn good picture,' Schyman said. 'I suggest we run it across the page, tightly cropped, still pixellated. We'll stick with anonymity, unless anyone has a different opinion?'

He looked at the editor-in-chief, who shook his head.

'Okay,' he said, 'so what have we got for the front instead?'

The whole of the Blue Cock Parade started rustling energetically, keen that something from their own departments should get the front page.

'How to make money on the new Telia share issue,' said the financial editor.

The others made disparaging remarks about his suggestion.

'I don't see anyone doing somersaults of joy,' Schyman said. 'What else?'

'We've found another politician buying private shopping on his party card,' Ingvar Johansson suggested.

They all groaned, every politician did that. If they could find a politician who didn't do it, then maybe they'd have a story.

'The local council has withdrawn funding for a carer for a mentally handicapped kid in Motala,' the head of news went on. 'The boy's being looked after by a single mum on benefits. The mother called us in floods of tears, saying she couldn't stand it any longer. The only question is whether we want to run with a story like that when we've only just had something similar.'

'There's a loose connection to the Paradise story,' Schyman said. 'We can keep an eye on it until we've run the rest of those articles. Anything else?'

'We should keep an eye on the JAS fighter-plane trials,' the social affairs editor said. 'You never know, another one may fall out of the sky on top of us.'

This woke them up. JAS trials? Where? When?

'They're starting trials at lunchtime today,' the social affairs editor explained. 'They've shipped in a load of potential foreign buyers to watch, and then there are the uninvited guests who are here to spy on it.'

'We'll have to look into that,' Schyman said. 'But whether or not it makes the paper depends on what we find. No recycled material. What else?'

'We're running an item on the new presenter of *Sofa Talk*,' the head of entertainment said. 'Some girl called Michelle Carlsson. Gorgeous.'

Enthusiastic response.

'Big tits?'

'Do you reckon she'd be up for a bit of body-painting?'

'Do we know what this year's must-have Christmas

418

present is?' Schyman asked thoughtfully. 'Or if Disney are thinking of cutting any classic moments from *Donald Duck* on Christmas Eve?'

Frowns. They all remembered the fuss when *Ferdinand the Bull* was cut. A hubbub of unfocused chat broke out, and Schyman let them talk. He looked at the editor-in-chief at the far end of the table, his forehead shiny with sweat. He was completely out of the loop.

The thought returned: *I'm a bad man.*

But on the other hand, he thought, *at least I know what I'm doing. Is it really any sort of kindness to let incompetence win? Should I really let Torstensson sink this paper, throwing several hundred people out of their jobs and removing an important voice in the media?*

'What do you think, Torstensson?' he asked gently. 'What do you think we should go with?'

The editor-in-chief stood up.

'I have a meeting to prepare for,' he said, pushing his chair back and walking out.

When the door clicked shut Anders Schyman shrugged demonstratively.

'Okay,' he said. 'Where were we?'

54

Annika got out of bed, cold and unable to think. She went out to the kitchen, still with the bitter, burnt taste of metal in her mouth. She brushed her teeth, harder and harder. She poured a bowl of yogurt and ate it, but it made her retch. She sat at the table for a while, staring at her grandmother's candelabra.

She had only vague and hazy memories of getting home the previous evening. She had walked from the wooden shack to the road, she didn't know long it had taken, but it wasn't long. She had emerged at the back of a 4H youth club, and had found a bus-stop. She had almost fallen asleep waiting for the bus, then it had turned up, the number 56. The people on the bus had been completely normal, no one had paid her any particular attention, no one had noticed that she was branded, marked out for death.

The night had been splintered by nightmares, she had woken to the sound of her own screams. The men from *Studio Six* had been trying to strangle her. She was having trouble breathing and got up from the kitchen table. The walls were collapsing in on her as she made her way into the living room. Her legs gave way and she slumped to the floor, wrapping her arms round her shins. Her breathing got shallower and harder, as if she were cramping. She lay there exhausted, aching all over and unable to get up. She fell asleep, only waking up when the phone rang. She didn't answer.

She climbed onto the sofa and shut her eyes. The white coffin danced in front of her eyes, the old officer's muttering echoed in her ears, the taste of metal jarred in her mouth.

She took several deep breaths, the walls rose and fell. *This will pass, it will pass.* She went into the kitchen. Grandma's brass candelabra sparkled, she drank water, lots of water, trying to get rid of the taste of metal, crying. She opened the kitchen cupboards, stared at the box of pills again, twenty-five foil-packed 15mg doses of Oxazepam. She could hear the doctor's voice: *You can't overdose on them, but don't take them with alcohol, that can make them dangerous.*

She took the blister-packs out of the box and pressed the plastic, making the pills jump around in their little hollows. Holding the pack over a mug, she popped the pills out one by one, every one, until she had a small collection of pills at the bottom of the mug.

She sniffed. Nothing. She tasted one. Bitter. She swirled them round in the mug, shut her eyes, felt the pressure building across her chest. She took a deep breath, gasped, and tears began to fall, trickling down her neck.

Don't take them with alcohol.

She put the mug on the draining board, went out into the hall and pulled on her shoes. Wiping her tears, she went downstairs, clutching the handrail. Sticking close to the buildings along Agnegatan and Garvargatan, she made her way to the rear entrance of the off-licence on Kungsholmstorg. It was almost empty, just a few old dears and a group of tramps. She picked up a copy of the previous day's *Evening Post* from one of the benches, and stood with her back to everyone else, her eyes stubbornly refusing to decipher the black headlines. She was trembling and stammering when her number was called, and the sales assistant looked at her suspiciously. She bought a large bottle of vodka. She went home the same way, weaving along the narrow pavement, the plastic bag bumping against her leg, the newspaper clutched under her arm. She finally made it home, exhausted and frozen. She went into the kitchen and put the mug of pills, the paper and the bottle of vodka next to the candelabra on the kitchen table, then sat down and cried.

She didn't want to carry on. She couldn't do it. *Paradise's victims tell their stories, pages 8, 9, 10 and 11.*

She leaned forward and rested her head on her arms, closed her eyes, listened to the sound of her breathing. It was all over for Aida, she didn't have to fight any more.

Annika sat up, reached for the vodka and broke the seal.

There was no point putting it off any longer. She may as well get it over and done with.

Taking the pills in one hand and the vodka in the other, she closed her eyes. The glass bottle was colder than the porcelain mug.

There's nothing left now, she thought.

And opened her eyes.

Out of the frying-pan and into the fire. Mia Eriksson, one of the women deceived and exploited by Paradise talks exclusively to the *Evening Post* about the foundation's reign of terror. Her revelations continue today.

Annika hesitated, then went into the living room and sat on the sofa, taking the pills, vodka and newspaper with her.

Her article about Mia was on page eight, and on page nine Berit's interviews with the women from Nacka and Österåker. Pages ten and eleven featured quotes from other victims, evidently people who had contacted the paper since the articles started to appear.

She put the paper down and leaned back in the sofa. She was responsible for Aida's death; Rebecka had given away her whereabouts, but it was her fault that Rebecka had had the chance to do that. She put her hands over her eyes and the funeral replayed in her mind, the sunlight on the roof, happiest in open landscapes.

Porutschnick miischitch, porutschnick miischitch, porutschnick miischitch.

The phone rang again, but she still didn't answer, just waited for the noise to stop. The silence that followed was dense and oppressive. She sat up in the sofa, took the top off the bottle of vodka. Her stomach was churning, the baby. She swirled the pills in their mug, as self-pity throbbed inside her.

Oh God, she thought. *Everyone's got it so tough. Poor Aida, poor Mia.* She picked up the paper, flattened the page out and read her own words.

The man who was father to Mia's first child abused her, threatened her, stalked her, raped her. When Mia got married and had another child, his behaviour got even worse. He smashed every single window in their house. Attacked Mia's husband one dark night. Tried to run Mia and the children over with his car. Tried to cut his daughter's throat to stop her talking.

The authorities had been helpless. They had done what they could, but that wasn't much. They installed bars on the windows of the family home. They provided social workers to accompany Mia every time she went out. In the end the social services department had concluded that the family would have to go underground.

For two years they had moved around, staying in shabby motel rooms. They weren't able to tell anyone where they were. They were instructed never to go out. Not even Mia's parents knew if they were alive or dead. And now the courts had decided that the family wouldn't be able to live a normal life in Sweden for the foreseeable future. They would have to emigrate, the only question was where. Rebecka had claimed to have the solution, but they had gone from the frying-pan into the fire.

Annika lowered the paper to her lap and started to cry.

People were forced to live such terrible lives. Why should young girls be wounded in war and forced to flee all the way across Europe? Why didn't we accept our responsibility? Why did we leave those we love to die? Why couldn't Mia have a decent life? Why shouldn't she live a completely normal life, just like everyone else, with her husband and children and job and daily routines?

She got up and fetched a glass of water. Sank back with the article on her lap again.

Human problems ought to be limited to what sort of Christmas decorations you put in the window for Advent. Or whether you're going to visit your grandmother on Friday or Saturday, or try to get promoted at work, or live in a flat or buy a house. Mia would have loved problems like that, but she wasn't allowed to have them.

She stared at the article, her phrases, her own conclusions.

The right to a husband and children and a job and a normal life.

Not just for Mia and Aida, but for her as well.

She held her breath as the realization hit her. She stared at the mug of pills and the bottle of vodka, sitting absolutely still as clarity spread through her body.

She was the one who was giving up. She was the one surrendering, giving in, getting off before the ride was over, letting the world carry on without ever finding out how the story ended.

She could hear her mother's voice in her head: *You never see anything through. You always fail. You're weak and lazy, you're nothing but trouble!*

Annika put her hand to her cheek, still feeling the force of her mother's blow, twenty years later.

No, Mum, she thought, *you were wrong, it wasn't like that at all. Of course I would have seen things through, but I always saw so many steps ahead, thinking out new alternatives, that it made you angry, and you thought I was just lazy. Birgitta was never lazy.*

She was sitting quite still, she hadn't thought about her early childhood for years. Why now?

When you told us to draw a bird, Birgitta drew a bird, and I drew a forest full of birds and other animals, which made you angry, because I was doing it wrong, I never did as you said.

Other scenes came to mind, how angry her mother would get when they went skiing, or to the beach, or did the cleaning on a Saturday. Her mother always found a reason to start shouting at her. If she hurried the cleaning she was doing it badly, if she did it carefully she was taking too long. If she slipped backwards when they were skiing up a slope she was ruining their outing, if she skied too fast she was spoiling things, if she stayed with them she was in the way.

I could never do anything right, Annika thought, amazed at the thought, wondering where it had come from.

But it wasn't my fault.

The thought was physical, it made her fingertips tingle.

Her outbursts had nothing to do with her, they were her mother's problem. Her mother hadn't been able to handle her own life, and she had made Annika pay for it.

Annika was staring into space, slack-jawed. A veil had been pulled aside in front of her, revealing a landscape she never even knew existed. She could see cause and effect, consequences and contexts.

Her mother had never made the effort to love her. It was sad and painful, but she couldn't do anything about it. Her mother had done the best she could, she just hadn't succeeded very well. The question now was how long Annika was going to punish herself for that. When was she going to take responsibility for her own life, break the cycle of behaviour and grow up?

She could carry on letting Barbro decide how things were going to be, and meekly fulfil the role allocated to her: hopeless Annika who always spoiled things for other people, who was always in the way, who never succeeded at anything.

Her life was her own, and she had the right to achieve whatever she wanted. Who was going to stop her, apart from herself?

She burst out crying again. Not harsh tears, but warm, sad tears.

There was practically no security here these days. No one would believe that this had been a well-functioning society just ten years ago.

Ratko was walking quickly, with determined steps and his hands in his pockets. When the city had been called Leningrad there were no small-time gangsters, and whores could walk through the city centre in the middle of the night without having to consider that it might be dangerous. Nowadays everyone, including him, needed eyes in the back of their heads. No one seemed to have any control over the gangs, and pretty much anyone could roll in from the country and make a living out of murder and robbery.

Capitalism, he thought scornfully. *This just shows that it doesn't work.*

He tried to relax. Nevsky Prospect was still reasonably safe – the main roads usually were. Just two blocks along Mayakovskaya and he would be there.

The side street was darker, he could see figures flitting among the shadows, and he jogged across the street to avoid them, ashamed, aware that he was growing paranoid.

The door was locked and he pressed the entry-phone. The lock clicked open without him having to say anything, and he glanced up at the hidden security camera above the door.

The stairwell stank. On every landing were bins full of rubbish and filth. The paint was hanging off the walls, heaps of fallen plaster in the corners.

Some things haven't changed, he thought. *Why can't people ever keep things clean?*

The top floor of the building, no lift. The bell didn't work and he knocked gently on the shabby wooden door. It glided open soundlessly, the inside covered with a layer of reinforced steel.

'Ratko! You old devil, I heard they were after you!'

His old friend in the east had grown even fatter. They embraced and exchanged kisses.

'We must celebrate, get some drink!'

Several young men scampered about like rats with vodka and glasses and cigars. He followed his friend along the corridor with its worn flock wallpaper. The boards beneath the linoleum floor creaked. They walked into the room at the far end and sat down. When the drink had been delivered, his friend yelled at the rats to leave them in peace.

The door was closed and his friend poured two glasses. They drank, and moved on to business.

'I need money,' Ratko said quietly. 'I've got a big investment on the go.'

He told his friend about his plans, how his new business would be organized, the customers, contacts, partners.

His friend listened without interrupting, sitting with his legs stretched wide, his head bowed and the glass in his hand.

'I have seven million cash in Swedish kronor,' Ratko said. 'But, as you can understand, I need more to get this up and running. I have to find the right people.'

His friend emptied his glass and nodded.

'So what's in it for us?'

Ratko smiled. 'This market is in its infancy. It's going to grow like hell. It's all about getting in at the start.'

'The usual terms?'

'Of course,' Ratko said.

His friend sighed asthmatically. 'How are you going to get there?'

'Direct flight to Cape Town. My passport's hot, Norwegian, it cost a lot to get here, and even more to get out again. I have to leave tonight.'

His friend didn't respond, didn't move. They had another drink.

'How much do you need?'

Ratko smiled again.

Thursday 6 December

55

The Swedish Association of Local Authorities was based in a discreet location a couple of blocks from the big junction between Södermalm and Gamla stan, Slussen. Thomas stared for a moment at the austere, yellow-plastered façade, the seat of power. His career goal, or at least one of them. He took a deep breath. His hands felt clammy.

God, he was desperate to get this job.

The foyer was light and airy, a woman in a headset sat behind a glass screen. She looked busy. Thomas told her who he was, then sat down with his briefcase on a group of sofas beside the entrance. He tried to read the *Metro*, but couldn't concentrate.

'Thomas Samuelsson? Great to meet you!'

He stood up and tried to smile as the director headed towards him from the lifts. He shook Thomas's right hand in his, and patted him jovially on the shoulder with his left hand.

'It's great that you could pop in at such short notice. Have you been here before?'

The director didn't seem to expect an answer. He led Thomas up a flight of stairs, through a corridor, out into a courtyard, into a lift and up several storeys.

I'm never going to find my way out of this labyrinth, Thomas thought.

Doors floated past, closed, open, people everywhere, talking, debating, reading.

What do they all do? he thought, bemused.

Finally they reached the director's office, a fine room on the seventh floor, with a view of the rooftops along Hornsgatan. They sat down on opposite sides of a group of comfortable sofas. A woman glided in and then vanished again, leaving coffee, Danish pastries and biscuits behind her.

Thomas swallowed, and concentrated on looking relaxed.

'Social security payments cost local authorities more than twelve billion every year,' the director said, pouring coffee into two mugs bearing the association's logo. 'The cost keeps going up, while our politicians would like us to cut them.'

The director leaned back and blew on his coffee. Thomas looked into his inquisitive, intelligent eyes.

'The people who receive social security payments are always the lowest priority for local politicians,' the director went on. 'To be brutally honest, they're regarded as uninteresting parasites. More than two-thirds of all politicians believe that the demands placed on the recipients of social security benefits are too low. And this has had devastating consequences for our citizens. Please, help yourself, they're fresh today.'

Thomas obediently took a bite of one of the pastries, it was shockingly sweet.

'The County Administrative Boards have looked at the way social security actually worked in local authorities last year,' the director went on. 'They paint a very depressing picture. I believe we have to take these criticisms on board.'

The director handed a report to Thomas and he opened it and glanced through.

'In general terms, the public has a negative perception of social services, they are seen as cold and unsympathetic,' the director said. 'It's difficult to get an appointment to see a social worker. A lot of applications never get further than first contact, whether in person or on the phone: people are turned away simply by being told they don't have the right to any support. And because no formal decision has actually been taken, it can't even be challenged. This all amounts to an unacceptable breach of individual rights.'

Thomas leafed through the report.

'More and more people believe that the way social services behave is offensive,' the director went on. 'But this isn't the fault of the staff. Most social workers do as much as they can, but their workload has increased, and along with it the risk of them burning out or making mistakes. We simply can't allow this to continue.'

Thomas shut the report.

'To be honest,' the director said, 'I'm seriously worried. We have no control over increasing social segregation. Out in our local authorities we ought to have the opportunity to break negative and alarming trends, but we have neither the skills nor the resources to do so. I had a call this morning from a desperate woman in Motala. She's been looking after her handicapped son full time for the past ten years, living on social security benefits. The council withdrew support for the boy in October, and since then she's been looking after him alone, twenty-four hours a day. She couldn't stop crying. That sort of thing makes me feel completely powerless, and it simply shouldn't happen.'

The director rubbed his eyes. Thomas noted with

some surprise that the man's agitation was completely genuine.

'That has to be a breach of local authority law,' Thomas said. 'A decision of that sort can be appealed against, surely?'

'I tried to explain that,' the director said, 'but this poor woman doesn't even have the energy to get dressed any more. It would have been patronizing and inappropriate to go through the relevant legislation with her and explain the way an appeal would work. I called the emergency desk in Motala and told them about the woman's situation; they said they'd look into it.'

Thomas stared down at the report in his lap. God, some people had terrible lives.

'We have to coordinate our skills and our resources,' the director said. 'And this is where you come in. People applying for social security benefits are treated in very different ways, depending on where they live, how the local departments are organized, and which member of staff they see. What we need are clear guidelines, a common strategy for all local authorities. We have to arrange regular case conferences, and try to find ways for people to make appointments to see their social worker in person. And there has to be clear leadership, protocol set up for internal monitoring of cases, as well as proper procedures for efficient cooperation, both internally and externally. And there has to be unimpeachable documentation of every case.'

The director sighed, then smiled. 'Are you our man?'

Thomas smiled back.

'Definitely,' he said.

Annika got out of the shower, feeling sore from jogging. She had forgotten how much she loved running, how good it felt when your body was flying over the tarmac.

She shuffled across the courtyard in her dressing-gown and wellington boots, climbed up the stairs, her pulse racing.

She prepared a huge breakfast, made coffee, then sat down in the living room with the papers.

When she saw the front page of the *Evening Post* her brain started to buzz. Rebecka had been arrested, she'd been caught.

Paradise had been demoted from the most prominent place on the front page, but there was a reference to it above the title of the paper. With trembling hands Annika turned to pages six and seven. Rebecka, still anonymous, her head pixellated, was being led away by three policemen. Yes!

She stared at the picture, focusing on the details: Rebecka's light clothing, her neat boots, the overgrown bushes behind her. It had to be the house in Olovslund. She got more coffee, then sat with the phone in her lap, hesitating. Then she dialled the direct number of her contact in police headquarters.

'Bloody hell,' Q said. 'Long time no hear.'

Annika smiled.

'Have you had a chance to talk to my friend Rebecka Björkstig?'

'She really loves you,' the officer said. 'You certainly know how to make friends with people.'

Annika stopped smiling.

'What do you mean?'

'If everything you've written in the paper is true, maybe you should start taking extra care,' he said. 'You're pretty much the only person who really went public about what Rebecka was doing.'

'I thought she had other things on her mind right now,' Annika said. 'Like talking to you, for instance.'

'For instance,' Q said. 'What do you want?'

'Is she guilty?'

'Of what? Debts, changes of identity, ripping off local councils? Yes, definitely, in so far as that's criminal. Conspiracy to murder? I'm not as sure about that as you are.'

'Do you know if any part of her organization actually worked?'

'Yes, in one case: she managed to erase herself. She's no fool. The question is whether she actually meant well, or was consciously guilty of criminal activity.'

'But all the changes of identity? That's pretty dodgy, isn't it?'

'You reckon? First she took her mother's maiden name and changed her first name, then she came up with an entirely new surname. Things like that happen every day.'

They fell silent.

'Anything else?' he asked.

'The murders in Frihamnen,' Annika said. 'Have you got any closer to solving them?'

A deep sigh down the line.

'The answer to that is no,' Q said. 'We're still not completely sure. It's got something to do with the Yugoslavian mafia and the missing load of cigarettes, but we don't know how it all fits together. It isn't the usual smuggling story, there's something else underneath that, and we just don't know what.'

Annika took a deep breath.

'Has it got anything to do with Aida Begovic?'

Q was quiet.

'Probably,' he said tersely.

'Has it got anything to do with Rebecka Björkstig?'

'We're looking into the possibility.'

'She said she was once threatened by the Yugoslavian mafia. Is there any truth to that?'

The officer sighed.

'Look,' he said, 'the Yugoslavian mafia does a hell of a lot of things that no one knows anything about, but they also get the blame for a lot of things they haven't actually done. Björkstig has trotted out the story of the threat against her to us as well, and evidently someone she owed money to, name of Andersson, tried to scare her with his mafia contacts.'

'So there's no connection between Rebecka and the Serbs?'

'*Nyet.*'

Annika shut her eyes, hesitating.

'Ratko?' she said. 'The leader of the tobacco mafia, do you know where he is at the moment?'

'In Serbia, probably, the only place in Europe where he can feel relatively safe. He couldn't move around freely anywhere else.'

'Could he be in Sweden?'

'It would have to be a very short and surreptitious visit, if he was. Why do you ask?'

She swallowed hard, thinking, the metallic taste still in her mouth.

'By the way,' she said, 'what does *porutschn . . . porutschnick miischitch* mean?'

'What?' the detective said.

'*Porutschnick miischitch*? It's Serbo-Croat. I think.'

'Sorry,' Q said, 'but I'm afraid I'm not fluent in every last one of the world's languages.'

'This is important,' Annika said. 'Do you know anyone who would know?'

He groaned.

'We have interpreters here,' he said. 'How important?'

'Very.'

There was a thud in Annika's ear as the policeman put the phone down, and she could hear his steps as he walked out of the room. She heard a distant 'Nikola!' and 'What the hell does *porutschnick miischitch* mean?'

The steps came back.

'It's a rank and surname,' he said. '*Porucnik* means colonel, and *Misic* is a fairly common surname.'

'Oh shit,' Annika said.

'What? Okay, now I'm curious.'

'A man turned up at Aida's funeral yesterday, he had loads of decorations and medals on his uniform.'

'Really?' Q said. 'Probably some old relative. And?'

'He arrived in embassy cars. Doesn't that seem a bit weird?'

'He's probably here for the JAS trials, just like a whole load of other fairly shady characters. What did the decorations look like?'

Annika thought hard.

'Leaves,' she said.

'Leaves?'

'Yes, sort of like leaves. And loads of medals.'

'Did you see what it said on any of them?'

She closed her eyes and sighed.

'One of them said Santa something on it, I think.'

Q whistled.

'Are you sure?'

'Of course I'm not. What do you think, that I've got some sort of photographic memory?'

'He could be from the KOS,' Q said. 'Although they've pretty much been wiped out.'

She lay back on the sofa, looking up at the ceiling.

'What's the KOS? What are you talking about?'

'Well, for you it's probably just a holiday island, isn't it? KOS was the Yugoslav military's counter-espionage unit. Milosevic has more or less dismantled the entire organization. During the past fifteen years there's been one mighty power struggle between the KOS and the

RDB, and the KOS lost. There's a hell of a lot of bitterness hidden away in those old soldiers.'

'RDB?' Annika said, confused.

'Slobodan's boys, the security police, the elite of the elite. They're in charge of both the criminals and the police in Serbia. Tough guys.'

Annika absorbed this information for a few seconds.

'Sorry,' she said, 'but what the hell did you used to do before you ended up in violent crime?'

'That's classified,' he said in English. She could almost hear him grinning.

'So where would a KOS colonel stay if he was in Stockholm for the JAS trials?'

'If he likes the RDB boys at the embassy, he'd stay there. If not, he'd be at one of the big hotels in the city.'

'Such as . . . ?'

'I'd start with the Royal Viking.'

'Love you forever!' Annika said.

'God help me!' he said, and hung up.

56

Colonel Misic was staying at the Sergel Plaza. Annika stood outside his room for several minutes, her hand raised ready to knock. Her pulse was galloping. Finally she knocked on the wooden door. She heard a questioning '*Da*?' from within, and knocked again.

The door opened just a crack.

'*Da*?'

She could just make out the old face, unshaven, a hairy shoulder, a vest.

'Colonel Misic? My name is Annika Bengtzon. I'd very much like to talk to you.'

She tried to smile, but was too nervous.

The man looked at her, he was in shadow, she couldn't quite make out the expression on his face.

'Why?' he asked in a gravelly voice.

'I knew Aida,' she said, her voice too high, too nervous.

He didn't reply, but nor did he shut the door.

'I saw you at the funeral,' she said. 'I spoke to you.'

The man hesitated. Then, 'What do you want?'

'Just to talk,' she said quickly. 'I want to talk to someone who knew Aida from before.'

The old colonel took a step back and opened the door. He was barefoot, and had evidently just pulled on his trousers, his braces were dangling by his knees.

'Go in and sit down,' he said. 'I'll put a shirt on.'

Annika found herself in a small room with two narrow beds, a television, mini-bar, desk and one chrome-legged chair. The man had disappeared into the bathroom and for a moment she was seized with panic.

What if he comes out with a machine gun? Or a knife?

Maybe he was the one who killed Aida!

Her heart started racing even faster and she was on the point of running back out into the corridor when the man came out of the bathroom in an unbuttoned white shirt, carrying a pair of socks in one hand.

'How well did you know Aida?' he asked in broken English.

Annika lowered her eyes. 'Not very well.' She looked up and met the old man's hooded eyes. 'But I would have liked to get to know her better.'

'You're wearing her necklace,' the man said. 'The Bosnian lily, and the heart, for love. I bought it for Aida. There was another charm, the Serbian double-headed eagle. She must have taken it off.'

Annika's hand flew to the necklace. She felt herself blushing.

The old man sat down on one of the beds, lifted a foot to the other knee and pulled on a sock.

'Sit down,' he said.

She sank onto the bed opposite the colonel, her knees trembling. She let her bag fall to the floor at the end of the bed.

'So why are you doing this?' he asked.

Annika looked at the old man, his grey-specked cheeks, sunken shoulders, heavy frame, the shirt that would hardly cover his stomach, his thinning hair.

She realized that he had been broken by grief – the sort of grief that makes people ill.

Would anyone ever grieve for her that much?

Suddenly she felt her tears overflow. She hid her face in her hands.

The man stayed where he was, silent, still.

'Sorry,' she whispered eventually, wiping her face with the back of her hand. 'My grandmother died recently, I haven't been myself lately.'

The colonel stood up and went into the bathroom; he came back with a roll of toilet paper.

'Thank you,' Annika said, taking it from him and blowing her nose.

The man was studying her carefully, but not with any malice.

'I met Aida a couple of days before she died,' Annika said. 'She wasn't well, and she was very frightened. I'm a journalist, Aida called the paper where I work, asking for help. I tried to help her . . .'

'How?'

Annika took a deep breath, then let it out silently.

'She was so alone. There wasn't anyone who could help her. She was being hunted by a man, and she was terrified. I went to see her because she had information about two murders that had been committed here. But I couldn't leave her like that, because she was so ill, so I gave her the phone number of an organization called Paradise . . . I thought they'd be able to help her.'

She glanced at the man. He was listening intently but showed no reaction when she mentioned the name 'Paradise'.

'The woman behind the foundation turned out to be a fraud,' Annika said. 'I feel extremely guilty for luring Aida into her organization.'

She bowed her head, feeling tears well up again, and waited for his outburst.

It didn't come.

'It's a good thing to help other people,' he said. 'Aida

442

must have appreciated what you tried to do, seeing as she gave you her necklace.'

'I'm so sorry,' she whispered.

The old soldier got up and went over to the window, and looked out over Sergels torg.

'She died here,' he muttered. 'This is where Aida died.'

The silence was oppressive. She sensed his despair, could see his shoulders heaving. She sat where she was, uncertain, her hands cold and clumsy. In the end she tore off a length of toilet paper, got up and walked slowly over to the window. Tears were rolling down the old man's cheeks into his stubble. He made no attempt to take the paper from her.

'I'm sorry,' Annika said softly. 'I thought I was helping her.'

The man cast a quick glance at her, then went back to staring out at the square again.

'Why should you feel guilty about it?' he asked.

'The woman behind Paradise, I'm afraid she . . .'

The man quickly turned round and went over to the fridge, where he took out a bottle of Slivovitz and poured a small measure into a glass.

'Aida chose to die,' he said, holding the bottle out to Annika. She shook her head and he replaced the lid and put it away again. He went back to the bed and sat down, making the mattress creak.

'Who exactly was Aida?' Annika asked. 'How did you know her?'

'I was born in Bijeljina,' the old man said, 'just like Aida.'

Annika sat down opposite him.

'Do you know Bijeljina?'

She tried to smile. 'No, but I've seen pictures of Bosnia. It looks beautiful, mountains, palm trees—'

'There's nothing like that in Bijeljina,' the colonel

said. 'The city lies on a plain, just to the north-east of Tuzla. The winters are hard, and the springs wet as hell.'

He was staring at some random point just above her head.

'Not even the river is particularly beautiful.'

He sighed and looked at Annika.

'You've probably seen pictures of that, the river Drina, it runs along the border with Serbia. Mind you, those famous pictures were taken a long way downstream, outside Gorazde.'

She shook her head.

'Piles of bodies,' he said. 'Bodies that were thrown in the river Drina and eventually drifted ashore near Gorazde. A Danish photographer got through our lines and took pictures, and they ended up being published all over the world.'

Annika swallowed. Yes, she remembered, she had read a book about it, and the *Evening Post* had bought the Swedish rights to the pictures.

He fell silent, and his eyes were staring distantly into space again. Annika waited.

'So you're . . . a Serb?' she asked.

The old soldier looked at her tiredly.

'In those days you grew up without ever thinking about what you were,' he said. 'I was an only child, and my closest childhood friend was like a brother to me. He was Aida's father. Jovan was fiercely intelligent, but because he was Muslim he couldn't get a career with the state. He became a baker, and a very good one at that.'

The man fell silent again and rubbed his eyes with his hairy hands.

'But you didn't become a baker,' Annika said quietly.

'I made my career in the military,' the old man said. 'Just like my father and grandfather before me. I never married. Jovan, on the other hand, had a wonderful

444

family, a beautiful wife and three talented children. I used to visit them every year, in the summer and at Christmas. The daughter was my favourite, Aida. She was lovely as an angel, and could sing like a bird . . .'

The old man downed his glass in one, then wiped his mouth with the back of his hand.

'Why do you care about Aida?' he asked.

'I'm a journalist,' she said. 'It's my job to write about things that are important, things that are true, about the way people live—'

'Ha!' the man burst out. 'Journalists are lackeys, just like soldiers. You just fight with lies instead of guns.'

Annika blinked, unprepared for his outburst.

'That's not true,' she said carefully. 'Truth is my only guide.'

The old soldier looked down at his empty glass.

'Oh, you're on the side of the virtuous, are you? So you don't get paid for the work you do?'

She threw out her hands.

'Of course I do, I'm employed by an independent newspaper, we have no editorial restraints—'

'A commercial newspaper, sold for money? How can it be independent, then? Its voice can be bought, and that makes it unreliable, corrupt.'

The man stood up again and refilled his glass. He didn't bother to offer Annika any this time. When he sat down opposite her once more she saw a spark in his eye. This was a man who had once loved debate, who had possessed both power itself and the power of words.

'Capital is its own truth,' he said. 'It seeks only to reproduce and spread, at any cost.'

'That's not true,' she said, surprised over how combative she felt. 'Only with a free and independent press can democracy be—'

'Democracy, ha! That merely creates competition and instability, politicians who offer themselves to the voters like whores, capitalists who exploit their fellow man. I don't think much of your democracy.'

'So what's the alternative?' Annika asked. 'A totalitarian state with a censored press?'

The man leaned forward, almost smiling.

'Only the state can take responsibility for the people,' he said. 'The state ought not to have any other goal but the well-being of the people. The press should inform and educate without the need to make a profit. It isn't freedom that speaks through your newspapers and television channels, it's capitalism.'

Annika shook her head.

'You're wrong,' she said. 'How good is life really in Serbia, under Slobodan Milosevic?'

The man's mood darkened. Annika could have bitten her tongue, what the hell was she saying?

'Sorry,' she whispered, 'I didn't mean to upset you . . .'

'Milosevic is a peasant,' the old man said gruffly. 'Look at what he's done to my country! He destroyed the KOS, the only organization that could maintain law and order; he cut our budget until there was nothing left, and gave the money to the RDB.'

He hit the bedside table with his fist, making Annika jump.

'Damn RDB, just look what they've done to my country! They've allowed criminal peasants to ruin Serbia. If the KOS was still in charge, Yugoslavia would still be a great power, an undivided Greater Serbia. We would never have let the country fall apart.'

He was sitting slumped, his head bowed, his elbows on his knees. Annika didn't dare move.

'Up until the nineteen eighties we had a morality in the Balkans,' he said quietly. 'Perfectly normal attitudes and values, then all hell broke loose. Men like Ratko came to power, buffoons, criminal idiots.'

Annika licked her lips, refusing to remember the taste of metal.

'Who exactly is Ratko?'

The old man sighed and straightened up.

'He came from a wealthy family that lost all its assets when the communists expropriated everything, distributing wealth from the rich to the poor. His father became a foundry worker, a good, decent profession, but that upset the family. Ratko decided that he was going to be a Somebody. He came here, to Sweden, to make his fortune, but ended up working on the assembly line of a lorry factory. He saw his compatriots succumb to industrial injuries, and chose a different path: that of the career criminal.'

He took a sip from his glass.

'Ratko and his father seemed to think that the new laws didn't apply to them. They thought Communism's laws had stolen everything they had, including their history and human dignity. The law was Ratko's enemy, and to obey it would have meant defeat. The only thing driving humanity is greed, avarice, the desire for material wealth.'

'That's not true,' Annika said.

'The only thing that can take responsibility for the people is the state,' the man said.

'But we are the state,' Annika said. 'It can never be better than the people it represents.'

He looked at her.

'Society is always greater than the people. Seeing us as isolated individuals means the victory of the ego.'

'Not necessarily,' Annika said. 'The state is its citizens, and we can't shove the responsibility onto anyone else but ourselves. We ourselves determine our future, we are the state. We have responsibility for one another and we have to take that responsibility. A single individual can make a huge contribution!'

'And then it all goes to hell!' the man exclaimed, banging the bedside table again. 'Look at Serbia! When Milosevic set himself up above the state it went to the devil! The RDB doesn't have the necessary skill, even though it got all the resources. It uses them all wrongly, for its own gain, it abuses its power, supports criminal activity . . .'

He fell silent, slightly out of breath.

Annika stared at him, as the sweat glistened on his scalp.

'How much do you know?' she asked quietly.

'I know everything.'

'Everything?'

'Everything.'

'About the mafia as well?'

The man looked at her intently, examining her face, hair, hands.

'The defender of the free word,' he said. 'Can you write any sort of truth?'

Annika blinked.

'If I can hold the truths together, and if they're of interest to our readers.'

'Aha!' the man said. 'Who takes that decision?'

'Me, to start with, and then the editorial management of the paper.'

'Censors,' the old man concluded.

'No!' Annika said. 'We serve no one but the truth.'

'You wouldn't dare publish my truth,' the old man said. 'No one would publish everything I know.'

'I can't answer that, I have no idea what you know.'

The man looked at her for a long while, and her skin started to crawl. She felt naked.

'Have you got a pen on you? Something to write on? Well, write down my story. Let's see if you dare to print it.'

Annika leaned over and hauled up her bag, and took out her pen and notebook.

'So?' she said.

'The mafia is the state,' the old man said, 'and the state is the mafia. Everything is controlled by Belgrade. The RDB – the security police – are pulling all the strings. Weapons smuggling is their largest and most important source of income. Three-quarters of the money comes from arms sales. They've cleansed the whole of the former Yugoslavia of weapons, and are storing them in huge weapons dumps. They've got enough there to last until Doomsday. Or to bring it about themselves. They do a lot of business with the Middle East, Iraq. North Korea's interested in chemical weapons, and Belgrade can help them with that. They're keeping a whole load of conflicts in Africa going, supplying African states with arms. They use Polish boats out of Gdansk. They load them in Serbia and take them down through the Suez Canal, where all the customs officials are bribed.'

Annika was just staring at him, hadn't written a word yet.

'What do you mean?' she said. 'Is this true?'

'Tobacco smuggling is another important part of the business,' the old man went on, 'along with spirits, drugs, prostitution. The cigarettes are made in big pirate factories, given false labels like Marlboro, then loaded onto lorries, sealed up for transport and driven up through the whole of Europe towards Finland. In Sweden the seals are broken, the shipments removed, then they head for the embassy and get a new seal put on. This only works because the state acts as the agent.

449

Then they drive to Finland and unload a few empty cardboard boxes.'

Annika lowered her head.

'Hang on a minute,' she said. 'Can you run through that first bit again? Weapons, Africa, North Korea?'

The old man patiently repeated some of the details.

'With the prostitution racket,' he went on, 'most of the women come from Ukraine and Belarus, and are shipped to brothels in central Europe, mostly Germany, Hungary, the Czech Republic and Poland. The drugs come mainly from Afghanistan. It's the opposition rather than the Taliban who are responsible for the heroin trade. The route goes through Turkey, and these days most of that section of the chain is run by the Kosovo Albanians. Once they've brought the raw materials in, they sell it to the Serbs. The Serbs transform the raw material into saleable heroin. There are whole hospitals involved in the business, along with large sections of the agriculture industry.'

Annika felt her head spinning. She was scribbling so hard her arm was aching. Was this really possible?

'The drink is manufactured in large factories, then given false labels, twelve-year-old malt whisky from Scotland, Finnish vodka, and so on. If any of this came to a halt, the country would collapse in a matter of days. The workers wouldn't get paid, the whole system would fall apart.'

The man sighed. 'The RDB hands out all sorts of different passports: Scandinavian, French, American. They have a well-developed network covering the whole of Europe in the form of bars, nightclubs, Serbian associations, chess clubs and so on.'

He laughed mirthlessly.

'The Serbian security services have one peculiar characteristic,' he said. 'They only spring into action

450

on Wednesdays. If you can make it past Wednesday, you're safe until next week. Their city patrols work in teams of between three and five men. If they're working in foreign countries they use embassies and consulates as their exit routes. Here in Sweden the consulate in Trelleborg is extremely active.'

His voice faded away. Annika finished writing, then sat there with pen to paper.

'How can I get confirmation of any of this?' she asked.

The old man got up and went over to the wardrobe. He entered the combination of a small inbuilt safe and came back with several documents, some of them a striking blue colour.

'I stole these from the embassy,' he said. 'Two TIR-certificates. They'll realize they're missing before too long.'

He put them down on the bed beside Annika. She stared at them, then looked up at the man. She was feeling completely bewildered.

'But how can this be possible?' she said.

The man sat down heavily.

'There are caches of weapons throughout Sweden,' he said. 'As well as stores of drugs, spirits, cigarettes, whole buildings full of Serbs without residence permits, trailers, vehicles, boats.'

Annika swallowed.

'Do you know where they are?'

He looked at her and nodded.

And told her.

57

When he had finished Annika could feel her veins pumping with adrenalin. This was incredible.

'But what's going to happen if I publish this under my own name?' she asked. 'Won't the mafia come after me?'

The old man looked at her wearily.

'Worried about your own safety? So you're more important than the truth? Isn't your state, made up of free citizens as it is, capable of protecting you?'

She lowered her gaze and blushed.

'You have to understand this isn't personal,' the man said, 'this is just business. Ratko has no friends left, no one's going to get rid of you as some sort of personal vendetta. If you bring down the criminal machinery, there'll be no one left who could do you any harm, and there would no longer be any point anyway.'

Annika looked up.

'But what about the embassy? If what you say is true, then they're behind it all.'

'The Serbian Embassy will be your best life insurance. It will be in their interests that nothing happens to you. But I wouldn't advise you to travel to the Balkans any time soon. You might just bump into the wrong people.'

She looked down at her notes and cleared her throat.

'What about Ratko?'

The man hesitated.

'Ratko's gone, no one knows where. The day he shows himself in Europe he's a dead man. My guess is that he's gone to Africa, to one of the places that buys arms from him.'

'What about you?'

The man looked intently at her.

'I've done my bit,' he said. 'Everything that ever mattered to me is gone. Aida was the last one.'

'What happened?' Annika whispered.

The old man got up, walked over to the window and looked out over the square, grey in the twilight.

'Ratko killed the whole family apart from Aida. That was what kicked off the violence in Bosnia. March nineteen ninety-two.'

Annika gasped.

'God, the whole family?'

'Jovan, his wife, their pregnant daughter-in-law, their youngest son, he was only nine years old. Their older boy was in the army and died at the front six months later.'

'He killed them?'

The man was staring at the triangular paving of the square below as he spoke.

'Ratko and his Panthers. The political tension had been building for some time, battle was raging in Croatia, but the massacre in Bijeljina was the first time Bosnia flared up.'

'And Aida's family was caught up in it?'

'I don't know how she survived, she never told me.'

Annika had tears trickling down her face again. God, the world was a terrible place.

'What happened to her? How did she get here?'

The man stared out at the square, snowflakes had begun to fall.

'She was seventeen years old at the time. As far as I know, she walked to Tuzla immediately after the killings. She got a lift to Sarajevo and joined up with the Armija BiH. Her uncle, Jovan's younger brother, lived in Sarajevo. He arranged for her to be put in the *speciale diversanskij group*.'

Annika waited for him to go on, holding her breath. Tears were hanging from her lips.

'And?' she said.

'The *speciale diversanskij group*,' the man said, stressing each word heavily. 'She became a shooter. When I found out, I washed my hands of her, and broke off all contact.'

Annika blinked uncomprehendingly.

'A sniper,' the old man said, sounding exhausted. 'She trained to become a sniper, lying on roofs and shooting at people down in the streets, men, women, children, without discriminating.'

Annika couldn't breathe.

'No . . .'

He turned and looked at her.

'I can assure you,' he said, 'she got to be very good at it. Only God knows how many people Aida killed.'

He sat down opposite her again.

'You didn't know?' he said.

Annika shook her head.

'How,' she said, then gulped, 'how did she end up here? In Stockholm?'

The old man rubbed his eyes.

'She got wounded, and was carried out of Sarajevo through the tunnel, up to Mount Igman. She arranged to go with a group of women and children gathered by the Red Cross. They had trouble getting out of Bosnia.

On one occasion the bus was stopped and some of the younger women were dragged out of the bus by drunk soldiers, barbarians. We don't know what happened, but when the bus set off again two soldiers were lying dead at the checkpoint, shot in the mouth with their own weapons. That could only have been Aida.'

The man bowed his head. Annika was starting to feel sick.

'Why did she want to get to Sweden?' she whispered.

'She had heard that Ratko was here. She'd sworn to get her revenge. That was the only thing that mattered to her any more. He had taken her family away from her, her whole life. I didn't hear from her for years. It used to upset me. I did the wrong thing. I should have stayed in touch. People can't cope alone. Aida might have needed me.'

Annika suddenly felt the necklace scorching her throat, heavy and hot, the gratitude of a killer.

'And then she wrote to me,' he said breathlessly. 'Saturday, the third of November this year. She wrote that her task was almost complete. She had made contact with Ratko, they were going to meet, one of them was going to die.'

'She contacted him?' Annika said. 'Are you sure she chose to contact Ratko herself? They met on her initiative? No one betrayed her to him?'

The man lowered his head.

'She was going to confront Ratko, once and for all,' he said quietly. 'She asked me to finish the job if she failed. I had survived all the purges, I still had Milosevic's ear, I could ruin Ratko's life.'

His shoulders rocked once more and he put his hand over his eyes.

'Go,' he said.

Annika gulped.

'But . . .'

'Go.'

She leaned over and put her pen and notebook in her bag. She hesitated for a moment, then put the old man's documents in as well, the TIR-certificates from the Yugoslav Embassy.

'Thank you, for everything,' she whispered.

The man didn't reply.

She left him, opening the door quietly and stepping out into the corridor.

The old soldier sat on the bed as darkness fell. His shoulders ached, his back, his hands. His feet felt cold, numb. The young journalist had taken the TIR-certification with her, good. They would never be able to prove that he had taken them, even if they might well suspect him.

He decided to take a bath. He went into the bathroom, turned on the light, put the plug in, ran the hot water. He sat on the toilet seat as the bath filled, the cold from the tiled floor seeping up into his legs, a welcome pain. When the water started to overflow onto the floor and reached his toes, he turned off the tap. He left the room, going out into the darkness again, took off his clothes, folding them and putting them neatly on a chair.

He sank into the hot water, right up to his chin, closed his eyes for a long time, and let his body unwind.

When the water started to get cold, he got out, dried himself carefully, shaved, combed his hair, and put on his dress uniform again, with all his honours and medals for particular achievements. He dressed slowly and carefully, running his hands over his uniform to smooth any creases, fixing the cap firmly on his head. Then he went over to the safe and took out his service revolver.

He looked at his reflection in the mirror, the whole of his back-to-front hotel room floating above the triangular paving of Sergels torg. He looked into his own eyes, calm, resolved. Then he focused instead on the square outside, fixing his eyes on the place where she had died.

Together, he thought, as he put the barrel in his mouth and squeezed the trigger.

58

Eleonor rubbed her forehead with the back of her hand.

'The steak's ready,' she said. 'How's the gratin doing?'

Thomas opened the oven and tested the middle of the dish.

'It needs a bit longer.'

'Do you think it needs to be covered with foil to stop it burning?'

'I think it'll be okay,' Thomas said.

Eleonor rinsed her hands under the kitchen tap, dried them on her apron, let out a deep breath.

'Are my cheeks red?' she asked with a smile.

He swallowed and smiled back.

'You look charming,' he said.

She untied the apron and hung it up in its place, then went into the bedroom to change her shoes. Thomas went out into the dining room with the bowl of salad, positioning it between the crystal glasses, the English bone-china plates and silver cutlery. He checked the table: the cold antipasto starter, napkins, mineral water, salad. It was all there apart from the wine.

He sighed. He felt tired, and would have liked to just lie and watch television, thinking about his new project. He had spent the afternoon reading the report detailing what people living on social security benefits thought of it, how life on the margins of society wore them down, how difficult it was to have to explain that you needed new shoes, the stressed attitude of their social workers, the constant feeling of having to accept hand-outs, the humiliation. How they had to choose between going to the dentist or paying for a doctor's prescription. Never being able to afford to eat meat. Their children's pleas for skates or a bicycle.

The despair these people felt had worked its way into him, and it wasn't letting go. He was carrying it around like a physical wound.

If only I had the power to change things, he thought, closing his eyes.

Then he heard car-doors closing out on the drive, and waited for the sound of footsteps on the gritted path.

'They're here!' he called to the bedroom.

The doorbell rang out its tinkling melody. Thomas wiped his hands and went out into the hall to open the door.

'Welcome, come in, take your things off, can I help you with your fur . . . ?'

Nils from the bank, the branch managers from Täby and Djursholm, and the regional manager from Stockholm: three men, one woman.

Eleonor came in as he was serving drinks, cool, smiling, beautiful.

'How lovely to see you here,' she said. 'Welcome!'

'Well, we've got a lot to celebrate,' the regional manager said. 'What a lovely house!'

He kissed her on both cheeks. Thomas noted with some annoyance that Eleonor blushed.

'Thanks, we love it here.'

She glanced at Thomas. He was smiling in a slightly forced way.

They drank a toast.

459

'Shall I give you the guided tour?' Eleonor wondered.

Enthusiastic agreement. They all followed her out, leaving Thomas alone in the living room. He could hear his wife's voice through the walls.

'We're thinking of having the kitchen redone,' she was saying. 'We'd like to get a gas stove, we love cooking so much, and gas is so much more responsive . . . We're going to have under-floor heating put in, marble, preferably green, it's such a peaceful colour . . . And down here we've got the basement, we'd like to install a wine-cellar, we're starting to think we need to look after our collection a bit better . . .'

He put his drink down, and noticed that his hand was shaking. What fucking wine collection? Eleonor's parents had a decent cellar out in the country, some seriously good stuff, but they hadn't even started to build up their own, there hadn't been time.

Suddenly he could feel himself start to panic; he felt completely cold.

No, he pleaded, *not now. Just let me hold it together this evening, this is so important to Eleonor.*

He went into the kitchen, opened the red wine to let it breathe, uncorked the bubbly with a pop and filled the champagne glasses.

'What a wonderful home you have!' the regional manager said as they came up from the recreation room. 'And so many great plans for the place.'

Thomas tried to smile, but felt he didn't really succeed.

'Shall we sit down?' he said.

Eleonor was smiling nervously.

'Well, we live quite modestly,' she said. 'Both Thomas and I work very hard. Thomas is head of finance at Vaxholm Council.'

'Finance officer for social services,' Thomas said.

Eleonor led the way into the dining room. 'Nils, you're there, Leopold here, next to me, Gunvor . . .'

The guests seemed to appreciate the food and wine, and the atmosphere quickly became convivial. Thomas heard fragments of the conversation, about profit, results, markets. He tried to eat, but every mouthful seemed to swell in his mouth, and he felt flat and giddy. Eventually the regional manager tapped his glass.

'I'd like to propose a toast to Eleonor,' he said ceremoniously. 'To our hostess for this lovely evening, and for the wonderful results she has achieved at the bank over this past year. You should know, Eleonor, that the senior management at the bank has noted your success, your determination and your enthusiasm. To Eleonor!'

Thomas looked at his wife, her cheeks were glowing with the praise.

'And as the icing on the cake, I should like to reveal to you this evening the form in which the management's appreciation will be expressed.'

The four bank officials stretched out. Thomas knew that this was the highpoint of the evening, the moment they played their trump card.

'You each represent the branches with the best results in central Sweden,' the regional manager said. 'The dividend on our investments has increased once again this year, and surveys of both business and private customers indicate high levels of satisfaction.'

He made a dramatic pause.

'I can also reveal that a study of staff opinions of branch managers has been completed, and that you all emerge at the top of that, too. As a result,' he said, enjoying the moment, 'it is with the greatest of pleasure that the bank's senior management has decided to increase both your bonuses and your profit share.'

Eleonor gasped, her eyes shining with delight.

461

'And,' the regional manager said, leaning over the table, 'you will also be given the right to enter the bank's management option programme next year!'

The four officials were unable to stay quiet any longer, and began to make little squeaks of happiness.

'As well as that,' the regional manager went on, 'you will also be given extremely advantageous health insurance, paid for by the bank. This means that not only will you be able to bypass the queues in the health service, but so will your spouses!'

Eleonor looked at Thomas, beside herself with joy.

'Did you hear that, darling? Isn't that wonderful!'

Then she turned back to the regional manager.

'Oh, Leopold, how can we possibly live up to this incredible vote of confidence from the board. What a responsibility!'

The regional manager stood up.

'To our mutual success!'

The others followed suit.

'To our mutual success!'

Thomas suddenly felt that he was going to be sick. He rushed out of the dining room, along the corridor and into the bathroom. He locked the door and slumped over the toilet, panting for breath. He had sweat on his brow and felt ready to faint.

Eleonor knocked anxiously on the door.

'Darling, what is it? What's happened?'

He didn't answer, just felt like crying.

'Thomas!'

'I'm not feeling well,' he said. 'Go back to the others, I'm going to go to bed.'

'But I thought you could make coffee for us!'

He shut his eyes, feeling the bitter taste of suppressed vomit in his throat.

'I can't,' he whispered. 'I can't do this any more.'

Friday 7 December

59

Annika woke up at three minutes to six, thirsty and starving. The winter night was still impenetrable outside the window, black and cold. She lay on her side looking at the illuminated numbers on the alarm-clock. It was set to ring in eighteen minutes.

She was due at Södermalm hospital at seven. She wasn't allowed to eat or drink before the anaesthetic. They were going to stretch her cervix and hoover out the contents of her uterus.

A boy, she thought. *Fair-haired, like his dad*.

She rolled onto her back and stared up at the ceiling, but couldn't see any patterns in the dark.

There's no rush. I've got plenty of time.

She shut her eyes and listened to the new day as it started to stir into life. At six o'clock the ventilation unit in the courtyard began to whirr, the brakes on the number 48 bus squealed, and she heard the theme-tune of the radio news through the floor from her downstairs neighbour. Familiar sounds, warm, everyday. She stretched her arms up, then put them behind her head and stared into the darkness.

The old soldier glided across her vision, weighed down, bitter, alone. He didn't believe in humanity, only in the state, and he chose to do so, there was always a choice.

Aida had been a sniper, a killer, she chose to be that. Our circumstances shape us, but the choice is always our own.

Annika suddenly felt the weight of the heavy necklace in her hands and sat up, feeling for the catch. It was fiddly, but she managed to undo it, and put it in front of the alarm clock on the bedside table. The illuminated numbers made the metal glow bright green.

She didn't want a killer's gratitude.

She turned off the alarm, threw the duvet aside, put on her dressing-gown and boots. She grabbed her sponge-bag and ran down to the shower on the other side of the courtyard. She washed her hair, careful not to swallow any water as she brushed her teeth.

She went back up to her flat. Maybe she ought to subscribe to one of the morning papers after all, it would be nice to have something to read over breakfast. She opened the fridge, she had juice, yogurt, eggs, bacon, garlic cheese, air-cured Italian ham, all of it bought from the nasty little Ica-supermarket the previous evening. She stared into the fridge, one hand on the door and the other on her stomach.

The choice is always our own.

She took a deep breath. It was so easy. She burst out laughing, it really wasn't difficult at all.

She took out the juice and poured herself a large glass. She turned the stove on and pulled out the frying-pan.

She drank. And drank.

She cracked eggs into the pan, then chopped some bacon into it. Toasted some bread, spread garlic cheese on top, and ate it as she stirred the omelette.

She ate. And ate.

She let the food settle in her stomach, then drank some hot coffee, feeling the heat radiate through her, feeling the caffeine kicking in. She lit the candles on the table, her grandmother's wedding present, the brass candelabra from Lyckebo. She watched the flames flicker and dance. She smiled at her reflection in the window, the woman in her dressing-gown with wet hair, the woman with candles who was going to have a baby.

She went into the bedroom, turned on the light, saw the gold glittering on the bedside table. She got dressed, picked up the necklace and weighed it in her hand.

Heavy. So bloody heavy.

For the first time in over a month she went into the room behind the kitchen, the bare little maid's room, with just a table in the corner and a chair with a broken back. She never used the room, still thought of it as Patricia's, her old flatmate.

Here, she thought. *I could sit and write here.*

She looked at the time. Almost seven. That was when the goldsmith over the street opened up. She had gone in once before by mistake when she was looking for a pair of earrings for Anne Snapphane's birthday. A big, bald man in a heavy leather apron had appeared before her, and she had gulped and asked if she was in the right place. She was, the goldsmith actually did sell earrings, and she had bought a pair of old lady's dropped gold pearls out of sheer anxiety.

She blew out the candles, dried her hair with a towel, pulled on a woollen hat, put on her jacket and shoes and went downstairs.

It had snowed overnight, and there was still a soft covering on the pavements. Her feet made a trail from her door, over the street, to his.

He had already opened up, the same thick apron, the same cheery expression.

467

'You're out early,' he said brightly. 'Christmas shopping?'

She smiled and shook her head, and handed him Aida's necklace.

'That's quite some chain,' he said, weighing it in his hands.

Annika saw the metal glint in his huge fists. He could probably make something beautiful out of the killer's gratitude.

'Is it gold?' she asked.

The man scraped at the chain beside the fastening, turned away and did something with it.

'At least eighteen carat,' he said. 'Do you want to get rid of it?'

Annika nodded, and the smith weighed it on some scales.

'It's bloody heavy,' he said. 'One hundred and ninety grams, at forty-eight kronor a gram.'

He tapped on a pocket calculator.

'Nine thousand, one hundred and twenty kronor, how does that sound?'

She nodded again. The goldsmith disappeared into a back room, then came out with the money and a receipt.

'There you are,' he said. 'Don't spend it all at once!'

'Oh, I don't know,' she smiled. 'That's exactly what I was thinking of doing.'

The computer whizz-kids round the corner didn't really open until nine, but she saw one of them tapping at a keyboard in a room behind the shop. She knocked on the glass and the man looked up. She smiled and waved, and he came out into the shop and opened the door.

'I know I'm too early,' Annika said, 'but I'd like to buy a computer.'

He opened the door with a laugh.

'And you just can't wait until we open?'

She smiled. 'What have you got for nine thousand, one hundred and twenty kronor?'

'Mac or PC?'

'Don't care,' she said. 'As long as it doesn't keep crashing.'

The young man looked around the mess in the shop. They sold both new and used computers, repaired them, programed them, ran servers, offered support, designed websites, all according to the sign in the window. Annika passed their shop something like eight times a day, and they seemed to spend most of their time playing computer games.

'This one,' the man said, lifting a large grey box onto a table. 'It's second-hand, but it's got a new processor and a hell of a lot of memory. What do you want it for?'

'As a word processor,' Annika said. 'And a bit of surfing.'

The young man patted the box.

'Then this one's ideal. It's all in there already, things like Word, Excel, Explorer—'

'I'll take it,' she interrupted. 'And a screen and all that as well.'

The man hesitated.

'And you want all that for nine thousand?'

'Nine thousand, one hundred and twenty. You did say the hard disk was second-hand.'

He sighed. 'Okay, but only because it's so damn early.'

The young man left her in the shop and went into the back room to fetch a small screen.

'This isn't very big,' he said, 'but it's recommended by the civil service. It doesn't flare much, which is something to look out for. Old screens make my head spin, they make your brain itch. Anything else? Disks?'

'I've only got nine thousand, one hundred and twenty kronor.'

He sighed again, took out a large paper bag and threw in a pair of speakers, a mouse, mouse-mat, a few packs of disks, cables and a keyboard.

'And a printer,' Annika said.

'You're joking?' the man said. 'For nine thousand, one hundred and twenty kronor?'

'I don't mind second-hand,' Annika said.

He went back out into the storeroom again and returned with a large box with the name Hewlett on the side.

'Okay, you're getting the hard-disk for nothing now,' he said. 'Anything else we can give you?'

She laughed. 'I think that'll do, but how am I going to get them home?'

'And that's where the boundary is!' the young man said. 'You'll have to carry them yourself. I know you live locally, I've seen you before.'

Annika blushed.

'Have you?'

He smiled awkwardly. He was quite cute, dark, curly hair.

'You're always walking past,' he said. 'Usually in a hurry. You must lead a very interesting life.'

She took a deep breath. 'Yes, I do, actually,' she said. 'But I'm not very strong, so I probably need some help to carry everything.'

He groaned and rolled his eyes, then took a better grip of the printer and headed towards the door.

'I hope you live nearby,' he said.

'On the top floor, with no lift,' Annika said with a smile.

60

The sky was starting to get lighter when she finally sat down at the table in the maid's room, her notebook beside her, staring out at the house opposite, with its swaying straw stars.

This is a nice room, she thought. *Why haven't I ever used it before?*

She went through everything, over and over again, typing, deleting, amending. She found herself in the zone where time and space vanish, and let the words come, the letters dance.

Suddenly she realized she was hungry again. She ran down and got a pizza from the place on the corner and ate it at the computer.

By the time the incredibly slow old inkjet printer had finished, it was already getting dark. She put the printout in a plastic sleeve, saved the file on a disk and headed over to police headquarters.

'You can't just march in here whenever you like,' Q said, sounding annoyed as he came down to see her in reception. 'What do you want?'

'I've written an article that I'd like your opinion on,' she said.

He groaned out loud.

'And I suppose it's just as urgent as usual?'

'Yep.'

'Okay, let's go and get coffee.'

They went out to the sandwich bar round the corner and ordered coffee and some sandwiches. Annika pulled out the plastic folder.

'I don't know if this will ever be published,' she said. 'I'm going to go up to the paper and hand it over to them when we're finished here.'

The detective took a long look at her, then picked up the printout.

He read in silence, leafed through it, then read it again.

'This,' he said, 'is a comprehensive overview of the activities of the Yugoslavian mafia, both internationally and in Sweden. The locations of their stores, offices, vehicles, details of contacts, routines . . .'

She nodded. He stared at her.

'You're fucking incredible,' he said. 'Where the hell did you get hold of information like this?'

'I've got two TIR-certificates in my bag. They're permits issued under strictly controlled conditions, to allow the free passage of goods across international borders,' she said.

He leaned back in his chair, letting his hands hang down over the back.

'Now I get it,' he said. 'You have a strange ability to make people die.'

Annika stiffened, feeling his words stab at her chest.

'What do you mean?'

He stared at her for several seconds, remembering the report on his desk, the suicide at the Sergel Plaza the night before, the Yugoslav colonel with the diplomatic passport.

'Nothing,' he said.

He leaned forward again and finished his coffee.

'Nothing. Just being stupid. Sorry.'

'What do you think?' she said. 'Is it correct?'

He thought for a moment.

'I'd have to check before I said for certain. This pizzeria in Gothenburg, for instance, that might not have anything to do with the mafia.'

She sighed silently.

'When will you be able to check?' she asked quietly.

'Well,' he said, 'hopefully before you publish all this information, because I don't suppose it would be much use afterwards.'

'I need confirmation before I do that,' she said. 'I only have one source.'

He looked intently at her.

'And if I don't want to?'

She leaned forward, lowering her voice still further.

'All I want you to do is take a look and tell me if the information stands up or not.'

'I'd have to check out the locations themselves to give you an answer,' he said, 'and the moment we knock on the first door, the alarm would go out. It would be too late.'

She nodded. 'Okay. I've thought this through. What if we look at it like this: I've got detailed information about where the mafia hang out, where their stores are and so on, but because I can't get confirmation I can't publish them. Which means I can refer to them in general terms, but not in detail. The addresses aren't the most important part of the story anyway. When you've done your checks, we'll know the answer, won't we?'

He hesitated, then nodded.

She smiled nervously.

'So can I assume that the police would be planning a coordinated series of raids sometime early one morning? Possibly the day the first part of the story goes to press?'

'And when might that be?'

'I can't say for certain yet, but the first edition always prints just after six in the morning.'

'How many people will have seen the article by then?'

She thought. 'Fewer than twenty in total. The night team and the men in charge of the presses down at the printers.'

'So there's no chance of it leaking? Okay, in that case I think I can safely say that we'll be checking these addresses at six a.m. precisely one morning very soon.'

Annika packed her things away.

'I can probably say that we may well have quite a few photographers out and about that morning, sometime around when we usually go to press.'

Q pushed his coffee cup aside and stood up.

'We do our job for the public,' he said. 'Not for anyone else.'

Annika pulled on her jacket.

'Same here.'

Anders Schyman was leafing through that day's paper. He started at the picture on the front page. Anneli from Motala together with her handicapped son Alexander, let down by their local council, desperate, isolated. Carl Wennergren's list of the various ways the social services department had broken their obligation of care under local authorities legislation. The council's hollow excuses.

God, some people have tough lives, Schyman thought. He wished he had some whisky in his office. He was longing to get back to his wife, their dog, the sofa in his house out in Saltsjöbaden. It had been a rough week. Torstensson's abrupt resumption of the post of editor-in-chief had antagonized him more than he liked to admit. Torstensson had to go. If the paper was to survive, there was no alternative.

Schyman scratched his hair and sighed. He reckoned they had three years to turn the paper around, certainly no longer. If the paper was going to survive the transition to new technologies, the new age, it would be up to him. He was planning to fight, and he wanted whisky. A large one. Now.

There was a knock on the door. What the hell? He really didn't want to have to deal with anything else right now.

Annika Bengtzon stuck her head in.

'Have you got a minute?'

He closed his eyes.

'I was just about to go home. What is it?'

She pulled the door shut behind her and walked over to his desk. She dropped her bag and coat on the floor.

'I've written an article,' she said.

Hallelujah, he thought.

'And?' he said.

'I think you ought to read it. You could say that it's a bit controversial.'

'Really?' he muttered, taking the disk she offered him.

He spun round on his chair and pushed the disk into the slot on his computer and waited for the file to load. He double-clicked. This wouldn't take long.

His heart sank.

'This is three articles,' he said.

'Just look at the first one, to start with,' she said, sitting down on one of the uncomfortable chairs he had for visitors.

It was a long article, a complete overview of the structure of the Yugoslavian mafia in Belgrade, what their activities were, what the different groups had responsibility for.

The second text was a description of the extent and the activities of the Yugoslavian mafia in Sweden, including exact addresses associated with their drug-dealing, cigarette smuggling, illegal alcohol, human trafficking, prostitution . . .

The third was similar, but without the addresses.

'I thought you were off sick?' he said.

'I stumbled over something interesting,' she said.

He read the articles again, then sighed. 'We can't publish this.'

'Which bit?' Annika asked.

He sighed again. 'This business with the TIR-certificates,' he said. 'It's absurd to suggest that the embassy is behind that, how on earth could we ever prove it?'

She leaned over to her bag and pulled out a bundle of documents that she laid on the desk.

'Two TIR-certificates,' she said. 'Stolen from the Yugoslavian Embassy.'

His jaw dropped as she delved into her bag again.

'As far as their activities in Sweden are concerned,' she said, 'I happen to know that the police are planning a massive raid on all these addresses simultaneously. It's going to happen at six o'clock in the morning, one day in the very near future.'

'How do you know that?' he said.

She looked him in the eye.

'Because I've given the list to the police,' she said. 'We have to coordinate publication with their raids.'

He shook his head.

'What on earth are you doing? What have you let yourself in for?'

'I got the information from a reliable source, but only

one. I know the articles can't be printed as they are, at least not at the moment, because I need confirmation of everything before they can be published. Only the police can provide that confirmation, and in order to get that from them, I had to ask them, if you see what I mean?'

He rubbed his forehead.

'We can run the first and third articles on day one,' she said. 'That's the general picture of the mafia internationally, and the situation in Sweden, but without the details. As the paper goes to press, we're out covering the police raids. That'll give us material for day two. "After the *Evening Post*'s revelations", blah, blah, blah. You know the sort of thing. Officially the embassy will welcome the chance to clear out the stable. The suggestion that the embassy has participated in any form of criminal activity will be regarded as malicious propaganda, and the TIR-certificates as fakes.'

He stared at her.

'How have you managed to cook this up?'

The young woman shrugged. 'Do what you like. I wrote the articles in my free time and I don't need to be paid for them. The police will carry out their raids anyway, with or without our photographers in position outside. It's up to you to decide if the paper is going to be part of this or not. I'm on sick-leave, after all.' She got up. 'You know where I am.'

'Hold on,' he said.

'No,' she said. 'I'm tired of hearing the same old story from you. I don't want to carry on slogging my way through the nightshift. I've bought a computer, so I can sit at home and write, freelance, if I don't fit as a reporter on this paper. For fuck's sake, you're head-editor, you have to be able to make your own decisions and stand by them.'

She closed the door behind her as she left.

He stared after her, watching her disappear across the newsroom, not talking to anyone, not saying hello. She was troublesome, she was a lone wolf, and she was serious. She definitely fitted in as a reporter, but he had no money for recruitment. It was mad to let her go. And, in comparison with all the other reporters, she was on a very low salary.

He picked up the phone and called the reception desk downstairs. He got through to Tore Brand, working Fridays as usual so he could have the weekend off.

'Annika Bengtzon's on her way down,' he said. 'Can you catch her for me?'

'What do you think I am, some sort of fisherman?' the caretaker snapped.

'This is important,' Schyman said.

'You're all so bloody important up there . . .'

He sat with the phone in his hand, thoughts running round his head. The Yugoslavian story seemed improbable, but it was bloody good. Collaborating with the police like that was controversial, but it was the fastest and safest way of checking the truth of the story. The way the deal had been worked out would doubtless lead to debate, but that was nothing but a good thing. He was more than willing to turn up at the Newspapermen's Professional Association and defend both the paper and freedom of the press generally. It was time to come out fighting.

Publish and be damned, Anders Schyman thought.

'Bengtzon, there's a call for you!'

There was a lot of noise on the line as Tore Brand passed her the phone under the glass hatch.

'What?' Annika asked down the line.

'You're a reporter as of the first of January,' Anders

478

Schyman said. 'You can chose between the night crew, crime or miscellaneous.'

Apart from Tore Brand's muttering in the background, the line was quiet.

'Hello?' Schyman said.

'Crime,' Annika said. 'I want to work on the crime team.'

They have brought me to account.

They have caught up with me. Together they have formulated the charges against me, my sentence, my punishment.

The violence, the guilt and the shame. My three comrades, my fuel, my guiding stars.

Welcome!

Violence, you who appeared first, you who framed my fate, I took you to my heart, I made you mine.

That spring day, it had been raining all day, grey, wet, in the afternoon it stopped, a low sun shining on the town.

I ran down to the market, the roots and vegetables were wretched, it took me an age to choose.

I saw the men between the houses, black clothes, black berets.

I didn't know you were coming. I didn't recognize the face of violence.

I was standing in front of Stojiljkovic's café when the man who turned out to be Ratko dragged my father out of the bakery. I watched as he put the pistol to my father's temple and fired. I saw Papi collapse on the street, I heard Mamma screaming. Another man in black, he shot her in the chest. My sister-in-law Mariam, my brother's wife, she was only a year older than me, they shot her in the stomach, over and over again. She was pregnant.

Then they dragged out Petar, my little brother, the light of my life, only nine years old. He was screaming – oh, how he screamed – and then he caught sight of me in front of Stojiljkovic's café. He pulled himself free and he ran, screaming, 'Aida, Aida, help me,' his outstretched hands, his bottomless terror.

And I hid.

I crept behind the fence outside Stojiljkovic's café and looked through the railings as Ratko raised his gun, I saw him take aim and fire.

My Petar, my little brother, how could I ever get absolution?

He lay in the mud calling my name, 'Aida, Aida, help me, Aida,' and I didn't dare step out, I couldn't, I crouched there sobbing behind the fence of Stojiljkovic's café and saw Ratko walk over, I saw him turn your face towards him, I saw him take aim and fire.

Forgive me, Petar, forgive me. You shouldn't have had to die alone. Forgive me my betrayal.

Welcome, guilt. Welcome, shame. It was your turn to take over.

And I used violence to hold you at bay.

I paid off the guilt with death, the right sort of death, the death of Serbs. It didn't help. With every death, more guilt was born, more hatred, shame for someone else who was guilty of betrayal.

For me the shame was constant, it lived in every breath, every moment of my life, because the shame was that I was alive.

Then I heard that Ratko, the leader of the Black Panthers, was in Sweden. When I got injured, it was time.

I had to be strong to use violence against its originator, the man who had planted it in my chest. I made my way into his circle, I slept with his men, I slept with him, but death wasn't enough, he had to feel the guilt and the shame too, and so I sabotaged his work, I destroyed his life.

I feel sorry for the young men from Kosovo, the poor idiots I fooled into coming along. They were only supposed to drive the lorry away, I would sort out everything else. And they stole the wrong vehicle. The trailer with the cigarettes is still in Frihamnen in Stockholm. Ironic.

But violence betrayed me, refused to obey.

It started with the storm, the terrible storm, ripping into buildings and people alike.

I had to be so incredibly careful, clambering up onto the roof, dragging my bag up there.

The butt and the firing mechanism were in one section. The barrel, telescopic sight, flash damper and bolt in another. I took out the butt and screwed the barrel onto it. I constructed the frame and attached the telescopic sight with chin support. Finally I screwed the flash damper onto the barrel. The short distance meant I didn't need a tripod.

Using my left hand as a support against the ridge of the roof, I leaned the rifle on my hand, a Remington sniper with a plastic barrel.

They came together, three of them, black in the yellow light. Ratko was a little behind the others, fighting against the wind off the sea.

I took the first one in the head, the entry wound fairly high up on one side. A second to reload, then the second one fell. A second later and Ratko was gone, swallowed up by the storm.

I hurried down from the roof, my rifle stuffed into my bag. I was rushing to make sure I didn't end up caught in a trap.

But violence betrayed me. I had to flee. My power drained away in my sickness.

When I had bided my time, got back on my feet again, I contacted him. Arranged a meeting.

I knew he would come.

But violence wasn't with me.

The square was full of people, my chosen position, on top of the roof of Kulturhuset, with its perfect view, was completely useless.

I had to meet him on the ground instead.

When he put the barrel against my neck I knew I had won, no matter what happened.

'That's enough,' he whispered. 'You lose.'

He was wrong. He snarled something else, pathetically.

'Bijeljina,' he whispered. 'Do you remember Bijeljina?'

I pulled away, took out my pistol, but there was a pushchair in the way, and he hit me and I let go of the gun, it tumbled away from me and I saw my only chance disappear. Cold metal against my neck.

And he pronounced my sentence, the wages of violence guilt shame.

'You can never win,' I whispered. 'I've destroyed your life.'

I saw him out of the corner of my eye.

Smiled.

Charges, sentence, punishment.

Absolution.

Epilogue

It had started to snow again, large soft flakes that slowly wound their way towards the tarmac. Annika headed down towards Rålambshovsvägen, calm, heavy, she had been eating all day. It was windy, pushing her forward, and she felt slightly sick, but that was the baby, her son, her little fair-haired boy. She walked over to the taxi-rank by the fast-food kiosk, jumped into the back seat and asked the driver to take her out to Vaxholm.

'The traffic's terrible,' he said.

'I don't mind,' Annika said. 'I've got all the time in the world.'

It took forty minutes to get out of the city. Annika sat in the warm back seat, the car radio was playing old Madonna hits on low volume, the Christmas window displays glided past, as excited children pointed at mechanical Santas and plastic toys. She tried to glance up at the sky, but couldn't see it past the snow and coloured lamps.

I wonder if they celebrate anything like Christmas on other planets.

The traffic thinned out when they reached the motorway, and the 274 towards the coast was almost deserted. The fields were white, lighting up the dark afternoon, the trees wearing heavy gowns, their branches bowed to the ground.

'Where do you want me to let you out?'

'Östra Ekuddsgatan,' she said. 'I'd like you to drive past first, I just want to see if they're home.'

She showed him where to turn off. As the taxi turned sharp right and headed up the hill, her nerves began to get the better of her. Her mouth went dry and she felt her palms getting clammy. Her heart started to hammer in her chest. She craned her neck to see, which house was it?

There. There it was. Cladding, and his green Toyota outside. There were lights on inside, someone was home.

'Do you want me to stop, or what?' the taxi-driver asked.

'No!' she said. 'Drive on!'

She pressed herself into the seat, looking away as they glided past, invisible.

They came to the end of the road.

'What now?' the taxi-driver asked. 'Back to Stockholm?'

Annika closed her eyes, clasping her hands together tightly in front of her mouth. Her pulse was racing, she felt quite breathless.

'No,' she said. 'Go round the block again.'

The taxi-driver sighed, then glanced at the meter. Well, it wasn't his money.

They did the circuit again. Annika studied the house as they drove past. How ugly it was. Okay, so it fronted onto the sea, but it was so bland, so 1960s.

'Pull up after the next bend,' she said.

The journey was expensive, and she paid by credit card. She was left standing on the pavement as the car slid away into the darkness and snow, brake-lights coming on, the indicator pointing the way back to the city. She took a deep breath in an attempt to calm down, but failed. She thrust her hands, dripping from nerves, deep into her pockets. She walked slowly back towards the house, the house where Thomas and his wife lived. Östra Ekuddsgatan, millionaires' row.

The front door was brown and well-oiled, on either side were coloured windows to let in the light. A doorbell with a name under it, Samuelsson.

She closed her eyes, almost unable to breathe at all, suddenly on the verge of tears.

A stupid little tune rang out inside the house.

Nothing happened.

Then he opened, his hair all over the place, his shirt unbuttoned, nothing but socks on his feet, and with a pen in his mouth.

She forced herself to breathe, as her eyes filled up.

'Hello,' she whispered.

Thomas stared at her, completely pale, and took the pen out of his mouth.

'I'm not a ghost,' she said, her tears overflowing.

He took a step backwards and held the door open.

'Come in,' he said.

She walked into the hall, suddenly aware that she was freezing.

He closed the door and cleared his throat.

'What are you doing here?' he asked cautiously. 'What's wrong?'

'Sorry,' she said in a muffled voice. 'Sorry, I really didn't think I was going to burst into tears.'

She glanced up at him. Damn it, she always looked so ugly when she cried.

'Do you need help?' he asked.

Annika swallowed.

'Is she . . . home?'

'Eleonor? No, she's still at the bank.'

Annika pulled off her jacket and kicked off her shoes. Thomas vanished into a door on the right, leaving her standing in the hall. She looked round. Designer furniture from R.O.O.M., some inherited pieces, ugly pictures. A staircase down to another level.

'Can I come in?'

She didn't wait for him to answer, and followed him into the kitchen. Thomas was standing at the sink, pouring coffee.

'Do you want some?' he asked.

She nodded and sat down.

'You're not working?'

He put two mugs on the kitchen table.

'Oh yes,' he said. 'Working from home today. I've got a new job, managing a big project for the Association of Local Authorities. I'm going to be doing some of the work from home, and some in the city.'

Annika hid her hands under the tabletop, tried to stop them shaking.

'Has something happened?' he asked as he sat down, staring at her.

She looked into his eyes and took a deep breath. She had no idea how he was going to react, no idea at all.

'I'm pregnant,' she said.

He blinked, but the expression on his face didn't change.

'What?' he said.

She cleared her throat, clenched her fists under the table, holding his gaze.

'You're the father. There's no doubt at all about that. I haven't been with anyone else since . . . since Sven died.'

She looked down at the table, feeling him staring at her.

'Pregnant?' he said. 'With me?'

She nodded, on the verge of tears again.

'I want to keep the baby,' she said.

At that moment the front door opened and she could see Thomas stiffen. Her own pulse started to race.

'Darling? Hello?'

Eleonor wiped her feet, brushed off her coat and closed the door behind her.

'Thomas?'

Annika looked at Thomas, and he stared back blankly, his face completely white.

'In the kitchen,' he said, standing up and going out into the hall.

'What terrible weather,' Eleonor said. Annika heard her kiss her husband on the cheek. 'Have you started dinner yet?'

He muttered something. Annika was staring out of the window, paralysed. In the reflection she saw Eleonor come into the kitchen and stop abruptly.

'This is Annika Bengtzon,' Thomas said in an unsteady voice. 'The journalist who wrote those articles about the Paradise Foundation.'

Annika took a deep breath and looked up at Eleonor.

Thomas's wife, a moss-green collarless dress, a thin gold necklace round her neck.

'Pleased to meet you,' the woman said, smiling and holding out her hand. 'You know your article gave Thomas a real boost to his career?'

Annika shook hands, her own cold and clammy. Her mouth was dry as dust.

'Thomas and I are going to have a baby,' she said.

The woman carried on smiling, and several seconds passed. Thomas was standing behind his wife, and he put his hands over his face, visibly crumbling.

'What?' Eleonor said, still smiling quizzically.

Annika let go of the woman's hand and looked down at the table.

'I'm pregnant. We're having a baby.'

Eleonor stopped smiling and turned to stare at Thomas.

'Is this some sort of joke?' she said.

Thomas said nothing, pushed his hair back, shut his eyes.

'Due at the end of July next year,' Annika said. 'I think it's a boy.'

Eleonor spun round and stared at Annika, all colour draining from her face. The whites of her eyes seemed to shrink and turn red.

'What have you done?' Eleonor snarled. Annika stood up and backed away, and Eleonor turned to face Thomas again.

'What have you done? Have you slept with this . . . this person?'

His wife went over to Thomas but he didn't move, just stood there staring at the floor.

'Bloody hell!' the woman said in a low voice. 'Bringing a load of germs and God knows what home to *me*!'

Thomas looked into his wife's eyes.

'Eleonor, I . . . it just happened.'

'It *just happened*? How did it just happen, Thomas? What the hell were you thinking?'

He rubbed his brow. Annika felt her brain shrinking; *I'm going to die.* She grabbed the table to stop herself collapsing.

'Have you any idea what this means?' Eleonor said, trying to collect herself. 'You'll have to pay for eighteen years, you're going to be held financially responsible until the kid grows up. Was it worth it? Was it?'

Thomas was staring at his wife like he didn't know her.

'You're unbelievable,' he said.

Eleonor tried to laugh. 'Me? Am I the one in the wrong

490

here? You've been unfaithful, and now you're going to end up with an illegitimate brat. Do you imagine I'm just going to accept that?'

Annika suddenly felt she couldn't breathe, there was no air in the house, she had to get out, get away, go home. She forced herself to move, went round the table and out to the hall and the front door, her knees trembling. Eleonor saw her in the corner of her eye and spun towards her, bitterness etched in her face.

'Get out of my house!' she screamed.

Annika stopped, let the woman's hatred hit her with its full force. She caught Thomas's eye and looked at him calmly.

'Are you coming?' she said. Thomas stared at her.

'Get out, you *whore*!'

The woman took a threatening step towards her. Annika held her ground.

'Thomas,' she said, 'come with me.'

Thomas moved, went out into the hall, got his coat and Annika's jacket.

'What are you doing?' Eleonor said, bewildered. 'What on earth are you doing?'

He went over to his wife, pulling his coat and shoes on.

'We have to sort this out,' Thomas said. 'I'll call you.'

His wife gasped, grabbed the lapel of his coat.

'If you go,' she said, 'if you step out of that door, you'll never be welcome here again.'

Thomas sighed.

'Eleonor,' he said, 'don't be so—'

'You *bastard*!' she shouted. 'If you go through that door now, you can never come back. *Never*!'

Annika was standing by the door, holding the handle. She could only see Thomas's back, the way his glossy hair hung over his collar. She saw him raise his hands and take hold of his wife's.

Shit, he's going to stay, their ties are too strong, he can't break out.

'I'll be in touch,' he said.

Thomas turned, his eyes fixed on the floor, his lips pursed.

Then he looked up at Annika, his eyes clear and wide-open.

'Come on, let's go,' he said.

Woman Accused of Fraud Speaks Out Ahead of Verdict

STOCKHOLM: The 31-year-old woman behind the Paradise Foundation has chosen to speak out for the first time.

On Monday she will be told the verdict of the high-profile court case in which she stands accused of conspiracy to murder, among other charges.

'This whole process has been a witch hunt,' she says. 'The *Evening Post* has ruined my life.'

In December last year the *Evening Post* published a series of articles about the Paradise Foundation and its activities. The manager of Paradise, the 31-year-old woman, was accused by the paper of attempted fraud, threatening behaviour, physical abuse and conspiracy to murder.

'I never got a chance to defend myself,' the woman says. 'I didn't have time to gather my thoughts before the paper went to press. It was all just a misunderstanding. I could have explained everything.'

The newspaper spoke to several women who said they had been fooled by you.

'You have to remember that these are people who were in a terribly fragile state. They don't always know what's best for them. We were well on the way to helping one of the families when they chose to run away from us.'

Several local authorities believe that they have been the subject of fraud.

'Our organization had only just been set up. It's true that things weren't working entirely smoothly. But our aim was to help people. It wasn't a public organization in any way. The whole point of our work was to avoid having too much scrutiny from official bodies. And that was something that the various social services departments evidently had trouble accepting.'

You've been charged with constructive fraud, false accounting, aggravated tax evasion and impeding tax supervision.

'I've tried to run a business in this country, to provide employment for others. Sometimes I've ended up working with people who've let me down, tricked me. But I have never tried to get money from anyone under false pretences, not the state, not local authorities, and not private individuals. I've had financial problems, certainly, but most of my debts have been dealt with.'

The prosecutor alleges that you arranged the murder of Aida Begovic in Sergels torg in November last year.

'That's the worst thing of all. I don't understand how anyone can be so cruel as to accuse me of something like that. I did all I could to help Aida, but she was sadly too damaged by her experiences of the war in Bosnia to accept any help.'

You are also accused of conspiracy in a case of grievous bodily harm and unlawful kidnapping against social services official Thomas Samuelsson.

'He was the one whose behaviour was criminal. He forced his way into the foundation's premises and threatened us. My brother and I were merely trying to defend ourselves, but we were too heavy-handed, and I apologize for that.'

Are you nervous about the verdict?

'Not really, I have faith in justice. But I feel violated. Misunderstood. Crushed. I spent three years working to set up Paradise, that's why my financial situation became so precarious. But I gave it my all, and I only ever wanted to help other people. A society that has put me in this position does not deserve to call itself civilized.'

Associated Press telegram

Date: 18 April

Subject: News

War Criminal Sets Up Private Army

South Africa (AP): The Serbian war criminal Ratko, suspected of participating in the massacres in Vukovar and Bijeljina at the beginning of the Bosnian War, has set up a private professional army in southern Africa, according to sources in Cape Town.

The army is active across central and southern Africa, working under the auspices of both governments and multi-national corporations.

Ratko is reported to have built up his army with money from the illegal trade of Serbian cigarettes to Scandinavia, as well as with loans from the Russian mafia.

London, 4 July

Dear Annika,

I hope you had a good Midsummer!

My family and I celebrated the holiday in the traditional way at the cottage we rented when we left Paradise. All is well with us.

I thought I'd just drop you a line from Gatwick Airport outside London. We have a few hours to kill before our connecting flight.

Our residence permits have come through, so we're finally on our way to a new country. This is our final flight. It feels hard to leave Sweden, but everything will be so much better from now on, especially for the children.

Very best wishes,

Mia Eriksson

News Agency Memo

Subject: Domestic
Author: Sjölander
Date: 10 August

Russians Take Over

The peace didn't last long. Crime is back to the level it was at before the police raids on the Yugoslavian mafia.

'The Russians have taken over,' a police source has told the *Evening Post*.

On 13 December last year, Lucia Day, the *Evening Post* revealed the structure of the Yugoslavian mafia in Sweden. The articles led to the largest coordinated set of raids the police have ever conducted against organized crime. More than thirty-five buildings, vehicles, boats and trailers were searched or seized during the raids, which took a whole day to complete. Large quantities of weapons, drugs, spirits and cigarettes were confiscated. More than fifty illegal migrants have already been expelled.

Questioning of the suspects has been going on all summer, but detectives say there is still a lot of work to do before any case can be brought to court.

'This investigation is proving very slow. All the suspects deny involvement in anything at all,' a police source reveals. 'We can't bring charges until we have a complete picture of the organization.'

The decline in crime statistics that followed the raids has vanished, according to the police.

'The conclusion we have come to is that the vacuum left by the Yugoslavian mafia has been filled sooner than we anticipated,' a police source says. 'The Russian mafia has simply moved in and taken over.'

So all those arrests were actually in vain?

'We can never allow ourselves to think like that. Every criminal who is caught is a victory for our law-abiding society.'

The Ally

no. 9, *21 September*

INTERNAL MAGAZINE FOR THE SWEDISH
ASSOCIATION OF LOCAL AUTHORITIES

NEW RECRUITS

Thomas Samuelsson, project leader of the recently completed investigation into quality assurance in social services, has been appointed an investigating officer for the negotiation delegation.

Thomas Samuelsson previously spent seven years as the finance officer for social services in Vaxholm. He lives on Kungsholmen with his fiancée and his newborn son.

THE END

Liza Marklund on *Vanished*

During the autumn of 1991 I worked as a night reporter in the newsroom of the *Expressen* newspaper in Stockholm.

One evening I received a peculiar phone-call. It was passed on to me by a male colleague who thought it was more suitable for me.

There was a young woman on the line who wanted to tell me about a completely new and fantastic organization: a foundation that would hide and erase the records of persecuted people from every public database, helping them to disappear completely. Because this sort of persecution affects women and children most of all, I decided to listen.

I ended up meeting the woman several times over the following six months. To start with I was deeply impressed by her passion and knowledge – she gave a very competent and credible impression.

But whenever I tried to check her information, I hit a brick wall. Nothing she had told me could be verified, because everything was so secret.

As a journalist I couldn't write anything I couldn't verify and prove, which meant that the articles were delayed. And I couldn't make any sense of the information about the funding and finances of the foundation.

In the end I contacted a woman who had been drawn in deep inside the foundation. I knew who she was already, we had spoken several times. She came to be known as Maria Eriksson.

With Mia's help I was able to uncover the foundation and the lies it was based on. The articles were published in *Expressen* one year after my first contact with the foundation's manager.

This made me wonder about what we actually do to each other as human beings – how we function and how we take responsibility for each other.

During the early years of the 1990s, large parts of the social sector were deregulated. Care homes were privatised, and suddenly it was possible to earn money from other people's addictions, old-age and illnesses. Who really has responsibility for the sick and the poor? Society? Capitalism? Or the family?

If Grandma looked after me when I was little, is it my responsibility to look after her when she gets ill?

Or take a marriage where the two parties are developing in different directions and acquiring different values: what is your primary responsibility: to the partner you promised to love, for better or worse, or to yourself and your own conviction?

These aren't easy questions.

What happens when the state itself becomes the bad guy, as happened during the war in the Balkans?

I spent several years thinking hard about these questions, and this book is the result.

Vanished is perhaps my saddest book. It was chosen as Book of the Year in 2002 by the readers of *QX* magazine.

Liza Marklund
Stockholm, January 2012

Author's Acknowledgements

This is fiction. All the characters are entirely the product of the author's imagination, with one exception: Maria Eriksson. Mia is based on an existing person, and her story is described in the documentary novel *Gömda* (*Buried Alive*). Mia has read and given her approval to the way she is portrayed in this work of fiction.

Otherwise any similarities to real people are purely coincidental. Neither the *Evening Post* nor the Paradise Foundation exist. Both have been inspired by a number of organizations, but are in this novel the product of the author's imagination.

The depiction of Serbian criminality, both in the former Yugoslavia and in Sweden, is the work of the author's own invention and conclusions.

Information about other criminal groups and their areas of activity are based upon previously published facts, primarily from the *Aftonbladet* newspaper.

In a few instances I have made use of the author's prerogative to change certain details relating to existing buildings, places and roads.

I would like to thank everyone who has answered my occasionally bizarre questions. They are:

Shqiptar Oseku, spokesman for the Kosovo Information Office in Scandinavia, for advice on the activities of various Balkan groups.

Peter Rönnerfalk, doctor and health advisor, for detailed knowledge about medical matters.

Ann-Sofie Mårtensson, public relations manager for Stockholm Harbours, for information and a guided tour of Frihamnen in Stockholm and all its activities, buildings, history and geography.

Rolf Holmgren, customs officer with the border control unit in Stockholm, for information about the routines surrounding the international transportation of goods, as well as a demonstration of the ingenuity of tobacco smugglers and how to catch them.

Jonas Gummesson, head of domestic news at TV4, for assistance regarding Social Democratic domestic policies.

Lotta Snickare, head of management training at FöreningsSparbanken, for her knowledge of the banking industry and the activities of local authorities.

Thomas Snickare, project manager for Telia, for his insights into the internal workings of a social services committee.

Pär Westin, regional manager of Stockholm's Cemeteries Authority, and his staff, for expertise concerning funeral ceremonies and burials.

Jan Guillou, author and journalist, who has helped me with details about weapons, ammunition and their effect on the human body.

Kaj and Maria Hellström, for information about Södermanland.

Niclas Salomonsson, my literary agent, and his staff at Salomonsson Agency in Stockholm, for all their great work.

Emma Buckley, my British editor, and Neil Smith, the translator, for their capacity and dedication.

And finally, last but not least, my genius Swedish editor, author and dramatist Tove Alsterdal.

Thank you, everyone.

Any mistakes or errors which have crept in are, as always, entirely my own.

Liza Marklund

Name: Eva Elisabeth Marklund (which only the bank statement calls her. To the rest of the world, she's Liza).

Family: Husband and three children.

Home: A house in the suburbs of Stockholm, and a townhouse in southern Spain.

Born: In the small village of Pålmark in northern Sweden, in the vast forests just below the Arctic Circle.

Drives: A 2001 Chrysler Sebring LX (a convertible, much more suitable for Spain than Pålmark).

Five Interesting Facts About Liza

1. She once walked from Tel Aviv to London. It took all of one summer, but she made it. Sometimes she hitchhiked as well, sometimes she sneaked on board trains. When her money ran out she took various odd jobs, including working in an Italian circus. Sadly she had to give that up when it turned out she was allergic to tigers.

2. Liza used to live in Hollywood. Not because she wanted to be a film star, but because that was where her

first husband was from. In the early 1980s she had a two-room apartment on Citrus Avenue, a narrow side-street just a couple of blocks from Mann's Chinese Theatre (the cinema on Hollywood Boulevard with all the stars' hand and footprints). She moved back to Sweden to study journalism in Kalix.

3. She was once arrested for vagrancy in Athens. Together with fifty other young people from all corners of the world she was locked in a garage full of motorbikes. But Liza was released after just quarter of an hour: she had asked to meet the head of police, commended him on his work, and passed on greetings from her father, the head of police in Stockholm. This was a blatant lie: Liza's father runs a tractor-repair workshop in Pålmark.

4. Liza's eldest daughter is an actress and model. Annika, who lends her name to the heroine of Liza's novels, was the seductress in the film adaptation of Mikael Niemi's bestseller *Popular Music from Vittula*. Mikael and Liza have also been good friends from the time when they both lived in Luleå in the mid-1980s. Mikael was one of Liza's tutors when she studied journalism in Kalix.

5. Liza got married in Leningrad in 1986. She married a Russian computer programmer to help him get out of the Soviet Union. The sham marriage worked; he was able to escape, taking his brother and parents with him. Today the whole family is living and working in the USA.

Liza's Favourites

Book: *History* by Elsa Morante

Film: *Happiness* by Todd Solondz

Modern music: Rammstein (German hard rock)

Classical music: Mozart's 25th Symphony in G-minor. And his Requiem, of course.

Idols: Nelson Mandela, Madeleine Albright and Amelia Adamo (the Swedish media queen).

Liza's Top Holiday Destinations

1. North Korea. The most isolated country in the world, and the last iron curtain. Liza has seen it from the outside, looking into North Korea from the South, at the Bridge of No Return on the 38th parallel.

2. Masai Mara, Kenya. Her family co-owns a safari camp in the Entumoto valley.

3. Rarotonga, the main island in Cook archipelago in the South Pacific. The coolest paradise on the planet.

4. Los Angeles. Going 'home' is always brilliant.

5. Andalucia in southern Spain. The best climate in Europe, dramatic scenery, fantastic food and excellent wine. Not too far away, and cheap to fly to!

Join Annika Bengtzon at the start of her career
as a journalist in *EXPOSED* . . .

Turn the page to read the first chapter.

Prologue

The first thing she saw was the pair of knickers hanging from a bush. They were swaying gently, their salmon pink standing out against the lush greenery. Her immediate reaction was anger. Young people had no respect for anything! They couldn't even let the dead rest in peace.

She began to contemplate the decline of society while her dog explored further along the iron railings. She followed the animal down the south side of the cemetery, round the thin trees, and that was where she caught sight of a leg. Her fury rose: how dare they! She saw them every evening, wandering the pavements with their skimpy clothes and their loud voices, offering themselves to men. The fact that the weather was hot was no excuse.

The dog did a little sausage in the grass next to the railings. She looked away and pretended she hadn't seen. There was no one about at this time of day. Why bother putting it in a bag?

'Come on, Jesper,' she said, pulling the dog towards the eastern end of the park. 'Come on, boy.'

She glanced back over her shoulder as she walked away from the railings. The leg was no longer visible, hidden by the thick foliage.

It was going to be another hot day. She could feel beads of sweat forming on her forehead even though the sun had only just risen. She was breathing heavily as she struggled up the slope. The dog was pulling on the lead. His tongue was hanging so far out that it was touching the grass.

How on earth could you just fall asleep in a cemetery, the final resting place of the dead? Was that what feminism was all about, giving young girls a licence to behave badly and show a complete lack of respect?

She was still annoyed. The steep hill was making her mood even worse.

I ought to get rid of this dog, she thought, then felt guilty for thinking it. To make up for her uncharitable thought she bent down to let the dog off the lead, and picked him up for a cuddle. The dog struggled free and rushed off after a squirrel. She sighed. What was the point of trying to be nice?

With another deep sigh she settled onto a bench while Jesper tried to catch the squirrel. After a while the dog had worn himself out and came to a halt under the tree where the little rodent was hiding. She didn't move until the dog had finished dashing about, then she got to her feet again, her dress sticking to her back. The thought of the sweat stains down her spine made her feel embarrassed.

'Come on, Jesper darling. Over here . . .'

She waved a plastic bag full of dog treats, and the short-legged bull-terrier set off towards her. His tongue was hanging out, swinging back and forth, making it look like he was laughing.

'Is this what you want, then? Yes, I thought it might be . . .'

She fed the dog the entire contents of the bag, and took the opportunity to put him back on the lead. It was time to go home. Jesper had had his treats. Now it was her turn: coffee and a Danish pastry.

The dog showed no inclination to go back. He'd caught sight of the squirrel again, and all those dog treats had only renewed his energy for the chase. He protested noisily and furiously.

'I don't want to be out here any longer,' she complained. 'Come on, Jesper!'

They took a different path to avoid the steep slope back home. Going uphill was just about okay, but going down always made her knees ache.

She was walking down the path towards the north-eastern corner of the cemetery when she saw the body. It was lying in thick undergrowth, stretched out, with its arms up behind a broken granite headstone. A fragment of a Star of David was lying next to the head. She felt suddenly afraid. The body was naked, completely motionless and white. The dog pulled loose and rushed at the railings, the lead dancing like an angry snake behind him.

'Jesper!'

He managed to squeeze between two rails and set off towards the dead woman.

'Jesper, come here!'

She was shouting as loud as she dared, because she didn't want to wake anyone living nearby. A lot of people slept with their windows open in this heat; the stone buildings of the city centre never had time to cool down during the short summer nights. She fumbled frantically for more dog treats, but they were all gone.

The bull-terrier stopped beside the woman and eyed her curiously. Then he began to sniff, at first hesitantly, then more eagerly. When he got to her groin he could no longer contain himself.

'JESPER! Come here at once!'

513

The dog looked up but showed no signs of obeying. Instead he moved up to the woman's head, then started stiffing at the hands. The woman watched in horror as her dog started to chew on the corpse's fingers. Feeling sick, she grabbed at the black railings. She moved slightly to the left and bent down, peering through the headstones. She stared into the dead woman's eyes, just two metres away. They were glazed, slightly clouded, dull and cold. She had a strange sense of all sound around her vanishing; there was just a faint buzzing noise in her left ear.

I have to get the dog away from here, she thought. *I can't tell anyone that Jesper has been chewing on her.*

She got down on her knees and stuck her hand as far as she could through the railings. Her outstretched fingers were pointing right at the woman's dead eyes. Her upper arm was so plump that she almost got stuck, but she just managed to catch hold of the lead. The dog whined as she pulled on the leather strap. He was in no mood to let go of his prey. His jaw was clamped onto the body, which moved slightly.

'You stupid bloody dog!'

With a thud and a whimper he crashed against the railings. She pulled him back through with trembling hands, clutching him like never before, both hands clasped firmly round his stomach. She hurried down to the street, her heels sliding on the grass and straining her thighs.

It wasn't until she had locked the door of her flat behind her and caught sight of the pieces of flesh in the dog's mouth that she started to retch.

Part One
JULY

1

'There's a dead girl in Kronoberg Park.'

The voice was breathless, the words slurred, suggesting drug use. Annika Bengtzon looked away from her screen and fumbled for a pen amongst the mess on her desk.

'How do you know?' she asked, sounding more sceptical than was strictly called for.

'Because I'm standing right next to it, for fuck's sake!'

The voice rose to a falsetto and Annika had to hold the phone away from her ear.

'Okay, how dead?' she said, aware that the question sounded ridiculous.

'Bloody hell, completely dead! How dead can you be?'

Annika looked around the newsroom uneasily. Spike, the head of news, was sitting over at the newsdesk, talking on the phone. Anne Snapphane was fanning herself with a pad of paper behind the desk opposite, and Picture-Pelle had just switched on his Mac over at the picture desk.

'I see,' she said, as she found a Biro in an empty coffee cup and an old printout of a news agency telegram, which she started making notes on the back of.

'In Kronoberg Park, you said. Whereabouts?'

'Behind a headstone.'

'Headstone?'

The man on the other end started to cry. Annika waited in silence for a few seconds. She didn't know what to do next. The tip-off line – officially known as the Hotline but only ever referred to in the office as Cold Calls – was almost only ever used by pranksters and nutters. This one was a strong candidate for the latter.

'Hello . . . ?' Annika said cautiously.

The man blew his nose. He took several deep breaths and started talking. Anne Snapphane was watching Annika from the other side of the desk.

'I don't know how you keep answering those calls,' she said when Annika had hung up.

Annika didn't respond, and just carried on making notes on the back of the telegram.

'I have to have another ice-cream or I'll die. Do you want anything from the canteen?' Anne Snapphane asked, standing up.

'I just need to check something first,' Annika said, picking up the phone and dialling the police emergency desk. It was true. Four minutes ago they had received a report of a dead body in the section of the park facing Kronobergsgatan.

Annika got up and went over to the newsdesk, holding the telegram in her hand. Spike was still talking on the phone, his feet up on the desk. Annika stood right in front of him, demanding his attention. The head of news looked up, annoyed.

'Suspected murder, a young girl,' Annika said, waving the printout.

Spike ended his call abruptly by simply putting the phone down, and dropped his feet to the floor.

'Is it from one of the agencies?' he wondered, turning towards his screen.

'No, Cold Calls.'

'Confirmed?'

'The emergency desk have got it, at any rate.'

Spike looked out over the newsroom.

'Okay,' he said. 'Who have we got here?'

Annika made her move. 'It's my tip-off.'

'Berit!' Spike yelled, getting up. 'This year's summer killing!'

Berit Hamrin, one of the paper's older reporters, picked up her handbag and came over to the newsdesk.

'Where's Carl Wennergren? Is he working today?'

'No, he's on holiday, sailing round Gotland,' Annika said. 'This is my tip-off; I took the call.'

'Pelle, pictures!' Spike yelled towards the picture desk.

The picture editor gave him a thumbs-up. 'Bertil Strand,' he shouted.

'Okay,' the head of news said, turning to Annika. 'So what have we got?'

Annika looked down at her scribbled notes, suddenly aware of how nervous she was.

'A dead girl, found behind a headstone in the Jewish Cemetery in Kronoberg Park on Kungsholmen.'

'So it isn't necessarily a murder, is it?'

'She's naked and was strangled.'

Spike looked at Annika intently. 'And you want to do this one yourself?'

Annika swallowed and nodded, and the head of news sat down again and pulled out a pad of paper.

'Okay,' he said. 'You can go with Berit and Bertil. Make sure we get good pictures. We can sort the rest out later, but we have to get good pictures.'

The photographer was pulling on the rucksack

containing his equipment as he walked past the newsdesk.

'Where is it, again?' he said, aiming his question at Spike.

'Kronoberg Prison,' Spike said, picking up the phone.

'Park,' Annika said, looking to see where her bag was. 'Kronoberg Park. The Jewish Cemetery.'

'Just make sure it isn't a domestic row,' Spike said, before dialling a London number.

Berit and Bertil Strand were already on their way to the lift down to the garage, but Annika paused.

'What do you mean by that?' she said.

'Exactly what I said. We aren't interested in domestics.'

The head of news turned his back on her demonstratively. Annika felt her anger rise through her body and hit her brain like a shot.

'That wouldn't make the girl any less dead, would it?' she said.

Spike's call was picked up at the other end and she realized the discussion was over. She looked up and saw that Berit and Bertil had already disappeared. She hurried to her desk, pulled out her bag from beneath the desk drawers and ran after her colleagues. The lift had gone, so she took the stairs. Fuck, fuck, why did she always have to argue? She was about to miss her first big story just because she wanted to put the head of news in his place.

'Idiot!' she said out loud to herself.

She caught up with the reporter and photographer at the entrance to the garage.

'Okay, we stick together until there's a good reason to split up,' Berit said, making notes in her pad as she walked. 'I'm Berit Hamrin, by the way. I don't think we've been introduced.'

520

The older woman smiled at Annika, and they shook hands as they got into Bertil Strand's Saab, Annika in the back and Berit in the front.

'There's no need to slam the door so hard,' Bertil Strand said, looking at Annika reproachfully over his shoulder. 'You'll damage the paintwork.'

Good God, Annika thought.

'Oh, sorry,' she said.

The photographers treated the newspaper's vehicles as their personal company cars. Almost all of them took their responsibilities extremely seriously. Maybe that was because the photographers, without exception, were all men, Annika thought. Even though she'd only been at the *Evening Post* for seven weeks, she was already well aware of the sanctity of the photographers' cars. She'd had to postpone several interviews because various photographers had been busy putting their cars through the carwash. And that also gave her an indication of just how important people thought her articles were.

'It's probably best to avoid Fridhemsplan and approach the park by the side streets,' Berit said as the car approached Rålambsvägen. Bertil Strand put his foot down and just made the lights, heading off down Gjörwellsgatan towards Norr Mälarstrand.

'Can you run through what the bloke on the phone told you?' Berit said, swivelling in her chair so she could look back at Annika.

Annika pulled out the crumpled telegram.

'Well, there's a young girl lying dead behind a head-stone in Kronoberg Park. Naked, probably strangled.'

'Who was the caller?'

'Some junkie, from the sound of it. His mate was taking a piss against the railings and caught sight of her through the bushes.'

'Why did they think she'd been strangled?'

Annika turned the paper to read something she'd written along the edge of the sheet.

'There was no blood, her eyes were wide open and there were marks on her neck.'

'That doesn't necessarily mean she was strangled, or even murdered,' Berit said, turning to look ahead again.

Annika didn't answer. She looked out through the Saab's tinted windows at the people sunbathing in Rålambshov Park. The glittering waters of Riddarfjärden spread out ahead of them. She had to squint, in spite of the tinted glass. There were two windsurfers heading towards the island of Långholmen, but they weren't doing terribly well. There was scarcely any breeze to lift the heat today.

'What a great summer we're having,' Bertil Strand said, turning left into Polhemsgatan. 'Pretty unexpected, after all the rain we had in the spring.'

'Yes, I was lucky,' Berit said. 'I've just had my four weeks off. Sun every single day. We can leave the car just behind the fire station.'

The Saab cruised the last few blocks of Bergsgatan. Berit had undone her seatbelt before Bertil Strand even hit the brakes, and was out of the car before it stopped. Annika hurried after her, momentarily taken aback as the heat outside hit her.

Bertil Strand parked in a turning circle as Berit and Annika headed off along the side of a red-brick building from the fifties. The tarmac path was narrow, with a stone kerb along the edge of the park.

'There's a flight of steps up here,' Berit said, already out of breath.

Six steps later and they were up in the park itself. They jogged along a tarmac path that led to an elaborate playground.

To their right were several sheds; Annika read the words 'Park Games' as she ran past. There was a sandpit, benches, picnic tables, climbing frames, slides, swings and other things for kids to climb and play on. A few mothers and their children were in the playground, but it looked like they were packing up. At the far end two uniformed policemen were talking to another mother.

'I think the cemetery's a bit further down, towards Sankt Göransgatan,' Berit said.

'You certainly know your way around,' Annika said. 'Do you live near here?'

'No,' Berit said. 'This isn't the first murder in this park.'

Annika saw that the police were busy unrolling their blue and white tape to cordon off the area. So they were emptying the playground and closing it off to the public.

'It's a good job we got here quickly,' she muttered to herself.

They turned off to the right, following a path that led to the top of the hill.

'Down to the left,' Berit said.

Annika ran on ahead, crossing two more paths, and suddenly there it was. She saw a row of black Stars of David standing out against the greenery.

'I can see it,' she shouted behind her, and from the corner of her eye saw that Bertil Strand had almost caught up with Berit.

The railings were black, and attractively ornate. The iron uprights were linked by metal circles and bows. Each railing was crowned by a stylized Star of David. She was running into her own shadow and realized that she was approaching the cemetery from the south.

She stopped on the little hill overlooking the graves, where she could get a good view. The police hadn't cordoned off this section of the park yet, but she could see that the northern and western approaches had already been blocked.

'Hurry up!' she called to Berit and Bertil Strand.

The railings enclosed the little Jewish cemetery and its worn granite headstones. Annika quickly counted thirty or so of them. The vegetation had almost taken over and the whole area looked overgrown and neglected. The cemetery covered an area of some thirty metres by forty. On the far side, the railings were little more than a metre and a half high. The entrance was on the western side, towards Kronobergsgatan and Fridhemsplan. She saw the team from the other evening paper stop at the cordon. A group of men, all of them in plain clothes, were inside the railings, at the east side of the cemetery. She realized why they were there: that was where the woman's body was.

Read the complete book – available now

EXPOSED

LIZA MARKLUND

How far would you go to
protect your secrets?

Trainee journalist **Annika
Bengtzon** has secured
a summer placement at
Sweden's biggest tabloid
newspaper. She's desperate
for this to be her big break,
although manning the
tip-off phoneline isn't quite
what she had in mind . . .

Until a caller tells her that
the naked body of a young
woman has been found in a
nearby cemetery.

As she pieces together details of the young woman's
life, Annika stumbles across video footage that places
the main suspect hundreds of miles from the crime
scene, right at the time of the murder.

Are the police looking for the wrong man? There is
suddenly far more at stake here than Annika's career,
and the more questions she asks, the more she leaves
herself dangerously **exposed**.

'No one tells a story like Liza Marklund'
Karin Slaughter

THE BOMBER

LIZA MARKLUND

SEVEN DAYS. THREE KILLINGS.
ONE WOMAN WHO KNOWS
TOO MUCH . . .

Crime reporter **Annika Bengtzon** is woken by a phonecall in the early hours of a wintry morning. An explosion has ripped apart the Olympic Stadium. And a victim has been blow to pieces.

As Annika delves into the details of the bombing and the background of the victim, there is a second explosion.

When her police source reveals they are hot on the heels of the bomber, Annika is guaranteed an exclusive with her name on it. But it soon becomes clear that she has uncovered too much, as she finds herself the target of a deranged serial killer . . .

> '*Edge-of-your-seat suspense*'
> **Harlan Coben**

> '*Nail-biting action and excitement*'
> **Daily Express**

The number one international bestseller

RED WOLF
LIZA MARKLUND

AN ACCIDENTAL DEATH?

Reporter **Annika Bengtzon**
is working on the story of
a devastating crime when
she hears that a journalist
investigating the same incident
has been killed. It appears to
be a hit-and-run accident.

A SERIES OF MURDERS

Several brutal killings follow –
all linked by handwritten letters
sent to the victims' relatives. When
Annika unravels a connection
with the story she's writing,
she is thrown on to the trail
of a deadly psychopath.

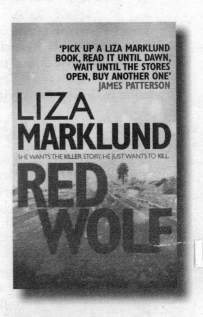

THE HUNT IS ON

Caught in a frenzied spiral of secrets and violence,
Annika finds herself and her marriage at breaking
point. Will her refusal to stop pursuing the truth
eventually destroy her?

*'An exceptionally well-crafted and
suspenseful work'*
Daily Mirror

POSTCARD KILLERS

JAMES PATTERSON & LIZA MARKLUND

James Patterson teams up with number one bestselling author Liza Marklund to create the most terrifying holiday thriller ever written.

NYPD detective Jacob Kanon is on a tour of Europe's most gorgeous cities. But the sights aren't what draw him – he sees each museum, each cathedral, and each café through the eyes of his daughter's killer.

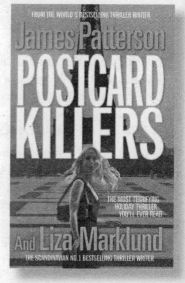

Kanon's daughter, Kimmy, and her fiancé were murdered while on holiday in Rome. Since then, young couples in Madrid, Salzburg, Amsterdam, Berlin, Athens and Paris have been found dead. Little connects the murders, other than a postcard sent to the local newspaper prior to each attack.

Now Kanon teams up with the Swedish reporter, Dessie Larsson, who has just received a postcard in Stockholm – and they think they know where the next victims will be.